LOVE Among the RUINS

LOVE

Among the

RUINS

A NOVEL

Robert Clark

W. W. Norton & Company New York | London

Grateful acknowledgment is made for permission to reprint an excerpt from "Make Our
Garden Grow," words and music by Leonard Bernstein and Richard Wilbur. Copyright ©
1955, 1974 Universal-PolyGram International Publishing, Inc., a division of Universal Studios,
Inc. (ASCAP). International Copyright Secured. All Rights Reserved.

Grateful acknowledgment is made for permission to reprint an excerpt from "Time of
the Season" by Rod Argent, copyright © 1968 Verulam Music Co. Ltd. International
copyright secured. All rights reserved. Reprinted by permission of Mainstay Music Inc.,
on behalf of Verulam Music Co. Ltd.

For information about permission to reproduce selections from this book, write to Permissions,
W. W. Norton & Company, Inc., 500 Fifth Avenue, New York, NY 10110

The text of this book is composed in Electra
with the display set in Ribbon and Distance
Composition by Tom Ernst
Manufacturing by Quebecor Fairfield
Book design by Chris Welch
Production manager: Julia Druskin

Library of Congress Cataloging-in-Publication Data

Clark, Robert, 1952–
Love among the ruins : a novel / by Robert Clark.
p. cm.
ISBN 0-393-02015-0
1. Vietnamese Conflict, 1961–1975—Middle West—Fiction. 2. Middle West—Fiction.
3. Teenagers—Fiction. I. Title.

PS3553.L2878 L68 2001
813'.54—dc21   2001018006

W. W. Norton & Company, Inc., 500 Fifth Avenue, New York, N.Y. 10110
www.wwnorton.com

W. W. Norton & Company Ltd., Castle House, 75/76 Wells Street, London W1T 3QT

1 2 3 4 5 6 7 8 9 0

For Tessa

Love bade me welcome, yet my soul drew back,
    Guilty of dust and sin.
But quick-ey'd Love, observing me grow slack
    From my first entrance in,
Drew nearer to me, sweetly questioning
    If I lack'd any thing.

                  —George Herbert, 1633

Just

Now

D ear Emily,
    I went up north this last week, up to the boundary country, and I wanted to write to you about it.

It hasn't changed much, even in thirty years. It was cool (doubtless outright cold at night) and there was some snow in the forest, though it was scarcely November. But I remember the water being almost warm in September, swimming naked with you.

What the hell were we—was I, I suppose, really—thinking, that we could live there?

There's a blacktop road to the lake now and I canoed out to the island. The island's even smaller than I remembered and I didn't have much trouble finding the site. There isn't much evidence we were ever there, and I don't think anyone's been there since. I could just make out the fire pit, not much more than a depression in the rock with some rusted metal in it, which I suppose we left there. I looked for some of the caches we made. I remember that I lined those things with a ton of rocks, but I couldn't find even one of them. I suppose the ground just swallowed them up.

You'd be glad to know the tree's still there, half rotted away and fallen in on itself where the hollow was. I don't suppose anything larger than a squirrel could sleep there now. But that's what thirty years of snow and decay will do, I suppose.

After that, I canoed back to the car and tried to find the place where the house was, and by dumb luck I found it. There's a nice road in there now, but the cabin is the same. The name on the driveway is the same too—Jorgensen. I suppose it's the same family, but a different generation. I think we figured the owners must have been in their fifties when we were there, which makes them eighty-plus now, in nursing homes or dead. So it must be their children that have the place now. I suppose they must all be about fifty now too. I've only got two years left until I'm there myself.

I like to imagine you happy and prosperous out in California. I imagine you married to somebody, too, and maybe playing tennis all day, or maybe designing computer chips. But I imagine you with children, pretty much grown.

My dad is still living out there. My mom's just the same, living in the apartment. I've got two children, Mark and Jenny, aged twenty and eighteen and both in college. Their mother and I split up some years ago, and I haven't remarried.

I love my children very much, but I guess the great discovery of my middle age is how inadequately I do so. I always feel that I have failed them, but I can't put my finger on *how* I have failed them, and that vague sense of omission, of dereliction, haunts me these days. To look at and listen to my kids, you wouldn't think *they* felt that way. They are cool as cucumbers, and I suppose are resigned to my inadequacies. But then I almost think they—and all their friends—were born to disappointment, to resignation at everything this world could throw at them, incapable of surprise.

Everyone I know feels this way about their kids, faults them for their lack of idealism, of engagement with everything. They don't feel that imperative to *make* a better world; they are content to take life as it comes and make do. But maybe that is their only option. Maybe when we were young, we, their parents, took history and idealism and used them up, sucked them dry. Or just somehow sullied them. And maybe what I feel bad about is having stolen those things from them. Then blamed them for not having the stuff we spent up in our "misspent" youth. Does that make any sense?

But what we did—I suppose it was a crazy thing, though it seemed so necessary at the time. Now I can't put my finger on the feeling anymore. The fear of the draft and the cops and some sort of impending totalitarian state, kind of shaggy and half-formed, like something out of the Brothers Grimm. Maybe to understand it you just had to be there. I guess in a way you're still there, where I left you.

I wish you could write me back. Even now, after all this time, I find myself still wanting to know everything about you.

All my best wishes and, yes, even now, love,

Bill

One

The

Beguilement

1

THE FIRST TIME WILLIAM LOWRY WROTE EMILY Byrne was more than thirty years before, in the war summer of 1968. After he had written the letter and sealed it in an envelope, William asked his mother, "Is it trespassing or anything to go up on someone's porch to put something in their mailbox?"

His mother looked up from her magazine. She picked up her cigarette from the ashtray and drew on it quickly and said, "Oh, I don't think so." She put the cigarette back down and took up her coffee mug. "Is it a letter?"

"Yeah."

"Then you could just mail it. Do you need a stamp?"

"They're in the desk in the hall."

"So there you are." She tapped her fingertips on the kitchen table and closed her magazine. On the cover there was a drawing of the president, dressed in knight's armor and holding a lance that drooped like a tired vegetable.

"Thanks," William said. "I'm going to go out until dinner. On my bike."

"Sure," said his mother as she tamped out her cigarette and began to dig in her pack for another. "Pick us up a pound of butter, okay? Money's in my purse."

Bill nodded. He went to the little rolltop desk in the hall and got a stamp from the roll in the drawer and fished a dollar bill out of his mother's woven straw bag. He put the stamp on the letter, pushed the money into his back pants pocket, and went out the door, into the hallway of the apartment house, and down the half flight of steps to the back entrance, where his bicycle was padlocked to the stair rail.

Mounting the bicycle, he wove down the alley, clutching the letter against the left-hand handlebar, gaining speed. It took him perhaps ten minutes to ride to Emily's house and he pedaled by at headlong speed, taking in the address—919—with a furtive sidelong glance. He thought he could mail the letter in a corner mailbox, but he realized he had no pen with which to write in the address. And he did not want to take the chance that on the very day he mailed this letter, someone would an hour later drop a cherry bomb into the box or, under cover of darkness, boost up a friend by the knees so he could piss through the open slot onto the letters heaped up inside.

William rode downtown, down the great hill to the main post office by the train station, and he took a pen and wrote in Emily's address and double-checked her zip code in the massive directory, and took the letter up to a window and watched the clerk carry it and drop it into the canvas hamper on wheels. Then, after another clerk came and rolled away the hamper into the back of the building, William went back outside to his bicycle and pedaled up the great hill home.

Twenty minutes later, as he was about to turn into the alley that led to the back door of the apartment house, he realized he had not bought the butter. He spun the wheel around and began to pedal off towards the grocery store, and then he stopped, suddenly aware that mischance was about to settle itself upon him.

He felt inside the back pocket of his pants but retrieved nothing more than the foil butt of a spent roll of Life Savers. He dug into his other pockets, which yielded only his wallet (whose sole occupants, his driver's license and a library card, faced each other on either side of the fold, a diptych of a life as yet unoccupied and so, it might seem, unlived) and twenty cents in change.

William explored his pockets once more, and concluded, more in embarrassment than despair, that the dollar bill had worked its way out of his pocket at some point, most likely as he pumped the bicycle up the hill. His own funds would neither cover the cost of the butter nor allow for the change his mother would expect. He did not for one second consider reporting what seemed to be the truth, which in any case seemed much less credible than any number of other explanations he was already beginning to concoct. He imagined his clumsy shame as he recounted how the dollar bill had, through some kind of Ouija-style self-propelling friction, wiggled its way out of his pocket and fallen unnoticed on the long asphalt path that ascended the cathedral hill; imagined his mother's cresting eyebrows meeting her brow wrinkled in exasperation, then the incredulous sputter launched on an exhalation of smoke, and—worst of all—her laughing at him.

William, had, in the space of perhaps twenty seconds, constructed two narratives. In the first, which he thought would appeal to his mother's sensibility and interests, he had encountered a group of college students downtown who were raising money for the farmworkers in California and was so moved that he handed the dollar over to them without a thought; in the second, which he found the more dramatically compelling, he had been accosted by a group of hoods in the vaguely seedy quarter between Seven Corners and the bottom of the hill and they had taken the dollar and let him escape with his Raleigh and his life.

He chained his bicycle and went inside. He opened the door, went down the hall, and, eyes downcast, found his mother in the kitchen, washing asparagus.

He looked up at her and then addressed the toecaps of his sneakers. "The money? For the butter? I don't have it. . . ."

William's mother set down an asparagus spear on the drainboard and turned to face him. Her mouth formed a tight, brittle smile, and she said, "I suppose you bought magic beans instead." Then she set her hands on her hips.

"No," William said, and he felt himself push off, riding the sled of his fabrication as it barreled down the hill. "There were some Mexican kids. In Rice Park. They said they needed some money to get home to California, to Delano, to pick grapes. And they were kind of tough. So—"

"Billy. Please. I've got people coming for dinner and the election returns. I don't have time. I've got to make hollandaise." Her hands dropped from her hips and shaped a plaintive gesture. "Take another dollar from my purse," she enunciated. "Actually, take two. Get me a bottle of quinine water too. Schweppes, not Canada Dry."

William nodded. His face had colored and now he felt it cooling. He spun around and returned to the straw bag in the hall, the bicycle on the chain and the lock, and rode off. The street was roofed over with elm leaves. He was moving through its shadows like dark places in water, inconsequential as a minnow, ruddy-faced, tight-breathed, with the tingle of being caught out still unreeling itself in his solar plexus.

2

O N   T H E   D A Y   I N   J U N E   T H A T   W I L L I A M   M A I L E D   H I S
very first letter to Emily Byrne, her father, Edward, had spent the
better part of the day prowling the Medical Arts Building on St. Peter
Street. He was talking up his company's new tranquilizer, Placidox,
and something new they had just gotten approval on and would be
releasing in the fall called Melanchor, a tricyclic antidepressant.

The doctors took their samples, the notepads, the pen and pencil
sets, and the paperweights with a model of a dendrite caught in it like a
house spider in aspic. They took them with grunts, with nods, sometimes with the brush of a hand across Edward's forearm or his shoulder
blade, kindly but distractedly. They rarely had time to talk, although
Edward had signed on fifteen years before because it was the only job
in the sales business where a college-educated man could routinely
talk to other college-educated men about science.

In all the Medical Arts Building, only old Dr. Fields could be
counted on for a real conversation. Edward thought he might have fan-
cied himself a philosopher, or that medicine had made him into one,
as though through all that contact with human bodies and their frailties
he had absorbed a certain worldly wisdom.

The nurse brought him into Fields's inner office, and Fields passed
him the cigarette box and they smoked together. It had been four
months since their last encounter, and as Edward replied to Fields's
various queries about the state of the pharmaceutical business, he felt
that Fields might be taking a history of the body politic.

"It was a good spring for Histamane," Edward was saying.

"Good pollen counts. The wife was just commenting on how well the garden is going, excepting the weeds."

"So how are you finding Placidox? Anything worth noting to head-quarters?"

"Oh no," Fields said, exhaling smoke and leaning forward as he slid his chair back a little. "Swell stuff. Mother's milk. Cracker Jacks. The brains of half the membership of the Junior League are awash in it."

"We're pretty excited about this new thing, Melanchor."

"That's for depression?" Fields put down his cigarette, cupped his hands behind his head, and leaned back, gazing up at the ceiling for a moment. "I think that's the coming thing," he said, and looked again at Edward. "Stress followed by despair. There's a historical pattern to it. Like when I was in college. World War I: the horror of the trenches, the exhilaration of victory, then the tawdriness of Versailles and the influenza epidemic. All *that* for nothing more than *this*. And so feelings of worthlessness, torpor, anomie, flat-out nothingness."

"The last war didn't end that way. With twenty-three years and counting."

"Maybe give it time. Anyhow, that was different. Watch how the current one turns out. You'll sell a ton of this—what do you call it—Melchior?" Fields halted. "No, that's one of the three wise men, the Negro, I think."

"Melanchor. So the Age of . . . what, Anxiety's over?"

"Superseded. At least some time soon. By the Age of Black Bile. Of Acedia."

"Which is . . ." Edward queried.

"The denial of God's love, his reality, I guess, on account of spiritual sloth, of despair." Fields grinned and then formed an expression of feigned wistfulness. "You could call your drug Acedex, or some such thing. Or Despond, after the infamous slough."

Edward stood, rising lazily. "Well, doctor, I have dope to peddle." Edward picked up his case. "Anything I can offer you? Notepads, playing cards, desk calendars? I have a nice cast model of a bladder we're using in connection with Micturon."

"I think I've got one of those. How about something more exotic—a vagina dentata, or some such?"

"I'm a good Catholic boy," said Edward. "I don't want to know what that means."

"If you're a good Catholic boy, you know enough Latin to already know what it means."

"So maybe I do. But we like to have it both ways. It's the distinguishing mark of our faith."

"Nice work if you can get it."

"It's been a pleasure, doctor," said Edward.

"Until next time, Ed. Come and see us again."

Edward's case was nearly empty, and it was a few minutes before five. He drove home in the apotheosis of the afternoon to his wife and his daughter. It was the first Tuesday in June, a beautiful day, and life was good, better, he sensed, than he could begin to know. For example, as he drove up the hill, a piece of paper blew across the road in front of him, which he could have sworn was not litter but a crisp new dollar bill.

*J*ust before dinnertime, Emily found her parents in the kitchen, as was their wont. Her mother stood at the counter while her father sat at the breakfast table near the back door. He held a cocktail, which he had the habit of regarding while he caused its contents—scotch whisky, water, and ice cubes—to swirl in the tumbler, and as he did this he talked to Emily's mother.

"Not a bad day at all. I spent the whole day in the Medical Arts Building. Finished up with a drink with old Dr. Fields." He cocked his wrist and set his glass in motion, watched the liquor spin and gazed into it. "Smartest man I know. Wears his age so gracefully. Wise and funny. And he says our new line is going to sell like hotcakes."

"Which is?" Virginia asked, still kneading egg into ground beef for the meat loaf she was preparing.

"The next thing after tranquilizers. Antidepressants. Mood elevators."

"Like bennies?"

"Like elevator shoes? Or Otis elevators?" Emily chirped from the doorway. Her father glanced over to her and smiled, and Emily might well have thought she was, after Dr. Fields, the second-wisest person he knew.

Edward turned back towards his wife. "Nothing so crude as that, as pep pills. These really address the underlying brain chemistry, the depression at its core."

His wife scooped a cup of oatmeal into the bowl before her and said, "I thought people—unhappy people, anyway—were more anxious than depressed."

"Neurotic people, you mean. Anxiety neurosis, it's called." Edward drank. "Maybe it seems that way. But this is the coming thing, the new frontier."

"People are going to be more sad?" Emily asked.

"Not in so many words. At least I don't think so. We're just going to be treating the same conditions from a different angle. Because maybe a lot of anxiety neurosis—"

"Antsiness," Emily interjected.

"—Antsiness, if you want, is really suppressed sadness. Someone's presenting anxiety, but it's really depression."

" 'Presenting,' " Virginia remarked. "You're spending too much time around doctors."

"Presenting, from Hollywood, in Living Color, anxiety, depression, and the neurosis orchestra," Emily proclaimed. Her father smiled— when could Emily not make her father smile?—and so did her mother.

But then, in a mild yet serious manner, Virginia looked at Emily and noted, "But of course it's scarcely a laughing matter. Not really."

Emily nodded her assent. This was what adults did—her mother and the nuns at school in particular—when you began to have too much fun with them. They let you know that you were being permitted on their turf—their right to say and do pretty much as they wanted— only by their sufferance. Perhaps they wanted to let you know who was boss, or perhaps they feared you'd run amok, that you would career off some precipice and never recover from the fall.

Had she dwelt on her mother's admonition, Emily might have felt hurt, but her father quickly added, "And of course, that's why it's so great that we can do something about it," rather as if they were all in perfect agreement and were entitled to some congratulations for their right thinking. This indeed made everything all right, at least for Emily, and seemingly for her mother, who slapped the finished contents of her mixing bowl into a ball and said, "Of course."

Emily did not really know anyone who was mentally ill or even neurotic, save through books and movies. She knew people, mostly people her own age, who were unhappy, but this was a temporary condition having to do with what one lacked or would prefer to lack. Her friend Monica Reardon, for example, lacked a boyfriend and was heavy in the knees, and these were simple enough problems, save in her imagining that the latter was the cause of the former. All would be well (this was a line from a prayer that her favorite nun of her whole life, Sister Mary Benedict, had taught her in kindergarten), for all the adults she knew were, in fact, happy—they were free (even the nuns with their vows, if you thought about it in the right way)—and her parents most of all.

Her father was looking into his drink again. He gave it a final swirl and downed the last of it, sighing as though he had completed a great and fruitful labor. "No, it was a lovely day, all in all. A lucky day." He stood and put his hands on top of the chair he had just vacated and looked up. "Why, on the way home, while I was driving up the hill by the cathedral, I could swear a dollar bill blew across the road, right in front of the car. Had to be. No mistaking it." He looked at his wife as though she might disbelieve him, and then to Emily with an assurance that she could somehow confirm what he was saying. "I suppose I could have stopped and grabbed it. But there was a breeze and I wanted to get home. Still, I see it"—and he grinned a little sheepishly, as if to say you could take him for a fool if you were so inclined, but that was no concern to him—"as a sign."

3

A s was his habit, William rose before seven,
well before his mother, whose sleep he never disturbed. He
ambled out of his room and through the kitchen, filled with the detri-
tus of his mother's guests the evening before: the brimming ashtrays,
the shriveled lemon slices, the bottles and glasses in whose bilges stood
the residues of various liquors and mixes, the curds of waxen hollandaise bobbing in the dishwater in the sink.

William took a box of raisin bran from the top of the refrigerator and
milk from inside it and put them on the kitchen table. He sat down
and then rose again to get a spoon, and as he leaned over the silver
drawer, he heard the sound of the newspaper against the front door.

He opened the door in time to hear the steps of the paperboy echoing in the hall and the lobby door slam in his wake. He picked up the
paper. The headline ran flat and heavy across the top of the front page,
as if it had been laid on with tempera and a stencil:

KENNEDY SHOT IN CALIFORNIA
Primary Victor Targeted in Los Angeles Hotel Kitchen

William read the headline twice, and then the first paragraph of the
news story, less to absorb its content than to let the last motes of sleep clear
from his eyes and his mind, to determine what he was supposed to do.

He never disturbed his mother, whose custom was both to retire and
to rise late, in the mornings, and often they did not see each other until
lunchtime or, when school was in session, until late in the afternoon.

But he knew with a certainty that had been rare to him in his life that he ought to wake her for this as surely as if their house were on fire.

*E*mily's father had gone out on his rounds that morning and then come home for good at lunch. There was detectable throughout the city a tacit agreement that the business of the day should be slowed if not halted outright pending reports from the hospital in Los Angeles.

Edward ate toast and tomato soup with Virginia in the kitchen while Emily took her lunch in the den, before the scarcely audible television, the broadcast day cleft into slices of game shows and soap operas set between bulletins from Los Angeles.

Virginia heard the squeaky rasp of the letter slot opening and the mail falling to the floor in the vestibule. She called out to the den, "Emmy, would you get the mail please?" and then she turned back to Edward. Emily had been half-overhearing them, and when she came back to the den and began to sift through the mail in her lap she continued listening.

"They did it because he was Catholic, because he was Catholic and he was going to win." Her plate rang out as she set her soup spoon down.

"It's not quite that simple," Edward said. "Surely."

"They shot him because he's Catholic just like they shot the other because he was colored."

"Negro."

"A Negro. But it's the same thing," Emily's mother insisted. It was, Emily thought, her mother's way to insist on things.

"Things are almost never the same thing. Which is not to say it's not terrible," Emily heard her father add quickly. It was her father's way to insist that things were not as her mother insisted, although he always allowed that they were undoubtedly a little bit that way.

"I know." Virginia paused and added, "I'm going to mass."

"That's good. That's fine." Emily heard the sound of her parents standing and, she guessed, her father picking up the two bowls, two plates, and two spoons and carrying them to the sink, then their thud and clatter against the stainless steel. Virginia called into the den, "Emmy, what did the postman bring?"

"Nothing much. Some bills. A letter."

*V*irginia kept her vigil in St. Luke's Church, before the shrine of the Blessed Virgin. William's mother, whose name was Jane, kept hers at her kitchen table, inscribed in coffee marks and stubbed-out cigarette ends. The coiled cord of the wall telephone trailed across the floor to her chair, bore the length and breadth of her conversations with her friends, the people she had seen only last night: Jack, the union foreman and precinct organizer from the brewery below the hill; Mark and Sally, the university professor and his Montessori teacher wife; Frances, her high school girlfriend who ran the library at the county art museum and also curated husbands, showing her last accession the door a scant seven months ago.

In the late afternoon and early evening they gathered around her, replenishing her larder with liquor, cigarettes, and potato chips. William stood in the doorway or sat off to one side, watching and listening, leaving only long enough to fetch another bag of ice from Ramaley's. He pedaled through the sultry and deserted streets, steering one-handed, the side of his chest closest to his heart numbing by slow degrees as he clutched the bag against it, while the other side sweltered. It was a curious sensation.

By eight o'clock, although there had been no word from California, they spoke as if Bobby were dead, or so it seemed to William, who sat on a stool next to the refrigerator and watched them through a thickening bank of smoke.

"Regardless, he's out of the race," said Mark.

"So it's just us against Hubert," said Frances.

"What I want to know is, who gets his delegates?"

"Please don't be crass, Jack. Just for now," said William's mother.

William sat and watched and overheard these things, and it seemed to him the very epitome of adult power and glory: how merely by sitting and talking (as he might sit and talk with his friends on the wall at the top of the park, their bicycles heaped around their feet), history and the future were made, or at least undeniably shaped, extruded from the press of grown-up worry, opinion, and surmise. Or so it seemed to William, for these were the most important and impressive people William had yet known and they were speaking of important things in a time of crisis.

*A*t Emily's house, the Byrnes were at their prayers. The notion that they ought to say the rosary together had struck Virginia during mass, and she bore it home like a hot supper whose very readiness precludes any argument against it. Edward and Emily could only assent. Emily fetched her rosary from the drawer in her nightstand where it rested between a jar of Noxzema and a red-haired troll mascot.

Edward thought he had a rosary somewhere, but could not think where it might be. Emily supposed it was in the tackle box above and to one side of the workbench in the basement in which were contained his combat ribbons, his fraternity pin, tokens and prizes won at carnival booths and fairs, ammunition in various sizes and configurations, foreign coins of several nations and denominations, scapulars issued thirty years before at Sacred Heart School—things that when Emily had looked through them had struck her as assuredly the property of a boy who had subsequently become a young man. But that this young man might have thereafter metamorphosed into her father seemed unaccountably strange, for surely he had always been her father, immutably so.

Edward sat empty-handed at the edge of the ottoman in the living room as Virginia began to say the first decade and Emily's voice fell in just behind hers. Edward joined in, muttering, droning a bass line beneath his wife's and daughter's sopranos.

Nor could it be said to what end this was done; perhaps to no end at all, but entirely as means. It was the buzz and hum of God, the sound, more real than any belief or inkling or assent, that assured Emily that God indeed existed; existed more, rather than less, than other things. The voices and the prayers riding on them were a current, a breeze on which the world was being held aloft, not by will but by submission. In theory they were saying, imploring, *Let Robert F. Kennedy live, or if not live, let this be enough because we cannot bear anymore.* But in practice, all that could be said was *Have mercy* on the one hand and *Thy will be done* on the other; in all, nothing more than *Let be what will be*. And yet they prayed as though if they stopped, their very house might collapse on their heads.

Emily knew the mind might wander but would return, that they were doing entirely the thing that they ought to be doing. For her mother, Emily supposed, it was as a shawl she was wrapping herself in, the same shawl that had warmed her as a girl and had warmed her mother and her mother's mother. She could—as she could not in the case of her father—picture her mother being a child, if not necessarily a girl much like her. But for Emily herself, prayer partook less of memory and time than of time bound to motion, as when, scarcely aware she was doing it, she rocked herself in her bed, a pendulum swung from the tender clockwork of her body, tipping itself into dreams, into peace.

Emily did not wonder if it was wrong or even a sin when she thought of the letter she had received today in the midst of their prayers. She knew Our Lady would bring her back to Herself, even as she recollected the words not of the Hail Mary (which was less a set of words than a tune she might almost wordlessly hum) but of the letter, parsing yet again the sentences, recollecting once more what she could remember of him—something of his hair, the shy insistence of something he had once said in her presence, something of the girth of his calves.

After they were done, there was still no news from California, and there was nothing more to be done but sleep. They shut their doors. Emily heard her parents undress and wash, and then nothing more. She wondered, as she had occasionally found herself doing in the last few years, if they made love, and by what sounds or signs this might be indicated. She wondered if worry and sadness, as on a night like this one, precluded it or perhaps encouraged it.

Emily sat in her bed with the light on. She was writing the boy, or thinking about what she would write him when she wrote him. She wrote the whole letter in her head, and then she said another prayer and switched out the light.

At a quarter of four in the morning, when the world is as asleep as it ever becomes—when if either Jane or Edward and Virginia had crept into their children's rooms they would have found them as deeply encradled in slumber as infants—Robert Kennedy was pronounced dead. That, so much of the time, is how history befalls us.

4

ON THURSDAY HIS BODY WAS FLOWN FROM LOS Angeles to New York, and on Friday there was the mass, and the train bearing the coffin to Washington through the stifling heat, and the burial in the evening at Arlington; and in all that time, although it seemed that William never left the kitchen or the charcoal glare of the little television on the table—that the death was a kind of water beneath which they were all now submerged—he never let Emily slip his mind. He had been tracking his letter to her all that while, in the little corner of himself that was not stunned or frightened by what had happened in California. He imagined the letter sleeping among the other letters at the big downtown post office, passing along belts and through tubes and slots and at last into a sack that was trucked up the hill to a substation and then to a military-green transfer box in Emily's neighborhood. Then—and it must be in the midmorning, with the heat beginning to build on the lawn, but the cool still hanging damply under the shadow of her porch—he heard the postman's steps ringing up her steps and the yawn of the mail slot and slap of the letter descending at last onto her hallway floor.

But in love—and what else is there to call such regard, such attentiveness, such constant mindfulness?—everything is a sign, an augury that demands interpretation. Nor does it brook any gaps in its knowledge: A silence is not a silence but a message; an absence is not an absence but a reminder of presence elsewhere; the failure of something to occur does not suggest that it is as yet undone, but that a different thing altogether has been willed.

So even as William pictured his letter homing towards Emily and settling like a dove onto her threshold, he imagined it going astray, fallen into a floor grate at the post office, entangled in the pages of a magazine and delivered to the wrong address, or sailing over Emily's doormat, catching some heretofore unknown floor draft, and gliding under a hallway table or chest of drawers never to be discovered until Emily's parents moved out seventeen years hence to retire in Arizona. Or more simply and therefore more likely, one or the other parent would intercept the letter, open it, and confront her with it, and Emily would be entirely on his account in grave trouble, grounded or shipped off to a boarding school deep in New Hampshire, and, needless to say, would hate him.

William had calculated that he might receive a reply by telephone as soon as Wednesday or a letter by Thursday. So when he had neither by Friday (and because of the funeral it was unclear whether there would be mail at all that day) he began to despair, and a vision of the most appalling outcome imaginable began to congeal in his mind: that she would read his letter, assay its contents, and share it with Monica Reardon as the dumbest, absurdest, dorkiest, stupidest thing ever to befall her in her whole life. With their rising titters and shrieks of laughter, word of it would spread through Annunciation and on to the guys at Sacred Heart and so even to the Academy, where he would be upbraided not only for striking out with a girl, but striking out with a Catholic girl. Throughout the city, or at least the swath of it from Snelling Avenue in the west to Dale in the east, he would be mocked, scorned, and laughed at. Guys would cruise the apartment house, braying over their radios as they drove by. The worst of them would put burning sacks of dog shit on his doorstep.

There was nothing Friday, and Saturday dawned doubly hollow in the wake of the funeral, in the absence of word. Then the postman brought Emily's letter at ten-thirty, or rather, with his big key, he opened the bank of eight letter boxes in the lobby and thrust it into the Lowrys' niche together with a Red Owl supermarket flyer and a manila envelope containing Jane's credentials for the Democratic-Farmer-Labor Party convention on June 22.

Somewhere in his heart, for the walls were too thick, the morning air too heavy, the postman too considerate to go around slamming things, William heard the postman's departure, and ran into the hall, flung open the door, leaped over the four steps down to the lobby, and skidded to a stop before the letter boxes. He rooted in his pocket for the key, opened the little brass door, and beheld the letter. The envelope was yellow, and as he took it into his hand, he saw there was a border of looping daisies on the back. And above them was her writing, her address inscribed in blue ballpoint, the paper where her hand had lain while she wrote, the flap whose gum her mouth had moistened.

William took the letter back to his room, cradling it loosely in his hands like a fledging he might too easily crush. He slit it open with the Swiss Army knife he had received from his father two Christmases ago and read and read again. It was more than he had hoped for, perhaps a little jocular in tone, a little sophomoric in its exclamation marks and interjections (although Emily had, in fact, just completed her sophomore year), but these were not defects but bonuses, traits that he would surely come to adore. She had suggested that, given the weightiness of recent events, he call her next week, but meanwhile, she wanted him to write back. She wanted more words from him, and now she had made him speechless with all the things that needed to be said.

$\mathcal{J}$ane awoke more or less at the time the mail arrived, and as she poured her orange juice and set the percolator up, her son ambled into the kitchen. She turned and regarded him, looked down to split an English muffin, and looked up to regard him again.

"You seem chipper this morning." She inserted the muffin halves into the toaster.

"I feel okay," he allowed.

"That's an achievement under the circumstances."

He cast his eyes up and met her eyes. He said, "I really believe everything's going to be all right."

"Well." She paused. "Bully for you. Really." He said nothing in response. The muffin halves bolted up out of the toaster and she gave a start. She laughed. "My nerves. Everything's like . . . a shot. You know?"

"I know," he said, and smiled at her.

Jane collected herself, brought the English muffins and the jam to the table, and sat down. "So," she said. "Did you win something? Or maybe it's . . . yes, maybe it's a girl?"

At last he looked away, down and away, where she was used to his gaze being. He said, more quietly, "Maybe something like that. But better."

"Tell me about it when you feel like it. Just be careful, okay? Of you. Of her."

"Sure," said William, and turned and strode down the hall to his room, a man with urgent and manifold labors before him.

*I*n his bedroom—a single window facing east into the gathering algaeous green of what will be a hot summer day—William Lowry is imagining himself for posterity, or at least for the purposes of the letter he is about to write. For this—walls bedecked with posters of Clyde Barrow and Bonnie Parker, Spider-Man, and Ben Shahn's *The Passion of Sacco and Vanzetti*; the desultory heaps of clothes; the works of Isaac Asimov and Ian Fleming, lesser quantities of the Lawrences (D. H., T. E., and Ferlinghetti), A. S. Neill's *Summerhill School*, Alan Watts's *The Book: On the Taboo Against Knowing Who You Are*, and Paul Goodman's *Growing Up Absurd*; and, in drawers, cigar boxes, and under a loose floorboard in the closet, talismans, souvenirs, and fetishes (jackknives and pocket nailclippers, matchbooks, stones, feathers, bones, rabbit's feet, pinecones, horoscopes, baseball cards, screws and bolts, summer-camp riflery badges, a penny flattened courtesy of the Great Northern Railway, and a pfennig courtesy of the Third Reich by way of the Third Infantry and the former Corporal Franklin Lowry—is the totality of him, or was until a half hour ago.

It is so great in scope and yet so little in sum; a historical museum whose exhibits are largely composed, on close examination, of lint, nail parings, and pencil stubs. So what shall William tell Emily about himself? In William's mind the matter of them has been until now entirely about *her*; her qualities and their contemplation. Assuming William has any qualities at all, would it not be really conceited to enumerate them?

William had set himself the task of replying to Emily's letter by the end of the day, by five o'clock when the post office closed, so that she would have it Monday (tomorrow was Sunday), and then he would call her Wednesday. He got the most elegant stationery he could lay his hands on, onionskin typing paper from the bureau in the living room, and set to work. There were, in the end, six drafts, excluding false starts and smudged or spoiled copies (William's penmanship had a tendency to lurch, or, rather, drain off to the lower right corner of the page, as if towards a sump). The final version was penned in permanent blue Scripto ink and sealed in a #10 envelope; William had considered using one of the elegant blue-and-red airmail envelopes emblazoned with the motto PAR AVION, but feared some post office clerk might take the instruction literally and ship Emily's letter to Furness and Victoria Streets by way of O'Hare or even Orly.

He was finished shortly after one o'clock and the letter was mailed by two. Happy enough, he went to the main library to browse *National Geographic, Evergreen Review,* and *Motor Trend,* ate a late lunch at the Seven Corners White Castle, and arrived home at five. But alone, in his room again, sequestered with Emily's letter and his various drafts of reply, he suddenly felt emptied out, false and hollow, although he could not say whether he was the cheat or the cheated, the liar or the dupe. Perhaps now he doubted with the same force that a mere hour before he had believed. Emily's letter (already limp, fraying at the folds with handling) no longer seemed so straightforward, nor did his reply—which he had no exact copy of—seem an adequate attempt at whatever response it was the letter invited.

William shuffled into the kitchen at dinner no longer the man he was at breakfast. After his mother pushed a hamburger patty onto his plate, she went back to the sink to continue washing spinach for the salad she was preparing for her friends, who were coming by to talk about the war, to count delegates, and to drink with her.

William watched her in these preparations, and then, as he was about to get up from the table, she stopped and raised her finger in a gesture telling him to halt. She went down the hall to her bag and returned with two dollars and laid them before William. "Why don't you go to a movie? Or do something with a friend? With Jim? Or whomever?" Her son looked up at her, and seemed to release a great breath he had been holding all that while, and smiled a smile of great relief.

*W*illiam got hold of his friend Jim without difficulty and within ten minutes, Jim's '60 Pontiac Bonneville pulled up, a hulking beast of decrepitude, oozing exhaust, thrumming and belching with carburetic dyspepsia, the chorus of "Judy in Disguise (with Glasses)" leaking from its inoperative power windows.

They drove down the hill without a word, the radio and the fact of being in motion—of moving through space *with* the music—rendering conversation superfluous. Finally, as they stopped for a red light a block from the Orpheum Theatre, William said, "I think I'm going to go out with Emily Byrne this next week."

"That's different."

William's hackles rose a little at this response. "How's it 'different'?"

"Well, didn't you like Sarah?"

"I never liked Sarah."

"I heard she kind of liked you, but you never called her after the dance."

"I never called her because I was only doing you a favor taking her in the first place."

"I think maybe I was doing *you* a favor, getting you a date." Jim put his foot on the gas and the car shuddered forward. "She's kind of sexy. You could do worse."

"She wasn't my type. Shit, she wasn't your type either," William said with a sense of having settled the matter. "And Emily's . . ."

"Sexy?" Jim whistled sardonically.

"Not sexy. Not like . . . Ann-Margret." William tried to get his tongue around the concept he was prodding at in his mind. "I mean that for me it's like she's someone you'd read about or see in a picture, in a painting."

There was a gravity in William's voice whose earnestness Jim fully comprehended, but that also cried out to be mocked. Jim tried to find some middle ground. "We called her carrothead when she was little. But her hair's kind of darkened down now."

William said nothing in response. He let his silence settle over Jim in warning, and Jim, now trying without much success to parallel-park the car, was flailing. Pulling out again, wrenching his neck over the backseat, and cutting the wheel hard, he said, "Look. I don't really know her." He set the parking break. "Good luck, okay? I mean, for real."

William and Jim got out of the car. They had not discussed what movie they would see. They had no reason to. It would be the same as the last time, three weeks before. They sat in the front row, practically blinded by the glass-beaded screen and the roar of the light. Then the bone rose in the air, became a ship wheeling among the stars, and then there was the astronaut, living as a dead man in the empty hulk, and then the black slab, himself meeting himself, and the child, whose bones were the stars from which, thought William, the first bone must have been made.

He and Jim walked to the car, silent, stunned, as though in grief or wonder. To say anything would be not just inadequate but a kind of profanation of beauty. Finally, nearly at the curb of his house, William said, "You see, it's *that* heavy."

"I know. I get it," said Jim, and William got out, and the Pontiac lumbered away.

5

T O LOOK AT HER, EMILY HAD A CERTAIN QUIETNESS
of demeanor; a smallness of mouth, a largeness of eyes, hair
worn shorter than was the fashion, and a roundness in her features
that made her look younger than she was. But Emily was known both
to her mother and the nuns to be a little impetuous, "impetuous"
being a term for juvenile conduct that was not delinquent or even
worrisome, but bore watching lest it boil over into something more
untoward. Now Emily was only "a little" impetuous and thus bore
less watching than most, and in her father's eyes she was nothing less
than faultless.

Still, Emily's conversation had a habit of putting others unfamiliar
with her somewhat on the defensive; of asking questions slightly too
pointed, of delving into areas her interlocutors were not yet quite prepared to broach. Emily's grandmother had a habit of greeting her with
the salutation "Well, come over here and let me get a good *look* at
you"; and Emily's own approach to human relations embodied exactly
this approach. Had she been a character in English storybooks of a certain time, she would doubtless have been portrayed as, say, a hedgehog
with spectacles, albeit a winsome one.

Emily was more self-possessed than William (who in that selfsame
storybook would have been the mole dressed in clericals) and more so
than many girls. But her self-possession was in no way founded on the
full-fledged possession of a self, which, being the holy grail of all
William's self-pursuit, was both what drew him to her and would most
deeply puzzle him about her.

The sun was still high at seven o'clock, a glorious thing, and Virginia had prepared a supper of summer foods, and of things that she knew Emily liked, in honor of her first day at work at Dayton's "New Wave" department. There was fruit salad with miniature marshmallows and hot dogs and baked beans, served on paper plates on the picnic table in the backyard. It had, effortlessly, the air of a birthday, minus the cake, and Emily was happy as Virginia knew she would be; happier still on account of having received a letter in this morning's post. The entire occasion was warm but bracing; and although she had never given conscious thought to it, that was what Emily liked about these foods: the cheery shocks and mischievous slaps of sweet and sour against creamy and bland, of maraschino cherries and grapefruit sections and green relish and yellow mustard, their boisterousness amid the somnolence of meat and salad.

Emily wore a bright yellow sleeveless A-line shift cut mid-thigh, and the shape of the dress and her demeanor suggested you might string her on a Christmas tree or hang her in a belfry and simply ring her. The dress was the first of Emily's purchases made at the employee discount, which would tend to have the effect of returning to her employer virtually every dollar it gave her in wages, but money was not the point of Emily's employment any more than charity was the ultimate end of her mother's church and civic volunteerism. The dress, and perhaps one or two more like it, would suffice, as would the chance to pass the summer in a store (really a "boutique") full of such dresses and girls wearing them and selling them to other girls.

It was to be the last summer of such dresses in those colors just short of gumdrop in shade, closer perhaps to Necco Wafers or tiny Valentine candy hearts: pink, green, lavender, turquoise, and of course Emily's yellow. They would never again be short in quite this way; every girl a little girl, every woman a teenager; nor would the motif of the dress—triangular, like stick-women's skirts, like paper dolls—be so perfectly replicated in the hair, which itself was A-line, triangular, worn long with flips thrusting out like serifs at the feet of the "A." Emily did not have the flips (she had no patience for rollers), but she had the rest: optimism, energy, and youth.

Emily had picked up the letter from the hall table when she came in, a little breathless, and was more breathless still by the time she had shouted a greeting down the hall towards the kitchen, run up the stairs to her room, shut the door, and settled herself onto the edge of her bed, legs dangling. She examined the envelope, caught the thrust of his handwriting. The letter itself she read perhaps four times before she put it in her bedside drawer. He had written things about the assassination—could it have been only last week?—that made her sad, but they, too, were sweet, they were not sobs or wails of grief; they were tender.

At supper, she ate and drank deeply, and her father regarded her as he might a daffodil that had erupted out of their fallow spring lawn. Her arms were bare, unmarked as yet by the sun or by anything at all save the tiny efflorescence of the vaccination scar just below her shoulder. He had seen the letter on the hall table when he had come home and he asked Emily about it, he who could ask Emily anything.

"So who's your correspondent? A dark and mysterious stranger?"

Emily looked up at him and let her fork rest against the side of the plate. She smiled and said, "None of your beeswax."

"Come on," Edward said. "Seriously."

"A boy," Emily said, and she let the words settle with a kind of glug of a stone dropped into a still pool, and in the gap before her father spoke again, she swore she could hear water lapping at the edge of the yard.

"Any particular boy? Or just your standard-issue boy—snakes, puppy-dog tails, and so forth?" Now the truth was, Edward could ask Emily anything, and he could press his luck as far as it would go: He could tease her.

"His name is Bill Lowry. He's a friend of Monica's. And Jimmy Donnelly's."

Edward turned to Virginia as though she were the family archivist and registrar of voters. "Is that anyone we know?" he asked, turning back to Emily.

"I don't know," Emily said, and a moment later, having completed her researches and tabulations, Virginia added, "I don't think so," and continuing, asked Emily, "Where does he go to school?"

"The Academy," Emily said.

"Oh, my," said her father. "I suppose his father is a lawyer or a doctor or a player at railroads and such."

"I don't think he has a father," said Emily. "I mean, his parents are divorced."

Virginia looked deeply at Emily. "How sad for him."

"So a broken home," said Edward. "But presumably a good one."

"I suppose," Emily said. "I know they're Democrats."

Edward tilted his head. "Well, that's rather charming, considering the school."

"And Catholics?" asked Virginia.

"I don't think so."

"Well, nothing wrong with that," Edward said. "And so he . . ."

"Invited me to . . . a concert. Thursday night. Near the U."

"Nothing wrong with that either. And he *wrote* to extend you this invitation. Impressive," said Edward. "So this is a string quartet or something?"

"It's folk music."

Virginia said, "So it's a college crowd? With drinking and so forth?"

"It's a coffeehouse," Emily said, now feeling a little pressed. "They serve *coffee*."

Edward put his hand on Virginia's forearm as if to restrain her and smiled. "So there'll be beatniks and poets?"

Virginia broke in. "I don't like—"

"It's okay," said Edward, increasing his pressure on his wife's arm. "More likely to be earnest, serious types. Penny loafers. Crewneck sweaters. Clean for Gene."

"I guess," said Emily unsteadily, now not quite sure which way the consensus was tilting.

"I think it'll be fine," said Edward. "What about you, Mother?"

Virginia said at last, "I think it's perfectly all right."

*I*t was only Monday night, which meant that Emily was not due to hear from William for two days, and then, presumably, to see him the evening after that. But now she was sorely tempted to call him.

Instead, she called her friend Monica Reardon, in order that Monica might talk her out of it. And Monica did not fail her, putting forward an analysis that was at once deep, elegant, and tidy: "You might think you want to call him, and you might even think he wants you to call him, and he might even think he'd like you to. But really, he doesn't want you to—not if he thought about it."

This line of reasoning was, it seemed to Emily, unanswerable. Yet later, in her bed, she conceived a wonderful compromise. She took up her pen and stationery set and wrote him simply to say that she thanked him for his letter, that she was looking forward to hearing from him again, and that she understood what he meant about everything.

Satisfied, she sealed the envelope and set it on the bedside table, leaning against the base of the lamp where, even after she switched the lamp off, she could look at it, at his name emblazoned on the envelope, his name written in her handwriting.

Then she prayed, as it seemed to her that her mother had bidden her especially this night to do so. She prayed the usual prayers for the usual people and the usual intentions, and when she was done with those she wondered if she ought to pray for the boy, for Bill, and if so, what she ought to pray. After she had thought it up, she prayed it, set it, as it were, in motion and pushed it out into the night, paddling through the stars: "Keep him safe, for me, until Wednesday."

6

WHAT DOES ONE DO WITH UNWANTED TIME; TIME unbidden and undesired, nuisance time that grows like hair and cannot be merely thrown away but must be spent? That was the character of Tuesday and the better part of Wednesday for William, and he wished, for once, that he had a summer job. He had not done well in employment in the past. Last summer he had been set up with a sweetheart job as a carpenter's helper on a construction site through the offices of a family friend. The pay was a mind-boggling three dollars per hour, and all he had to do was lift, shift, or haul as and when he was told to, and otherwise—the bulk of his workday—he simply sat on a pallet or a bundle of shingles and waited for orders.

Only a fool would complain about such an arrangement. But after little more than a week, William, bored and discontent, went to the foreman and suggested that his time might be more wisely used: that he wanted to make a contribution, to perform honest labor, that this enforced indolence was false and hollow. Perhaps, William suggested, they could find something *more*, something *better*, for him to do?

The foreman looked at him, first with annoyance, then befuddlement, and at last pity, perhaps not pity without mercy, but at any rate pity at a loss as to what to do with itself. "I think you better just go home. I think you're missing something here. I don't know what, but there you are. We'll send you what you're owed."

What William was owed, he discovered a few days later, was not much shy of one hundred dollars, and that went into his passbook account at the First Grand Avenue Bank. He passed the summer riding in various cars or sitting with his Raleigh on the banks of various front yards and the walls and stoops of alleys, parks, and minor public edifices. With what he already had prior to his job and with further windfalls later in the year from his father, he had in excess of $350 by the time the present summer arrived. His allowance (five dollars) covered a new record album or book every week, and so there seemed little point in earning additional income.

But now he found himself pressed upon not by lack of funds but by the unwanted interval between now and Wednesday night—well, surely it would be okay to call Wednesday afternoon?—that whined in his ear like a mosquito and made reading or listening to music impossible. He pressed lying around to its extremes—on sofas, chairs, ottomans, the floor, and in combination; in postures sprawled and balled up, with legs hooked, splayed, or tucked and with arms flung or knotted in various modes of akimboment—but found no peace in it. He masturbated (which only made him think of Emily) until he could masturbate no more, and in the last resort, pulled himself on the Raleigh and simply rode and rode and rode.

Emily was more content. She had not only the diversion of her job, but the belief that William's interest in her was but a further bonus in a life abrim with good things; that at worst, if she found she did not like him, she could simply let the matter rest, let the letters return, as it were, to sender, and her life to where it had been before June 5, 1968. But the truth was, as even by Tuesday lunchtime she could not resist intimating to her workmates, that she already thought she probably liked him.

Emily might have asked on what grounds this could be, for William was someone with whom she was scarcely acquainted, never mind someone she could in any sense of the word claim to know. But that kind of knowledge is rather beside the point. The one boy Emily previously liked—Roger Ericksen, whom she had kissed deeply on many occasions over the course of six weeks and who had touched her breasts and once even between her legs—she had liked before they had spoken directly, and she did not stop liking him once she knew him, even though she could not say he acted exactly the way she would have liked him to. When they broke up, she didn't then *dis*like him, but the liking had run its course and was spent, like a great enthusiasm; like the summer a couple of years ago she had spent most of making potholders out of cotton loops on a little red frame with spikes around the edges. She had liked it and then it was used up. Someone might say that is really immature and stupid, but that is exactly how it was.

Perhaps William simply asked Emily to like him, and Emily simply agreed to his request. Although one of Emily's teachers, Sister Mary Catherine, had said we ought to be careful about asking for what we think we *want* rather than what God knows we need, sometimes someone does indeed ask and it is given unto them, just like that. And it does not seem that there was much more to it than that they asked, and someone else didn't. But there is more. For surely Emily in some way was expecting and awaiting this, and was in some way disposed to respond to it in the affirmative. Something particular to that time and place befell her or shaped her in some guise or took her up into itself, so that her head had already begun to nod, her lips to form a whispered "yes," even as she was unsealing the first of William's letters.

At lunch that day, in the employee cafeteria, in the basement where the naked, unwigged manikins lined the corridors like chemotherapy patients under the fluorescent lamps, like schizophrenics queued up for the Pneumanol syrup Emily's father sold to the state hospital, someone asked Emily if she liked anyone.

Emily picked up a french fry, desiccated from spending an hour under the heat lamp at the far end of the steam table next to the sullen, faintly mustachioed cashier lady. She said, "Yeah, there's a guy I like."

That is how love comes, how it shows itself: not ardent or loud, aflame and thundering, nor, on the other hand, timid, weary, and faint. It is but a yes that merely says, in reply to the declaration "I am," "Indeed you are."

7

WILLIAM PUT THE BRIGHT YELLOW PAGE BACK into its matching envelope—a slice of grace, of sun on sun, of butter on sweet corn—and went down the hall and into the apartment, intent on the phone, but then realized he would have to get Emily's phone number from her earlier letter that was cached in his room. He dove into his closet, pushed aside its debris of loafers, ice skates, and sneakers stiff as dried codfish, and retrieved the letter from under the floorboard. He returned to the hall, went to the living room, and picked up the telephone extension there, ready to dial, to seal his fate.

He heard Jane's voice. "—and of course all the farm counties belong to Hubert," and then, "Billy? Is that you? I'm talking with Frances. I'll just be a minute more."

"Okay," William said, and put down the receiver. He idled on the sofa, one ear cocked toward the kitchen, towards the distant susurrations of his mother, and leafed through the new *Life*, with RFK on the cover, running on the beach with a dog, his feet sprung, spiraling upward as though he were going to pirouette right off the sand. He regarded that and then the contents inside. There was an advertisement for the Pontiac GTO in exactly the shade of olivey green he coveted. Then he was conscious of silence from the kitchen, of footsteps coming toward him, and his mother put her head in the door. "It's all yours now," she said.

"Thanks," William said, and after allowing an interval for his mother to return to her perch at the kitchen table, he dialed, and with each rotation and winding back of the dial he felt he was doing the bravest and most momentous thing of his life, that he was risking everything in a moment that was nothing less, he thought, than existential.

The first ring purred and then the second and by the third he was hoping no one would answer, so that he could put down the receiver and this could stop. But just then a voice came on and said, "Hello." It was the voice of an adult, possessed of authority, of the well-exercised capacity to issue edicts and assessments and prison sentences.

William said, "Is Emily there?"

"No, she's at work," the voice said. "This is her mother. May I tell her who called?"

"Um . . . it's Bill—William Lowry, please. Mrs. Byrne, I mean."

There was a pause. The voice said, "Oh . . . I see." Then more briskly, "Shall I have her call you, William?"

He thought for a moment. He did not know the protocol. But then, as he decided that in any case he would not be able to bear the waiting for her call, the voice interjected, "I expect she'll be home by five-thirty."

"I'll call her then," William said. There was a silence for what seemed a moment too long. "Okay?" he added.

"Yes. Very well then," the voice said. "Goodbye."

"Bye," he said softly, and wondered what it was or wasn't that was "very well." He leaned back into the sofa. He felt as awful as he had at any moment during the last three days. Although nothing had materially changed from a half hour before, William could not see himself bearing the wait until five-thirty; no amount of magazines or bicycle pedaling or touching his penis could stanch the flow of what was leaching out of him.

It is cynics that are said not to believe in love, or at least who are willing to utter the thought publicly. But we are all so often faithless in that way. We deny and betray it; we cannot hold it safe in our hearts even from noon to the end of the day.

*E*mily's mother had alerted her to William's earlier call when she came home, just ahead of schedule at twenty past five. There were three telephones in the Byrnes' house, one in the front hall on the table, another in the kitchen, and a third in Emily's parents' bed-room. Emily's mother was in the kitchen, assembling dinner, and Emily could not decide whether to position herself by the front-hall telephone or the kitchen door, where she would be in a position to get to the receiver there before her mother would have a chance to pick it up.

In the end, she hovered between the two, just behind the landing of the stairs, at the head of the hallway that ran ten feet back to the kitchen. She took her place at almost precisely five-thirty. The tele-phone rang at five thirty-eight, and Emily shouted, "I'll get it," in the direction of the kitchen, spun herself around, and sprinted towards the hall table, arriving just as the second ring began. She put her hand on the receiver and felt its vibration run up her arm. With her other arm she touched her hair, regarding herself in the mirror that hung over the hall table. Then, the second ring barely having spent itself, she picked up the receiver.

"Hello," she said, or—so it seemed to her—she croaked.

"Ah . . . is Emily there?" said a voice, thin as water.

Emily tried to clear her throat silently. Then she said, more loudly than before, "This is her. I mean she." There seemed to be no response. She pitched herself a half octave higher. "I mean, it's me. It's Emily."

"Hi, Emily," said the voice, taking a swallow in mid-phrase, and then, with an upturn at the end as though it were putting a question, "It's Bill Lowry."

"I know," said Emily. "I mean, I guessed. My mom said you'd called before."

"Yeah, it was really stupid of me . . ."

". . . but I was at work."

"Right. But your letter was really nice so I thought . . ."

"Your letters were really nice too . . ."

". . . that I'd call a little early . . ."

". . . kind of thoughtful. Not dopey and immature."

". . . because I couldn't wait. So I'm sorry . . ."

"There's nothing to be sorry about."

". . . unless you don't want me to be."

"No, I don't want you to," concluded Emily. "So . . ." she added.

"So . . ." said William. "Do you want—do you still want to go to the Scholar with me? Tomorrow? I can drive. . . ."

Emily thought for a moment that she could not speak, that her mouth and throat were dried beyond the possibility of utterance. But what she said was, "Yes, I'd really, really like to."

8

AFTER WILLIAM'S PHONE CALL — AFTER THEY worked through the details of his picking her up, during which Emily had turned her back to the wall and settled herself to the floor — Emily told Virginia their plans and Virginia, sliding the casserole into the oven, agreed to them. Then Emily went upstairs and sat very quietly on the edge of her bed for a minute, before she stood, went to her parents' room, and telephoned Monica Reardon.

Monica, who had been a comparatively disinterested party in her previous conversations with Emily about William Lowry, now demanded and received without resistance a full debriefing and transcription of the telephone call. They peeled it like a tangerine whose rind they planned to preserve entire, which took nearly ten minutes, whereas the conversation itself had taken scarcely two. When they were done, Monica did not offer an opinion about the wisdom or prospects of what was to occur the following evening. (She privately held that William was, if not an out-and-out spastic, more than a little weird, but then she also thought Emily was just a shade kooky herself.) She did ask Emily what she was going to wear.

"God, I don't know," Emily said. "Maybe my yellow shift."

"Not to the West Bank," said Monica, a little darkly.

"Well, I can't wear . . . dungarees or something. It's a date. It's like a concert."

"It's a coffeehouse, so they dress like college kids. Some of them like Ivy League, some like hippies or art students."

"I don't know about art students."

"It's pretty much beatnik, only no sandals and always all black."

"I don't have anything like that."

"It's not really your look anyhow," said Monica. "Just think of Joan Baez or Judy Collins."

"I'm not sure I have anything like that," Emily said. Then she brightened. "But there's things in New Wave. I get the discount, and one of the girls told me the manager will even sort of advance you stuff. Because I don't get paid for ten more days."

"Well, that'd be cool," Monica allowed.

And that was how the matter was left. The next day at work, Emily reconnoitered, and in concert with the department manager (who was herself a junior at the U) found a dress in exactly the mode Monica had suggested, a floral print in purple, blue, and apricot, A-line, cut mid-thigh, but with short sleeves and gathered at the bodice to accentuate the bust a little. With these she would wear the round-toed single-strap shoes with slightly stacked heels. She would wear no stockings, a scrawl of eye pencil, and earrings, tiny pink-and-green wedges of watermelon.

William also put some thought into his attire, but emerged from his room with considerably less confidence that he had made the right choices. All he had to choose from was various combinations of shirts and pants—khaki and twill, button-down, polo, or surfer-style—that were much the same. But the question at hand was not so much *what* he was going to wear but *who* he was going to be. He could find, in six or seven pages of *Life*, three or four characters that were conceivably aspects of himself, persons he was or felt he ought to be: the serious-minded college student (Dartmouth? Columbia?), a political science or sociology major volunteering spring quarter for McCarthy; the guitar player and poet in a fringe jacket sitting cross-legged in the panhandle of Golden Gate Park whose girlfriend is studying mime; the guy with sunglasses and a tan (with, as well, the sailboat, and the blond girl, also in sunglasses) who drives the olive-green GTO.

On close inspection his closet and chest of drawers yielded only a yellow long-sleeved button-down shirt, a navy turtleneck, and a pair of slightly rumpled but fundamentally clean khaki pants. Choosing the turtleneck over the button-down, he strode to his mother's car as the

Dartmouth student from the waist down and the poet/guitarist or the GTO owner from the waist up.

In the car, which he had washed that morning before the heat could leave cloudy spots of evaporated rinse water on the hood and roof, he turned on the radio and drove slowly in the direction of Emily's house. The distance might be covered in less than five minutes, but William had left twenty-five minutes before their appointed meeting time of seven o'clock. He had, once again, time to kill, to burn up like a jet-liner dumping fuel in order to land, and he circled the perimeter of Emily's neighborhood, and with each circuit moved a street closer to her, bearing down on her. Finally he docked the car just west of her house and waited until the clock in the car said seven. He pulled the car forward the thirty feet to the curb in front of her house, set the parking brake, and got out, looking first across the street and then up it to the east, as though to give the impression that he was not quite sure which house was Emily's. Then he ambled (or rather feigned ambling) up to Emily's door.

William worried as he pressed the bell that the father would answer; that he would be called upon to engage in that combination of fore-lock-tugging obsequiousness and punch-in-the-arm joshing that characterizes intercourse between young men and older men that are neither relatives nor authority figures, but to whom both respect and cordiality need to be shown; who need to be feared but in a friendly sort of way. But he did not much relish the alternative, the mother, whose tone on the phone seemed more than a little formidable, like Joan Crawford in her capacity as chairwoman of the Pepsi Company.

But he saw it was Emily who opened the door, or rather someone who looked like Emily but was different from Emily as he had heretofore seen her, either in life or in his mind. He seemed to look at her for a long time, forgetting that he ought to greet her, that he ought to do anything other than regard her. For he had always thought Emily was pretty (although in most of the world's estimation she was merely "cute"), but now she had become more than that. She had acquired another dimension, that of depth, and William could see around her, could see her distinct from the background in which she stood, against which, it seemed to him, she now shone, although she was nothing more than a girl stand-ing in the doorway of a house on a summer's evening.

"Hi," Emily said. She was conscious that this boy was for all intents staring at her, and she wondered if there was something on her face or stuck in her teeth.

His eyes met hers and then refocused, and he said, "Hi." He began, it seemed to Emily, to put out his hand in order to have it shaken, but then he pulled it back and put it in his pocket. "I'm Bill," he said.

"I know." She laughed, not, she hoped, in a way he would take as mockery.

"Just checking, I guess," William said, and then laughed himself, and looked at his feet. He met her eyes again for an instant and then, hands still in his pockets, swung his gaze back down to and around the floor of the porch, as though he were making an estimate. "So," he said, and his eyes drifted up towards hers again, "are you ready?"

"Um . . . sure," Emily said, although she felt that niceties that some-how ought to be attended to were being ignored, that, far from being swept away, she was being hoisted off her front porch like a piece of furni-ture destined for the moving van. Then she saw that he was looking at her again as he had done in that very first instant, and it felt a little heady, a lit-tle thrilling and dizzying, to be looked at in this way, almost as though she were naked and his gaze were a heat lamp or a spotlight or both.

What William was seeing then and in the car on the freeway was simply beauty, but he had never seen beauty in a girl before. He had of course seen knockouts and stunners and lookers in films and on the television, and he had encountered some remarkably pretty girls at dis-tances of under ten feet. But those were things he had merely seen, that were as pictures: He had never been in the presence of beauty before, felt it light and warm his own skin, had it sitting next to him not two feet away. As he drove, he stole glances of Emily, trying to take her in, and more particularly to isolate and pinpoint what it was that seemed different about her. He saw that she was wearing a purple hair band and green-and-pink earrings, and that because her hair was back a little he could see her ears, which presumably he had never been in a position to see before. He saw that her nose was small and rather upright and jocular, that there was a dusting of acne to either side of it, and that overall her complexion was very fair, almost a floury white, but he was sure he had noticed all that before.

William parked at the side of the coffeehouse, which was in a narrow old brick building fronting on a wide and rather dingy street that was in the process of being bridged for a freeway. William had intended to go around and open Emily's door for her, but she exited the car at the same time he did and stood waiting for him on the sidewalk, her hands clasped together in front of her. William looked at her as he rounded the front of the car, Emily just standing there, and he thought he had never seen anyone stand in exactly that way before, just waiting, eyes downcast, shifting weight from foot to foot, yet radiating something that he hoped only he could see, that was perhaps his alone to apprehend.

They went inside. The room was high-ceilinged, brick-walled, and studded with tables and candles thrust in wine bottles. Along one wall there was a piano and to its left a sort of stage, although it was perhaps only the crate the piano had come in, laid on its side. William motioned to a little round table to the left of it, and he and Emily sat down. There were perhaps a dozen people in the whole place, plus a waitress dressed in the style Monica had called "art student." After a time, the waitress came over to them and asked them what they would like. William ordered himself something called a mocha cappuccino and suggested Emily might like the same. "I guess so," she said, for having looked around the room and observed the other occupants, all college people and really mature-looking, she now felt a little out of her depth. She was liking William—who still had not actually spoken more than a few words to her—for simply having been here before, for not being intimidated by it. She was also getting used to the way his eyes darted up from his lap to look at her, his lips parted slightly as though in surprise.

When the coffee came, they began to talk. He told her about the Academy and she told him about Annunciation; they talked about which teachers were nice and which subjects they liked, about which kids they hated and why, about how stupid it was and how they couldn't wait to get out and how, all in all, it was okay. Then the music began, and in truth, that was a relief. Because talking is hard and music talked for them by proxy. It told them what they thought and what they felt, knowing these things before they did. This, the music said, is how it is; is what is important; is the name of the thing you feel.

The musician was a guitarist with a large head, a babyish face, and wavy hair. He sat on a stool and positioned two microphones before him, one aimed at his guitar and the other at his face. Without a word he began to play. Most of what he played were instrumentals (although he sometimes sang in a rusty moan of whimsy or resignation) and were not exactly what Emily or William understood to be folk music, being neither rousing nor satiric nor sad in direct and straightforward ways. But it was serious and thoughtful, and for Emily and William music was both history and prophecy. It showed them how to see the world and themselves, not because they were empty-headed, but because there was such a surfeit of world and selves to see; because you could sit and stare as William stared at Emily—just one girl in one medium-sized city of no particular account—and be dumbfounded. The music the guitarist played for Emily and William had a kind of melancholy air that reflected the place they lived in, or perhaps a place a little to the north of it. It was music—most of it wordless—that evoked refrigerators and wringer washing machines sitting derelict in fields; cars abandoned on the ice of a frozen lake, waiting forlornly for the thaw; things forsaken and unseen, yet achingly real. The music was a response to the question "If a tree falls in the forest, and no one hears it, did it make a noise, did it fall? Does it even exist?" and the music answered yes. It is a particularly northern view of things. It is a way to smile in the face of a cold so cold that it might freeze a person from the inside out, starting with the heart.

By the time the guitarist stopped for his break, Emily was both a little giddy from the caffeine and susceptible to whatever influence might present itself and enter her through the tender wound the music had worn in her. After the guitarist stepped down from the stage, she and William faced each other—the table they sat at was scarcely eighteen inches across—and for the first time were able to look at each other without flinching, without turning away every few moments in order to let their gaze catch its breath.

"He sure is good, isn't he?" William said.

"It's like . . . bells or something."

"That's because it's a twelve-string."

"So you play?"

"Not really," William said. "I mean, I can play 'Michael Row the Boat Ashore' and 'Hey Joe' and the intro of 'The House of the Rising Sun.' Which is, I guess, what just about everyone can play." William laughed. "I pretty much stopped last year."

"But you still have a guitar?"

"A Gibson. My dad got it for me."

The latter was a subject Emily was curious about, and even as she sensed her own vulnerability in the wake of the music, she understood that this was a matter she might now enter into. "So your dad . . ."

"Doesn't live with us. I mean, he lives in California."

"Wow, that's cool," said Emily. "I mean that he lives in California, not that he doesn't live with you. Do you get to go visit him?"

"I guess I could, but I haven't. Once in a while he comes here. He and my mom don't get along."

Emily paused and then said, "So they're . . . divorced." She uttered this last word cautiously, as though it might have been "insane" or "dead."

"Yeah, since I was six or so." William looked away, and then, bravely, he looked at Emily again. "It's no big deal."

There were several things Emily thought of saying at this juncture, and all of them, she felt, were the wrong thing. Here what seemed called for was not a response so much as an acknowledgment that she had understood what he meant. But she could not say what it was he meant. It was, she felt, something like what the music had been saying.

"I know," she said at last, and if she hadn't stopped to ask herself what Monica might advise in this situation, she might have put her hand on top of his for a moment. But she felt she had at least gotten the tone right and that it contained nothing of "Poor baby," because he clearly wanted no sympathy for the fact of his coming from a "broken home."

William understood that there was no easy transition that she might make to a related subject with which to keep the conversation in motion, for example, "Oh, my parents are divorced too," or "Well, when I get older I'm planning on getting divorced." But as her simple reply settled on him, it came to him that it required no elaboration or extension: that another subject might now be embarked upon, but that the choice of it properly lay with him. But rake his mind as he could, he was unable to find a thing to ask or say to her that did not ring false and hollow, for what he really wanted to know was as yet unspeakable: "Do you like me? Do you really like me?" At last he hit on a serviceable question.

"Do you like poetry?"

Emily looked at him as though he had by some peculiar genius unique to him guessed the innermost secret of her heart. "Oh, yes," she said. "I really, really do."

Sensing his success, William plunged on. "Do you like Emily Dickinson?"

"Oh. Yeah, I really, really do. I like 'The Chariot' especially."

William was suddenly in a little over his head, for his own acquaintance with this poet was slight, his knowledge of her confined to the fact that she seemed to be one whom girls generally liked. He did not want to say he was familiar with the poem, for that would be a lie, and he believed a lie would poison the atmosphere that seemed to have so nicely risen up around and between them. He thought he might nod, although this was a half-lie, an implication of knowing something he didn't really know. Then he felt an urge—from where he could not say—to risk everything.

"I don't know that one."

"I could read it to you sometime," Emily said. "I could read you that and maybe some Elizabeth Barrett Browning. I like her too."

That was another poet William had been given to understand girls liked. "That'd be nice. I'd really like that." William felt doubly blessed, first by Emily's response to this line of questioning, and, second, as it came to him, by the realization that the problem of raising the matter of their seeing each other again had been preempted and successfully overcome.

He added, "I've written some poems myself," and at that moment the guitarist, clutching a glass of ice water, walked past them and hoisted himself up on the platform. As he adjusted his microphones, the waitress came by and asked if they wanted more coffee. Emily, who felt her heart was racing now and that her thoughts were beginning to ferret about more than she cared for, declined, and William declined because she declined. Then, before anything more could be said—all they could do was look at each other, their eyes meeting for the first time at exactly the same moment and same matrix (one might have drawn perfectly parallel lines from Emily's pupils to William's)—the music began again.

It was in much the same mood as before, and for Emily, it was Dickinsonian, although it must be admitted that Emily's knowledge of Dickinson was limited, having been filtered through both the exigencies of a high school curriculum and the sensibility of Sister Mary Catherine. But that was not really of much concern, because for girls and boys of a certain age and time—approximately the thirty-fifth year of the existential era and one year after the Summer of Love—being was more crucial than doing, and so *being* the sort of person who read Emily Dickinson mattered rather more than doing the reading itself.

William was of the same persuasion, not that he had needed any persuading: not after watching the bilgewater of the war in Asia rise through the whole transit of his adolescence; not after being fired by Mortensen Home Builders, Inc., for merely being principled (not to say helpful); not with the equally distasteful alternatives of college or the draft facing him in less than a year. But the touchstones of his conviction were more diffuse than Emily's. If he had been pressed he would have named the beat poets together with Alan Watts, Paul Goodman, and A. S. Neill as his chief mentors, although, in common with Emily, he had not read deeply in any of them save for one volume of Neill, which he read twice. (He had lobbied his mother for the better part of a year to send him to Neill's free school in England, Summerhill, until she convinced him that it was very far away and that he wouldn't like the food.)

But it was really Jack London for whom William had the greatest affinity, although in an odd reversal of the being/doing principle of knowledge, William had no acquaintance with London. For William would have liked nothing so much as to face down the entire Canadian boreal zone with three matches, a jackknife, and, for tinder, the last remaining documentary proof of his claim to the richest vein in the Yukon. Emily might like to live contemplatively, growing ever smarter and more whimsical, in an empty parsonage (friends could visit; there could be a phone, she supposed), but William would, all things being equal, like to howl at the moon. Prior to *Summerhill*, the first and only book that had produced an epiphany in him was the story (read aloud over a succession of weeks by William's pretty third-grade teacher) of a city boy who runs away to the Adirondacks and lives in a hollow tree.

After the music was over, or had to be over for them, since Emily needed to be home by ten o'clock, they walked to the car, side by side, William's hands in his pockets but his left elbow nearly touching Emily's arm. The sun had gone down perhaps half an hour before, the air beginning to cool but still thick with the day's residual heat, now pressed into waves between the pulsing of the crickets. They walked together to the passenger door, and they stood there a moment, neither William attempting to unlock it nor Emily to open it. It seemed like something of importance or great necessity was going to be said or done, but when the sensation came into William and Emily's con-sciousness, they backed away from it, from each other.

William got the key from his pocket and unlocked Emily's door. He opened it and she slid in, closing it from her side before he had a chance to shut it himself. Then she reached over and pulled up the lock on his door so that all he had to do was open it and get in. The vinyl seat was cool and dry. It might have been a shelf of rock at the edge of a lake where they sat watching the water lap.

William put the key in the ignition and started the motor, saying, "That was nice."

"That was *really* nice," Emily said, not to correct him, but to encour-age him, to thank him. William took the remark as it was intended; he could scarcely mistake it. It seemed to have the same quality of being projected as did the presence of her beauty earlier in the evening, of being a kind of weather or light that emanated from her.

They drove mostly in silence as before, but it was not the silence of chatter repressed or paralyzed, but of the music. They were moving, in the sodium light of the freeway and the hum of the tires, as though gliding or skating on that same beautiful ice of desolation. "I could do that again," Emily said.

"Next week if you want," he said, blurting it out before realizing that voicing the idea ought to cause him anxiety.

"Sure."

"I'll call you about it."

"Sure, anytime you like."

"You could read me the poem. 'The— ' "

" 'The Chariot,' " she said. "Like this," she added, patting the seat of the car.

"A Buick. Some chariot." William continued, "You could read it to me on the phone."

"You could come over. My parents don't bite."

"I could," William agreed, and thought how suddenly, in the space of a couple of hours, everything was abrim with potential, with what could be.

He pulled the car up to the curb in front of her house and put the transmission into park. "So . . ." he said.

"So," she said, and smoothed her dress over her legs. "So you'll call me?"

"Tomorrow. Or the next day."

"Okay." She smoothed her dress again and looked at him. "I suppose we'd better do this now instead of at the door," she said, and she put her hands on his shoulders and kissed him on his right cheek and let her lips rest there awhile before pulling away, so that he would know that he ought to come back to her, that she would be waiting. He began to open the door, to go around and get her, and, for a moment, he cupped his hand to his cheek as if he were clasping something against it.

9

EMILY RODE THE NUMBER THREE BUS THAT NEXT morning in a state perhaps not of elation but of confident hope. She was not by any stretch of the imagination head over heels or snowed or sodden or sappy with love for William Lowry. She did not really know quite what to make of him, or herself in relation to him. She knew that she liked him, that she thought he was cute, but also that there was, as Monica had said, something a little weird about him. On further reflection, however, as the bus careened down the Oakland Avenue hill, she thought that perhaps she also liked whatever this thing was that was a little weird about him.

That thing was a little hard to put her finger on. In part, it had something to do with his gaze swiveling around like a lighthouse beam, intent upon you, and then petering out and off in other directions and then coming back after a moment full force. That vague and indeterminate impression was the best Emily could do, but in fact, she had stumbled upon the essential truth of the matter: William Lowry was, at bottom, vague and indeterminate. He was, at least viewed from without, liquid rather than solid; he moved through the world in waves, lappings, drips, and oozes.

As William drove his Raleigh towards downtown about an hour after Emily had been riding the number three in the selfsame direction he was, however, a tsunami of intention. He had hit on the idea (or, more accurately, the idea had hit upon him) that since Emily had a job, he ought to have a job; that it was a good way to pass the day, and would yield funds for further visits to the Scholar and the like. His mother had a friend who worked at Brower's downtown, and he had determined to see if they could do anything for him in the line of being a stockboy or whatever.

Once an intention had discovered William, it propelled him forward like a ball from a cannon, and this is why although others might see him as vague, it was not his experience of himself. Admittedly, the time William spent in this mode was small in relation to that he spent waiting to be seized by whatever the thing would be that would launch him into it.

It should be understood that, for all this, William was not especially malleable or susceptible to either passion or reason. Things might strike him and take him over entirely, but they had to do so at the right time, from the right angle. So if Emily imagined that since William seemed vague, she might remake him according to her own lights, she was mistaken. Moreover, when in the grip of one of his intentions, William could be quite persuasive. He was possessed of a bit of what people then called "charisma," although in truth the word is perhaps a bit strong to describe the angular boy, somehow not quite at home in, not quite fully *composed* in, his body, who ambled into Brower's at about ten-thirty that morning. He had the luck to be greeted by his mother's friend and would-be suitor Louis Campion, who, rebuffed but not yet discouraged, was just now gathering his forces with a view to making another play for her.

"Hey, Billy," said Louis. "How's tricks? How's your mom?"

"Oh, fine. She's fine. Busy."

"Not too busy, I hope."

"Just on account of the DFL convention coming up, I think."

"And you? What can we do for you?" William noticed that Louis's questions were, in the manner of many grown-ups trying to befriend young people, really declarations and even demands. "Going to camp? Need some gear?"

"Well . . ."

"We stock the good stuff. Gear that's stood the test of time. Voyageurs. Trappers. Expeditions. Leather and canvas, not nylon and plastic. Lasts a lifetime."

"Actually, I was wondering about a job." William tossed this out, just as bald as that.

Louis was caught off guard. "Well, I don't know what we've got going. Of course, it's our busy season. Camping, canoeing, hunting season coming up, lots of weddings." Brower's was an emporium whose main line of hunting gear, outdoor clothing, and sporting goods was supplemented by domestic objects—tableware, lamps, wastebaskets, and prints emblazoned with traditional icons and fetishes such as mallards and spaniels—that might tastefully furnish a new home.

Louis paused thoughtfully, as though making a decision that was his alone to reach and merely needed to be affirmed by others as a matter of courtesy. "Let me see what I can do," he said at last. "Why don't you stop back after lunch?"

"Okay," William said with an assurance that suggested he thought this follow-up visit was only a formality, which indeed it was, for Louis's boss had mentioned only two days before his intention to look for a stockboy. Thus by the fortunate happenstance of this boy (somehow simultaneously both diffident and cocky in his bearing, Louis thought) wandering in at the optimum moment, Louis would score points with his boss and be positioned for a further attempt upon Jane Lowry. By twelve-thirty, at which time William was perched at the counter of the White Castle, consuming the third of five hamburgers in the wake of an intense session in the library periodical room, Louis had indeed secured William a position, to commence Monday, eight to three, five days a week, at the wage of $1.65 per hour.

After he had returned to Brower's, been briefed on his duties (vacuuming the store before it opened and thereafter doing as instructed in the stockroom and basement and on the loading dock), and been told to return on Monday morning, William could not but reflect that, against what he felt was his usual grain, he had scarcely put a foot wrong in the last twenty-four hours. He briefly considered dropping into Dayton's to steal a glance at Emily, but thought better of it. As things stood, he had only to wait a few hours to call her (tonight? No, better tomorrow morning), and by merely standing aside and letting events already ordained follow their course, he would see her again soon.

Oddly, it was Emily who felt a flutter of misgiving rise in her chest as the day wore on. She wondered if it had been a good idea to kiss him. It was only a kiss on the cheek, but somehow she had found herself putting her hands on his shoulders and exerting a certain downward pressure on them, and that—that, and the length of what she had intended to be a peck—had, she feared, changed things. That and perhaps seeming a little too eager to see him again. Plus mentioning "The Chariot," a poem she had just selected at random as being by Dickinson, but which she now remembered was kind of serious, even sad. As the afternoon wore on, as business in the New Wave department came to a virtual standstill around three o'clock and she had time to think, it seemed to her that she might well have managed to incorporate the worst of two apparently contradictory worlds, coming off as being both fast and gloomy.

Emily had not called Monica last night. It had not even occurred to her; the experience of the evening had not required Monica's explication to make it comprehensible and complete. It was wholly itself, and wholly Emily's to hold on her own, as her own. But now Emily would have liked Monica to tell her what to make of it, even though she had a pretty good idea what Monica would say, having absorbed the entirety of Monica's wisdom on the subject of boys.

What Monica would have said was this: that if a boy had indeed formed the impression of Emily that Emily feared—the slutty and bookish spinster, the man-eater of Amherst—he would either bolt or stick around to see how far he could get. And with that conclusion drawn, Emily felt utterly at sea, lost if not quite despairing. Monica seemed very small to her, certainly no bigger or smarter than herself; and Emily found herself wanting the counsel of her mother, of her father. Should she not have let her lips linger on William's cheek? Should she have said that her favorite poem was "The Cremation of Sam McGee"? But there was no one she could query about these matters who would have an answer. Except, she supposed, William himself.

It says somewhere that love seeks only itself, which may or may not be true. For Emily, at any rate, her dilemma forced her deeper into her dilemma, deeper into the matter of her and William, which could only be resolved within itself, on its own self-enclosing terms. Sensing this, folding cotton tops and checking sizes against their labels, Emily had little choice but to go forward. What was left for her to decide was in what spirit she would proceed, in dread or in hope, in doubt or in faith, which is to say, in fear or in love. She recollected the way he looks, and in particular the way he looks as he looks at her, and she decides. She believes.

That evening, William went riding with Jim Donnelly. That was what he usually did on Friday nights, and, indeed, on most nights when there was nothing else to do, which tended to be almost all nights during the summer. You might say they were really listening to music, since the radio was always on and often regarded with great attention. You might also say they were sightseeing, except that they rarely went anywhere they had not driven before. You might even say they were socializing, promenading, for several times they joined the procession of cars that made a circuit between Seventh and Ninth Streets downtown, many of whose drivers and passengers were familiar to them.

But it was truly none of those things. Rather, they were treading water, holding themselves aloft as the current of the night swept under and around them.

"So how'd it go?" Jim asked, broaching the question after thirty minutes of guiding the sullen and brooding Pontiac between the river and downtown.

"How'd what go?" William was not going to be easily drawn. He, to whom nothing ever happened, wanted to pay this story out slowly and with care.

"Emily Byrne."

"Fine."

Jim waited for more, realized it was not going to be forthcoming, and harrumphed (as much as any seventeen-year-old can harrumph). "That's all?" he said.

"We had a good time," William offered.

"How good?"

"Heard some good twelve-string. Drank some good coffee."

"Anything else? Good, I mean?" Jim was narrowing down his inquiry. William knew where he was going, but feigned ignorance.

"Did you get . . ." said Jim, trailing off, reduced to a desperation he now felt it was unbecoming for a friend to let him flail about in. "You know," he added, almost pleadingly.

"I'm not saying," William said, knowing full well that such a reply not only created the impression of success but was ethically impeccable. In truth, he felt, and the impression had only grown as the day went on, that Emily Byrne had given herself over to him, not in the dirty way Jim was imagining, but in some other manner that took the form of a promise, a pledge.

"Okay, so do you like her? Better than Sarah?"

"I never liked Sarah."

Jim sensed a chance to get a little of his own back. "Oh, you liked her. She just didn't like *you*."

"Suit yourself," said William.

Jim was feeling his oats again. "So, do you? Come on."

"Yeah. I do."

"And her? Do you think she likes you back?"

"Yeah," William said, almost wearily. "I think she does."

"Well, well, well," said Jim, letting his voice trail off into a whistle.

William seized the opportunity to change the subject. "I got a job today. At Brower's."

"How'd you manage that?"

"Walked in. Asked."

"Just like that?" Jim wasn't buying this as presented, and William sensed he had better provide a little more, lest Jim return to the subject of Emily.

"Well, my mom has a friend there. Mr. Campion. He kind of arranged it. But they were looking for somebody anyhow."

"Hey, that's Louie Campion, right? I heard he's a 'mo. I heard he tried to 'mo Rich Banner in the University Club locker room. Better be careful. Better wear a nut cup." Jim laughed deeply, and the Pontiac burped, seeming to join him.

"He went out with my mom once. He's always asking about her. I don't get how he'd be a 'mo."

"Maybe he's confused. Or ambidextrous." Jim decided to stick his neck out. "I mean, your mom's . . . not like other moms. So maybe they were just being friends," Jim added quickly.

William indeed took umbrage, but recast it as riposte.

"Yeah, she's got a little more on her mind than sunbathing and tennis." From June to September, Jim's mother was to be found mostly on the court or slathered with Coppertone in their yard. "And if you want to talk about being a 'mo, what was that you did a couple of years ago?"

Jim was now firmly back in his place. "You did it too," he said weakly. "And it wasn't really 'moing. Not like a couple of fags, cornholing and everything. Everybody does it. At least when they're kids."

"How do you know? Nobody ever says they do."

"Everybody jacks off, and nobody says so."

"I suppose." This was indisputable yet troubling because it stubbornly resisted confirmation from anybody, rather like the question of sexual intercourse between parents; like what nuns looked like out of their habits; like the dark side of the moon. And he had always wondered if people like Jim (and maybe, now, Mr. Campion) just *said* that everybody jacked off as a way of talking people into jacking off with them, and in fact nobody did, except the sorry few who had been suckered into it and were now themselves for all intents and purposes 'mo initiates. William had done nothing else with other guys since those times with Jim two summers earlier, but he had to admit that as for jacking off, he was pretty much beyond cure.

For his part, Jim sensed that while he had restored the equilibrium between William and himself, he had gone a little too far and that now the forward momentum of the evening had stalled. He pulled himself up straight on the seat. "Want to get something to eat? Drive out University, go to Porky's?"

They were all of eight blocks from William's house. William said, he hoped without any trace of sadness, "No. I think I'd better just go home."

*A*lthough she had already established there was nothing of use that Monica could tell her, Emily called Monica that evening, because it was owed to Monica under the rules of their friendship. Moreover, Emily did indeed want to put what had happened into words for another person so as to make it real for herself; to set the previous evening before the two of them and examine it together objectively.

After Emily had done this—saying she had "kissed him good night" but leaving out the fact of her hands bearing down on him, which was the troubling part, the part that would have set off alarms—she let Monica summarize for both of them.

"So, that sounds pretty good. And he was nice. And he didn't do or say anything weird." This last was a little more inflected towards the interrogative.

"No, he was fine."

"So are you going to see him again?"

"Oh, yeah. Maybe this weekend."

"That's kind of soon."

"Well, it's not a date or anything. We might just get together."

"For what?"

"Just to hang out." Emily was not sure how precise she ought to be.

"Like at the park?"

"Maybe." Emily couldn't stop herself. "Actually, there's some stuff I want to show him. Some things . . . I've been reading. Some poems."

"Some poems. That's kind of . . . heavy."

"He really likes poetry."

"He *really* does? Or he says he does?" Monica, who was not much for poetry, sounded skeptical.

"He really does."

"Because guys will say things like that. To get in your . . ."

"It's not like that," Emily put in quickly, and Monica felt her swerve the line of conversation.

"I s'pose not. He's pretty serious," Monica said, and exhaled. "So where are you going to go?"

"I don't know. He's supposed to call about it. Maybe I'll go to his house."

"Emily, you can't go to his house." This, Emily realized, was true.

"So maybe I'll invite him over here. During the day."

"That's better. It's kind of fast, but it's better."

"Fast?"

"Well, not *fast* fast. Just kind of *soon* fast."

"It could be like he was coming over to do homework," Emily proposed.

"Yeah, I guess it could. That would be okay. Even though it's summer."

After Emily was finished with Monica, after Monica was finished with Emily, after the situation with William had been put through the mill of casuistry and protocol, Emily went to her mother.

Virginia was sitting on her bed—the double bed that she and Edward had occupied for nineteen years—reading a magazine, and when Emily came in she looked up, smiled at her, and said, "Yes."

"Well," said Emily, and swung her hands around behind her back and locked them together there. "You know, Bill Lowry. The boy I . . ."

Virginia jumped in, to save Emily from describing the exact nature of the relation. "Yes?"

"We thought we might get together to look at some books, kind of like summer enrichment?"

"Yes."

"Maybe over here. Maybe tomorrow or Sunday."

"What time of day?"

"Say, in the afternoon?"

"And what kind of books?"

"Well, you remember how I told you he likes poetry. . . ."

"Oh, yes. You did."

"Well, that kind of thing. Is what we'd be doing. Reading. Together."

"Well, that seems perfectly fine," and Virginia seemed to be sincere in this assessment. She continued, "So when exactly is he planning to come?"

"Actually, I'm not sure. Probably this weekend. He's supposed to call."

"Well, when he does, you just fill us in, okay?"

"Sure," Emily said, and her body at last relaxed. "Thanks, Mom," she said.

"You're welcome," her mother said, and returned her eyes to the magazine that still lay on her lap.

10

WILLIAM AND EMILY SAT ON THE GRASS IN THE Byrnes' backyard, Emily's book open before her. William had called at nine-thirty and come by a little before noon. Emily's mother made them lunch. William sat at the kitchen table, sculling dutifully in his tomato soup and nibbling at the grilled cheese sandwich as he answered Mrs. Byrne's questions with brief but polite replies, feeling as though his feet did not quite reach the floor, but it was less of an ordeal than he imagined. The room did not reek of fish, although he supposed they had been eating it just the night before, it having been Friday.

Emily was wearing cutoff jeans and a sleeveless striped cotton top with her hair tied back. This was how girls of that time and place generally dressed themselves on hot weekend days. She was not for this less beautiful than she had been two nights before, for it seemed to William that the casualness of her appearance granted him an intimacy with that beauty that was deeper, if less outwardly glorious; a kind of nakedness, the beauty beneath the beauty.

Emily was reading as William was thinking this, or forming the impression that amounted to it, and he wondered if he was getting an erection. Then she finished and said, "That's the one I told you about at the Scholar." She looked at him and said, "I guess it's kind of gloomy. You don't mind, I hope? That kind of thing?"

William had scarcely heard a word of the poem save something about death and horses and eternity, and he said, "Oh, no. Maybe it's not gloomy. Maybe it's just important. Profound." The latter was a word he had been waiting to use for some weeks.

"Yeah," Emily said. "And besides, she's not really gloomy. It's like she thinks it's all a little funny and odd—how people are and how God is." Emily thought of another poem, and flipped through the pages of her book.

"Listen," she said. " 'God is indeed a jealous God/He cannot bear to see/That we had rather not with Him/But with each other play.' "

This time William had been listening, and thought he understood what she was getting at. He wondered how to respond and finally said, "Kind of sacrilegious, isn't it? Like she's making fun of God?"

"It's not like that. Because it's not like God's really jealous, like he really minds. The joke's really on us—that we're like children."

"Like we're having too much fun playing to sit around and worry about God." William was not sure this last comment had been such a good idea.

"So do you worry about God?" she asked. Her voice was friendly but a little impish. "Or maybe you're like an agnostic. Like a lot of kids." William could not tell if this last remark was meant to be helpful.

He struggled to frame a reply. Ordinarily, the term "agnostic" was one that, like "profound," he would have savored the opportunity to make use of. It did, after all, describe something like what he thought (or felt or intimated). It made his doubt (his confusion, to be more precise) sound considered. It was rather like the way his mother allowed that she thought of herself as a "socialist" rather than a "communist," although most people in Minnesota were hard pressed to see the difference.

"It's like I'm a little like that," William began. "I mean, I think there's a God, but I don't know exactly what's he's like. If he's like a spirit or a ruler or an idea." William continued in this vein, and was soon tangled in analogies, the ground around him strewn with "likes" and "sort ofs" and "kind ofs."

This reliance on "like," on analogy, among adolescents tends to be chalked up to their imprecision of thought, to the callow diction of half-baked and lazy minds. But William's mind was scarcely lazy, and Emily's was at times stridently energetic. So perhaps when they grappled with the great questions of existence (which becomes rather a penchant when existential terror can be induced by the thought of making a phone call;

of choosing high-top over low-top sneakers; of doing or saying any one particular thing rather than another) they were on to something in adopting this mode of discourse. For we do not apprehend ultimate things directly, but approximately. They are unseen and unseeable, we can only picture them—imagine them—sidelong; we are not able to say what they are, but only what they are *like*.

After a minute or so, William concluded with something along the lines of "So God is like the air. He's everywhere and in everything, but the whole system, our whole society, is set up to keep you from seeing that." He thought that was rather fine, and so felt no compunction in asking Emily the same question she had asked him.

"So what do you believe?"

"That God made me to know Him, to love Him, and to serve Him in this world, and to be happy with Him forever in the next," Emily said in a cheery, singsongy voice. Then she smiled and rested her hands in her lap.

William was not entirely sure what he ought to make of this, although he sensed that some levity was intended. "So that's it? Or are you kind of teasing me?"

"I'm kind of doing both. It's what we learned when we were little. *And* I suppose it's what I believe." Emily saw that William was, if not troubled, a little at a loss for words. He was getting, before her eyes, a little vague, vaporizing into a curtain of fumes that floated and twisted in the heat. "But you ought to believe whatever you want," she added. "I mean, I liked what you said."

"I'm glad," William said. And then he had an idea, a notion that he thought would please them both, that would recover what had been lost in the last five minutes and record what had been gained. "That last poem, the one about how God's jealous. It's short. So you could write it down for me? Couldn't you?"

"Sure. And then maybe another time you could show me your poems, the ones you wrote."

"Sure, if you want. I mean, they're kind of personal. I mean, you might not really like them. I mean, they're not very good," William said. "But you can see them. If you want."

"I want," Emily said.

*E*mily said her prayers that night, and she prayed all her usual intentions, which now included the health and safety of William, just as they did that of Monica and Emily's other friends. She wondered about what William had said about God and why he said it so apologetically when in fact it was more or less what everyone believed these days, even Emily. It was not that she did not still believe the catechism she had parroted for William. But she did not so much believe it as she loved it beyond any mere assent or conviction; she loved it as something she had known from childhood, as she loved her father and mother and sister and grandmother; she loved it with an assurance that entitled her to mock it, as she had done with William.

But the truth was that if she were pressed to talk about it as the college kids at the Scholar doubtless did, she would probably say the kind of things William had said. She wondered if to speak of God in that way—leaving out all the things the church said God does as opposed to merely is—was a sin. If it was a sin, surely it was a sin of omission, made in the interest of getting along with other people. It was, she supposed, ecumenical.

Emily's prayers tolled silently over the city and fell upon its roofs as dust or ash from a fire, unseen. William was still awake as she was praying. He was reading his poems, all six of them, which he had written last winter and typed (entirely in capital letters) on his mother's Olympia portable. He read them, and despite what he had said to Emily, he thought they were pretty good; they had some catchy lines, like the best songs do. But he was a little chagrined to find that they contained a lot of swear words—one of the things he had thought made them good at the time he composed them—and worried that Emily might be put off by this. There was one poem, for example, that had no theme other than the sheer joy of inscribing curse words on paper: "GOD IT'S A GAS HOW I CAN TYPE/FUCKANDSHITANDASS AND ALLTHAT/PUTTING A GUN TO THE HEAD OF EVERY CLEANANDMORAL-MINDED AMERICAN/AND I CAN'T GET NO IMPRIMATUR FROM CARDINAL-SPELLMAN." He thought it just as well that Emily not see this one.

Of the remainder, William set one aside as unfinished (the almost preternaturally Nietzschian "THE PHILOSOPHER FUCKING MOTHER-EARTH") and another as charming but jejune ("SUPPOSING THAT WE ALL WALK OUT OF HERE/AND SPREAD OUR WINGS/AND FLY/AND DROP SHIT ON THEHUMANRACE/I'LL BE THE BOMBARDIER IF YOU'LL HOLD MY HAND/AND WE'LL DUMP THE SYSTEM RIGHT ON THEM"). He thought he would just show her his best effort and leave it at that:

> i've been watching myself and wondering
> who i am
> and looking at the sun burning my eyes
> i could do something better
> so they tell me
> if i only had the guts to leave or stay
> go out there and play jesus
> or i could stay where i am and pretend nothing
> exists but my little schzoid sphere and help myself
> but who wishes they were me?
> i'm sort of walking the line now pretending i'm doing one
> or the other
> talking to the disciples and defenders of the realm
> bitching
> bullshitting
> loving every minute
> asking the questions children ask:
> why?

This was, William thought, if not a good poem, at least a very sincere one. It was the truest thing he had written and also the hardest. It was his confession. It was his prayer.

11

MONDAY WAS WILLIAM'S FIRST DAY OF WORK.
He locked his bicycle in the alley behind Brower's and went in
the freight entrance. No one was there excerpt Mr. Murkowski, the
warehouseman to whom William had been told to report by Louis
Campion. Mr. Murkowski didn't so much explain William's duties to
him as grunt and shrug and gesticulate towards various piles of goods
that needed to be shifted from one place to another. And that, more or
less, was William's job.

It was dull work moving, say, 125 boxes of Bass Weejuns from a pallet to the shoe stockroom, and stacking them by size and color
(William had not even known they came in black). But the place itself
had a certain museumlike fascination for him. The main stockroom
and its ancillary chambers were larger than the showroom and two stories high, with catwalks and balconies and a little office from which
Mr. Murkowski watched him. There were canoes lying on the rafters
and stacks of paddles, fishing rods packed in metal tubes, Hudson's Bay
blankets, tents and tent poles, Dutch ovens, fire grates, lanterns, and
boots, especially boots, the item Brower's was most noted for.

William himself had his eye on a pair of boots, the model called the
Boot Sauvage, named in honor of the voyageurs who explored and
trapped in the far north woods, along the boundary and northward to the
boreal zone and the verge of the Arctic. Louis Campion had told him
that he could buy items from the store at a thirty percent employee discount, and in addition to the boots (thirty-five dollars), William figured
he would investigate a Duluth pack, the traditional haversack of the

voyageurs (distinguished by the head strap that helps bear its weight). At home, he had a fair amount of camping equipment—a hatchet, a canteen, a sleeping bag, and a small tent, mostly unused and untried—but what he wanted most of all was a canoe, although by reason of price and practicality (he had no more means to move or to store a canoe than a jetliner) he seemed unlikely ever to attain one. Still, the idea could not but preoccupy him, for every time he looked up to the rafters from his pallets and crates and cartons, there sailed the canoes, six or eight of them in aluminum, fiberglass, and wood laminate.

That was what he told Emily about when they went to the Scholar again that Wednesday night; of dull and pointless work in a chamber full of what were for him fabulous curiosities, of Mr. Murkowski watching him like a fish in a tank, of what seemed to him to be his own daily submersion in the wondrous aroma of leather, canvas, gun oil, and clean wool. All that, and earning almost twelve dollars a day for his trouble, money he didn't really need; money that, he calculated, could indeed accumulate to an amount equal to the price of a canoe in thirty or so such days.

"You ought to have a canoe, if that's what you really want," Emily said. Emily had been to canoe camp in the north of the state.

William was feeling ebullient and a little silly. "What I really want is a GTO. But I'd be at Brower's until I was twenty-one to save that much," he said. "I'd be awfully tired of hauling shoe boxes by then."

"Do you really care about cars that much? About driving around and engines and stuff?"

"I guess not. But it's beautiful, that car. It's the most beautiful thing—well maybe not thing, but most beautiful machine I've ever seen. Especially in the metallic green, with the front bumper that's made of this new material so it's green too. It's the coolest thing you've ever seen."

"I know," Emily said, though it was hard to say if she meant she was familiar with the car in this regard or if she was expressing a deeper but more general sympathy. "But what do you *really* want?"

"You mean that I could really have?" This seemed a tricky question, for William felt the correct answer was something along the lines of "world peace" or "the end of poverty" or "civil rights." But while those were desirable goods that he certainly willed, what he really wanted was the canoe, and more than that, Emily, in the way he was enjoying her right now, but also in every possible way there might be to know and to love her.

"I guess I'd really like the canoe with you and me being able to go in it somewhere," William said at last.

Emily smiled and then looked away, down at her lap, not in embarrassment or discomfiture but because this remark numbered among the kindest things anyone had ever said to her. It spoke of wanting her and yet of requiring nothing of her save her presence, the mere fact of her being.

William felt that she must have understood what he said in the intended spirit, but then wondered, as she was looking down, if her interpretation might be taking some more negative turn as she pondered it, as she held it in her hands in her lap and examined it.

"That's what I'd really like," he finally repeated, as though to underline his intentions.

Emily looked up, and meeting his eyes with hers—which William now saw were a grayish blue, like lake water—said, "I know." She said this as she might have said "Yeah," its subject having no apparent object, no particular thing it claimed to know. But William heard it differently, and heard it rightly. Emily knew, and what she knew, what she wanted to know, was William.

Such moments, which depend more on what is heard than what is said, are rare, and rarer still for young people like William and Emily who imagine their every utterance as an inchoate stammer—as opposed to adults, who believe their words are solid objects, like poker chips or cabbages or cakes of soap. And so you might look up and around and see how very ordinary everything is, as from a daydream, and quite reasonably decide that you had not heard the thing you thought you heard, or had attached some fanciful and mistaken meaning to it.

William and Emily did not do this immediately, as they broke the surface of the lake they had been beneath together and saw that it was the same place and the same day as when they had begun. Their hands

were still, so to speak, touching, more entangled in each other than in
the circumstances and contingencies that were beginning to press in
around them demanding to be recognized, to be accorded their due as
reality. But whatever had descended upon them had largely vanished
by the time they left the Scholar. On the freeway home, the sodium
light poured down on them like a wrung-out sun and the tires ground
against the concrete and last winter's pulverized sand and road salt, taking all the beauty away.

When they parked just down from Emily's house, they were exactly
where they had been a week before. Emily had not forgotten her worries about the way she had kissed William, and despite the harmony of
her relations with him on Saturday (when the constant presence of one
or the other of her parents afforded no opportunity to kiss him again)
and tonight, she worried about it now. William's unmistakable regard
for her had registered, but so too had the logic of the inadvisability of
the previous week's kiss.

So when William put the car into park and shifted his body in her
direction and looked at her, she looked away and seemed to hold herself—arms pinned to her sides, hands knotted together—not simply
self-protectively, but *away* from him. William's lips had parted slightly,
and they might have spoken something, but he held himself still and
finally bent over decorously, brushed her cheek with his lips as he
might have done with his hand, and pulled himself back. She looked
up, and by way of response nodded in a cursory manner, as though
some business had been concluded.

They recovered themselves a little on the way to the door of Emily's
parents' house. Emily said, "So I'll see you this weekend?"

"I suppose." The instant William said it, he knew it had come out
stung, petulant, inflected with a kind of obsequious disdain. He quickly
added, "I mean, sure."

Emily read his unhappiness clearly, though she could not tell whether
its source was innocent, honest emotional injury or thwarted selfish
desire. She offered reassurance as best she could. At the door she touched
his hand lightly and said, "It was really nice tonight. It was good."

"Sure," William said, but in trying to drain out the bitterness he had drained out every other feeling the word might have. He said, "Good night," and she said, more tenderly than he could now hear, "See you soon," and William shambled down the steps of Emily's house and into the dark.

That was the end of William's peace and contentment. He worked joylessly in the warehouse, Mr. Murkowski all the while watching him as though expecting him to steal something. And William felt like stealing something, or more likely hurling a decoy or a set of fireplace tools through Mr. Murkowski's office window.

He had ruined things with Emily, their past, present, and future. He must have done something wrong, but in endless replays of the evening's events he could not locate the misstep he had apparently made, the crime for which she wanted to punish him. He imagined and quickly rejected the thought that he had completely misconstrued her behavior: that she had sat back in the car seat not disdainfully but in fact demurely, letting him make the first move, waiting for him to more or less ravish her, as a kind of test of his masculine mettle. But that did not seem to be borne out by the other facts of the evening, nor by what he knew of Emily's character, which was not cunning or perverse—or at least hadn't seemed so until now.

That was as far as William could get with Emily's side of it. As for his, he had in everything he had done (and was doing, for it was Friday and he had not called her, half in confusion and fear, half in spite) made matters worse. He should not have kissed her when she did not kiss him; or should not have kissed her in that way, but in some other way. He should not have been sarcastic—or whatever it was—with her. He should not have skulked off. He should have, right then and there (or maybe after a little cooling-off period), asked her if everything was all right, or he should have just ignored the whole thing and acted like nothing had happened, or maybe he should just take the fucking hint: that she'd changed her mind about him, or he had misread everything from the beginning.

Now, as he worked, as he swept, as he tried to carry one too many shoe boxes at once and the whole tower of Weejuns collapsed and fell from his arms and he could have sat down right then and there and wept, he was checkmated and miserable. They could break up, although it was doubtful they had ever been together. They could reconcile, but that involved meeting each other in some way, somebody making an overture, and she would not call him because he was supposed to apologize to *her* (and girls didn't make overtures anyway) and he wouldn't call her because she was supposed to apologize to *him* (and guys didn't make overtures when they'd been given to understand that overtures were unwanted). So there they were. William supposed he could do nothing at all, and then they would meet when they were both very old and she would say her whole life had been wasted, that she had been waiting all this time for him to call.

Mr. Murkowski walked by, as if on his way somewhere, but doubtless to establish the source of the noise he had heard. He found William on his knees, sorting B's from C's, brown from cordovan, and when William looked up and began to explain, their eyes met and Mr. Murkowski smiled and seemed to take great satisfaction in William's present posture. He made no move to help pick up the boxes or to return their contents to them. Finally, he clicked his tongue and said, "Mind the merchandise, son," and then, "Don't bite off more than you can chew," and finally, as he began to turn in the direction of his office, "Make haste *slowly*."

"Fuck you," William said.

12

IT HAD NOT BEEN LOST ON EMILY THAT WILLIAM had turned cold towards her at the end of Wednesday evening and that the kiss was the cause. But she had, at the moment itself, done her best to mollify him, and in the following days she did not worry over the matter. Working in the New Wave department did not encourage introspection, and even in quiet moments, when she was folding and hanging clothes, the garments themselves—extrovert and glossy in form, color, and substance—promoted the view that life was all horizon, broad rather than deep.

That is not to say that she never thought about William, or the note upon which they had parted. She thought particularly about what he had said to her at the Scholar and how nice it was, and the fact that if he had meant it, he wouldn't have gone cool on her, particularly not over something like the kiss, which was hers to withhold, it being her kiss. He had kissed her anyway, and she hadn't objected; she had been a little disappointed, in retrospect, that he hadn't kissed her longer or on the mouth.

So he had no right to be angry. It wasn't fair. Moreover, it bore out the logic of Monica's argument, for he was only angry because he hadn't gotten more of something to which he wasn't especially entitled in the first place and which might have been giving him the wrong idea about Emily (not that the idea that he apparently now entertained of her was the one she had in mind, Emily had to admit). At any rate the ball was in his court, and she would simply wait to see if he called and what he said when he did; although if he didn't, that would only prove what his interest was to begin with, unless, Emily thought, he was thinking something entirely different—some hermetic and unfathomable boy thing—which could only be discovered by her calling him, which, of course, she could not do.

*B*y the end of the day on Friday, William could still not decide how to proceed. The correct meaning of Emily's behavior remained a mystery, a matted and tangled skein of surmises, second and third guesses, dreads and bewilderments that told no more of a coherent story than something he might fish out of the bathtub drain. Thus flummoxed, he could well have simply surrendered and called Emily except for the fact that one of the few credible readings that remained on the table was that she meant for him not to call, not ever.

William decided to go riding with Jim Donnelly to clear his mind (if that is the correct word to describe sealing himself inside the hulk of the Pontiac with Jim's fulminating 100mm cigarettes and the beast's own emissions of gasoline, carbon monoxide, and blue gusts of combusted motor oil). Over the course of an hour's driving William had no compunction in ladling out his whole dilemma until his friend had a good taste of it.

Nor are friends like Jim and William shy about offering advice when faced with a problem, no more than they are when the hood of a malfunctioning car is raised and every male within a radius of a mile closes in on it to take a shot at reading the entrails. Jim knew rather less about girls than Monica Reardon knew about boys, which was not very much at all. But on this occasion he was on the money as uncannily as the time when, the best automotive minds of Sacred Heart High School having been stumped, he sidled up to an Olds almost bereft of vital signs and quietly noted that the coil wire was missing.

Jim said two things, neither of which was strictly true, but which nonetheless effected a solution to William's dilemma. First he said, with no particular conviction or commitment, "Sounds like she's kind of testing you."

"How's she doing that?" William asked.

"Maybe to see what you'll do. To see if you're serious or whatever."

"Whether I'm serious . . ."

"I mean, you said she didn't really freeze you out or anything. That she . . ."

"Just sort of . . . hung back," William confirmed.

"So it's a test, like the damsels with the Knights of the Round Table. Like with mice, like with B. F. Skinner."

"He's like A. S. Neill, right?"

"I guess. Anyway, she just wanted to see what you would do."

"What if I did the wrong thing?"

"There's no right or wrong thing to do, unless you did something really stupid."

"I kind of . . ." William was struggling to gauge exactly what he had done. "I kind of . . . well, pouted."

"Pouted?" Jim snorted. "That's cool. You mean you stuck out your lip at her?"

"No, I just sort of acted a little put-out."

"And did she act pissed-off back?"

"No."

"So no big deal. So do you want to call her?"

"I don't know if I'm supposed to."

"That's not what I asked."

William pondered this, and realized that all the feelings of the last two days had come to a tinge of regret overlain by an unnamable sadness. Then he said, "Yeah, I guess I want to call her," and with that succeeded in putting a name to his affliction: that he missed her, and that was pretty much all of it.

"So do it," Jim said.

"Suppose she doesn't want me to?"

"Then she can hang up. Or she'll have her mom tell you she's doing her homework."

"School's out."

"Okay. Then she's douching or something." Jim snorted again, and the Pontiac's sclerotic exhaust manifold seemed to echo him.

William would have liked to hit Jim for that, but he needed Jim to give him a ride home. He mentioned then, only in passing, that he had been fired from Brower's, and, as Jim pressed him, explained the exact cause.

"Boy, you've got some mouth," Jim said, swinging his head in admiration. "I didn't know you had it in you."

"Neither did I."

"Better learn some respect for authority, boy," Jim said as they pulled up outside William's house. "Gonna get yourself drafted."

"I probably will anyway," said William, and with that he got out of the car and went inside.

Jane and her friends were in the kitchen, oiling themselves with liquor for the convention tomorrow, and William moved scarcely noticed through their muttered conversation and smoke. He went to the living room, took the phone, settled sideways onto the love seat, scissoring his legs over the arm, and began to dial. Three digits into Emily's number (now committed to memory as fixedly as his bike-lock combination), he felt his breath leave him, replaced by a woozy upward pressure from his gut ending in his throat at the point where nausea generally begins to form. But he kept dialing. A voice answered, and it was Emily's father's voice.

"Is Emily there?" William asked.

"I'll see," said the voice, level, bland, and dark with authority. Then in the same tone it added, "Can I say who's calling?" and with that second obstacle set down, the voice seemed that not merely of a guard or a cop, but of the three-headed dog that minds the door to Hell. William coughed out his name and then he heard steps going away and a burst of television noise, and then other steps, brisker, lighter, the tapping of the heels a little slurred as they skipped here and there in their passage; then, like an exhalation after a long holding of breath, a voice.

"Hello?"

"Emily?"

"Yeah?"

"It's Bill."

"I know." Emily said this half a beat too early and too brightly for it to register the hint of slight indifference, of coolness, that she and Monica had settled on as the optimal response to William's call when it came. Instead, coming so soon after William's announcement of his presence, his name, it seemed to affirm these, even to convey excitement at the prospect of them. Or that is how William took it, and so in turn he abandoned the plan that he and Jim had concocted: that he should simply pretend nothing unusual or untoward had ever taken place.

Instead it required whole bolts and spools of restraint to prevent himself from blurting "I'm sorry" and "I missed you" and to settle on the more moderate course of "So, hi. How are you? I really—" at which point Emily fortunately cut him off with "Oh, fine!" Emily was still thinking she might be able to reel herself in a little, but then William said, "I'm really glad," which made the flat and neutral tone she had been considering sound not self-possessed but petulant. She almost said "I'm glad you're glad," but caught herself. Trying to slow down, she responded, finally, "So how have you been?"—the "been" underlined in a fashion that would have caused Monica to wag her head sideways in despair.

"Oh, fine," William said. He still wanted to say that he had missed her, but settled for "Actually, I lost my job."

"Really?" Emily said.

"The foreman had it in for me."

"So he got you fired?"

"I told him off." Because I was thinking about you, William might have said. Instead he offered, "It's a long story."

"So what are you going to do? With the rest of the summer?"

"Oh, I'll find something." William coiled himself and lurched forward into the question. "So are you doing anything tomorrow?"

"No. Not really."

"So do you want to meet up?"

"Sure." The notion of "neutral ground" came into Emily's mind. "Maybe the park?"

William had a notion too, and it did not include crossing paths with his friends or, more likely, her friends and getting tangled up in hanging out with them en masse. "How about the park by Summit and Western. The one with the statue." He added, "It's nice there."

That had not been what Emily had in mind. The fraction of herself that was still determined to approach William as much on her terms as possible had indeed calculated the advantage of being able to withdraw to the cover of the friends likely to be in St. Clair Park. But as their conversation progressed it was less and less clear exactly what those terms consisted of, or even if her "terms" had any relation to her "desires," to what she wanted, which was now, she understood, to see William on whatever terms presented themselves.

"Sure," she said.

"Maybe around one?"

"Sure," said Emily, and added, as though to signify that the water had closed over the breach between them so that it almost might never have existed, "And bring your poems, okay?"

*L*ove wants to shout itself from the rooftops but in equal measure wants to be secret—both to proclaim itself to the world and take shelter against the world, to be herald and prophet, hermit and mute. It is that way, too, with persons of Emily's and William's age: The self that they are not busy disclosing they are busy concealing. Perhaps on that account they are seen to be deceitful when in fact they are merely protecting and conserving from profanation what is sacred and meant to be unseen and unsaid.

So when Emily told Virginia that she was that afternoon going to "the park," correctly presuming that her mother would assume this meant St. Clair Park, Emily was learning a little of the grown-up truth about telling the truth: that sometimes in deciding in what way to speak it, we are not offered a choice between good and evil, but between larger and lesser harms.

Emily walked all the way down Summit Avenue, moving like a fish through pools of light and shade, over the sidewalk, over pavers cracked and heaved by roots and frost like a fractured icefield, like a sea of floating headstones. She came into the park as into an arena from a tunnel, an arena ringed with trees, the air a green mist of heat and leaf-filtered light. William was sitting on the grass, his bike splayed beside him, and as she pressed past the trees and through the hedge, out into the space where he was, he began to rise.

"So, hi," William said.

"Hi," Emily said.

William put out his hand palm up and parallel to the ground, bidding her to take a seat. She settled into the grass and crossed her legs beneath her. They were sitting not quite opposite each other, Emily being a little to the left of him. Neither had given any real thought to what they would do next or what they would say, and they were without music or her parents' house or any other particular context that might inform their actions or direct their speech. They were in the grass with the sky overhead and the elms looming all around and the temperature just cresting eighty-five degrees.

Emily broke the silence. "So how'd you lose your job?"

"This guy, this Mr. Murkowski who runs the warehouse, he was looking for an excuse. Watching me all the time, waiting for me to screw up without ever telling me what I was supposed to really be doing."

"So . . ."

"So I dropped a bunch of stuff, a bunch of shoe boxes, nothing breakable, and he comes over and just stands there. Not helping, just kind of laughing at me, but not out loud. Then he started laying these . . . proverbs on me. So I told him to, well, fuck off."

"Wow," Emily said. "Just like that."

"Just like that."

"So you kind of lost your temper?"

"Kind of. But when I said it, it was like I was really calm. Like I was taking a stand. Like nonviolence. Like King."

"And then?"

"Then he went off and got me a check and I was out of there by two o'clock. I got maybe thirty bucks."

"That seems like a lot," Emily said.

"They were paying me one sixty-five an hour."

"That's a lot more than I get."

"Well, it's like warehouse work. I suppose guys from the Teamsters do it, usually."

"So now what?"

"I don't know. Take it easy. Read. Relax," William said. "It's my last summer before I graduate. Before I go to college. Or into the army. So

I might as well enjoy it." And with that William lowered himself onto his elbow and cradled his head in his hand.

Emily leaned forward. "Did you bring your poems?"

"Yeah, a couple." He reached into his back pocket and removed some sheets of paper, folded in four. He opened them out and offered them to Emily. "They're really meant to be read, you know, silently. So if you want . . ."

Emily nodded and took the pages. She began to read, and as she read she lowered herself onto the grass, onto her belly and elbows, with her calves and feet in the air. William watched her and saw that her feet were moving, as though tapping against the sky. He lay a little deeper in the grass, now prone himself, pulling out a leaf here and there and regarding the curiously raw-looking striations the grass had made on his elbow where he'd rested on it. There was birdsong, the sound of a far-off plane, and the hiss and seethe of the warming air.

Emily, too, was conscious of the bite of the grass against her elbows, and the strata of heat and shade lying over them. But she truly was reading William's poems, reading them more than once. She might have thought they had a certain pulse to them and a kind of heedless, headlong energy and also that as poetry they were pretty dreadful. But she was not so much reading them as poetry as she was regarding them like snapshots or pages in an album, as records and traces of things that William had once done or said, as the residue of moods and feelings in which he had once been immersed. So she did not expect them to aspire to the condition of art—to contain those occasions within them, transformed into signs that were now themselves occasions—and that was probably a good thing. What, after all, is a poem or a painting or even a symphony, when you are fashioning your whole life—its scherzos and silences, its rhythms and themes, its lines and chiaroscuros—each day; when you are just now, lying belly down in the grass, embarking on its magnum opus, the work about love and loving?

Emily looked up.

"So?" William asked.

"I really like them."

"Really?"

"Really," Emily said. "I mean, they're really kind of . . . *you*. Really feeling these things, really . . ." Emily was a little lost. "Really . . ." she finally concluded, "passionately."

"You mean like Browning or Byron or somebody?" William was not sure these were apt examples, but had heard they were considered "romantic," which must be very similar to "passionate."

"Maybe like *Elizabeth* Browning," said Emily in a tone that suggested some expertise.

"You mean like 'romantic'?"

"I mean really felt deeply. Like the passion of Jesus or something."

William fingered the grass, a little puzzled. "You mean Jesus was in love? I thought he was . . . above that kind of thing."

"It doesn't really mean that kind of passion. It's more like his suffering, the pain he felt."

William looked at Emily a little apologetically. "I didn't mean them to be mopey or anything."

"They're not. They just have a lot of feeling in them." Emily realized that she felt rather comfortable this way, lying on the grass, explaining something—what? himself?—to William that he didn't know. "I mean feeling sad. Or angry about how things are. It's only natural."

"That's what got me fired." William, too, liked this; liked the great reassurance that Emily was bestowing upon him, breathing out and blanketing him with, her face all of two feet away.

"Sure. Like you saw it was unfair and you got mad."

"Actually, I was kind of sad. Not about the job."

"About . . . ?"

"Something else," William said. "But it's okay now, I guess." William pulled himself up to a sitting position, resting his hands on his knees, and looked around the park. "Do you want to walk a little?"

Emily was infinitely happy just where she was, but obliged him. "Sure," she said.

"There's another park across the street. Do you want to go see it?"

"Sure," Emily said. Emily knew of this park, but had never been in it, for it was not a park trafficked by children or young people. That was odd, because it had begun its existence as a vacant lot much frequented by neighborhood kids for games and various adventures. But that had been half a century ago. Shortly thereafter, in the 1920s, an heiress—it was said she gave off an aura not only of benefaction but of longstanding and perennial grief—purchased the property, deeded it to the city as a park, and had it furnished with a fountain and a bronze sculpture by an eminent artist. The sculpture, in the middle of the fountain, was of an Indian youth running with his dog, clutching his bow. Adjacent to this was a little stone-and-brick shelter in a Gothic style—like a shrine or a chantry in which an anchorite might shut herself away—with a bench and a poem carved above it. The theme of the poem was the death of childhood. The poem seemed to have infected the place in some manner. At any rate, it was not now a place children were inclined to go.

William walked his bike across the street with Emily beside him, and they went in. Emily regarded the sculpture and said, "It's pretty."

William said, "He's meant to be in the woods. He's a hunter. He knows all the woodcraft and stories and stuff."

"I suppose." Emily looked at the stone shelter. She wished it would rain so she and William could go in it and have a reason to sit and do what they had been doing back across the street; so she could tell him a few more things about himself, and, if it rained for long enough, he could return the favor.

William had apparently also been looking at the shelter, but had seized on the inscription. "Read it," he said. He gave her a moment to skim the words, and then said, "I don't get it. But it's gloomy."

Emily read:

As from the house your mother sees
You playing round the garden trees,
So you may see, if you will look
Through the windows of this book,
Another child, far, far away
And in another garden, play.
But do not think you can at all,
By knocking on the window, call

That child to hear you. He intent
Is all on his play-business bent.
He does not hear; he will not look,
Nor yet be lured out of this book.
For, long ago, the truth to say,
He has grown up and gone away,
And it is but a child of air
That lingers in the garden there.

"I don't think I get it either," she said. The poem made her reconsider wanting to sit there. She looked at William. "So . . ."

"You want to get something to drink? Or eat?" William asked. "There's not much around here. But my house is just a couple of blocks away." William said this without considering what he was saying, any more than if he had said it to Jim Donnelly or some kid he might have met here in a pickup football scrimmage. "I mean, we have Coke and stuff."

The "we" eased Emily's mind a little, implying the presence of William's mother, who, being a mother, must be more or less like her mother. Not that Emily was going to ask him straight out, "Is your mother at home?" Anyway, she was hot and thirsty and she felt happy; and the happiness was not unconnected to this boy.

"Okay," she said, after what was not really very much of a pause at all. They began to walk, the bicycle between them like a pet or an infant they were tending, and William steered it and them down the street a few blocks and then turned left. This was not a part of town that Emily was much familiar with, since it was separated from her own by the breadth of Summit Avenue. Moreover it bordered on an area that was considered a little risky, and was itself slightly down-at-heel, populated by houses similar in style, age, and size to the ones on her street, but rather less kempt, as well as by apartment buildings, which were virtually unknown in her neighborhood. Emily did not know of anyone living in an apartment except for people's grandmothers.

It was not until they turned towards his door that Emily realized that William lived in such a place, entered by way not of a door and a

threshold, but of a lobby, as though it were an office or a hotel or a hospital; it had mailboxes set in the wall like teeth and floors that looked as
though they were buffed with a machine.

That made Emily a little uncomfortable. And when William remarked
in an offhand manner as he unlocked the door that his mother was not in
fact home, she was a little alarmed. It seemed to her that this was clearly
someplace they should not be; that they entered it as trespassers or thieves
or fools blundering into a haunted house. Then William felt it too: that
this was the home of people he did not know; of real but unknown persons whose presences echoed in its sleeping carpets and vacated furniture,
its rightful inhabitants having left some hours before.

William guided Emily through the rooms, or rather pointed at them
as though they were exhibits in a museum devoted to the anthropology
and culture of the people who used to live there. He did not turn on any
lights until they got to the kitchen. Emily looked around. It was not like
the kitchen at her house. It had a bay window on the far wall through
which came the only sunshine. The overhead light William switched
on was covered by a round shade made of paper segmented into con-
centric rings like a Chinese lantern. The walls were an orangey dark
red, and there were two framed prints hanging on them, one by the
artist she knew as Sister Corita and the other, in a rather similar style,
child-like, as though drawn in crayon, of a hand clasping a bouquet.
There were magazines piled on the table and on the radiator, and the
room smelled of lemon or vinegar and herbs and cigarette smoke.

William opened the refrigerator. "There's no Coke," he said.
"There's orange juice, though."

"Okay," Emily said. "I mean, that's fine."

William poured some juice into a clear glass tumbler that was very
tall and thin. "Do you want ice? I'm getting some ice water."

"No. That's okay."

William withdrew an ice tray from the freezer and ratcheted the
handle upward. "So where's your mom?" Emily asked.

"At the state convention. The Democrats, I mean. She's a delegate."

"Oh. That's kind of cool. So she gets to vote on stuff, like who gets
nominated?"

"Yeah. And maybe go to the national convention too," William said. "But I think it's pretty much already decided. For Humphrey, I mean."

"Your mom likes McCarthy, right?"

"Yeah."

"But you liked Kennedy."

"Yeah," William said. "But don't tell my mom." He laughed.

"I guess my parents would have voted for Kennedy. Because he's a Kennedy. Because he's Catholic. Now I suppose they're for Humphrey. Don't tell your mother," she added.

"I won't." William filled his glass at the tap and turned around. "So do you want to sit down? In the living room?"

Emily had just begun to feel some ease, but this query unnerved her a little again. "Sure," she said. "I suppose." She was afraid, but of what she could not say.

They went back down the dark hall, past the front door, and into the room that William had indicated earlier. There were curtains of a material a little like burlap and furniture upholstered in brown and orangey red, a small sofa and two armchairs, plus a coffee table. Against the wall stood another table with a record player—white and modern-looking and configured in several parts—with records stacked upright beneath it.

"You have a lot of albums," Emily commented. She was trying to figure out where and in what manner to sit.

"They're mostly my mom's."

"That's weird. I mean, it's different. My parents hardly have any. They have *South Pacific* and some Christmas carols."

"My mom's got a lot of classical stuff. And Dave Brubeck." William sat down on the little sofa, and Emily sat down on the edge of one of the armchairs opposite him and a little to the left, and it was as if this mere change of posture had rendered both of them mute.

William reached out and put his glass down on the coffee table, onto a magazine with pictures of Sirhan Sirhan and James Earl Ray on the cover. He opened his mouth and what came out was "So . . . ?" and his face devolved into an expression of panic or futile desperation. Or that is how it seemed to Emily, who felt these same things, whether

William did or did not. They were already as mirrors to each other, and placed together in an empty space with few or no distractions, what they saw was a little unbearable.

William said, "I could . . ." although he was unable to say what he might or might not do. And Emily said, before he could finish, "That's okay."

William picked up his glass, drank from it, and licked the water from his lips. Then, suddenly, with his other hand he grabbed the magazine the glass had been resting on and held it up. "So did you see . . ." and it seemed that he might not know what it was he was going to refer to. "Did you see the pictures of the train—of all the people waiting for it to go by?"

"No," Emily said.

"I'll show you," William said, and he pulled the magazine towards him, as though to pull Emily with it.

"Okay," Emily said. She got up and came around the edge of the coffee table and sat at the edge of the couch, close to William, because the couch was small.

"Here," William said. But he couldn't say any more because he'd stopped breathing, or else all his breath had gathered into the top of his throat and would not go back down. He opened the magazine, and took her hand, his own hand shaking, and put it down on a page as though he were steering her fingers across a line of Braille. "See?" he managed.

Emily nodded, his hand still atop her hand, and then her hand lifted and found his back, his waist, his belt near a belt loop, and rested there. And William's hand found the same place on her, only a little higher, and then they had turned and were facing each other and Emily kissed him, not on the cheek, but on the mouth, because that was somehow where their faces simply met. They kissed that way for a long time, and you could not really say if William was kissing Emily or Emily was kissing William.

After a time, they stopped—stopping together just as they had started together—and opened their eyes as if awaking in a strange room; to see, as it were, who it was they had been kissing.

William's panic had translated itself to a glorious urgency, and he was still breathless. He looked at Emily, who indeed looked a little as if she had awoken from a nap, her hair a bit disheveled, her face a bit ruddy and damp. He looked at her and smiled. "I thought you didn't want . . ."

"To . . . ?"

"Do . . ."

"That?"

"I mean, in the car. The other night."

"Oh, that," she said. "Silly . . ." And they began to kiss again. Their hands did not move. They merely pulled each other closer, pulled each other in.

When they stopped, William continued, "I mean, it seemed like you didn't want to the way you did the first time."

Emily was enjoying this kissing very much and took almost an off-hand if not scolding tone with him for interrupting it. "It's not that I didn't want to. It's that I didn't want you to think that I wanted to . . . too much."

"So you wanted to, but you didn't want me to think you wanted to."

"More or less."

"Well, that's pretty silly too."

William, who two minutes earlier could not have told you his own last name, had now recovered enough self-possession to think thoughts along these lines and to utter them as well. But Emily was in her body, just as you might say she was in the water if she were swimming. She was happy to listen to and respond to (in a rather cursory manner) William's words, but they came to her as though through water, refracted and vague, as though William in those brief moments had thrust his head above the surface to speak.

They went back to what they had been doing, which was really not much more than a very urgent sort of cuddling, save for the fact they were deeply connected at the mouth. It was nothing they had not done before with other people. But it was different in degree, in amplitude: more pleasurable and more joyful, but also more driven, as if by an imperative that had to do with ordinary desire, but also by some other powerful outside influence. You might say they kissed almost in desperation, as though they were fighting for breath itself.

Emily was in her body, but William, although just as caught up in the moment, had thoughts: in the first instance, whether this was really happening to him and, when he ascertained that it indeed was, what if anything he needed to do about it to sustain or further it. "Further" is perhaps the crucial word, for his main preoccupation was to what extent he might go in that direction. Certainly the erection butting against his fly weighed in on the matter; so too did his hands, which had tracked their way up from Emily's waist and whose thumbs were now cradled in the concavities of her shoulder blades, whose fingers were now mulling over the buried outlines of her bra straps.

But his answer to the question of "further?" was "no," not unless there was some tacit encouragement from Emily herself; not given their recent misunderstanding about the kiss last Wednesday. And that was a wise decision. For although Emily might very well have, in the heat of the moment (nearly ninety outside; God knows how hot at various points of flesh contact between William and Emily), permitted him to go further and might very well have enjoyed his doing so, it would have been problematic in the long run. Because what they were presently doing was not in Emily's estimation being "fast" in social terms or "unchaste" in moral and/or theological ones, whereas moving beyond that into the territory covered by "further" would entail a reassessment.

So it was that Emily and William continued in this mode, and were very content with it, for twenty minutes or more. When they finally pulled themselves apart far enough to see each other in the way they had seen each other until now—as distinct objects framed by space and air and light, rather than mingled together in the humid soup of making out—it was unclear to either of them what they ought to say. It was a little like coming out with a friend into the daylight from a movie one had been moved by and wondering what to say about it, because maybe the friend hadn't felt that way at all.

William was more troubled by this than Emily. It was, after all, his house, his couch. He was, so to speak, the host, but the idea of inquiring just now whether Emily would like some more juice did not seem a way of extricating himself from the moment. Emily saved him.

"Ummm," she said, stretching her arms upward as though awaking from a long and pleasant nap. "That was . . . nice." She drew this last word out, not unchastely, but rather as her cat might have done after a good rub around the ears and beneath the chin. William was both pleased and a little taken aback by this: pleased that she had no objection to what had happened between them, but taken aback that her reaction was so frank and seemed to have as its object not him or them together, but a kind of "that," an activity or pastime in which it was pleasant to engage. With him. Or maybe with anybody.

William did not dwell on this latter possibility. It did not accord with anything he knew about love or about Emily. But it puzzled him even as he put it out of his mind, as he laid it down among those riddles and mysteries which he would take out and examine from time to time for the rest of his life and put away again, unsolved. For it seemed to him unfathomable that whatever it was he and Emily were doing (or perhaps *making*) together was not unique to them or was somehow merely physical, that it was not a particular expression of *them* rather than something that anybody could do, interchangeably, with anybody else, less a one-of-a-kind painting or poem than a croquet set that anyone possessed of a body might use.

But for William the pressing issue of the moment was what to say or do that was not too jarring, because for a while they had been so tightly joined that, now separated, it seemed as if they might not recognize each other; that they would blink and then say, "Oh, it's you," their intimacy in some uncanny way having made them strangers. Which is why it would have been nice to say "I love you," not as a pledge or a declaration, but as the merest sign of recognition, as if to say "We are just you and me again, but I haven't forgotten us." But what William said was, mirroring Emily, "Yeah, that *was* nice"; and then he did indeed ask her if she would like some more juice, for who is to say that, too, is not a kind of tenderness?

None of this troubled Emily. It did not even occur to her. That was not because she was not thoughtful, but because the distinction between thought and sensation, between mind and body, was a little indistinct for her. She knew she had a soul and a body as she knew she had ten fingers and ten toes, and she knew she had the capacity for something called reason, but where a "mind" (was it more or less the same as a soul?) fit in was a matter neither the catechism nor the nuns had ever addressed. There had been a great deal of talk about chasteness, but this quality had as much to do with the soul as the body; and indeed argued for their inseparability, and so did seemingly everything else the church and the nuns taught her. For what was the whole drama of Christianity if not the fact of God taking on a body? What was the point of the mass if not the body of Christ? What made Our Lady's bodily assumption glorious if not Her body's being assumed? Emily lived in a nation and a culture at war with the body and its more troubling manifestations (its unseemly and inconvenient needs and wants and especially its penchant for death); a whole culture dedicated to pitting the virtues of the mind against pesky corporeality. But she—on account of her experience, her education, and her own disposition— secretly inhabited a realm in which the physical and the bodily was the expression of the divine, expressed in the body: the only way it could be expressed for us and also in us, its created creatures, its beautiful emanations. And if love had a voice, from what but a mouth could it speak?

So for Emily—as she stretched and tugged and fluffed her hair and sighed the sigh of her contentment that creation was so good that one creature might fit another so well—these things might be a mystery but they were not disturbing or puzzling as they were for William. Nor did what she had been doing with William conflict, as yet, with chasteness, for chasteness was not in opposition to the body, but belonged to it. It did not belong to the mind, whatever that was, nor was it meant to trouble the spirit. So the last thing in the world we might fairly say of Emily was that when she was in her body she had forgotten herself or what was important to her. But we also might say, from William's perspective, that when Emily was in her body, she was a little out of her mind.

13

IT WAS THE FOLLOWING WEEK THAT MONICA REARDON felt she might be losing her best friend. Monica did not, in fact, have as many friends as she had persuaded the world to believe, and by her own private standard of true friendship—no secrets, not ever—she had only one real friend, Emily Byrne. Emily herself did not know that she held this status, for Monica's air of certitude and self-confidence did not make it easy for Emily to entertain the idea that she might make such a claim.

Emily had been calling her infrequently, and when she did call, she was a little cagey with her, in particular about Bill Lowry. In truth, the more Emily saw of him and felt about him, the less she said about it to Monica, and by the middle of the week Monica imagined Emily disappearing from her life entirely, like a dot on the horizon, as she and Bill Lowry sailed out of sight on this voyage they were making together, as the sea and the sky swallowed them up.

Monica was perhaps being a little dramatic (a word adults had long applied to her, rather as they applied "impetuous" to Emily), because Emily had called her on both Sunday and Tuesday and told her that she had had a "friendly" time with Bill on Saturday, although she was somewhat unresponsive to further probing on Monica's part. But right now, as Monica fretted, on this very Wednesday night, Emily and William were, as Monica suspected, being as secret as CIA agents, as Rosicrucians, as leprechauns. After a cursory visit to the Scholar—just long enough to down two mocha cappuccinos and note who was on the program—Emily and William were parked along the river, doing more or less what they had been doing Saturday afternoon, except that they were doing it not on William's mother's couch but on the gray seat of her station wagon, the vinyl clinging and peeling away from their flesh like octopus suckers as they wiggled and writhed.

Secrecy was at the essence of everything they were doing, and there were mighty imperatives at work: first, that it wouldn't be a good idea for anyone to find out, especially Emily's parents (whom Emily could no more picture imagining or fathoming what she was doing than Sister Mary Immaculata); second, that it wasn't anybody's business; third, that what they were doing was necessarily secret—it wasn't a choice on their part, but essential to the thing itself. It was their thing, and if anybody else had been included, it would not merely be compromised but cease entirely to exist. And even if they had wanted to tell other people—really tell them—they could not have done so, for their secret was at bottom secret even from them. They could not say, individually or together, what it truly and really was that was passing between and over and through them.

When they paused in their kissing, they tended to talk about other secrets: to say things they would not ordinarily say; to confess things they would not ordinarily admit; and, when their talk turned to the larger world, to reflect upon *its* secrets, its hidden movers and hands. It was William who led the way, but Emily listened attentively, breathing the fog of their commingled breath while the moon poured down and the leaves and crickets hissed and clattered.

"If Goldwater had been elected last time, my mom was going to move us to Canada."

"But he didn't. He got pasted."

"But he could have been. He was the nominee. It could have been close. Think about it. It could happen next time."

"What could?"

"Phone taps, clamping down on free speech and protests. Escalation of the war. Secret files kept by the police. Dropping the bomb." William spoke of these things not as happenstances, but outcomes dictated by the iron law of history that had the intransigent inexorability of suction, of water gyring down a drain. There was no escaping what had been ordained to happen next.

"I suppose," Emily said. "Even the nuns say the war is evil."

"Immoral. Illegal too."

"But you think it's not just the war. That it's all connected." No one at Emily's house was much drawn to this kind of thinking, still less to the reflexive habit of believing that things are necessarily the opposite of what they seem. Yet while Emily lacked William's fuzzy-mindedness and tendency to speculate much on the basis of very little, when she was confronted with the choice between something and nothing—between presence and absence—Emily chose something every time, just as she chose the body over the mind. What William offered her was consistent with that, and it was consistent with what they did between discussing it, with the two of them and the body and all the secrets it contains, the greatest of which is love. That one, love, was the one they were keeping from each other and even, until now, from themselves. Let us say it was on this night, or a little afterward, that William knew he both loved and was in love with Emily, love being a motion and a state of being, a verb and a noun, a restlessness that is also a refuge, a secret hiding place.

14

THERE IS A MOMENT, AROUND THE FOURTH OF JULY, when the summer reaches its apex and begins its long course of days, one much like another, hot and hotter; a miasma of light and fetid air through which, for all the intention and conviction we can muster, we can only drift half blind, the days a syrup through which we wade. Emily and William each had their routines—Emily in the New Wave department, William delivering prescriptions part-time for Frost's Drugstore on his Raleigh—but the chief continuity in their lives was increasingly each other. Their usual Wednesday date was now supplemented by more casual meetings on other evenings and during the day on the weekends.

They spoke, too, on the telephone and sometimes at great length, for although love is supposed to stupefy its pilgrims or at least strike them dumb, they had become more rather than less articulate with each other. Where once the telephone could only amplify the mutual tripping-up, hem-treading, and general speaking at cross-purposes that afflicted their attempts at communication, now they could at least talk and make arrangements to meet, speaking one at a time and with almost total comprehension. And when they did meet, because they had begun to believe that they truly were being understood, they became more understandable—or so it seemed, at least to them.

With that confidence, Emily began to take William a little more in hand: to be firmer in asserting her own opinions and in feeling that William ought to assent to them, which he did, both sympathetically and eagerly, because to affirm what Emily said was to affirm Emily herself and thus the two of them and thus William himself. William in turn became less vague and more acute in Emily's mind, his opinions more grounded, less nebulous and high-flown. That was doubtless because many of them were increasingly Emily's opinions, or opinions of William's that Emily had adopted.

Those differed less in substance than in the way they were stated. In politics, they consisted of whatever Emily and William believed Robert Kennedy had believed. Emily felt, with some justification, that as a Catholic, she had an inside track to this, and also noticed that William had a tendency to speak from the head—despite the general disorder of his thoughts—rather than the heart; to become incensed not by the pity of poverty, war, and injustice but by their asymmetry to the ideal or, alternatively, their connection to other more general nefarious patterns he or his reading had detected.

That extended to his attitudes to poetry, and here Emily also tried to bring his sensibility more into line with her own. She had never consciously thought ill of William's poems—she sensed that to have found a boy who cared for poetry at all was serendipitous—but conceived that the feelings these expressed might be put more subtly and precisely. As they stood, they had the quality of an inchoate ideological rant, a sort of incantatory stomping and flailing. It was as if William had received a disagreeable letter outlining the world's condition and had torn it into little pieces and was now jumping up and down on them.

So it was that on the Friday after the Fourth of July, Emily was sitting in her room prior to going to bed, looking for a poem. She could not say whether she was searching for a poem which would suit William—rather as she might have chosen a necktie for her father—or one that expressed him, as a portrait might, or, better still, one that expressed them both, that described that zone of cross-hatching, of light and color, where the two of them overlapped. She was thumbing through a book she had of the Brownings, both Robert and Elizabeth, and simply stumbled across it, and it was one of his, surprisingly, rather than hers, and it was absolutely perfect. Then, as a kind of bonus, she came across a selection of their letters in the same volume; and these too were perfect. She marked two places in the book, kissed her parents good night, and went to sleep, deeply content, praying her prayers of thanksgiving.

That Saturday, after they had eaten the tuna fish sandwiches Virginia had brought them, they lay together on the lawn in Emily's yard. William dug his fingers into the turf, idly combing and twisting strands of grass, and Emily read him the poem, which began, "Where the quiet-colored end of evening smiles/Miles and miles/On the solitary pastures where our sheep/Half asleep/Tinkle homeward through the twilight, stray or stop/As they crop—/Was the site once of a city great and gay/(So they say)."

You could not have heard Emily reading unless you were very close by, because Emily's voice was a little small and because there was a slight wind that afternoon, moving the branches and singing in the telephone wires and even the grass they lay on. Add to that the singsong of the poem's rhyme scheme, and Emily's reading must have seemed a muttered chant, with the higher bell-tone of her voice tolling every few beats. You might well drift off to sleep.

But William was attentive, and more attentive as the stanzas went by and he understood that the poem was about a shepherd and shepherdess living in the overgrown ruins of a great nation's capital that had been destroyed—indeed, destroyed itself—in the pursuit of glory and war. Now nothing was left but pieces of fallen columns and the shepherds and the sheep. There was a book William had read once set in the wake of a nuclear war, and the whole earth is uninhabitable, save for a bit of Australia, where the last man and the last woman are left to restore the human race, just the two of them.

"It's like here. Like the war and everything," William said as Emily paused between stanzas, and Emily nodded and went on reading. She was getting to the part she thought William would like best, the part where the shepherd comes home from the fields to the shepherdess. It was, at any rate, the part she liked best:

When I do come, she will speak not, she will stand,
Either hand

On my shoulder, give her eyes the first embrace
Of my face,
Ere we rush, ere we extinguish sight and speech
Each on each.

Emily paused a little longer than usual at the end of that stanza. She could not tell whether William had gotten it yet—what was being alluded to—and then she went on and read the last stanza:

In one year they sent a million fighters forth
South and North,
And they built their gods a brazen pillar high
As the sky,
Yet reserved a thousand chariots in full force—
Gold, of course,
Oh heart! oh blood that freezes, blood that burns!
Earth's returns
For whole centuries of folly, noise and sin!
Shut them in,
With their triumphs and their glories and the rest!
Love is best!

Emily stopped and looked up, not at William, but in the direction of the back of the backyard, towards the garage and the alley and the sun burning white-hot in the sky.

"You know," William said, "it's exactly like now. Here. Johnson and McNamara."

Emily waited and then asked, "And us?"

"Yeah, and us."

This last remark satisfied Emily that William indeed understood; not just the apocalyptic aspect of the poem, but the love that is counterpoised to it. Just then, William looked up to see that neither of Emily's parents was in view, and put his hand on top of Emily's hand.

They lay that way for some time, without speaking, for they had by now learned not only to talk to each other without stammering, but to let the silences in their conversation run their natural course, to neither trip over them nor step on them. Finally, Emily said, "You know, her parents—Elizabeth Barrett's—wouldn't let her marry him, wouldn't let them be together. They waited and waited and her parents wouldn't give in. For years."

"For years?"

"Yeah. So finally she wrote Robert and said she didn't know what to do. She asked him. She said, 'Think for me.'" Emily opened her book again. "He wrote back and said, 'All our life is some form of religion, and all our action some belief. In your case, I do think you are called upon to do your duty to yourself; that is, to God in the end.'"

"So what did she do?"

"She ran away from home. With him. To Italy."

"Wow. So her parents went berserk?"

"Them and everybody else. It was a big scandal."

"So did they make them come back?"

"No. Italy was a long way away. Like from here to California. So they just stayed there, like exiles."

"Until everybody cooled down."

"I'm not sure everybody ever did cool down," Emily said. "And then after ten or fifteen years, she died." Emily paused. "He lived for a long, long time. But he always was thinking about her. And them, together."

"So it was like he wrote to her, that they were like their own religion to each other?" William said tentatively.

"Sort of," Emily said, thinking that in fact this was a great insight, perhaps only a hair short of the mark. "But not in a selfish, conceited way." Emily thumbed through her book and stopped. She said, "Yeah, there's another poem, and he says—here it is: 'All is beauty: And knowing this, is love, and love is duty.'"

"Like a cause. Like being *for* something."

"Yeah. And being against war and greed. That's kind of what the other poem says. About how love is best."

"And wins?"

"And wins. Over all the generals and businessmen and politicians."

At some point William's hand had removed itself from Emily's, although neither of them had noticed. It must have been when Emily was leafing through her book, and needed both of her hands free, and William's hand just settled back into the grass like a butterfly and resumed what it had been doing, the picking and combing and stroking. That was just as well, for a moment later, Emily's mother appeared before them, like a ghost or an angel. She knelt down, resting on her heels.

"So what are you two up to?" she asked.

"Reading. Poetry."

"Who?"

"The Brownings."

"Oh, that's nice," Emily's mother said. "They're very—" And happily Virginia did not say "romantic." She paused and finally she said, "—beautiful. They're very beautiful poems." And Emily nodded.

Virginia stood up and before she walked away, she turned back to William and said, "It's nice to see so much of you, Bill. You're almost like part of the family. Emily's father and I thought it might be nice to get to know your mother too. Suppose you both came over for a picnic. Next Saturday. Would you ask her if that would do?"

"Sure," said William. "I'll ask her right away."

That Wednesday, Emily and William forwent their usual evening date and simply walked to the park. On their way out the door, William had told Emily's mother that his mother would indeed be coming Saturday and would bring salad. This prompted an approving remark from Virginia and a friendly nod from Edward; and William could not help but feel that he did not mind Emily's parents that much at all.

Tonight William had brought a little olive-green rucksack with him that he had bought at an army surplus store, and as though in sympathy Emily wore an oversize jacket of the same material. It was a cool evening, scarcely above seventy degrees, and promised to turn cooler. When they entered the park, they did not stop in the main area where the warming house and playground and ball field were situated, but continued through to the other side, into the tall grass and down the hill. This was a long, rather steep bank that ran down towards the rail-road tracks and overlooked the river. You could lose yourself in it, unseen from either above or below, if you lay down in the vegetation, and this is what Emily and William did.

William had a transistor radio in the rucksack and he turned it on, very low, and laid it down next to him. Then he took what appeared to be a cigarette out, a hand-rolled cigarette, wrinkled and tapered at the ends, and looking a little the worse for wear. In truth, William had gotten it from Jim Donnelly some time ago and had saved it under the floorboard in his closet where he kept his money and his adult magazines. He showed it to Emily and Emily said, "Oh. Grass."

She said this unremarkably, but with a slight tone of intrigue, and certainly with no alarm. She had seen it before and smoked it a few times, without having a precise sense of what effect it really had upon her, beyond noting its swarthy, raunchy aroma and the tarred and gummy taste it had left in her mouth. There were kids for whom smoking grass was a complete vocation, but for Emily, as for William, it was a diversion rather than a compulsion, belonging in the same category as the alcoholic beverages (beer, sweet wine) they had on occasion imbibed. All were illegal and, for various reasons not exclusively having to do with adult disapproval or hysteria, were most of the time more trouble than they were worth. With anyone else, it would have been kind of a disreputable joke. With each other, it was a lark; it might even take on purity and beauty, sanctified by its being another of their secrets.

William lit the cigarette, inhaled, and passed it to Emily, who did the same. The cigarette sputtered and popped, and then the coal at the lit end fell off, and William had to relight it, and then they both drew on it again. William laid his head down in the tall grass next to Emily and they passed the cigarette back and forth and looked up as though they were watching the stars, although it was barely dusk and the stars hadn't come out yet.

After a time, Emily turned her head toward William and said, "So tell me a story."

"I don't know any stories. Not any good ones."

"Sure you do. Or tell me what stories you liked when you were a kid."

"I liked *Winnie the Pooh* and then later I liked *My Side of the Mountain.*"

"*My Side of the Mountain.* I loved that one."

"Really?" said William, and propped himself up on his elbows. "That's cool. I didn't really think it was a girl's story."

"So why isn't it?"

"Well, I mean living off the land, hunting and fishing, dressing in buckskin, making a house in a hollow tree—that's guy stuff."

"Girls love to make houses. Especially in a hollow tree." Emily laughed and then so did William, and he laid his head back down in the grass next to Emily's. They faced each other and kissed a few times, smelling and tasting the raw smoke in each other's mouth. Then, having dispensed with the cigarette, whose butt William nonchalantly ate, they looked back up at the sky and listened to the radio softly playing just above and behind their heads.

"So tell me about . . . tell me about all your other girlfriends," Emily said.

"*All* my other girlfriends?" William laughed. "Like all one and a half of them?"

"So just tell me about the ones you kissed. Or did more than that with."

"That makes about one-half. Excluding playing spin the bottle and stuff like that. Which doesn't count, right?"

"I suppose not. But what about Sarah Jacobsen?"

"Jeez. I am so tired of hearing about her, like we went together or anything."

"So you made out with her?"

"Not really."

"But you kissed her?"

"Sure, I guess."

"On the mouth? Deep, like you do with me?"

"I don't remember," William said. "You sure are curious."

"So did you? Make out with her?"

"Maybe a little. After the dance, just in the way you would after you've gone to a dance with somebody. It didn't mean anything."

"She has kind of . . . big breasts. Did you . . ." Emily trailed off.

"I don't know anything about them."

"Really?"

"Really," William said.

"So do you want to know about me?"

"About what?"

"Me and guys."

"What guys?"

"Just one, really. Roger."

"Roger Ericksen?"

"Yeah. Do you know him?"

"Not really. Just that he's kind of a jock."

"Yeah, I guess he is. It was a long time ago."

"So what did . . . you guys do?"

"You mean making out?" Emily laughed.

"Well, yeah."

"Well, we did. Yeah. But I didn't like it like I do with you."

"Did you do . . . more?"

"More than we do?" Emily asked. "I'm not going to lie," she added and looked up.

"So maybe I'm not sure I want to know."

"It's okay. It wasn't anything. It didn't mean anything."

"So you didn't . . ."

"No. Not nearly. Like I said, it wasn't—" Emily put her finger to her lips. "Listen. To the radio. It's us. Where I work."

The radio buzzed with a woman's whispered voice chanting repeatedly over an innocuous rhythm track:

New Wave
New Rave
Fashions for fall
Jumpers in plaid and cord
New Wave

New Rave
Fashions for fall
Minneapolis, 700 The Mall
Cedar Level, St. Paul.

The jingle stopped and another ad began. Emily grinned. "Wow. That's where I work. I mean, it's a stupid ad, but that's where I work. Like we're famous."

"I hope you didn't write that poem."

"No. They do all that over in Minneapolis. Or someplace. I don't know."

They turned again to face each other and kissed. Then they kissed some more and they ran their hands up and down each other's back. William could feel Emily's bottom against her jeans. Emily could feel William's erection through his pants where their stomachs and waists were pressed together.

Emily pulled away, not abruptly or as if she wished to stop what they were doing, but as if they had all the time in the world. "Hey, can I turn off that radio?" she said.

"Sure."

Emily turned the radio off and laid her head back down next to William's so they were breathing each other's breath. William smiled and said, "So now you'll have to sing to me. Since we don't have any music."

"Sing what?" Emily laughed. "I don't know anything."

"Sure you do. Just anything at all."

Emily paused and said, "Okay. Anything at all. She opened her mouth and sang in a whisper, " 'I'm walking my cat named dog. I'm walking my cat named dog.' " And then she laughed.

"Come on," said William. "More."

"That's all I know."

"So more. Of that."

Emily said, "Okay," and sang again and then said, "Now you."

"I don't think I know anything either."

"Come on."

"Okay." William stopped and put his lips very close to Emily's ear and his voice came out a little broken, breathy and deep and rhythmic, like waves. " 'What's your name? Who's your daddy? Is he rich like me? Has he taken any time to show you what you need to live? Tell it to me slowly. Tell you why, I really want to know.' "

"That's nice. It's cool," Emily said. "Where'd you hear it?"

"I'm not sure. I'm not even sure I have heard it. Not yet. Does that make sense?" William asked. "I guess I'm stoned."

"I guess."

William and Emily went back to what they had been doing, and after a time Emily took William's hand and kissed it on the palm and guided it inside her jacket, under her blouse. William let his hand rest there and kissed her and said, "Hey. Wow. You're not wearing a . . ."

"I don't really need one. Not like that Sarah. So I didn't. Not tonight."

"That's nice," William said. He kissed her again and feathered her breast with his fingers, with his palm. After a time, he slid his head down a little bit and pushed the layers of fabric upward and looked at it. The light had gone toward full dusk and the evening rose up around them, but he could still see. Emily's breast was very white where it wasn't grading off into pink and the nipple was red, like a tiny strawberry. Then he brushed his hand over the nipple and the breast again, and his hand was quaking and also giving and taking something that seemed to him very precious and rare. He did that for a while, breathing deep across her chest, into and under her clothes.

Emily cradled the back of his head with her palm and said, "You can do . . . more. If you want. We can. Do more."

William didn't look up, and her chin was resting on his head and his face was resting on her chest with his hand on her breast. He said, "That's okay. I don't need to. This is everything I could want, just for now, just . . . perfect."

It is so rare that we do the right thing, and rarer still that we say it, words being dull and clumsy tools indeed. We live our lives at cross-purposes to our intentions; we injure where we would heal; we abjure and insult what we mean purely to love. The peace among us depends on equivocation, guesswork, revisionism and reinterpretation, and brevity of memory. Yet William had stumbled across exactly the right thing and said it. And for his having said it, Emily then and there would have let him go—would have gone eagerly with him—as far as he might ever want to go.

They didn't, although they did a little more, but precisely where it took them and what it meant must remain just between the two of them. Because you had to be there to understand it: how the stars did indeed come up, and how wonderful that was. But you would have had to have been there, or graced with the kind of words William was able to speak that night. Otherwise, you might think it was nothing special, no big deal, or even that it was corny or silly. But if you had been there, you would have felt it was like watching the very first sunrise on the first day of creation.

15

AT THE END OF THE DAY THAT FRIDAY, EDWARD paid his customary visit to Dr. Fields. Since it was nearly five o'clock (or at least demonstrably after four-thirty), Dr. Fields sent the nurse home and fetched an ice tray from the refrigerator that housed his vaccines and specimens. He put the ice into a beaker and fetched two Dixie cups from the water cooler and set them on his desk, from whose bottom drawer he then extracted a bottle of scotch whisky. He dropped an ice cube into each cup and poured from a great height so the liquor slopped and lapped into the cups.

"Like water with that?" Fields asked. "Pneumanol?"

"Pneumanol would be redundant. And water's always contraindicated."

"Exactly my counsel, too." Fields took an ashtray from a drawer, pulled a pack of cigarettes from his lab coat pocket, and lit one, dragging deeply. "Can't smoke in front of the patients anymore. It wouldn't *do*, not nowadays."

"I 've given it up. Mostly. I didn't want my kids to start."

"Well, of course you don't. All things being equal." He drew again, and both he and Edward drank. "And of course, all things being equal, you will die. On account of something you did. Or didn't do. On account of your history. On account of having lived. If it happens to be specifically because of this, that doesn't change the outcome."

"It might hasten it."

"That's an imponderable that can't be calculated."

"Actually, it's a probability."

"You're going to start, aren't you? You can't help yourself, I suppose." Fields refilled his cup and motioned with the neck of the bottle over Edward's and Edward nodded. "Anyway, what is a fact rather than a probability is that tobacco has been one of the great consolations of my life. And that is that." He drank again and so did Edward. Then Fields said, "So, by the by, how are those children of yours?"

"Well enough. Susan's finished her first year at the U. Now she's working all summer as a camp counselor. Emily has a job at Dayton's. And a boyfriend." Edward took a sip from his cup and coughed lightly.

"And this gives you pause?"

"The boyfriend? Oh, some, I suppose. Emily's only sixteen."

"More than nubile, though. I suspect you had a girlfriend by that age. I suspect your wife—"

"Virginia."

"Virginia. Wonderful name. And with such a name surely she had boyfriends by that age too."

"I suspect," Edward said.

"You suspect? Surely you know all about each other in that regard. After all this time."

"Yes, I do. And she did. But with Emily, it's different. With kids today, it's different."

"I doubt it," Dr. Fields said, and ground out his cigarette in the ashtray.

"I'm also not sure if I like the kid she's seeing."

"He's a thug? Or a lout?"

"He's not a thug. Too mild. Mild but determined, somehow."

"Determined to ravish your daughter?"

"I don't know. I don't think Emily would let herself be ravished."

"So she's rather determined too."

"I suppose. He's been over. Twice. Just last night, in fact. And it's as if he still hasn't come through the front door. Like he's watching us without being observed."

"He's probably just shy. Or very nervous. After all, he knows that you know what he's come for."

"Which is?"

"To ravish your daughter."

"That's a little extreme. And anyway, there's nothing knowing about him. That's part of what's odd."

"And what do they do?"

"They just sit. On the lawn. Or last night, on the porch steps. Doing nothing in particular." Edward looked into his cup and saw it was empty. "And sometimes—I said this to Virginia—you have to remind yourself that they're not just playing together." Dr. Fields poured for them both again. "Because that's all they would have been doing a couple of years ago, and I wouldn't have had the slightest concern if they'd been down in the basement or up a tree or in the bedroom together."

"Whereas now . . ."

"I'd be a little alarmed. I mean, they seem young—Emily *seems* a little younger than other girls, than her friends—but of course they're fully capable of . . ."

"Reproduction?" Fields asked.

"Reproducing themselves. Yes. I guess," Edward said. "Although it's hard to think they'd even know what to do. Not technically, I suppose. But to go from playing house to—"

"Playing doctor. I've been doing it for years."

"—or jacks or whatever, and then to imagine them . . ."

"Making the beast with two backs?"

"Yes. More or less," Edward said.

"But really, the knowledge is already there. Built into the species. Surely no one needed to tell you what to do."

"On my wedding night? Or . . . whatever." Edward seemed to sigh. "I'd had other experiences. Before. While I was in the service. But as far as my own kind were concerned, I was rather a virgin when Virginia and I got married."

"With your own kind. That's a charming distinction. The others were . . . marsupials?" Fields coughed into his fist. "Never mind. I won't ask—since we're gentlemen." He lit another cigarette. "As regards your daughter, the point is, they don't simply *know* how, any more than they *know* how to breathe. It's much more elemental—more of the essence. They could find each other, blind, one hundred miles apart, in total darkness, and manage it."

"Because it's instinctive . . ."

"Because it's the end for which we are made. Not that I'm all that Darwinian. I think I'm more Pavlovian," Fields said, and let the smoke drift from his mouth in a languorous stream. "I don't think it's all constant sex and survival, screwing and fighting. I really do believe we can address ourselves to other things. Finding food. Study. Even truth and beauty. We can really quite totally concentrate on them. But then a bell rings, and we are called to this other business."

"Salivating."

"Yes, but it's not that crude. Because I think it's not just one bell, but a series of cues that fall together, like a very particular chord one hears. And it might be formed of previous memories and associations. Or it might be there from birth, and we're simply waiting—completely unwittingly—for the signal, to hear it. I don't know. But anyway, there you are, doing what you ordinarily do, and, say, a girl comes down the street on a bicycle with her hair behind her, wearing a skirt of a certain color, and there's the whir of the bicycle and maybe the sun at a certain angle to her and the smell of lilies and there you go. You would pretty much follow that girl to the ends of the earth, that particular one, for no particularly apparent reason."

"Powerless against it."

"Nearly. You can thwart it, but oh the misery involved—madness, tears, murders, war. Years of pining and second-guessing and melancholy."

Edward had finished his drink and was conscious of feeling his liquor. He held his hand over the top of the cup when Fields started to pour him another.

"Oh, that won't help," Fields said. "Abstinence. Trying to look the other way."

"I was just thinking of trying to drive home in one piece. To avoid temptation and trouble."

"That you might do. But this other thing is irresistible. Irresistible, yet voluntary."

"How so?"

"I can't say. It's only a theory. But surely it is something we want, something we desire. We're waiting for it, listening for it, even while we think we're doing other things. That sounds like volition to me." Fields tamped out his cigarette.

"This irresistible, preordained thing?"

"Well, no one wants to be born, never mind to die. But, as I said, that—along with this—is the end for which we are made."

"I think you lost me back there during the second drink," Edward said. "And as a practical matter"—he was trying to think what point he was attempting to put his finger on—"I see . . . seven or eight nurses a day, and maybe three of them are quite pretty. And in fifteen years on this job I have never felt the least bit . . . compuncted . . . ?"

"Compelled?"

"Compelled to follow . . . up . . . on any of them."

"Not even tempted?"

"Oh, tempted. Sure. But temptation is just ordinary life. It's just bread and butter. You just shrug. Confess whatever you yield to. Maybe avoid the occasion."

"The occasion?" Fields smiled. "Like birthdays, weddings, testimonial dinners?"

"The occasion of sin. The situation that gives rise to the temptation."

"And I thought we were doing so well keeping Mother Church out of the discussion."

"I'm sorry. But it's useful, really. You learn to stay out of the line of fire."

"So you wouldn't trust yourself alone in the autoclave room with one of the three pretty nurses."

"It's not a matter of trust. It's a matter of avoiding . . . steering clear of potential trouble."

Fields put his hand on the bottle, shook his head, then shrugged, and withdrew it. "But suppose you think that all this time you've been dodging bullets quite nicely, when in fact you haven't really been fired upon at all. That you just haven't heard . . ."

"The irresistible chord. Then I thank God I've been spared. I don't need that. Not at my age."

"Which is . . . perhaps forty-five?"

"Forty-four."

"And you talk like an old capon. When you're scarcely middle-aged. When you could sire an entire brood in a couple of afternoons."

"It's not what I want. And you said it's volitional."

"Sometimes it wants us. And becomes what we want."

"I'm happy," Edward said, and added, not as an afterthought but a conclusion, "I love my wife."

"Of course you do. I loved my wives. Both of them. Truly. I miss them. Especially now. In my dotage. In which I don't mean to harass you."

"Of course not."

"But these are things worth speaking about, don't you think? With a good drink, at the end of our labors. At the end of the day."

"Indeed," Edward said. "It's a good way to amuse oneself. Human folly."

"Oh, but it's sad," said Fields, without a trace of apparent sadness. "At least I always feel that way about it, after the fact. So melancholy and sadly earnest, the whole business. Deadly earnest, I suppose."

*E*dward was not thinking of these things as he drove to one hospital and then another the next morning, but his mind came back again to the boy and Emily. Midway between St. Luke's Hospital and Miller Hospital, he seemed to recollect that once he had stood in the dark outside a girl's house, and he had done this because she was an extremely pretty girl—even prettier than Virginia, he had to admit— and he had wanted to see her come out and possibly approach her.

As he remembered this, Edward waited at the stop light at the bottom of Ramsey Hill, and recalled her and felt something in his midriff that could only be called a pang, although, try as he might, he could not remember the girl's name at all.

The light changed, Edward drove on, and wondered if this boy was having pangs for Emily. He marveled at the recurrence of this sensation in himself after so many years. It struck him that it was almost exactly like the feeling he had when he recalled something from the past that was lost to him and the combination of sweetness and futile longing catalyzed into something that went uncomfortably beyond nostalgia or sentiment; that if gone into deeply enough could turn to grief and even despair, not so much for any one person, but for everything he had wanted and that had failed to be. Not pangs of love, but of mourning, the one pretty much indistinguishable from the other, except by the time of life in which they struck you.

Edward drove into the Miller Hospital parking lot, contemplating the absurdity of this boy's having pangs for his daughter and of the pangs being a kind of precursor or proxy of what amounted to grief. And this seemed to Edward, as he got out of the car and went around to the trunk to get his cases, to be both ridiculous and dangerous: this boy feeling things toward his daughter that rightfully appertained to the old and the dead; his love wish that contained a death wish.

16

WILLIAM RODE WITH HIS MOTHER TO EMILY'S
house that Saturday with decidedly mixed feelings. On the
one hand, the whole thing was on account of him, him and Emily.
But on the other hand, he wasn't sure he wanted anyone—particularly his mother— intruding on his and Emily's secrets and pleasures.
And riding in the car with his mother at the wheel, with neither of
them saying very much on their way to an *appointment*, was a little
reminiscent of her taking him to the doctor or the dentist or a par-
ent/teacher conference at school at which he would be talked about
like a laboratory specimen and spoken to with a level of condescen-
sion scarcely fit for a toddler.

But when they arrived at Emily's house, it was necessarily
William who led the way to the door, his mother carrying the salad,
covered with a shield of aluminum foil. Mrs. Byrne met them at the
door, and William heard her and his mother exchange choruses of
those chortling, bubbling, rumbling noises (like a water cooler or
what he imagined an Aqua-Lung sounded like) that adults use to
greet one another on first acquaintance. Then Emily's mother led
them back to the kitchen, and there they found Emily calling out
through the back screen door to her father, who was just then stoking the charcoal grill.

William's mother set down her salad on the kitchen counter and put
down a paper bag next to it. Emily and William watched her explain
herself to Emily's mother and watched Emily's mother take this in.

"Well," Jane began. "It's just something I threw together, and I

brought the dressing separately so we can just *toss* it at the last minute.
If that's all right. . . ."

"Oh, of course," said Virginia, a little diffidently, or so Emily
thought. Jane removed the foil, and they saw that what William's
mother had brought was contained in a mahogany-colored wooden
bowl, shiny with what must be oil, rather like Jim Donnelly's mother
poolside at the tennis club. Then from the bag Jane fetched a small
bottle that, Emily supposed, had once held capers or olives or cocktail
onions, but was now filled with a viscous green liquid, not far removed,
she thought, from something you might find on your windshield on a
hot day of high-speed travel.

"Just a few things," Jane was saying. "Mushrooms, bacon bits, hard-
boiled eggs, artichoke hearts."

"It's very exotic," Virginia said. "And here we're only having hamburgers and wieners."

"Oh, it's really casual, actually," Jane said. "Exactly the thing for a
meal *alfresco*."

Emily saw that her mother let this Gallicism or whatever it was slip
by unexplained, and wondered if her mother was beginning to think
that William's mother might be, as her granny put it, a little grand,
albeit in a curious fashion. For while she affected a folkishly plain manner of dress—a shift in bright orange, flat ballet-style shoes, and a rather
shapeless, outsize straw bag—these were offset by a bracelet of clunky
charms that must have come from Polynesia or Mexico and sunglasses,
sunglasses with huge, almost blackly opaque lenses.

"Well, I'm sure it's delicious," Virginia said. "Why don't we step outside and see how Edward's doing with the barbecue?"

Virginia led the way out the back door and down into the backyard,
Jane following, and Emily and William behind them like retainers.
When they were sure the grown-ups were fully distracted, they looked
at each other quizzically and shrugged.

"Edward, this is William's mother, Jane," Virginia said.

Edward took off his barbecue mitt and extended his hand.
"Pleased to meet you," he said pleasantly. Jane removed her sun-
glasses and shook his hand. "Bill's rather a fixture here these days,"
Edward continued.

"But not an imposition, I hope," Jane said. "He can be a little . . . relentless at times."

"Oh, no. Not at all. We're used to having lots of kids around. Love it."

"You and Mrs. Byrne have—"

"Please, *Virginia*," Virginia cut in, nicely enough.

"Ginny," Edward said, "and I have just the two, Sue and Emily."

Then Virginia, a little in the manner of someone presiding over a school assembly, said brightly, "Well, Edward. If you're ready, I'll bring out the hamburgers and wieners and you can set to work while Jane and I finish up the lovely salad she's brought." With that Jane and Virginia went back into the house, followed at a short distance by Emily.

William now stood alone about ten feet beyond Edward, closer to the garage, and watched Edward watch the women go inside and then return to prodding and poking the coals. He hoped Emily's father would not now commence to ask him questions or josh with him about sports. Happily, Edward continued to regard the fire bed absentmindedly, albeit as though it might at any instant somehow require great attention.

Inside, Virginia set about finding Jane the requisite tools for her salad, and came up with a silver serving spoon and a carving fork that sat a little uncomfortably alongside Jane's ethnic bowl. Emily was curious to see what "tossing" consisted of—probably, she supposed, some Isadora Duncanish dervishing of the lettuce. But her mother asked her to help carry the rest of the food out to the table. As she set the platter down on the little metal table next to the grill, she saw her mother and father exchange a series of microscopic eye-crinklings, imperceptible shrugs, and tiny mouthings. Moving back to where William was standing, Emily continued to watch them, trying to make out what signals were being passed, while William watched her and, assuming she was preoccupied with something a little grave, touched her gently on the hip and then removed his hand.

At this point, Jane emerged from the house, bearing her salad bowl and Virginia's wedding-silver implements. She approached the picnic table, already set with paper plates and napkins by Emily, and said, "Shall I just put this down here?"

"Oh, anywhere," Virginia replied, and added, "We'll need forks, I imagine. I'll go get them." She set off and then spun around and asked Jane, "And knives too?"

"Oh no," Jane said. "You don't need knives. It's very informal."

Virginia nodded and went back into the house while Edward poked and turned the meat on the grill. Jane came over and stood next to him and said, "Is there anything I can do?"

Edward, pulling back just half a foot or so, said, "Oh, no. We're . . . I'm fine. Just sit down and relax. Pour yourself some lemonade."

Jane backed away and sat down at the picnic table, still regarding Edward. "Well, I'll just go right ahead," she said with a laugh, half directed toward him, and half toward no one in particular. She poured herself a glass from the pitcher that stood on the table. It occurred to William that he had probably never seen his mother drink lemonade before. Virginia returned with a fistful of forks and set them around. Edward announced, "I've just about got the first bunch ready if you want to come over with your plates."

After they had each gotten a hamburger or a hot dog from the grill, they all sat down again, Edward at one end of the table, William and Emily on one side, and Jane and Virginia on the other, with Virginia positioned between her husband and Jane.

"Well," said Virginia, and looked at Edward, who looked back blankly and made the tiniest of shrugs, and Emily realized they were not going to say a blessing. Her mother shrugged back and said, "Well, shall we?" and everyone began to eat. William and Emily listened to the adults coo to each other about the food in a sort of variation on the earlier greeting rite.

Emily, and her mother, too, she suspected, worried that the conversation would not go well—that the adults would not have enough in common and that she and William would feel left out, pressured, or simply embarrassed—but she needn't have worried. William's mother was, if not adroit in social circumstances, gifted with connections and free associations that were fodder for talk. She had almost immediately announced that she had practically grown up on this very block, her best childhood friend, Anna, having lived just six doors down. Then she mentioned various people they must know in common, and indeed, Edward and Virginia were acquainted with some of these personages. Emily observed that Jane seemed to address herself chiefly to Edward while Virginia swung her gaze back and forth between them, as though one of them were about to slip away. During one particularly long exchange William's mother took off her sunglasses and set them before her, the better to see Edward, Emily supposed.

That had gotten them through the second round of hamburgers and hot dogs, and the bulk of the salad, which Edward ate with especially apparent pleasure. He remarked to Jane, rather merrily, as if his lemonade might have been fortified in some way, "So, Emily tells us you are a mover and shaker in politics."

"Hardly that," Jane said, and looked up at Edward. "But I am going to Chicago. To the national convention. I'm an alternate, really. But still . . ." She was looking at Edward straight on, but then, as though she were forgetting something, she turned to Virginia, ". . . it's nice to be included."

"It sounds very exciting," Virginia said.

"I suppose," Jane responded, "although right now I really rather despair of the whole business."

Edward said, "Because of the assassination and the way the nomination's going, I'd suppose."

Jane smiled at him. "Oh, yes. Exactly. I just don't see how it can end well, as far as the war is concerned. Which is what concerns me most."

"Of course," Edward said. Virginia glanced away. He added, "I gather you're also on the front lines of the war on poverty and so forth. At work, I mean."

"Oh, yes. I guess I am," Jane replied. "Of course, you can't really accomplish everything you'd like. These institutions and agencies move a little slowly—"

"We raise money for yours, I think," Virginia broke in. "At church. Bingo. Bring and Buy. Sodality and so forth."

Jane said, "Of course. It's very . . . good that you do. And important." She said this with an air of familiarity with what Virginia was referring to, although Emily wondered how or why she would be.

There was a pause and Virginia leaned over the table and lifted a sheet of waxed paper off another platter to reveal a bank of puffed-rice bars. William had two bars, and his mother took one. Emily noticed that although Jane ate hers, she did so as if holding it at arm's length, at the ends of her fingertips, as though it threatened to stick to her teeth.

When they were done, Virginia stood and volunteered to give Jane's salad bowl a quick wash before she left. "Oh, that's all right," Jane said. "Really, you're just supposed to wipe it out with a paper towel. To keep it nice and oiled." Virginia nodded, a little uncertainly.

Virginia stood with Edward in the front door and William eased around from behind them to join his mother. "I might come back later," he said, "if that's okay."

"Sure," said Edward, and Emily, now standing just behind her father, nodded.

"Of course," said Virginia.

The adults said their thank-yous and goodbyes, in more or less the same ebullient mutter they'd used to greet each other, and Emily walked with William and his mother to their car. Edward and Virginia remained in the doorway, and as Jane got into her side of the car, Virginia put her arm around her husband's waist and guided him ever so gently inside. A moment later, Emily returned and began to mount the stairs, but she paused just below and listened. From the kitchen hall, she heard her father say, "Well, that was painless."

"I suppose it's hard raising a boy by yourself," Virginia allowed, as though she were excusing something in William's mother's conduct.

"She's fine. Interesting woman."

Virginia did not affirm or deny this. Instead, she was silent for a moment and then said very gently, "You didn't say the blessing."

"Oh, that. I wondered if you'd mind." There was a pause. "I just thought since they're not Catholic, it would be a courtesy. It would be ecumenical."

"I suppose. Of course, this is a Catholic house. It's our house, and you could say the onus is on . . ."

"You could. But these things are a little awkward, aren't they? Both ways. Even for the kids. Didn't seem like they said a word the whole time. But . . . but everything went fine. And now it's done. And there you are." Then they each went their separate ways, Edward to the back-yard, Virginia to the kitchen, and Emily to her room.

That night Emily and William returned to the park, to the same place on the hill they had been a few nights before. The grass was still flattened where they had lain. It was their burrow, their nest, their bower. They sat down and waited for the dark to come like a flood tide, for the stars to descend out of the sky.

William said, "So do you think they liked my mom?"

"I think my dad did. My mom, I don't know."

"My mom didn't really act like my mom. She acted more cheerful. She didn't talk about politics and the war the whole time."

"Grown-ups always say to avoid talking about religion and politics."

"But they didn't avoid them. Not really."

"It was my dad, I think, that brought them up," Emily said. "My mom says sometimes he likes to put the cat among the pigeons. To stir things up."

"With my mom, things are always already stirred up. So they'd like each other."

"I think they did. Not that you can really tell. It's like everything they say to each other is in code."

"Suppose there's no code," said William. "Suppose it's all exactly like it sounds, and they never really say anything to each other. Or at least not what they really think."

"Maybe they're just trying to be polite," Emily said.

William turned towards her. "I mean, your parents are nice, but today, they all sat there for an hour and nobody said even one really true, unphony thing."

This was a little more than Emily was prepared to grant. "Just because somebody's not saying something . . . earth-shattering doesn't mean they're automatically lying."

"Okay. Not lying, but ignoring. Not speaking out."

"Your mom speaks out."

"Yeah. But sometimes I think it's just another way for her to make . . . an impression. Like, 'Hey, everybody, look at me.' Because, really, what difference does it make?"

"So what makes a difference?"

"I don't know anymore. Maybe helping people who need help. Changing things. But not just going to school and going to college and coming out and being a robot."

"So you want to be a hippie?" Emily laughed.

"Maybe we could. Maybe we could go to California," William said.

Emily laughed again. "We could?"

"Sure. If the kid in *My Side of the Mountain* can go live in the mountains, we can go live in California."

"What about school?"

"He didn't go to school. The woods was his education."

"But you're going to graduate next year."

"So? I don't care. The only reason to graduate is to go to college and do all the rest of it—not doing anything about anything that matters."

Emily laughed yet again. "Are you serious? I mean, you have to finish school."

"You know why you have to finish school? Because if you're not in school and then in college, you get drafted." William said this angrily, although Emily did not feel this anger had anything to do with her. William had his hand under her neck, his fingers in her hair.

He went on, "So you see, if you don't do what you're supposed to do, you go in the army and probably get killed. That's how they keep us in line. You can go to college, you can even protest a little bit, but you get your deferment. Otherwise . . ."

"So you do kind of have to stay in school."

"Or get away. Or go to Canada or something. Because I wouldn't let myself get drafted. It's a bad war. It's wrong to go." William turned his head away and said, "And I wouldn't want to anyway. I think I'd be afraid."

"I'd be afraid too. I'd be afraid for you," Emily said, and she did not want to say anything more or to have William say anything more.

But he did. "Besides," he continued, "I'd want to be with you. I'd want you with me."

Then Emily heard herself say, "And I'd go. With you." She had said this without apparent thought. Instead, it seemed a great gulf of purpose and conviction had suddenly opened itself up all around her.

"To Vietnam?" William looked at her and laughed.

"Not there. I wouldn't let them take you. Anywhere but there."

"Okay," he said. "I believe you. I really do." And he truly did. Emily pulled him close to her and kissed him, and he held her and pressed himself against her. They were down deep in the grass, and although it was a warm evening, they were trying to keep each other warm, out of harm's way.

*T*wo weeks later, on a Saturday afternoon, Emily found herself in church. She was killing time, on her way to meet William, and she felt a little sad, partly because she missed him, and partly because she missed what missing him—what coming to care for him so much—had displaced, which was the wide, shallow, and placid stream that used to be her life: not doing anything that she couldn't happily tell her mother and father about; thinking that working at the New Wave and getting dresses at a discount was the best possible way to pass the summer; being friends with Monica; being like she used to be; being a girl. Not that she wanted to undo anything.

She went to the Blessed Virgin's shrine and knelt and prayed, praying by rote, with all the other things that were on her mind streaming through her like a draft that became a wind and a roar. She finished, or rather—so she felt—she gave up, and lit a candle. Confessions were being heard, and on the same impulse that had caused her to pray, she found herself in line and then inside the confessional. She asked the priest—the young new curate, who was known to be "liberal," who played the guitar—to bless her and told him how long ago she had last made her confession: three months, she reckoned.

Then Emily confessed the things she habitually confessed: disobeying her parents, thinking ill of others, talking back, being prideful, and sometimes saying curse words, the same sins that she had confessed the very first time she had ever made a confession, years and years ago. And then because she had to, because it was time, she confessed that she had touched herself, and had been doing so even before her last confession or the one before that. The priest asked if there was more, along those lines.

"I let a boy touch me there. And I touched him back."

"More than once?"

"A couple of times. Maybe three. Or four. Just recently."

"I see. And is that all?"

"That's all, father."

"Well, you know the church says the last thing is a grave sin. Because it's masturbation and because, with the boy, it's sexual activity outside of marriage. You know that, don't you?"

"Yes."

"You see, I know how it is being a young person. And sometimes it's not so grave. But this is something you need to stop doing, to avoid in the future. Can you do that?"

"I don't know."

"If you can't avoid the occasion, then you have to avoid the person. And I suppose you feel strongly about him."

"Yes."

"So perhaps you should just try to be together when others are present. Just as friends."

"Yes," Emily said, although after she said it—because Emily always said yes to priests and nuns and, despite her reputation as a headstrong girl, to practically everybody—she realized what the priest was asking: that she do what she had already understood she couldn't do, even with all the will in the world, because it was too late.

The priest told her she should say a decade of the rosary every night and to ask Our Lady for chastity and forbearance in particular; that Our Lady was the exemplar of these virtues and would grant them to those who prayed to her.

"Make a good act of contrition and I'll give you absolution," the priest continued.

But Emily said, "I really can't. Not just now. I'm sorry." The priest said something else, something she could not or would not hear, and Emily said, "I'll come back later. Soon. Okay?" And she got up from her knees and left.

17

IT IS HIGH SUMMER SOMETIME IN AUGUST; THE TIME
when it will get no hotter, but only cooler; when there is a month or
so until harvest and the crops are in; when the tomatoes are as ripe as
they are going to get before they burst and rot. By the time it arrives, in
the middle of the month or just before, it seems as though it has always
been summer, that the heat and thrum of the air is the element in
which we have always lived, even if we know it will not be so for much
longer. It is a realm as close to paradise as we are vouchsafed on this
earth, for in it we might well do without clothes or shelter or concern
for our next meal, since we could easily go about naked under the sun
and sleep open under the stars and pluck our dinner from the vine or
the tree. It is a time in which surely one has no right to be unhappy; or
at least ought to be content.

That was when Emily and William became lovers in the full and
true sense, not much more than two months after their first date. You
may say that they were hasty or that they were a little timorous, but it
seemed to them they had exhausted every other possibility before
exploring this one, and that it could not be refused—not on account of
its being a craving or an urge, but because it was their history, the gravity by which they were falling through life. That, and also because it
seemed that all there was in the whole world was each other, and any
separation of one from the other, in body or soul, was intolerable.

It happened in their usual place, just as it was getting dark. They
had been touching each other for some weeks now, and because the
spot they lay in was pretty much invisible they had fallen into a com-

fortable routine, Emily's underpants removed and her dress above her hips, William's trousers and underpants down at knee level, pressing together, stroking, pressing. In one of these latter moments, the head of William's penis found itself farther between Emily's legs than it was usually accustomed to go. William and Emily looked at each other for a scant half-second, as though with a shrug of the shoulders, smiled to each other, and Emily put her hands on him and just guided him inside her.

It was done in no time at all, so little time that neither was sure they had technically completed the act they had begun. They lay very quietly together for a few minutes, and then William was hard again and they did it again, more slowly and surely and deliberately, and as William rocked in and out of her, Emily began to weep. He stopped and asked her what was wrong and she said, "Nothing. Nothing at all," and she pulled him back inside her and they went on, just them in the rustle of the grass and the boil of the crickets.

Later, when she climbed the steps of her parents' house, she had been thinking, That was really no big deal. But at the same time, as she reached the porch and went inside, she felt as though she were naked and carrying her clothing before her for modesty's sake, as though she had fallen into a lake and gotten thoroughly soaked.

She went inside and the rest of the evening passed like any other. She got ready for bed and her parents kissed her good night, and this was the way it always was, save in two particulars. First, when her father kissed her good night, she wondered if she must smell different in some detectable way, of a deep and metallic nitrogenous tang. Second, when her parents were gone and the light was out and Emily began to pray, and directed herself to Our Lady, as was her custom, she realized that her prayers were no longer the prayers of a virgin.

This worried her, but not because she suddenly felt ashamed or feared that her prayers were no longer efficacious. Emily had never imagined she was consecrated to virginity as the nuns were, but neither had she given much thought to being anyone's wife. Now she was somewhere between these two states, and she wondered whose prayers these really were and what purpose they might serve.

Jane left for Chicago on a Sunday afternoon, and William drove her to the airport. And since mass, a family visit to her grandmother, and lunch were all complete, Emily went with them, rather as if Emily and William were the parents and Jane were being sent off to college; and since Jane was not a little giddy in the face of her journey, that was not far from the truth.

Inside the terminal they waited together in a long line so that Jane could check her suitcase, and then they went down the concourse to the gate. They waited in another line and the woman at the desk peeled a sticker off a chart of the seats on the plane and put it on Jane's ticket. They waited a little more, and at last Jane went down the passage and into the plane, waving to them with one hand and rooting in her bag with the other as though she feared she had forgotten something. Then she turned around, waved to them one more time, and was gone.

William and Emily walked slowly back down the concourse, regarding the names of the destinations posted above the check-in desks. The airport was as far from home as you could go without leaving home: From here you could go to New York or California (nonstop, twice a day) and then pretty much anywhere you wanted, and they would show you a movie on the way. William proposed that they drive out by the end of the runway and watch the planes come and go, and Emily agreed this would be pretty cool.

There were one or two other cars parked when they arrived, and in the distance they could see a plane coming towards them, preparing to land. They got out and William took Emily's hand and pulled her up onto the hood of the car, and they sat there waiting. Then the plane roared over their heads—Emily thought she might almost reach up and brush the fat tires with her fingers—and touched down perhaps one hundred yards beyond them, its howl and racket shaking in their ears like a thundercrack. As the plane landed, another pulled up near the end of the runaway waiting to take off, and William decided this was probably his mother's plane. They watched it rumble off down the runway. After it was no more than a mote in the sky, William said, "So she's gone." He said this as though her return were in some doubt; as though his mother and her anti-Vietnam candidate might not only lose to Hubert Humphrey and the Lyndon Johnson war party, but perish in the effort.

William drove Emily home. He came in for an hour and they watched television and ate potato chips. Emily's mother suggested he come for dinner the next night. He said he would, and left Emily's house about five-thirty. The city was perhaps as quiet as it ever got during the daylight hours: the end of Sunday afternoon, tools and toys being put away, dinner being assembled, no one going anywhere, every creature in its home.

William opened the door to the apartment, and felt the vibration of its emptiness, the dust spinning in the window light like nebulae, the distant hum of the refrigerator, water somewhere trickling down a pipe; that—all that—and nothing more. It was terribly lonely, he felt, but only for an instant, because this feeling was quickly surmounted by a burgeoning vision of the freedom—absolute provided he didn't make too much noise and kept the shades down—he might now enjoy here. That freedom, which was really the condition of being perfectly hidden, seemed to belong completely to the sphere of his and Emily's secrets, but without its attendant anxiety, the fear—of discovery and punishment and shame—in which the secrets came wrapped and that could never be completely shed in the car or the hillside below the park.

This was a joyful realization, and the first thing William did was take off all his clothes and masturbate, brazenly and with luxurious deliberateness, right there in the living room, on the very couch on which he and Emily had made out. As was his custom, he called out Emily's name as he stroked himself, nearly sang it when his orgasm came and his ejaculation cannonballed over the back of the couch and landed on the lower stile of the frame containing his mother's print of Childe Hassam's *Late Afternoon, New York: Winter, 1900*. He ambled down the hall, a thread of fluid swinging from his penis, and fetched a tissue to clean himself and the picture frame up, and then he sat and flipped through the new issue of *Life*, already contemplating perhaps a follow-up bout of masturbation later in the evening, following a chopped sirloin TV dinner.

William has, of course, been aware of the possibilities of the coming week and even made some preparations (having, for example, filched a pack of prophylactics from the drugstore he delivers for), but he has forgone their contemplation until now. For example, it turns out Emily will be working only during the mornings this week, and thereafter not at all, since it is but a week until Labor Day. They will be able to pass the afternoons here, and, although it will necessitate a little dissembling, perhaps some evenings. The only intrusions will be his mother's phone calls from Chicago, and the first of these, the very next day, just before Emily arrives, is no impediment to anyone's pleasure: Jane in fact reports that contrary to her pessimism, there is much talk of a McCarthy/Edward Kennedy "dream ticket" or at least a last-ditch compromise Kennedy candidacy with a strongly worded antiwar plank in the party platform.

When Emily is at last inside the apartment and the front door is locked behind them, what William would like to happen is for both of them to shed their clothes then and there. But Emily is cagey, or perhaps is just savoring the moment. She walks through the apartment, William in tow, remarking on its rooms and fixtures in the manner of a real estate agent or a docent in a museum. Then, having come at last to William's room, Emily simply lies down, shoes and all, upon his bed, and William shuts the door and, unbidden, begins to undress her. He takes off her shoes and her socks; her cutoff shorts; her blouse; her bra (which she does indeed normally wear); and finally her underpants. Then he removes all his own clothes, and they are upon each other.

That part is fine, but the best is after. For they had never seen each other completely naked and they take the time to look at each other, to inspect and touch each other in places that until now have been a little off the map: Emily's little feet and toes; William's calves and shoulders; and both their derrières. Emily's inclination is to cover herself up with William's bedspread, but both the heat and William argue against this. Eventually, he persuades her to come out into the apartment with him, to walk down the hall, and finish up before the mirror on the closet door in his mother's room.

They stand there for some time. They stare as into a square frame: on the left is the dark of the open closet, the dresses and shoes and coats huddled in its shadows and depths; and on the right the brilliance of the mirror, with a man and a woman standing naked inside it. It is wondrous not just that William and Emily see each other naked together for the first time, but that they see each other together—separate from themselves as they look on—at all. Here, for the first time, they are real and substantial, undeniable. They have not been imagining themselves after all.

They are very beautiful. William is not that handsome and Emily is not that pretty, but here, framed in the shining glass and bounded by the perfectly ordinary world, they are beautiful. They are young, of course; every part of their skin and musculature defies shadow and gravity, but heretofore neither has had an especially good opinion of his or her physique, and at the worst of times both have hated and feared their own flesh as ungainly and even ugly. But together they seem very fine to each other, nor is their mutual appreciation purely awestruck or solemn. William's penis, which Emily has never before seen unerect, looks stringy and forlorn and a little insulted, like a fish dumped in the bottom of a boat. The hair on Emily's pubis betrays a little of her childhood red, and her stomach has a suggestion of toddler roundness; her rump is gloriously fleshy, and William would like to bury his face in and on it. Emily would like to cradle in the crotch of William's armpit and perhaps idly tousle his limp and docile penis. All that will happen, but what they do now—and this is the best thing of all—is return to William's room and William's bed and sleep together for an hour, tangled in arm and leg, breathing together like twins. And when they are done, they return to the mirror once more, just to make sure.

Those days were paradise, for what else is there to call freedom without so much as a whisper of obligation, want, or anxiety to spoil it? They spent the time, or rather the afternoons, much as just described, and in the morning William delivered a few prescriptions for the drugstore, tidied the apartment, and, on Tuesday, rode downtown, strode into Brower's, and bought himself a pair of Boots Sauvage as Louis Campion clucked over him and Mr. Murkowski glowered from the stockroom door.

On the way home he stopped off at the library periodical room and looked at magazines and newspapers. The latter were full of the Chicago convention, and, to a sometimes lesser or greater extent, recent events in Czechoslovakia. William knew very little of Czechoslovakia, except that it was one of the Central European places that used to be known for pastry, but now had been entrapped within the Iron Curtain; not totally, apparently, for of late the locals had inaugurated some democratic reforms and liberalizations, and now the Soviets were coming down on them. It seemed to William a little analogous to what was happening in the United States and even in his own life, for whenever anybody—societies or adolescents—tried to claim more freedom than authority—governments and grown-ups—thought was good for them, they got quashed. Now this was happening in the blatantly oppressive and totalitarian environment of Eastern Europe (which, however, Jane had told him, ought to be given some credit for at least *trying* socialism), and even in his darkest moments he did not imagine tanks and soldiers in American cities enforcing the status quo. As for his own present freedom—his and Emily's Prague spring—it was more a toy they had quietly borrowed for a week and would quietly put back, with no one being the wiser.

When Emily came that afternoon, they did pretty much as they had done the previous afternoon, albeit without the overtures and preambles (as a matter of fact, they undressed one another in the hallway and made love alongside the chest of drawers, the umbrellas and boots, and Jane's archival wicker basket of *New Yorker* magazines). Afterwards, they lay down on William's bed, but they did not sleep. William rested his hand on Emily's bottom and told her about his morning, and in particular about his triumphal return to Brower's. He left the bed to get the boots and show them to her, and this led in turn to his guiding her through some of his other possessions, including the cache in the closet floor (excluding, for modesty's sake, the magazines therein). He showed her his favorite books; his maps of the north woods; his knife and hatchet; his pack (the one item he had managed to obtain while still eligible for the Brower's employee discount); his canteen, mess kit, and set of nesting kettles and pans; his savings passbook (now exceeding five hundred dollars); and his father's boyhood copy of Ernest Thompson Seton's *Book of Woodcraft and Indian Lore.*

It seemed to William that he had told Emily a great deal about himself in presenting this display, and he added, as an afterthought, "If we went away, this stuff would come in handy." Emily nodded, but made no response, instead finding herself wishing that she too might do the same thing for him, in her own room, showing him without apology or hesitation her St. Teresa doll in its frayed and sandbox-scruffy habit, the stuffed rabbit toy whose ear she had habitually sucked as a toddler, her copy of Sartre's *La Nausée* (bought in Paris by Sister Mary Catherine), and even her autographed picture of Jon Provost (obtained in person when he and Lassie had come through town some years before). There was nothing Emily did not want to know about William, and nothing she did not want William to know about her, because knowing and loving, apprehension and adoration, had become, at least for now, one thing.

They passed the afternoon in this way, and at its end they agreed that for appearance's sake tomorrow they should imply they were going to the Scholar for a show that would begin early and run a little late (Emily's parents had become quite pliable about curfew times where William was concerned), but would in fact spend the evening here. He would make Emily dinner, maybe spaghetti.

*W*illiam's mother called a little after dinnertime, and her mood was less sanguine than the day before. The "dream ticket" had evaporated, the Vietnam plank being pushed through was one that Richard Nixon could comfortably run on, and there had been some confrontations between police and protesters in the big park downtown. There were police and soldiers everywhere.

"It's like Czechoslovakia, kind of," William offered.

His mother's sigh came down the telephone line, all the way from Chicago, like a groan of wind, like smoke. "It's worse. Because it's here. Where it's not supposed to happen."

"But it is."

"It is. Watch the TV. And watch the TV tomorrow night. That's the nomination. You might see me when they do the roll call."

"Wow."

He telephoned Emily, not to tell her about the distressing things unfolding at the convention, but about the possibility that his mother might be on television, or at least glimpsed among her delegation. He did not mention this on the phone, but he imagined they might watch the TV naked and perhaps smoke the rest of the grass he still had from Jim Donnelly.

The next evening, a little before six o'clock, William picked up Emily and drove her to the apartment. He had prepared most of the dinner in advance—spaghetti, tomato sauce, French bread with butter and garlic salt, and salad with the dressing you made in a special bottle with a packet of seasonings—so first they made love, quickly, on his bed, just by way of saying hello.

Afterwards, William stood naked before the stove finishing the cooking, and then, at Emily's suggestion, he put on the tawny burlap apron that his mother sometimes wore. He put the spaghetti into the pot and stirred it and Emily watched his bottom and his cock and balls, dipping in and out of sight. They ate at the kitchen table pretty much as anyone might eat, save for the fact they were both naked and that in mid-course William, overcome by the sight of Emily's breasts where he might normally have seen a stack of unread copies of *Ramparts* or *The Nation*, came over to her, knelt before her, and lapped her nipples with his tongue.

When they were done with dinner and the rest, they went into Jane's bedroom, sat on the floor at the foot of her bed, and watched the television. It was a black-and-white television; while William coveted a color television almost as much as he did a canoe, his mother could not be prodded into purchasing one. Perhaps if she had, everything—the sad and foolish things that followed this night—would have been different; perhaps William would have wanted to stay home, simply to watch everything there was to see or that he had already seen in this new and glorious form, in color.

As it happened, the coverage of the convention was in color, although William and Emily had no way of knowing this, and most of the rest of what they saw—the news film from outside the hall, from Grant Park and Michigan Avenue—was in black-and-white anyway. They were in any case chiefly watching out for William's mother, but the roll call seemed never to come, being interrupted not by commercials but by images of the police, the soldiers, and the protesters. There were speeches and more film from outside and William and Emily did indeed smoke the last of Jim Donnelly's grass. They watched, and at one point William said, "Wow. They're just . . . beating the shit out of them."

The roll call still didn't come, and then they realized it was time to go if Emily was going to be home by eleven o'clock. They had some trouble finding all their clothes, and their parting felt very odd, perhaps because of the grass, or what they had seen on TV, or the fact that the whole evening was in some sense imaginary, since they were supposed to have been at the Scholar, not cooking dinner and lolling naked together, watching the nation come apart at the seams.

They drove towards Emily's house through the dark and noiseless streets, the sound of the marchers and the truncheons and the bullhorns left behind them, stoppered inside the cooling television tube. It was inky and silent in the car and in the night, and with the dumb spinning of the tires, the mood deflated, turned somber, regretful, and discontented.

"So what happens," William said, "after this?"

"After what?"

"After this week. Next week. The week after that."

"When your mom's back?"

"And when school starts. What happens to us?"

Emily was not sure she was following what William was saying, but she felt scared. "How do you mean? Why should anything . . . ?"

"Because," William said, "all this ends next week. Being together."

"Well, we'll see each other. Just the way we did before, I guess."

"We'll be apart mostly."

"We'll see each other. All the time."

"I don't want to 'see each other, ' " William said. "I don't want to just go on 'dates, ' like stupid high school kids."

"It doesn't have to be like that. We'll find ways. And then next summer, you'll be free, and I'll just have another year."

"Yeah, free to get drafted or go to college. Neither of which I want to do." William had turned onto Emily's street and was coming up to her house. "What I want is us."

Emily was looking at her hands. She said, "So you just have to wait for me."

William brought the car to a stop in front of the house and turned to her. "For two years?"

Emily looked up at him. There were tears in the corners of her eyes, tiny glintings in the flat opacity of the dark. "It's not so long," she said.

William turned his face back towards the windshield. "It's still two years," he said quietly. "Two years ago there wasn't anything." He put his hand in Emily's lap and searched for her hand. When he found it and had taken it, he said, "Two years from now maybe there won't be anything either. I won't even be me. Like I am now. Not without you."

"And who do you think I'll be?"

"I don't know. I'm afraid to think about it," William said. "I mean, not about what you'll do, but about us. That we could change without even wanting to. Does that make sense? That things we don't even know about could change us. Unless we do something to stop it."

Emily had put her hand over William's hand so now their hands enveloped one another, shells within shells, cradled. "I know. Don't worry." Emily felt as if she were saying these things in a play or a movie or a song, and that made them more real; made her feel stronger. "We'll find a way," she said.

When William got home, he went back to the television and found the roll call had begun, and was in fact well into the letter M, with Michigan about to begin. So he only had to endure that one state, and then he began to look for his mother, and he thought he saw her, in what he guessed must be her yellow shift, as the numbers were bellowed out and repeated from the rostrum. Then he switched it off. He really didn't want any more.

He went to bed, and the bed was still full of the smells of him and Emily together. He fell asleep very quickly. Then, sometime later, the telephone rang. The experience of this—of the phone ringing in the dead of night, down the hall, like what he had always imagined the Gestapo coming to your door would be like—was so alien to him that he sat upright and did nothing for two or three rings. Then he got up and went to the kitchen and picked up the receiver. Maybe, somehow, it was Emily.

It was his mother. "Billy, I know it's very late. But I thought I ought to call—to make sure you're all right."

"I'm . . . fine. Why shouldn't I be?"

"Well, with everything going on, I was worried, I was scared. You watched, right?"

"Yeah. I think I saw you."

"That's nice. But you saw everything else too?"

"Yeah."

"It's awful. It's worse than I ever imagined."

"But it's over now?"

"I don't know. I don't think so. Because they're everywhere, the police and the army. And there are two more days and people are very, very angry. They should be, of course. But it could spread. Into the ghetto here, and to other cities. And then who knows what the military and Johnson would do? Would feel that they had to do?"

"I guess I didn't know it was that bad. I was with Emily. I made her some supper."

"That's very sweet. But I think you need to be very careful. That's why I really called. Because you need to be careful. Stay away from the police or crowds or anything like that. Maybe you should just stay inside."

"I will. If anything happens."

"I'm afraid it will, maybe even there. I'd come home, but . . ." Jane paused. "Do you want me to come home? It'd be difficult, but I could."

"No, it's really okay. Really. But you be careful. You're the one that's down there, Mom."

"Oh, I'll be fine. They'll probably just lock us all up inside the amphitheater. Where we can't do anything. We didn't do anything anyway, did we?"

"So it's Humphrey."

"Oh yes."

"I'm sorry."

"That's the least of it. It's really very bad, Billy. And no one knows where it's going to end. So I think you should just stay inside, until I get back Saturday."

William was not going to argue. He was very tired and it was very late. "Okay. I will. I promise," he said.

*W*hen William went down to the vestibule in the morning, he looked out the door of the apartment building and everything looked the same. The paper was full of the events in Chicago, but outside the street was quiet and the sun was angling down, hot and acute, through the trees. So of course he went out, leaving the phone off the hook so if his mother called she'd think the line was busy with him talking on it. He delivered a few things for the drugstore, and every house and street was normal and ordinary. There was no gunfire, no smoke or flames.

It was in all these ways a day like any other, except that when William went by Emily's house that afternoon no one was at home except Emily. He went inside and they had the whole place to themselves.

She took him upstairs, where he had never been before. They ascended the stairs in a hush, on tiptoe, and when they arrived on the upstairs landing it was as if they had reached the top of a tree they had climbed together, and there ought to have been long, vertiginous views and no sound save the wind.

It was indeed quiet and sunlit, and, from the walls to the curtains to the bedspreads in the bedrooms, very white. William held his arms against his sides and kept his hands in his pockets as he looked around, swaying a little. "It's really . . . clean," he said. "I mean, in a nice way."

"There's not really anyone here to make a mess. Just the three of us these days," Emily said. She pointed to a doorway at the side of the landing. "This one's mine. My room."

"I see," William said. "Is it okay? If I look?"

"Sure," Emily said, and led him in.

"It's nice. It's like I imagined it." William scanned the room nervously. "All your stuff."

"I suppose it's not much different from when I was little." Emily shrugged. "Dolls and things. Corny stuff." She pointed to a bookshelf, to a figure robed in a nun's habit. "That's Teresa. She was my favorite."

"She's . . . a nun or something?"

"A saint."

"Umm." William nodded. "And then there's all your books, right?"

"There's not much to it."

"But it's good. It really is."

Emily looked up at him. "But it doesn't seem to have much to do with anything anymore, you know?"

"I guess," William said. "I guess it's the same with my room. In my house." Then he backed out the door, as though he thought the room was very small and if he had turned around he might have knocked something over.

Out on the landing, Emily indicated another door to a room at the front of the house. "That's my mom and dad's."

They moved to the doorway together. William looked in and saw there was a bay window looking out onto the street, and opposite it, a big double bed with a white coverlet. His hand was on Emily's waist, almost as though to steady himself, and he put his index finger into one of her belt loops and drew her a little closer. He was looking at the bed and then at her. Each knew what the other was thinking, and they nearly shook their heads at the same time. No, they had both decided, that would be too weird.

Outside the door again, Emily said, "That's about it. My sister's room is back there." William looked down to the far end of the hall beyond the landing, to where the sun was pouring in.

He said, "There's an attic, isn't there? With a sort of terrace or something?"

"You mean like a balcony?"

"Yeah. I noticed it once."

"My dad calls it a widow's walk. It's like a crow's nest, where the sailors' wives could see when their husbands were coming home. There's no ocean, but it's still kind of cool. You want to see it?"

"Sure," William said.

Emily opened a door and they climbed a narrow, roughly finished staircase that emerged into a surprisingly large space, lit by a bank of windows at one end and a set of small French doors at the other. Between them were stacks of cartons, rolled-up carpets, suitcases and steamer trunks, high chairs and floor lamps, and, hung from the rafters, tennis rackets and old suits and dresses.

"That's Susan's dollhouse," said Emily, pointing towards the doors. "And this is my dad's trunk from the war. See the stencil? He was a captain. In Germany."

William was looking around, smiling and nodding. "It's like your family museum," he said.

Emily patted a big rectangular box from Schuneman's Department Store. "And here's my mom's wedding dress. And"—she gestured beyond them—"my crib."

"This is great. You could hide up here," William said. "Like Anne Frank." He laughed. "Like me, when the FBI draft guys come looking for me."

Emily cast her eyes down. She did not like it when William talked that way. It made her feel a little despairing and nauseated.

"Do you want to go out?" she said, indicating the French doors.

"Sure."

Emily opened the two doors, which came away a little stubbornly, and then they were standing at the rail, out among the treetops and the crests of neighboring roofs, up in the hot clear blue of the summer sky.

William looked out and then back to Emily. "A long time ago, before I really knew you, I'd come by your house and I'd look up here. And I guess I was thinking maybe you would come out and I'd see you."

"You mean you were thinking about me then?" said Emily.

"All the time. Even back then. I suppose that's kind of weird."

"No. It's sweet," Emily said, and took his hand. "And now here we are." They moved to face each other, to press up against each other.

"I want to," Emily said. "Right here." She looked at the floor of metal flashing and asphalt patching. "Maybe not *right* here," she added, and drew him by the hand back inside.

They went to a spot near the dollhouse, where two carpets were heaped side by side. They kneeled before each other, and each unfastened the other, and they touched each other while they kissed.

"I don't have a . . ." said William after a time.

"A safe?" said Emily. "I don't think it matters. I think I've pretty much got my . . . time." She stopped. Her breath was in his ear. "Do you care?"

"No. Not at all. I mean, I kind of want you that way," William said. "I mean, all the ways. All the ways you could be."

They lay down together. The breeze drifted in through the open doors and sometimes the distant buzz of a plane or the tires of a car rolling down Furness Street. After he had been inside her for a while, Emily clutched William's shoulder and watched a constellation of dust spin in the sunlight over her sister's dollhouse, and she said in a whisper, like a vapor or a sigh, "You know I would do anything for you."

*A*fter dinner Emily watched the convention with her parents and her sister, Susan. Susan had arrived at dinnertime from the end of her summer job—camp counseling up at Crane Lake—and would be staying through the weekend. Then she was going to visit some college friends in Wisconsin until it was time to return for fall semester. Susan sat on the couch with her parents while Emily perched in a chair. This was just like old times, Emily thought, except that when she was smaller she would have sat on the couch too, or right in front of it on the floor, at her father's feet.

On the TV were more speeches and even more rioting than the previous evening. Now people had been killed. People were going to storm the amphitheater. Edward, Virginia, Susan, and Emily watched in silence, save when Edward asked Susan, "So do you know any kids who are . . . involved in this?"

"I know some people who knew some people from Madison who were going to go. But it's not anything kids from our school are that much into. It's more a Madison, Ann Arbor kind of thing."

"I guess we should be happy about that," said Virginia.

"I think it's very important," said Emily. "It's evil. What's going on."

"It's very sad, if nothing else," said Edward. Emily thought that at this point Susan would weigh in as their resident expert on student-hood, opine something in that way of hers that sounded assured and grown-up but merely assented to adult suppositions, that was complaisance dressed up as maturity. But she said nothing.

They listened to Humphrey's acceptance speech, its exhortations to joy and to progress, for a while before preparing for bed. They knew as long-time constituents of his that it was likely as not to continue well past bedtime; that long after the earth was no more than a cinder or mankind had simply extinguished itself, the last thirty or so minutes of one or another Hubert Humphrey speech would still be rolling and echoing around distant galaxies.

After Emily's parents had retired, after Emily herself had finished what she was reading and was about to turn out her light, Susan put her head through Emily's door. "Can I come in?" she asked.

"Sure," said Emily, and Susan came and sat down at the side of the bed. She was attired not in a nightgown as was Emily, as Susan herself scarcely a year ago would have been, but in an outsize football jersey, big enough to reach nearly to her knees.

"So how've you been?" Emily's sister said to her.

"Oh, fine."

"Did you like your job?"

"Oh, yeah. It was great. I got" — and Emily thought here of going to her closet and showing Susan, but changed her mind — "some cool things. I saved almost three hundred dollars."

"That's great. Anything else exciting happen?"

"Not really."

Susan looked at her and smiled. Not with a friendly smile, for she and Emily had not really been friends since they had ceased to be play-mates, which was around the time Susan entered the fourth grade. So this was, Emily supposed, a sisterly smile, or a smile she had learned this summer at her job, for use in consoling homesick campers.

Finally Susan said, "Mom says you have a boyfriend."

Emily wanted to deny this, not because it wasn't true or on grounds of secrecy, but because she didn't want her sister saying it, appropriating her and William, defining them. Emily said, "Well, I guess it's a little like that. But not really. Or exactly."

"Do you like him?"

"Sure."

"A lot?"

"Maybe."

"Come on. I'm your big sister."

"None of your beeswax," Emily said, and Susan took this as a friendly, teasing rejoinder that amounted to confirmation, although Emily—smiling as she said it—was very much in earnest.

"Is he nice?" It seemed to Emily that in this phrase Susan sounded precisely like their mother.

"No," she said slowly. "He's an utter beast."

Susan laughed. "Come on," she said, and slid a little closer to her sister.

"He is. He only wants one thing."

"Oh, come on. Really."

"And what he wants, he *takes*."

"You're sure as silly as ever, Em," Susan said. "So really."

"Really what?"

"Are you guys . . . serious?"

"I don't know."

"Well, don't do anything dumb."

"What would that be?"

"Oh, come on," Susan said. "Like going all the way. You know."

Emily said nothing, and after moment, Susan put her hands on her thighs and leaned forward towards her sister. "You aren't, are you?"

Emily looked away, off over her shoulder, and said, "I already told you. How he is. I *daren't* say more."

"Oh stop," Susan laughed. "Anyway, don't do anything stupid, okay?" She lowered her voice. "Or if you think you might, use something."

"Something?" Emily said. "Something what?"

"You know." Susan lowered her voice yet another tone, to nearly a hiss. "You know what? It's a secret."

"What?"

"I got the pill. I'm taking it."

"From where? Why?"

"From the student health service."

"Isn't that against the law?"

"No. Not if you're college-age."

Emily suddenly felt strangely close to Susan; she regretted teasing her, mocking her without her even knowing she was being mocked; being cruel, secretly. She leaned towards her sister, and their heads were almost touching. "So is there someone you . . . like?" Emily said in a whisper. "That much?"

"No. Or maybe. We'll see when I get back to school."

"So why . . ."

"Just in case. Just to be ready." Susan paused. "You never know when it might happen."

"I guess not," Emily said, and shook her head in commiseration. She had not felt this close to her sister in a very long time. She wanted to take her in her arms and hug her. But then Susan said, as though completing a sentence she had already begun, "So you be careful. When you're ready. When you're older."

$\mathcal{T}$he next afternoon, Friday, in the apartment, William and Emily made love and looked at the newspaper, and he said to her, "So now do you see? About the system and the draft and everything?" He did not intend this to sound mean—he was merely in the grip of an intention, a new one undergirded by fear and panic—but it sounded cruel to Emily. It could almost have undone all that they had become to each other, except that the past five days had been perfect, and everything outside of them had been shown to be evil and false; and that, or at least the contrast between the two of them and the world, Emily understood with complete clarity.

"I see. And I didn't ever not believe you. Not ever," she said.

William felt the awful paltriness of his faith, his ingratitude and blindness, and the forgiveness Emily's response contained. "I know. I don't why I said that. I guess I'm scared."

"I'm scared too."

"So what do you do?"

"I'm not sure. I'm not you."

William said, "Yes you are. We're each other now, even if everything else falls apart. Right?"

Emily said, "Right." She said this not in acquiescence, but as a statement of fact, of what she believed entirely.

William went on. "So you be me. Tell me what we think."

Emily paused, and then she licked her lips and spoke. She told him that all our life is some form of religion, and all our action some belief. In his case, she thought he was called upon to do his duty to himself; that is, to God in the end.

William asked, "Are you going with me?"

And Emily said, "I suppose I am."

$\mathcal{T}$hey made their arrangements quietly. William's mother returned on that evening, and Emily's sister left on Sunday. Another five days passed. Then they told their parents that they were going to the big Grandstand concert at the State Fair on Tuesday, the last day of the fair and two days before school started. They would have to leave early, maybe as early as seven o'clock in the morning, to get in line and get tickets. The concert ran through the day and into the evening.

Emily had organized her gear the night before and concealed it under her bed. She rose at five-thirty, and the very last thing she did before she boarded the number three bus to meet William downtown at the depot was to mail the postcard. She opened the door to the mailbox that stood just half a block up from the bus stop, thrust her hand in, and, after a moment, let the card drop inside. There, she thought. Now I have to go. Because how else could I explain?

Two

The

Beggar

Maid

1

THE TUESDAY BEFORE THE DEMOCRATIC CONVENTION in Chicago, Edward was working in the Medical Arts Building, and at the far end of the hall, as he emerged from the office of Dr. Frederick Marling (Dermatology), he saw a figure he thought he recognized exiting the office of Dr. Anthony Petti (Internal Medicine). She wore a russet shift and flat shoes and had dark chin-length hair, with perhaps a streak of gray in it, and he realized this was the boy's mother.

He called out to her, and she turned and looked at him, trying to ascertain who it was and if she knew him. He moved down the hall towards her in long strides, reached her, and set his case down by his side. "Edward Byrne. Emily's father," he said.

"I know," Jane said, and looked at him with a smile and raised eyebrows, as though he was a little silly to think she would not know him.

"I was making some calls in the building and I saw you," Edward continued, sounding rather as if he was making an excuse for being there at all. "Are you well?" he said, and then, realizing that this was not an entirely unweighty question when asked in this particular situation, he added, "We really enjoyed having you come by."

"I'm perfectly fine. Just the usual annual checkup. To make sure I'm in fighting form for Chicago next week, I suppose."

"Oh, yes. The convention. You must be very excited."

Jane had turned her head away for a moment and brought her hand up and under her hair on the right side of her face, and she raked it absentmindedly with her fingers, slowly, exposing her ear and the

nether side of her throat. She said, "Oh, yes, I am. I guess I must be."
She laughed.

Edward was looking at her all this while, although he did not realize
this until her gaze intersected his and rested there a moment before
darting away, somewhere else—to her hands, her watch, her bag.
Edward thought perhaps he had been staring, that he might be making
her nervous. But then she looked back and began to speak.

"I saw your daughter with Billy yesterday. Walking down Summit
Avenue holding hands. Near the little park with the Indian brave. I
thought it was sweet. Like childhood's end." Jane shrugged. "Or something . . . enchanted, like that." Jane realized she was going off in some
direction and that she herself did not know where it lay or went. She
had been, she knew, rather distracted lately. "Anyway, she's a very nice
girl," Jane said, as though handily mopping up a small spill.

"We think so," Edward said. "And Bill's a nice boy."

"He seems that way, but what would I know?" They had been
regarding each other all this while, and then Jane smiled and looked
away, and Edward turned his head and cleared his throat, as though
coughing into his fist. He looked back and saw her eyes were slowly rising upward, towards him again. He was not sure what to do next. He
rather enjoyed conversing with this woman—not bantering, but just
standing there with a faintly incredulous but amused expression,
almost needling her, gently teasing her about her worldliness, her
earnest immersion in human tragedy and her own self. He sensed that
she rather liked it too; that they were sharing a private joke, invisible to
others, and that although it was a little at her expense, their amusement
was more or less congruent; that it arose from knowing each other a
very long time, although they had scarcely met.

"He seems very dependable," Edward said.

"Oh, he is. He'll be on his own next week, and it's the least of my
worries. I'll come back, and he will have washed the dishes and vacu-
umed the apartment."

"While you've been dodging ward heelers and bagmen in
Chicago?"

"And worse." Jane looked at Edward with utmost seriousness, without a shred of coyness or guile. "It could really have been something. Really accomplished something. We came *this* close."

"Maybe you still will."

"I don't think the numbers add up. But it's a nice idea."

This is what preoccupies her, Edward thought: beauty, goodness, and truth, or something akin to it. Everything the world fails to be for us; that we fail to be for each other. "We could have Bill over for dinner while you're gone," he said. "Just to give him some company, to make sure everything's okay."

"That's very kind. But I suspect he already imposes enough."

"Not at all."

"Well," Jane said. "I suppose you need to be going." That was true enough, but Edward did not particularly want to stop. He enjoyed what they were doing, even as he was aware that it made him a little uneasy; that it refused to declare its destination or purpose, the category of relation into which it might be put and thence filed away. It was as if, whether he said goodbye and walked away or not, this conversation would continue; as if it could not be brought to a close with the handing over of a sample or a pen and pencil set or a handshake or even a kiss on the cheek. The truth was, they needed to find something to talk to each other about, a subject that might be brought to a conclusion, agreement, or stalemate, some content to give a beginning, a middle, and an end to their interaction. As it stood, it was pure form, pure process, and it might as well go on indefinitely.

*A*fter her encounter with Edward, Jane drives home slowly. The days until Chicago are like an ice cube melting in her glass, the solid metamorphosing into the formless; at the last, a little chip of itself afloat in its own unraveling; and then not a trace. This is how time passes and perhaps how the world will end. It is, at the very least, the way this August seems, this one in particular.

Jane has not until now given much thought to the Byrnes. At their lunch together, she found Virginia to be rather the hausfrau and Edward the pedestrian husband and father, but strapping: He made

Jane a little bashful. Still, they are *nice* in the nicest possible way, and the girl is nice too. Her son could be worse occupied, and occupied he is indeed, almost every day. Sometimes she finds them in her kitchen, and once she spied them ensconced before the hi-fi in the living room. Another time, driving down Summit Avenue, she saw them walking, holding hands, and by the time she was done being charmed by this scene and then realized who it was, they were blots in the disappearing horizon of her rearview mirror; and the girl might very well have been someone Jane herself used to be, thirty summers ago.

That is not wistfulness or nostalgia or sentimentality. It is grasping the hard fact that time runs in only one direction, that we have already died a thousand deaths and will die a thousand more, and that there is no remedy for it but love, though we are sure we have never seen love except in the rearview mirror, in the sad and tawdry puddle at the bottom of the glass.

*A*t about the same time Jane is speaking with Virginia's husband, Virginia herself is taking a break from her chores. She leafs through the new issue of *McCall's* without much interest, but in fact she prays that its articles—their fretting over fractured families and troubled adolescents—will continue not to apply to her situation; that things will go on pretty much as they are.

Virginia has some reason to believe this might be the case. For example, her daughter Emily is not a secretive girl, and although she is closer to Edward, rather as Susan is closer to Virginia, Emily does not seem to regard her mother with the wary belligerence so common among teenage daughters. There is nothing about her life that Emily would not tell Virginia, Virginia feels; and there is next to nothing about Emily's life that Virginia does not, she feels, indeed already know.

But Virginia might wonder what Emily truly knows of her mother's life, for it is a life of parts, not one thing, but many. There is the cleaning and shopping and cooking and paying the bills and the maintenance of the house and yard, and at some amorphous boundary this realm leaches out into the street and the block (the Neighborhood

Association and Historical Preservation Society) and down to the church (Altar Guild, Holy Names, and Rosary Societies) and the school (parents association, plus fairs, pageants, and other events too numerous to count). And in the midst of all these activities Virginia somehow finds time to cut flowers for the hall table.

Yet to see her life only in relation to these things—which are less things than themselves relations, congeries, the sum of what her net hauls in each week—would be to miss its point, its great labor, which is no more than to bear her family, and, in her small way, every life that touches her life in body or mind, safely across the waters of this world.

Virginia, of course, would make no such claims for herself; it is not given to us to see the pattern of our lives save, perhaps, in retrospect, and even when we think we grasp it, we are likely to get it wrong. Jane Lowry, for example, would describe herself as every bit as busy as Virginia, and might even regard Virginia's life as the epitome of middle-class indolence. In fact, to her own mind, Jane is not merely busy but, as she perpetually puts it to her friend Frances, "swamped." Her life is a skiff whose bilge is never dry, and she is too busy bailing to ever set the sails.

This is how it feels, and it has always felt this way to some degree, but especially so since, ten years ago, Billy's father left. That term, "Billy's father," expresses well enough his condition (absent) and hers on account of it (alone and thus "swamped"). True, his check arrives from California every month, though she is aware of feeling more diminished than enriched each time she deposits it. And at Christmas and birthdays, and sometimes on random occasions, gifts arrive for Billy, generally things related to camping and woodcraft; things Billy's father would do with Billy if he were here, which he is not.

Now if the vessel Jane commands has a bridge it is the kitchen, and the round American oak kitchen table is its helm. And it is here that Jane feels her responsibilities most gravely. Yet it is also here, where she is most conscious of all that must be done, that she most feels that nothing is in fact getting done; that she is adrift. The evidence the table supplies can imply both action and stasis. There is, for example, the phone on its specially installed twenty-foot cord, ringing or its receiver scrunched between Jane's shoulder and jawbone as she chops, stirs, writes, smokes, drinks, rifles in the drawer for a pen, matches, her address book, the scrap of paper, receipt, or card that contains the vital thing this instant requires. But you might equally regard the towering slag heap that is the ashtray, the three or four coffee mugs—all launched solely by Jane during separate trips to the percolator just this morning—or the copies of *Ramparts*, *The New Republic*, *The New York Review of Books*, and *I. F. Stone's Weekly*, either manifestly unread or cocked open at points that suggest half-read articles that will never be returned to.

Of course, Jane has a job, which Virginia does not, and curiously it is with Catholic Social Services, where she works part-time as a counselor/caseworker. Jane—no Catholic herself but resolutely agnostic—majored in psychology in college and after the divorce she got a master's in social work at the university, having resigned herself to the fact that a Ph.D. was not in the cards for a mother raising a child alone, nor, that aside, for a personality, a character formation, that, truth to be told, has felt itself "swamped" since perhaps the age of four—no, longer still, since before she seemingly alone rowed herself ashore and landed in this life.

It is, Jane must admit, a curious thing to be so overwhelmed by obligations and duties—to have unfinished chores tugging at her hem while lined up behind them is the impending sense that some fundamental necessity has been completely overlooked—but also to experience moments of terrible clarity in which she sees that she is not busy, that in fact she is doing nothing. And that "nothing" is perhaps the substance which swamps her, the flood that threatens to sink her altogether. For it is not merely nothing in the sense of a moment of inactivity, of respite or pause. Nor is it the nothing of "nothing in particular," neither this nor that. It is, Jane sees when she looks up to see it hovering just above and in front of her, her thumb holding a place in a magazine article whose subject she has already forgotten, the index finger of the other hand clawing in the near-spent cigarette pack, "nothing at all." It is the kind of nothing that is a force in its own right, that precludes all the possible somethings one might try to put in its place; that marks the fact of everything one is not doing and, looming stupidly, heavily like humidity, renders starting impossible.

It hovers, and were Jane of Virginia's temperament, she might call it the Angel of Despair, perhaps the Angel of Death. But Jane's divinities, spirits, and emanations are of an older order, buried deep in the earth with the dead gods, Saturn and Cronus. She has come to this place alone, bone-weary with the rowing, and attended, if at all, by the dead gods' shades, by the ghosts of futility.

But now Virginia herself is about to begin "Can This Marriage Be Saved?"—a *McCall's* column she approaches each month with pity and, she has to admit, lurid fascination. Each story—each "case history," as they are called—is presented in the same format: the wife's version, the husband's, and then the counselor's, the marriage a sickly infant, colicky, sleepless, and failing, over whose wasting body they fight and fret and pray.

Virginia cannot imagine her own marriage ending. That is not to say she would rationally deny that it could end through some circumstance, but that she cannot *see* or picture what those circumstances could be or how life would go forward afterward, so much is her marriage, with her faith and her children and her ministrations to all of them, the ground of her being. So she reads "Can This Marriage Be Saved?" with a feeling of terrible dread, but dread at one remove—this is not going to happen to her—and it is thus bearable.

It might seem that Virginia is a bit overconfident in this belief, even a bit of a fool, although she is the great realist of her household; the one who sees with clear eyes where others are blind. It is she, for example, who sometimes feels that this world is going to hell in a handbasket and that it may even be her daughter that is this very moment carrying that selfsame basket through the woods and into Virginia's house. Maybe what is in the basket, ticking like a bomb, is this boy, William Lowry.

But it is more than complacency—however well founded—that allows Virginia to feel secure in her home with her husband and her daughter. Their mutual affection is as established as the constitution, and it is the perhaps unwitting genius of their relation that it weathers crisis so well. Not that they resolve their differences with complete dignity. Virginia and Edward have fought over wallpaper, for heaven's sake, over Edward's bringing home a black convertible with red upholstery that he thought would delight her, over a single occasion when Virginia turned away from Edward's bedtime tendernesses (aggravated, to be sure, by what Edward sees as Virginia's Jesuitical dithering about the problematics of rhythm versus her scarcely used diaphragm, which snickers at them from her lingerie drawer). And in the wake of these conflicts, misapprehensions, and eruptions of sheer cussedness, they have mutually inflicted and endured implacable bouts of silence, flaying one another with disregard, rowing their marriage onward like a slave ship to whose oars both of them are chained.

These stalemates do not so much resolve themselves as dissipate like weather. Usually, someone tires of the impasse and through a set of diplomatic signals standardized through years of a kind of cable traffic, back-channel mediation, and treaty-making, yields or agrees to a cease-fire. Sometimes it is Edward who yields and sometimes it is Virginia, and Edward yields because he wants to be steady and wise, like Solomon, and Virginia because she wants to yield as Mary yielded, not in passivity but in affirmation of what is great and good. But essentially, harmony is restored because on balance, it is better to be together than apart, and that impulse—which may be a fair definition of married love—triumphs over anger and pain and injustice.

The marriage of Jane and William's father—of which Virginia knows virtually nothing—seems to bear this out. For it was not fighting but the moment at which they at last, after over five years, *stopped* fighting that signaled the end; that revealed the truth that they had both concluded that there was nothing in their being together that was worth fighting *for*. That is not to say that the anger was instantly gone or that they did not in fact hate each other for a very long time. But they hated each other for having made fools of each other, for having wasted each other's time, for having depleted each other's limited store of hopes and aspirations, of innocent credulousness and goodwill. Now Jane has only William to fight with, and sometimes those fights are uncannily reminiscent of fights she had with William's father. But Jane should not worry, just as Virginia does not. What William takes away from their fights, in which sometimes it is he that yields and sometimes she, is the conclusion that it is better to be together than not; and in this she has taught him a little of what she feels she has never learned to do, which is to love beyond justice or reason.

2

AFTER CHICAGO, AFTER EVERYTHING, IT WAS Virginia who first understood what had happened. She and Edward had watched the ten-o'clock news, which featured a report from the State Fair and the concert Emily was supposed to be attending as it had broken up, an hour before. These things took a long time to empty out, of course; and that much longer to find your car and drive home. Edward suggested they go upstairs and go to bed. Perhaps, he implied, they might make love. And they did, although Virginia seemed distracted; seemed to be gazing at some mark or sign in the distance. When they were done, Edward said he would go downstairs and wait for Emily. Virginia waited in the bed with the light out, wide awake, still looking deeply at whatever it was she thought she was trying to make out, that was trying to speak to her.

A little after midnight, Edward came back upstairs. He said, "I just don't know where—"

Virginia interrupted him. "You call that woman, and ask her what her son's done with Emily."

Jane had been in bed a little while, reading something—everything she read might be one thing, so little of it did she seem to retain for more than an instant—when the angel of agony came and stood in her doorway; came and stood and looked upon her with an air that suggested she would be here some while.

Or in any case, the telephone rang. She noted that it was half past midnight, and answered.

"Mrs. Lowry? Jane, it's Edward Byrne. Emily's father. I'm sorry to call so late, but Emily hasn't come home and she was supposed to be with Bill, so we wondered . . ."

"They're not here. They're supposed to be at the fair, aren't they?"

"Well, yes. But we figure they should have been finished there by ten."

"I suppose it's crowded — that the buses are slow."

"They were taking the bus?"

"Oh, yes. I needed the car today. And Billy said he didn't want it anyway. They were going very early."

"I know. So I suppose they could still be on the bus, riding home."

"They might have had to wait a very long time, what with the crowds, and the night schedule and so forth."

"I suppose."

"I don't think I'd begin to worry just yet. Billy's very reliable about coming home. I don't think he even *likes* being out late. So they'll probably be turning up any minute."

"It still seems a bit late," Edward said. "Even allowing for the bus and so forth."

"Well, it's not unheard of for teenagers to get . . . diverted. To run into friends and decide to wander off with them. No sense of time at all. But I'm sure they're fine."

"I'm sure you're absolutely right. But Ginny's terribly wound up. I don't think Emily's been out past eleven in her life. Maybe for a prom or something. But not really."

"Oh, I'm sure they're fine."

"Of course," said Edward. "But just the same, could you give us a call when Bill comes in? And of course we'll do the same when Emily turns up."

"I'd be happy to do that. But I'm sure they're fine. I mean, it's not unheard of for teenagers to stay out all night. To watch the sun come up. And to be oblivious to the fact that the whole world is going mad with worry."

"I know. I know," said Edward, and he could not decide whether he ought to be irritated with Jane for her insouciance or with Virginia for her anxieties. "But call us all the same when he comes in, okay?"

"Of course. But you mustn't worry. Really, you mustn't, Ted."

No one had ever called him Ted. But there it was. He was not going to argue about it under the circumstances. He was not sure he didn't rather like it; didn't rather imagine that this "Ted" Jane had conjured up could bear up under the present situation better than could plain old ordinary Edward.

He said, "I won't. I'm sure it's nothing."

"Of course it's nothing," said Jane. "Trust me."

"All right. Sorry to have disturbed you. But do call, okay?"

"Of course," Jane said. "Now go and get some sleep, Ted."

"Okay. Good night. Thanks."

Jane returned to her reading, but had no appetite for it. She could not say she was worried. It was thirty-five minutes after midnight. She had been quite emphatic with Edward Byrne that there was nothing to it, and she supposed that, probably, this was the case. Her intent had been to ease his mind, but nothing is more readily misunderstood than a good intention, and perhaps what had been impressed upon Edward's mind was not comfort, but a notion that Jane was indifferent to their children, that she was not a good mother.

As she turned out the light, as she tried to sleep, it was this that lay upon and over her mind: that she ought indeed to be worried, not only about the world's estimation of her as a parent, but, as the minute hand of her alarm clock scoured the circuit of the dial, about William.

Jane is, of course, no stranger to anxiety—the Age of Anxiety, dating from around August 1945, is twenty-three years old this very month— and her daily life is in essence a sandbagging operation against its seas and their tides. But this is worry, and it is a little different from anxiety: Particular rather than pervasive, it arrives unannounced, without anxiety's harbingers, dread and foreboding, the fearful tea in which we steep awaiting oblivion. Instead, worry simply turns up on the doorstep, the overbearing, passive-aggressive out-of-town relative who insists he "won't be any trouble" even as he displaces every known routine and custom of the house for days and weeks on end; as he expropriates the sofa, the bathroom, the contents of the liquor cabinet and cigarette carton, and monopolizes the telephone and the ear of anyone within shouting distance. Worry displaces the entire mood, the entire ethos of the house—even if that mood hitherto consisted largely of anxiety—and replaces it with something more substantive, more real than a mere mood. You would be mightily pleased to have ordinary anxiety back in residence, for under worry there is no peace whatsoever, not even the peace of cynicism, pessimism, or despair. Even when all the rest of the world is abed, worry is awake, plundering the kitchen cupboards, raiding the refrigerator, playing the hi-fi, watching the late show until the national anthem closes the broadcast day; then noisily treading the halls, standing in your bedroom door, wondering if by chance you are still up (knowing that of course you are), breathing and casting its shadow upon you, the silhouette of its slope-shouldered hulk and its towering black wings.

*F*rom sheer exhaustion, Edward and Virginia drifted off to sleep a few times that night, but never for long. Every stirring and creak and yawn in the bones of the house hurled them out of the tangle of their unformed dreams to sit bolt upright in bed to wonder if this might be Emily's footfall. Edward went downstairs four or five times. Finally, around five-thirty, he settled in the living room, overlooking the street, and having transited irritation and anger at Emily, simply wept for want of his little girl.

Virginia heard him, or rather heard yet another unaccustomed sound, and called out to him. He told her it was nothing, for it was nothing indeed; the empty street, the icy light of the moon, the distant scatter of chirps from the earliest-rising birds. He watched the dawn come like a great reproach: Everything is rising, coming, coming into itself—everything there is—except your own heart's desire.

At seven, he went up to Virginia and told her he supposed they should call the police now. He would call William's mother first, and then he would get on with it. Virginia nodded and went downstairs to brew coffee.

Jane answered on the first ring, and Edward said, "I hope I didn't wake you."

"I've scarcely slept. I suppose I was too casual last night when you called. Then I woke up around three, and I thought, this is all wrong."

"So he hasn't come back? Called or anything?"

"No. Nothing."

"Well, we think we ought to call the police now."

"I suppose you—we—should. For all the good it'll do."

"I don't see what else there is. To do. Do you?" Edward was aware that an edge had risen in his voice; that he was chafing a little, caught between these two women, the one sitting in his kitchen dull and mute as stone, the other now muttering sullenly at him.

"I'm sorry," Jane said. "Of course we should. This is very hard. Will you tell me right away what they say? What we ought to do?"

It was understood that Edward would call, and that he would call on Jane's behalf as well as his and Virginia's, although how this arrangement had been effected you could not say, save that he was the male on the scene, and since Jane lacked such an agent, Edward would act for her.

Edward telephoned the police station, was put on hold, and finally was transferred to a voice that announced itself as Lieutenant O'Connor. Edward described how matters now stood.

"So she—they—should have been home when?" this O'Connor asked.

"Maybe by eleven. Last night."

"So they haven't been missing too long."

"Long enough that we're sick with—that we're very concerned."

"You see, the thing is, Mr. Lowry—"

"Byrne. The boy's name is Lowry. The boy's mother is Mrs. Lowry. There's no father. Well, there is, but . . ."

"Fine, fine, Mr. Byrne. The thing is, it hasn't even been twelve hours. I can't even take a missing-person report for twenty-four."

"What can you do? Now?" Edward said. He was beginning to fray already. The cup of coffee Virginia had set before him was cold.

"I can tell you to stay calm and not to worry too much. Most of the time, they turn up within a day. That's why we wait. If we didn't, we'd be processing false alarms right and left."

"You think they'll 'turn up'? That's swell," Edward said. Virginia had come over next to him, trying to listen to what the cop was saying, her hand heavy on his shoulder. "You think my daughter's a stray cat that just wandered off or something?"

"I don't think anything of the kind, Mr. Byrne."

"Sorry. But, hell, I mean, suppose something's happened to them. Is happening to them. Now. You don't worry about that until the clock strikes eleven or twelve or whatever?"

"If anything happened like what you're thinking we'd probably already know about it. Accidents, emergency rooms, we get all those reports. We'd know."

"So you think we should just relax and wait. When two perfectly reliable, dependable kids just disappear like this?"

"People don't disappear. They go somewhere, but you and I don't know where. Especially teenagers. And especially at the fair. We get maybe *double* these sorts of calls during the fair. There's ten thousand other kids there and they meet each other and off they go. Turn up the next day or so saying, 'Oh gee, I didn't know what time it was.' That's just what they're like. I don't have to tell you that."

"I suppose not," Edward said. He could see no profit in pressing the point that this was not what his daughter was "like." "So what's next? We wait until eleven-oh-one tonight and then I call you back?"

"I won't be here that late. But you can come in and file a report at the desk—"

"Oh, for Christ's sake—"

"Look. I'm sorry. I know this is very . . . frustrating. Tell you what. If they're not back this afternoon, you come down around three, before I go home, and we'll do it then. Okay?"

"All right."

"See, chances are they'll be back and we'll never have to bother. But there you go, okay?"

"Sure. That's in the Public Safety Building, right?"

"Second floor. Room 217. Now this Mrs. Lowry will need to file her own report for her son."

"But you'll extend this . . . courtesy to her as well? She can come too?"

"Sure. No problem. Makes sense to do them together."

"Good. Well, thanks. And we'll see you—"

"If you need to. Probably won't."

"Okay. Goodbye," Edward said. He hung up the phone, and looked at his wife. He had not looked at her, it seemed, since the night before, since before all this had begun. Other than being a little colorless and a little drawn, she looked like herself, but then he saw that her pallor was less a color overlying her skin than a transparency through which another face was visible, and it was an ancient face, the face perhaps of Virginia's mother, or some other long-dead person in her lineage. It was not, in any case, his wife, or so it seemed to him, even as he held her and explained the parts of his conversation with the police lieutenant that she had missed. For the rest of the day, as they waited, he did not really look at her again—although he said soothing things to her and squeezed her hand—for fear she might shatter, might flare and turn to cinders before his eyes.

$\mathcal{E}$dward had called Jane a little before eight o'clock and explained what could and could not be done as regarded the police. Then, at an hour which would normally find her scarcely beginning to stir, she realized she had the whole day before her. Now she might have taken Lieutenant O'Connor's advice (as relayed by Edward) not to worry, but this was of course no more practicable than not breathing, and in fact every other possibility besides worrying was severely circumscribed: She could not go out, for fear that Billy would then come home while she was gone; and she also could not go out because he or Edward or somebody might telephone; and she could not use the telephone herself for fear of tying up the line when Billy or Edward or somebody was trying to get through. She could, she supposed, ask to use a neighbor's phone, but that would be to risk missing the phone ringing here.

It is bad enough that worry induces a sense of paralysis, and worse when it imposes paralysis as a duty, as the best solution to the problem from which it has arisen. The world, of course, is deeply contingent, and we are doubtless fools to believe we are ever free from its accidents or the purposes and deeds of others. But we enjoy the illusion—or the promise, for those inclined to belief—that we can act a little in our lives and the lives of our fellows, and not always for the worse. Perhaps that is why worry leads so easily to despair, to existential doubt and disbelief, for we can do nothing good under its aspect but wait, and it is a passive, virtueless kind of waiting, a kind of timorous staying out of the way, standing atop a chair while the mouse of chance runs amok round the kitchen floor.

It took Jane the better part of an hour to devise a strategy whereby she might contact the outside world, or in particular her friend Frances, whose ear, she realized, she desperately needed; whose counsel, however self-regarding and jaded, would be a welcome alternative to the buzzing of the worry swarming around her. The strategy consisted of being rude, or at least abrupt, of abandoning every shred of telephonic finesse to deal with the emergency at hand. So it was that Jane dialed Frances's house and when the phone was answered, she more or less bellowed rapid-fire, "It's Jane. Billy's disappeared. Please come over right now. Can't talk. Don't call back."

Counting the rings, Jane figured it took all of ten seconds. She slammed the receiver back down into the cradle and kept her hand on it, holding it down for fear it might somehow levitate off by itself and render the line busy. Then she caught her breath, and making sure the phone was secure, she sat and waited, she hoped, for Frances to come, and tried not to think overmuch on the probability that the someone might have tried to call during those ten seconds, the ten she had willfully stolen from worry, and perhaps, if she was unlucky, from William's life entire.

Frances arrived twenty-five minutes later and burst into the apartment, breathless, as though both it and she were in flames. "What the hell is going on, Jane?" she said, and then, rather than let Jane answer too hastily, repeated herself. "What the hell is going on?"

"Billy's gone. He went to the State Fair with his girlfriend yesterday morning and they should have been home by eleven or twelve. But they never came back."

"So did you call the police?"

"Ted—the girl's father—did. We're going to go down and file a missing-person report if they're not back this afternoon."

Frances moved toward Jane and put her left arm around her and pulled her close, hugging her. "Poor baby," she said. "Poor baby." She stepped back and looked at Jane from head to foot, appraised her as though William might be hidden somewhere on her person. Then she said, "So do they think anything . . . untoward might have happened?"

"They think nothing happened—that they just wandered off the way kids will, and that they'll come home sooner or later."

"And what do you think?"

"I suppose they're right. He's not the Lindbergh baby, is he? And there haven't been any reports of accidents or . . . violence and so forth."

"But . . ."

"But this isn't like him, is it? They say this happens all the time, particularly at the fair. That some kids meet some other kids and go off. But Billy's not the kind to do that, is he? He's not very . . . social. So why would he go off with anybody? And he's very reliable, except when he forgets things."

"He's a sweet kid."

"So it's not like he's going to just forget to come home."

"What about the girl? Maybe she's the reason."

"Oh, she seems very normal. Quiet. Small. Girlish-looking. Irish Catholic family. The father's in pharmaceuticals. The mother does Junior Leaguey things—however Catholics do them. Virginia's her name."

"And she's . . . virginal?"

"She's not, not really. Maybe a little reserved. And he's very nice. He called the police. He's going to take me down to the station. If we have to go."

"So was Billy very involved with this girl?"

"I think so. You never know." Jane paused. "I mean, they don't *say*, do they? But they're always together, at least since June." Jane gestured down the hall. "Why don't we go in the kitchen? We'll have coffee."

Jane stopped in the kitchen doorway. "I think he wrote her love letters. I think maybe she wrote poems for him," she said, and then moved to the counter, to the percolator. "That's awfully sweet, isn't it?"

"So maybe they eloped."

"Nobody elopes anymore."

"I did. Once. To Iowa. With Jimmy McGowan."

"That was a long time ago."

"It was fun. Maybe it's still fun. Shame about Jimmy. Dull man."

They sat down at Jane's table and drank coffee and continued to talk in this way, elliptically, moving away from the matter of William for a time, and then returning to it. This gave Jane some ease, worrying openly for a minute or two, then taking shelter in familiar topics — politics, people they had gone to school with, men about whom Frances held opinions or with whom she had had experience — before coming back to worry. She attained a little more ease when, around eleven-thirty, she and Frances were simultaneously struck by the notion that, under the circumstances (and given the ascendant heat), a round of gin and tonic would be in order. And at twelve-thirty, Jane made egg salad sandwiches, and for the first time in twelve hours she felt optimism.

After a second round of drinks, Frances slipped away to visit her office and Jane made the bed and did the dishes. She did not make William's bed or even enter his room. She had begun to sense how far she might push herself, to what extent she might permit reality or active speculation about it to trespass in the precincts of her heart; how much the few strands of peace she had painstakingly woolgathered in the last few hours might withstand.

At two, Frances returned. At two-thirty the phone rang. It was Edward, saying they would be by in twenty minutes to pick her up to go see Lieutenant O'Connor. Jane excused herself for a few minutes to prepare for this; to put on a sober lightweight dress and to fix her hair and makeup. It was as though she was at last embarking upon the occasion this whole day had been planned to culminate in all along — a wedding or a funeral or a graduation ceremony.

She smoothed her dress, and asked Frances to check her. She was fine, Frances said — "They'll probably put you in the lineup" — and, yes, Frances would stay here in the apartment, for the sake of the phone, just in case.

*I*t is no slight thing, the facts parents know about their children, without even knowing that they know them. Answering the policeman's queries, Jane found that she could say without hesitation that Billy was five-eleven and weighed 160 pounds, even though she had some years ago given up attending the physical examinations where these statistics might be obtained. He had been born April 1, 1951 (always amusing, that one), and had brown eyes and brown hair. Jane could have easily recited his birth weight, the duration of her labor, and the blend of analgesics that had rendered her semisensate from the waist down, if the lieutenant had so desired. She could have told him things William himself did not know or had forgotten: His first word ("Da"); his shoe sizes at various points in his toddlerdom; the name (Ollie) of his favorite stuffed animal until he was five; his IQ (130) on the Stanford-Binet scale.

In turn, Jane learned that the Byrnes' daughter's full name was Emily Elizabeth; that she was born almost exactly a year after William on March 25, 1952, in exactly the same hospital; that she was five-four and about 110 pounds and had light blue eyes and auburn hair, although Jane noticed that the lieutenant translated this to "lt. br." on his form. And of course, Virginia could have given him all the same supplementary information about Emily that Jane possessed in regard to her son and then some: that Emily's baby-sitter when she was an infant was named Mrs. Kane (and that Mr. Kane had a drinking problem); that her confirmation name was Mary Agnes; that she had wanted to become a nun when she was seven and a geologist when she was eleven; that her menses had begun a few weeks after her thirteenth birthday; and that she adored her father and definitively preferred him to her mother, which was a little sad, but completely understandable in a girl of Emily's temperament.

After both questionnaires had been completed and the lieutenant had laid down his pencil, Edward said, "So now what?"

"Now," Lieutenant O'Connor began, "these get typed up and duplicated and you bring me a nice clear picture—like a school photo—and the whole package goes all around the department here and to all the sheriffs in the five-state area."

"And then they start looking?"

"Well, looking, maybe. Searching, not exactly. To be honest."

"I'm not following you," Edward said.

"Well, they probably get ten or twenty packages like this a week. We get more, being a metropolitan force. So, no, you can't go search—go actively looking—for all these kids, all these people. You just couldn't do it all."

"So what do all these sheriffs and cops do?"

"They're made aware of the matter. It goes into the files. So if they see something, notice something—kids who don't seem to belong locally—maybe they put two and two together."

"Maybe," Edward said. "But you, the police here, you search, you investigate, right?"

"We make an alert. Everybody knows. But, no," the lieutenant said, "we don't mount a search, do an investigation."

"You don't?" Virginia said.

"Well, what do you do? Just exactly?" Edward asked.

"I'm sure—" Jane found herself interjecting to no purpose; Jane, to whom the police, at least in theory, were but a precursor to some future gestapo.

Lieutenant O'Connor put his hands together on top of his desk and spoke slowly. "There hasn't been a crime. No abduction. No foul play. No law broken. They're not even truant, because they're both over sixteen."

"School starts tomorrow," Virginia offered, inanely, Jane thought. Then Jane reconsidered. It was the kind of thing one said to fill empty spaces, to keep the madness at bay while the moment passed, the madness Jane had to admit she was already up to her boottops in.

"So, really, you don't *do* anything," Edward was saying. "Strictly speaking." Edward—this Ted—Jane thought, sounded nobly prosecutorial, like Welch facing down Joe McCarthy. She was not sure what this might accomplish, but it heartened her.

"I wouldn't say that. Within our . . . brief, we do everything we can. But until there's evidence of a crime, we can—"

"So if Emily turns up in a ditch somewhere, you guys will get to work," Edward said. "That's really swell. Gives me every confidence."

"That's really not fair. Or how it works. We have a framework. From the city, the state, the district attorney, and that is where we have to be." Lieutenant O'Connor shifted his eyes from Edward to Jane, detecting in her a perhaps more willing interlocutor. "Now really, as far as investigation goes—figuring out what they might have done, where they might be—*you* people are actually better equipped than any cop. You know these kids, their friends, their associates, their interests, their habits. Right?"

"I suppose," Jane said. Edward was looking away, his hands knotted together. Virginia watched the lieutenant talk to Jane, whose eyes were riveted upon him.

"So first thing, what all of you do"—Lieutenant O'Connor looked over to Edward—"is call all their friends, ask questions. Then go through their rooms, their stuff. They're careless, even when they're trying to be secretive. So chances are there's something that will point you in the direction they went."

"So we get to sleuth this thing out while you—" Edward put in.

"Hush," Virginia said. "Let him finish."

"*Then* we have something to go on. For example, maybe they planned to go to San Francisco, so we can put a query in to the police there—something substantial, that they can maybe look into."

"Maybe look into. Swell," Edward said.

"So you're saying you think they ran away?" Virginia asked.

"I'm not thinking or saying anything. But it's an obvious possibility. And San Francisco, California in general, is where they all go these days. And the boy's father lives there, right?"

"Yes," said Jane. "But it's scarcely likely he'd go to him. The man doesn't take any interest—"

"Still, you have to consider these things. That's how it works. Little fact here, little fact there. See what you find. Then come back and see me."

Edward said, "So that's it. That's what you have to offer?"

The lieutenant nodded. "For right now, yes."

Edward stood, taking Virginia's elbow as he did, and she rose with him. He said, "Well, thank you. This is all very . . . helpful." Then the two of them moved out into the hall, and the lieutenant watched them speak briefly in whispers, the wife, he figured, chewing out the husband for being sarcastic.

The other woman remained for a moment, still in her chair, in nearly a daze. He decided to rouse her by standing up from his desk. "You think about this California thing, Mrs. Lowry. About the boy maybe going to look up his dad. It's pretty common."

Jane shook her head. "He wouldn't."

"All the same . . ." Lieutenant O'Connor finished, and finally Jane stood up, and he walked her out to the hall. She was an attractive woman, he saw, and he wanted to make nice to her, because he pitied her situation, if not necessarily the woman herself; she and all these other white-collar swells, with their spoiled mixed-up kids.

"Your address—475 Laurel. That's an apartment house, right?"

"Yes," Jane said, looking ahead.

"I had a case there when I was a rookie. Ground-floor apartment."

"That's us," Jane said, and looked at him. "You must mean the taxi-dancer thing."

"Yeah, that's it. Maybe twenty-five years ago, a little more." Lieutenant O'Connor continued, "Nice big apartments. Guy had a whole darkroom in one of the closets. That still there?"

"No. Not anymore. Not since we came."

"Too bad," Lieutenant O'Connor said. "Make a nice hobby for your boy. When he comes back."

*W*hen Edward and Virginia came home, Emily's postcard lay with the other mail on the vestibule floor. On the picture side there was a generic photo of a Minnesota lake, on the other, face up, her handwriting. Virginia fell upon the card, picked it up, and read it, still on her knees. She read it again, and then she handed it up to Edward. He read it aloud, expressionlessly, like a jury foreman announcing a verdict.

" 'Dear Mom and Dad. I am going away for a while with Bill. It's something we need to do. It's very serious and important, but we are not in any kind of trouble. Please don't worry. I love you very much. Emily.' " Edward's daughter's name came out of his mouth with a shudder, with an ache in his chest.

Virginia stood up, unsteadily. "So that's it," she said. "They ran away together."

Edward nodded.

"I suppose we ought to be relieved," Virginia said, and she brushed her hands against her skirt.

"I suppose we should," Edward said.

"But you know what? What it really does," and her voice was rising, but then it fell off. "What it really does is make me a little mad."

"Because . . . ?" Edward said, thinking he ought to know what she was going to say, but somehow did not.

"Because if she had the . . . the consideration to send us a card, she should have had the consideration to not do it in the first place," Virginia said. "Does that make sense?"

Edward thought about this for a moment, and said, "It makes, well, one kind of sense."

"I know this is all wrong, but I'd like to swat her one," and then Virginia began to cry, to shake with great quaking sobs.

Edward put his arm around her shoulder, which seemed to be the stooped and bony back of an old woman as the sobs traveled up through it. "I know," he said. "I understand," and he added, rather helplessly, "It'll all turn out," and Virginia said nothing in response to him at all.

Somehow, that night, all of them—Jane and Virginia and Edward—slept easier. Edward had called Jane about the postcard, and after he had told her what it said and she had thought about it, she wondered if she had not preferred the uncertainty of the earlier part of the day to the knowledge the card had afforded them. For then—and the same feeling stole upon the Byrnes—there had remained the possibility that the children would simply return: that whatever circumstance had impeded them had removed itself; that whoever had taken them had released them or had been escaped from; that, for whatever reason you cared to name, the whole business had been an accident, a temporary mistake.

But now everyone knew it was irrefutable and deliberate, a piece of childish willfulness grown huge and monstrous. Jane, Edward, and Virginia might go ahead and look for the children—try to find them so as to rescue and save them—but the children were intent on thwarting them; didn't want to be saved. After Edward turned out the light in their bedroom that night and laid his head on the pillow to begin staring at the dark ceiling, he heard Virginia mutter, " 'Please don't worry. I love you very much,' " and her tone was not far removed from sheer fury.

When the clock struck twelve, there had been, of course, no further word about anything; nothing to be hopeful about or even to speculate upon. But the meeting with the lieutenant had given them, if not a sense of purpose, some distractions: the rounding up of photographs, the searching of the rooms, the interrogation of friends. And the possibility of one distraction opened their imagination to others: Jane, for example, realized she had not played any music in the house since before her trip to Chicago, and determined to begin working her way through her entire record collection, albeit not at such volume as to make the phone inaudible. Virginia turned to prayer, understandably, although she would be the first to take umbrage at anyone's describing this as a distraction, for it was indeed *doing* something—taking action, perhaps the only effective action possible—about the situation.

Edward remained a little more at sea. He had found no reassurance in their meeting with Lieutenant O'Connor; had scarcely in fact been able to contain his livid despair at the police department's indifference, its condescending and ineffectual response to their dilemma, not much more than paper-shuffling, make-work, and do-it-yourself detection.

So although Edward slept that night, he also awoke many times; and on two of these occasions he thought he heard someone on the porch or at the door, and of course he thought it was Emily. Because she hadn't necessarily meant what she said in the postcard, had she? Or had changed her mind. And of course he went downstairs and there was no one there at all.

There is something called mother love, which is tender but girded by great fortitude, by a steely determination to protect and foster until the child can fend for itself, and thus moderated by a certain practicality which is soft-hearted but by no means soft-headed. Father love, or at least Edward's love for Emily, may be somewhat different: It is a little awestruck, and since in Edward's generation it is not much touched by the quotidian business of dressing and changing and feeding and supervising, it rather tends to remain that way. That this child is simply a child is glorious enough; that it is *his* child makes it doubly so. That it is a girl child, that it partakes of the beautiful and ineffable nature of woman, renders it a glorious mystery; and because it is his wife's child—because it contains her, her youth reborn, captured and held in check, as if redeeming death itself—it is surely a species of miracle. It goes without saying that the girl child ought to be good; that she proves to be good—in her perfect and unself-regarding beauty, and her uncontingent love for the world in general and him in particular—is unfathomable, almost unbearable.

This is not necessarily universal, and perhaps it only applies to Edward or to men like him. Even Edward himself would have to admit that while he adores Susan (who is prettier and steadier than Emily; and who never, of course, put him through what he is going through now), at some point after infancy or after her sister was born, she became something like her mother's second-in-command, unfailingly responsible, helpful, and unflappable, and so a little too uncomplaining, a little too self-possessed, a little too invulnerable to meet his own deeply vulnerable father love on its own terms.

With Emily, it is otherwise, and sometimes he wonders if Susan did not sacrifice something—perhaps willingly, as was her nature—so that he and Emily could be so very close. But now he has the other thing, and it is more than worry or agony. He looks at the empty porch, the empty street, and the darkened houses, and all he can conceive is emptiness, loss upon loss, nothing rather than something or everything or even anything at all. This is what Emily has left him; this is where his love, more foolish and heedless than anything he felt as an adolescent, has gotten him.

3

IN THE MORNING, EDWARD AND VIRGINIA AGREED that Edward ought to go to work; that there was nothing he could usefully do at home (Virginia would go through Emily's room; Edward was privately much relieved that he would not have to) and he could drop off the photograph at the police department and show O'Connor the postcard. Because they both thought of it, because he was kind and she was kind, he could even collect William's picture on the way, and save his mother the trouble and perhaps the pain.

When Edward arrived, Jane was up and cheerful, after a fashion. In the afternoon, she, too, was going to go to work for a couple of hours, and this morning she was going to play all twelve sides of *Tristan und Isolde*, and she was going to clean the house. She was going to carry a great stack of magazines down to the boiler room and let the custodian have at them.

Jane invited Edward in and asked him if he'd like coffee. Edward said, "I'd better not. I just thought I might save you a trip downtown with Billy's picture. For the lieutenant, or whatever he is."

"Oh, that's very . . . sweet of you. To think of that," Jane said. "Just let me look. They did one last winter for school." Jane began to rummage in a drawer in the hall, and then moved down the hall to the living room, calling after Edward to follow her. "I'm a little scatterbrained. Forgive me."

"More than understandable under the circumstances," Edward said, and looked around. He saw a little sofa, an impressionist print of some kind, and then he heard the music. "Oh, Wagner. Right?"

"Tristan."

"I thought so. I spent time in Germany after the war. Not that they were putting on much music."

"I suppose not," Jane said. She thrust her hand into another drawer and pulled out a five-by-seven print. "Here we are." She regarded the picture. "You know, he already doesn't quite look like this. He's already . . . older, more grown-up. Or more composed or something. But I guess it'll do." She handed the photograph to Edward.

He held it and looked down at it for a moment. "Ginny's going to check through Emily's room today. Rather daunting. With a teenager."

"I suppose I should do the same. But I don't know if I can bear it. Not the mess . . ." Jane had stopped, and Edward looked at her and saw that a tear was running down her cheek. He had to stop himself from reaching out his hand to wipe it away.

Instead, he spoke, very softly, and said, "You can wait. Until you're ready. There's no harm in it."

"I suppose."

"But it's very hard, isn't it? I suppose especially for you."

"I don't know. I suppose it is. But I thought I was doing better. Until just now."

"You'll do fine," Edward said, and moved toward the door. "I ought to go."

"Well," Jane said, "I'm sorry I couldn't get you anything. Some coffee. Maybe you can come by sometime—maybe later—and have a drink. You. And . . . Ginny. We can—I don't know—commiserate."

"Maybe we will," Edward said. He put his hand on the knob of the front door. "Maybe I will. When I get done today. Just to see how you are."

"That's awfully kind."

"Perhaps . . . I could help you. With Billy's things. His room."

"That would be a tremendous favor."

"Fine. I'll come around four-thirty or five, okay?"

"Of course."

"Maybe I'll drop by home and get Ginny. Or whatever. I'll see how the day goes."

"Wonderful," Jane said, and Edward slipped out.

$\mathcal{V}$irginia opened the door to her daughter's room. She could not say whether she or Edward had closed it, or on what impulse. The first thing she did was put up the shades, which were still down, and had been down since the last night Emily had slept here. Emily must have left them down when she rose the morning she went to the fair.

Virginia looked at the alarm clock on the bedside table and saw it was set for five-thirty. Emily had told them she wanted to leave the house by seven, but this implied it had been rather earlier than that; and this thought caused Virginia to recollect that neither she nor Edward had, of course, seen her that morning. The last time either of them had set eyes on her—had hugged her, had bidden her to pray for them—was the night before she went away.

Looking away from the alarm clock, Virginia noticed that the bed had been made. This was perfectly unremarkable. Emily always made her bed. So the fact that she had made it on that particular morning meant either she expected it would be an ordinary day or she had forgotten it was going to be extraordinary; or that she was completely aware of what she was doing and out of some sense of perverse consideration undertook to leave her room tidy before she walked out of it and out of their lives.

The lieutenant had not been very specific about how they should go about the searching of the children's rooms, but, in keeping with her observations of the bed and the alarm clock, she thought she ought to concentrate on what was different, on what might be missing. With that in mind, Virginia began with Emily's closet and clothing drawers. Virginia was familiar in a general sense with Emily's wardrobe, if only because all the laundry passed through her hands at some point, whether by way of the washing machine or across the ironing board. Now upon opening Emily's closet, Virginia noted three or four obviously new dresses that she had never seen before, but these, she realized, must be booty from the job in the New Wave department. The clothing Virginia was familiar with—the dresses Emily wore to mass, the blue jumpers and white blouses she wore to school, the outfits she might put on for a family party or to visit her grandmother—was all as it should be, undisturbed.

It was in going through Emily's chest of drawers that Virginia saw items missing, or their quantities depleted: only a couple of pairs of socks and underwear; no jeans or shorts or sweatshirts or casual tops whatsoever; only two sweaters where there ought to have been at least four; and on the closet floor, no tennis shoes or the boots she had gotten for CYO camp last year.

As her comprehension of these anomalies took shape—as she scanned the shelf in the closet and saw that the blue vinyl Northwest Orient flight bag that served as Emily's suitcase was also gone—she felt panic rise within her. In part it must have been because these missing objects confirmed once more the message of the postcard; the fact of Emily's intention; that she had weighed these actions before taking them. She had examined them and apprised herself of their consequences and decided to proceed. No one had stolen her away, no terrible accident had befallen her. That great evil had been averted, but here, in its stead, was this other evil, this other privation that was nothing less than Emily's decision to deprive those who loved her most, who conceived and bore her into this world, of that which they loved most.

Virginia has no heart to continue, but because she is Virginia, because what amounts to her love knows no bounds, she goes on all the same. She moves to the bookcase, to the nightstands on either side of Emily's bed and their drawers. Emily is not a messy child, but in common with children and adolescents, her possessions are laid out without apparent system, accumulated in heaps, accreted in layers, not by theme or form, but archaeologically. Thus Virginia finds in one drawer, beginning at the top, a Robert Kennedy bumper sticker, various pots and tubes of makeup, and a strand of leather bootlace Emily wore around her ankle for the better part of the previous summer; deeper down, instructions for Tampax, a rubber-faced troll, and a Red Cross junior lifesaver swimming badge; deepest of all, scapulars, pop-beads, feathers, stones, and shells.

On the other nightstand, there are books, and in the drawer, more books and papers: a slight and stern-looking volume titled *The Colossus*;

an essay with the heading "Edna St. Vincent Millay" (marked at the top, in blue pencil, "A!"); various notices and handouts from school; and a box of stationery. Virginia picks it up and opens it. Inside there are two pens, one ballpoint and one fountain, some rubber bands, and blank sheets of paper. The topmost leaf shows faint impressions of Emily's handwriting, traces of overlapping letters and words where she has borne down hard with her pen. There is another postcard just like the one she sent them. On the back there is a picture of a lake in northern Minnesota, the lake where she went to camp. In the box she also finds Emily's savings account passbook. The last entry, made five days ago, records that the account has been closed and that the entire balance, $296.83, has been withdrawn.

Virginia has been hoping that here she might find a diary or some record of Emily's thoughts or plans, but at the bottom of the box she finds only two letters. She reads the one with the earlier postmark:

> 475 Laurel Ave.
> St. Paul, Minn.
> 55102
> U.S.A.
> June 4, 1968
>
> Dear Emily,
>
> I don't know if you know that you know me. My name is Bill Lowry and I go to the Academy, but I hang out with a lot of kids from Blessed Sacrament. Jim Donnelly is a real good friend, and I know Mike Reardon pretty well, and I know you are friends with his twin sister Monica and you two are in the same class at Annunciation.
>
> I talked to you once, even though I can't quite remember what I said, and I know we sat around in St. Clair Park with some other kids a couple of times.
>
> Anyway, I am writing you to say I thought it would be fun to maybe do something sometime. For example, there's a place called the Scholar on the West Bank. It's a coffeehouse and they have folk music (or folk-rock, I guess) and these coffee drinks with whipped

cream and stuff in them. It's almost all people from the U that go there, but you can be in high school and still go there even though almost no high school kids go or even know about it.

I've had my license for a year and have a perfect driving record and we have a Buick wagon (feeble, but it goes!).

Anyway, I really hope you would like to go next week and you can call me at 226-5385 or I can call you or you can even write me back.

I think you are really cool and really pretty too and I bet we could have a lot of fun together.

Yours sincerely,

Bill

Then Virginia reads the other:

475 Laurel Ave.
St. Paul, 2, Minn.
June 8, 1968

Dear Emily,

It sure was great to get your letter. I got it this morning and now I am writing back first thing.

I only went to the prom with Sarah J. because Jim asked me to invite her so he could go with Linda Olson without Sarah feeling put out on account of Jim having kind of made it seem like he wanted to go with Sarah before he started liking Linda. I'm not really into dances anyway. I like to listen to music by myself, the kind of thing you mentioned, and also to read about psychology and social problems. I don't worry about how I dress or look, although I suppose I did a few years back when a lot of kids wanted to go around being fake surfers or Ivy League or whatever. I'm sorry I did-n't notice you at that birthday party, but that was four years ago and I was awfully young then.

I know what you mean about RFK. We are really McCarthy peo-ple in our house, or at least my mom is, but we all feel terrible. And I always liked Kennedy better, even though my mom thought it was kind of a cheat for him to get into the race when he did—like he'd let McCarthy do all the work and waited until Johnson was out of the way.

But I guess I think McCarthy is kind of, well, *dry*—good, I mean, but like a minister or something—and Bobby was cool and cared about the poor and the inner city and the farmworkers, not just about the war. And I know what you mean about JFK and the older kids, and how RFK would have been for *us*. But I haven't said that to anyone before, just to you, just now.

My mom and her friends—they're all friends because they're against the war—really feel rotten about it. But I guess they wonder mostly about whether McCarthy could beat Humphrey now, and if he can't what they should do, because they like Humphrey even less than they liked RFK. In fact, my mom says Nixon and Humphrey are just Tweedledee and Tweedledum—that it will just be more of what's happened with LBJ.

Because you asked, I will wait to call until Wednesday, and then maybe we could go out Thursday, if that's OK. And maybe I will write again just because you like letters.

Stay cool.

Yours sincerely,

Bill

Virginia puts the letters back in their envelopes. They have the smell of adolescence about them; of chewing gum and cheap cosmetics, of vapid sentiments. Then she sees a sheet of paper upon which Emily has copied out a poem in printed rather than cursive characters, as though to make a little poster. It is headed "For Bill—'Love Among the Ruins' by Robert Browning" and reads:

> *In one year they sent a million fighters forth*
> *South and North,*
> *And they built their gods a brazen pillar high*
> *As the sky,*
> *Yet reserved a thousand chariots in full force—*
> *Gold, of course,*

Oh heart! oh blood that freezes, blood that burns!
Earth's returns
For whole centuries of folly, noise and sin!
Shut them in,
With their triumphs and their glories and the rest!
Love is best!

Virginia reads this and it does not mean anything to her. It is but more childish nonsense—no more, it seems, than the troll or the disheveled rabbit that sits listing in the bookcase— and the best you could say for it is that it irritates Virginia, it makes her angry, which is a momentary alternative to her worry and horror. It is but another sign of the thoughtlessness and heedlessness which reigns in this room, in Emily's life: Trivialities become profundities and that which ought to mean everything means nothing at all. She writes down verses for a boy she scarcely knows—who can scarcely know her—and leaves her mother and her father this room, its empty made-up bed and vacated dresser drawers, as memorial to their love, to all their labors.

*W*hen Edward called her at lunchtime, Virginia apprised him of what she had found and not found in Emily's room. She related this in the tone a doctor might relay a bad prognosis, but more in the manner of a curse, a scourge, or at least of confirmation of a heretofore ineffable dread. The prognosis was, of course, theirs: his and hers.

For his part, Edward passed on Lieutenant O'Connor's reaction to the arrival of the postcard, which was scarcely a reaction at all: He had nodded and said this, too, was par for the course; that they ought to be grateful there'd been no accident or foul play; that they could narrow their efforts down to simply looking for two runaway kids. And maybe, in addition to California, they ought to think about the north woods as a possible destination. Maybe the choice of postcard was accidental, but maybe it was a kind of signal. With kids you never knew.

That was that, Edward told Virginia. Given his lifetime knack for judging what would suit Virginia at any given moment, Edward did not propose that she go with him to Jane's house that afternoon, assuming he even consciously thought of it at all. He did think, as he drove up the hill about half past four, that a drink would be rather nice, and that he was not averse to spending a little time with Jane Lowry.

When she answered the door, it seemed to him that scarcely any time at all had passed since he had seen her that morning; it seemed that even the exact same music was playing. She smiled and said, "Ted," as though his arrival were a very happy surprise to her. She motioned him into the hall, and he quickly told her what the lieutenant had said and what Virginia's search of Emily's room had yielded. Jane frowned and shrugged, and brushed her hand against her forehead. Finally, she said, "Let me get us something cold. Gin and tonic sound good?"

"Lovely," Edward said.

He was not sure whether he ought to follow her back to the kitchen, remain in the hall, or go make himself at home in the front room, where presumably they would take their refreshments; and then Jane's voice boomeranged from the kitchen door, "Have a seat in the living room. I'll just be a sec."

Edward sat down on the little sofa, first leaning back and then forward, with his hands on his knees and his feet set flat and evenly placed on the floor before him. It was the waiting-room posture, designed not for relaxation but for springing to one's feet and offering a handshake, and he spent much the better part of his days in it. Thus positioned, he might be expected to take up a magazine (*Life* and *The New Yorker* sat before him on the coffee table), not to read but to occupy his hands and eyes, lest it appear when his quarry finally came to him that the waiting had in a way inconvenienced him, that he might in fact have anything better to do than sit right here and inform himself of the contents of this particular weekly organ of news, opinion, and culture. And so he did, and although the copy of *Life* he found was an old one, from twelve weeks ago, with Sirhan Sirhan and James Earl Ray on the cover, this was of no import, one magazine being as good as another.

In point of fact, after he had been sitting for a moment, Edward found himself first diverted by and then nearly absorbed by the music, which was familiar to him, not just from that morning but from past hearings. You might imagine that it could not fail to be, for its chief quality was of circling, overlapping repetition, of one theme dipping and rising, flooding and ebbing, advancing a step and retreating back upon itself.

Jane came in, bearing two tall glasses already befogged with condensation. Edward took his, thanking her, and said, "Still working on your Wagner, I see."

"Well, there are six LPs to it. Comes in a box with a big fat book."

"An all-day sucker, so to speak."

"Exactly. Though it's almost done, I think. Maybe one more side."

Edward drank. "That's where the big lady in the helmet with horns dies of her agonies or something."

"Nearly. It's the lovers in this case. Tristan and Isolde." Jane sat down opposite him in an easy chair.

"It's very beautiful," Edward said, with a faint note of apology in his voice. He paused as though to listen for a moment, to give the music — now scaling another crescendo from which it would slither back in a minute — its due. "To tell the truth, I can understand it a little. I was an intelligence officer in Germany."

"A spy? Really."

"No. Just a translator. Newspapers and documents. Pretty stupid stuff. After the surrender. I'd picked it up in college."

"Still. How clever of you. And me with my schoolgirl French."

Edward shrugged and changed the subject. "That's quite a hi-fi, too. With the separate speakers and so forth. It's a . . ."

"KLH . . . " Jane said, as though she were not quite sure about the reliability of this information.

"It makes a beautiful sound."

"I suppose it's an indulgence, but I love music. Mind you, since the primary season, I've hardly listened."

"Politics," Edward said, and drank again, deeply.

"But now it's rather out of my hands. The election. Nixon and Hubert. May the worst man win." Jane halted and also drank. "I guess I have more important things to think about now. I've been . . . over-taken by other events."

Edward nodded and Jane added, "At least we know they weren't kid-napped or something."

"It's good. In that sense."

"But then I suppose you just worry about what's going to happen to them now."

"That," Edward said, and drained his glass. "That, and just trying to find an explanation."

"Of why they did it?"

"Yes. That in particular."

"But maybe that's a little inexplicable. I mean, teenagers . . ." Jane stopped. "Oh, let me get you another."

Edward thought about it, but not for long, and nodded. "Thanks very much," he said and continued, "Oh, I know it doesn't really help find them either. But you—or at least I do—you have to wonder why ever she—they, I suppose—would do this."

Jane looked at him, and Edward thought she was going to touch him and maybe call him Ted again. Instead, she looked down at her hands, at the two empty glasses she was holding. "Why they would do this?" she said. "Want to do this for themselves, for their own sakes? Or do you mean do this as in do this to *us?*"

"I don't know. Both, I guess. It seems like they have to be con-nected."

"I don't know either," Jane said, and walked away towards the kitchen.

Edward was by now sufficiently relaxed that while Jane went to the kitchen he really did sit back on the sofa and lose himself in thought a little, and in the music; and he did indeed catch a little of what was being sung, although—with his college classes and his tour of occu-pied Germany more than twenty years behind him—he compre-hended it in a very piecemeal fashion. He heard, for example, Tristan say something about *ein heiss-inbrünstig Lieben, aus Toddes-Wonne-Grauen jagt's mich,* which he understood correctly to refer to a species of enduring, flaming love.

It was rather a shame he did not understand more, because the answers to the questions he and Jane had just been putting to each other were there right in front of him. For example, what clearer explanation of what drove the children to do what they had done than that very line of Tristan's, which we might render "the ardent, indwelling love that has chased me from the blissful horror of death"? And as to where they had gone, is there a better answer than *Wo ich von je gewesen, wohin auf je ich geh': im weiten Reich der Weltennacht. Nur ein Wissen dort uns eigen: göttlich ew'ges Urvergessen*—"Where I had been for all time and where forever I shall go: the vast realm of universal night, where our sole knowledge is but divine, eternal all-forgetting"? But these are scarcely consoling answers, so perhaps it was just as well that Edward did not hear them.

Jane came back with their replenished glasses, set them down, and seated herself again. She said,"So what's your guess, Ted? Tell me, really."

"About where or about why?"

"Take your pick."

"Well, as for where, maybe the cop's right. There's the north, but California seems pretty obvious."

"I guess that's where I'd go if I ran away," Jane said, and laughed. "That's what my husband did."

Edward smiled. "I suppose anyone would."

"Would run away? Or go to California?"

"Go to California. As for wanting to run away, I haven't the slightest." He stopped and drank. "Particularly with Emily. She was the happiest, most . . . well-adjusted girl. . . ."

"So you just don't see her doing it at all?"

"Not at all. Neither does Ginny. Maybe that's what hurts—this delusion we were operating under."

"But you must understand how it is . . . to be young?"

"I thought I did," Edward said. "In fact, I thought being young was a pretty fair definition of happiness."

"Maybe. But maybe sometimes just the opposite." Jane reached for the cigarette box on the coffee table and held it out. "Want one?"

"Under the circumstances, what the hell," Edward said, and took a cigarette. Jane extracted another for herself, seized the lighter that sat next to the box, spun the wheel with her thumb, and held out the flame for Edward. He thrust his face forward and drew on the cigarette. Then Jane lit her own cigarette, pulling deeply. "What I mean is, maybe it's just as much a miserable time, being young. You, for example. Were you always happy then?"

"No. I suppose I wasn't. But then there was a war on, too."

"There's a war on now."

"It's hardly the same thing."

"It's worse. It's an illegal war. An *immoral* war. So you can't even support it—not if you have any kind of conscience."

"I know, I know." Sometimes Edward felt he had known Jane a very long time; that he might even say to her, in the gentlest possible way, "Please don't start," and she would understand it to be condescending in only the tenderest sense. "But it's quite a leap, isn't it? To say this thing that's happening a million miles away is going to cause a perfectly happy—"

"Who says anybody's perfectly happy?"

"Emily seemed awfully damned close." Edward stopped, and after doing so realized that he did not quite know what to say next and that apparently neither did Jane. They both drank and then drew on their cigarettes, hoping the wind impelling the conversation might pick up again. But they remained becalmed, for Edward and Jane had unwittingly broached a subject—or the implication of a subject—that was as unpleasant as it was impossible to wish away: that if Emily, being happy or at least content and above all innocent and thus pliable, had become discontent, it must have been because somebody plied her; and it went without saying who that person might be.

Among the virtues of deep convictions such as Jane was accustomed to hold about the world (if not about herself or the security of her place in it) is that it renders one pretty much immune to being affronted. So, rather than argue about Emily's alleged contentment and William's impact upon it, she proposed that she and Edward go forward with the task that Edward had earlier volunteered for.

"I wonder if we shouldn't get started on Billy's room," she said. "If you're still willing."

"Oh, sure," Edward said, and finished his drink and tamped out his cigarette. Jane did the same, and she led him down the hall, back into the depths of the apartment. They passed the kitchen, which bore, in Edward's quick glance therein, a distinctly modern air, of terra-cotta and sans-serif typefaces, like an Italian restaurant run by Scandinavian folklorists. They went down the hallway, past what must be Jane's bedroom, past the bathroom, and, at the end, where a nimbus of sun shone through a drawn curtain, they ended at the open door of the boy's room.

On entering it, Edward felt sad, for it was so clearly the empty room of a child, rather than the den of the malign influence he had so recently conjured. It had the fetid dishevelment that is unique to boys' rooms: the Gordian tangle of bedclothes; the abandoned socks littering the floor like worm castings; the forlorn and croaking, terminally untuned guitar; the heaps of paperback thrillers that looked as much pawed over as pored over; the shabby hulks of model airplanes; the sun-blasted poster (once meant to express outrage or libidinousness or both) hanging flaccidly by a few shreds of yellowing tape—in sum, less a home than a squatter's camp whose entire inventory of contents might best be handled with tongs.

"Shall we start?" said Jane. "I went through his bureau. I can't really say what's missing. The laundry just sort of . . . accumulates. Then when it's knee-deep, we just shovel it out and wash the whole lot." She paused and looked up at Edward. "That's not really fair. He's generally tidy. For a boy." She looked at him a little harder. "He's a good boy, you know."

Edward looked back at her, perhaps less intently, but still much possessed by the sadness that had overtaken him. "I know," he said. "Emily wouldn't have liked him otherwise." He was not sure this was quite the thing he ought to say, but it was what came out.

"Maybe we could look in the closet. To begin," Jane said.

Edward nodded and moved toward the closet door. Inside there were perhaps four or five blue oxford-cloth shirts and as many pairs of khaki trousers as well as a blue wool blazer and a pair of gray flannel slacks. At the bottom, among the dust bunnies and upon the battered and gaping floor planks, stood a pair of penny loafers and a pair of blue canvas deck shoes with holes in the toes.

"There's not much here," Jane said. "His coat and boots are gone. And all his camping equipment."

"His camping equipment?"

"He sort of collected it. He's hardly been camping, really. But he had a tent and a sleeping bag and so forth. A pack and a canteen. Even a hatchet."

"So they have that with them, I suppose."

"I'd imagine."

Edward's gaze returned to the floor. "Wait a minute," he said, and took his keys from his pocket. He reached down and inserted the shank of his house key between two boards, one of which easily lifted away.

"Oh," said Jane.

"Every boy's got one of these. I had one. It just came back to me." Edward knelt and began to remove the items contained in the cache beneath the floorboard. There were six or seven men's magazines whose bindings were in various stages of decomposition, as though from hard use; a half-empty box of .22-caliber rifle cartridges; two letters; and a bankbook. The letters, Edward saw, were from Emily, and he seized them, read them quickly, and passed them to Jane. "Nothing much in these," he said.

Jane read:

919 Furness St.
St. Paul, 5, Minn.
June 6, 1968

Dear Bill Lowry,

Thank you for your letter. I know who you are. In fact, I remember you from a bunch of times. You were at my cousin Jim's birthday party when he was 13, and I bet you didn't even know I was there.

Monica said something about you once, I don't know why. She said you had a funny sense of humor and that you used to be sort of Ivy League, but not in a stuck-up way like you had to always be wearing a yellow button-down and a burgundy V-neck. Also, that you went to your Junior Prom with Sarah Jacobsen. My dad says there's no accounting for taste. (Ha, just kidding!)

I know about the Scholar. I have a lot of albums of that kind of thing, not just Peter, Paul & Mary, but the authentic stuff like Joan Baez. So I would like to go, but usually I have to be home by 10 unless it's for something really special. My parents aren't really strict, but that's the way it is.

Things are kind of odd around here right now, so why don't you wait to call me (CA5-5382) until next week—or you can write again. I think letters are really kind of cool!

We are very sad here about Bobby Kennedy. I was only in the sixth grade when JFK was killed, and I didn't really take it in like my sister and her friends. So I kind of thought RFK would be our JFK, but it didn't work out that way, did it?

Stay cool!

Sincerely yours,

Emily

Jane shook her head and then read the other. It merely read, "Dear Bill, Thank you for your nice letter. I am really looking forward to talking to you. Yours truly, Emily," with the postscript "P.S. I know what you mean about RFK and everything. He (or somebody) could have been 'for us.' And now it is so sad to think we are alone. Do you know what I mean?" Jane let out a little sigh of what was surely pity.

Then Edward handed her the bankbook. She opened it and passed it back to Edward, holding the last page open. "Cleaned out," she said. Edward looked at the balance. "Not an inconsiderable sum for a young fellow," he said.

"He saved it all, I guess." Jane shrugged. "I don't know where he gets it. The impulse to . . . accumulate capital. His great-grandfather, I suppose. The rest of us were wastrels and spendthrifts."

Edward said nothing. "Perhaps we ought to check around the bed," he suggested, and Jane nodded. As they moved, Edward asked, "Is there a rifle that goes with those bullets?"

"No. I suppose he brought them home from camp. Just souvenirs. Charms. Fetishes."

"I imagine. I guess I had stuff like that too. In my secret place."

Edward and Jane now stood on opposite sides of the head of William's bed, and Edward turned to the bookcase to the left of it and regarded its contents. "Quite a reader, your son," he said. "Esoteric stuff. Buddhism. *Identity: Youth and Crisis. Growing Up Absurd.* My, my."

"He was always precocious that way. I thought it was fine—that he cared about serious things. That he was trying to understand."

"Emily is"—he had nearly said "was"—"rather that way too. Maybe more in a dreamy, sort of poetic way." Edward turned away from the books. "I don't suppose it makes for a very carefree childhood, though. Not like you'd like them to have."

"I'm not sure that's available anymore. Of course, for William— given what happened between his father and me—I suppose he was going to be disillusioned early." Jane pulled the drawer from the bedside table and put it down in the middle of the bed, and sat herself down next to it. "Maybe not disillusioned in the sense of jaded. Just serious. Very determined to get . . . *at* the heart of things. Does that make sense?"

"Yes. I think I understand." Edward sat down opposite her, on the other side of the drawer. "So what have we got here?"

Jane handed him a photograph and he saw it was the same school photo of Emily that he had dropped off to the police that morning. Edward took it and looked at it. "In the drawer by his bed," Jane said. "That's kind of sweet." Edward said nothing. He wasn't sure it was sweet, but perhaps more on the order of the bullets in the cache, the talisman by which the boy took possession of Emily, the way he divined and conjured and controlled her.

Edward saw there was a book in the drawer, close to him, on his side of it, and he picked it up. "Well, well. I had this." He held it up. "*The Book of Woodcraft and Indian Lore.* Campfire stories. Animal tracks. Knots and whittling." He opened the book and read, " 'When I was a boy I hungered beyond expression for just such information as I have tried herein to impart. It would be a great joy to me if I could reach and help a considerable number of such heart-hungry boys tormented with an insatiate instinct for the woods.' " Edward closed the book and patted the cover. "Indeed, indeed," he said.

"I think it was his father's."

"But you still think it's unlikely he'd go there—to California, to see him?"

"I don't think so. Maybe they went . . . camping. What with this book. And his equipment gone."

"Could be. I'd feel better if they had. Instead of San Francisco." Edward put the book down on the bed while Jane continued to sift through the drawer, through pencil stubs and loose mints and coins flattened on the railroad track. "You know, it's really a big thing when you're a boy. The woods." He smiled. "I suppose it still is. Must be. Because it's real and you want to get back to it. Be an Indian brave or a trapper or Scott of the Antarctic. Whoever." Edward was leaning back on his hands, sitting quite happily, and the dark impression of William that had struck him in regarding Emily's photograph was being replaced by a kind of fellow feeling for the boy; by the notion that the boy was but a younger manifestation of himself. He began to want to report his sense of this to Jane, who was still rifling in the drawer, and he said, "You know, we think kids are so different . . ."

But Jane held something up, and said, "Oh dear."

They both knew what it was. Any grown man or woman would: an empty foil envelope, a little over an inch square, torn open along one side.

"I suppose we shouldn't be surprised," Jane said with a sigh.

"I suppose not," Edward said after a long pause. "I suppose it was Emily." Jane nodded. "But I didn't really want to know."

"It's different with a girl. I know," Jane added, and even as she said it, she knew it was the wrong thing, and that she was going to say another wrong thing. "I'm pretty sure he had never been with anyone before. He wasn't . . ." And then she thought she had better stop.

"I'm sure she hadn't been either," said Edward. "If that matters. If it's either here or there," he added a little sharply.

"At least they took precautions."

"Oh, that's a great consolation," Edward said. He at last looked over to Jane again and said, "I'm sorry. This isn't anyone's fault."

Jane was looking at her hands. She said, "I'm happy you said that. I mean, the boy's usually seen as . . . the culprit." Jane stood up from the bed, and so did Edward.

"I know," he said. "And maybe that's not fair. Or at least it's more complicated."

They rounded either side of the bed, meeting at its foot. Edward might have put out his hands and rested them on Jane's shoulders, to comfort her or to explain himself. But he just stood, close enough to smell her breath, the juniper berries and tart scent of what they had been drinking together, and said, "It's silly. But I just didn't want to know this. Not on top of everything else."

*E*dward came home to Furness Street a little before six. He had decided on the way that he would not tell Virginia everything they had discovered: that it wasn't really material, that it was no surprise under the circumstances, that it would only hurt her. Everything else merely confirmed what Virginia had surmised from her search of Emily's room. They had planned to run away, they had nearly nine hundred dollars between them, and they were perhaps planning on camping somewhere.

Virginia listened to Edward summarize this, and then she reported that she had been on the phone to Monica's mother, who had impressed upon her daughter the gravity of the situation and then put her on the line. "Monica said she was completely surprised, that she and Emily hadn't talked much recently, that she was spending all her time with the boy. Afterwards, Pat told me she was sure she was being truthful—that Monica had already been complaining that she and Emily weren't close anymore."

"So it wasn't very helpful," Edward said.

"Not really. Did his mother talk to his friends? She should. He goes around with the Donnelly boy."

"I don't know. I'll ask her."

"I'm surprised you didn't." Virginia, Edward saw, was looking not at him, but past him, over his shoulder. "You were over there . . . for what? An hour?"

"Thereabouts. It took a while to go through the boy's room. Kind of a rat's nest." Edward added, "She gave me a drink. We talked."

"How nice of her," Virginia said. It had indeed been Edward's intent to communicate the fact of Jane's niceness, but that was not how it struck Virginia. "How nice of you. To take the time." There was an edge, an inflection, to her voice that was quite alien to her, and Edward found himself wanting to say "This isn't you," but thought it might be better to let it pass. It did indeed pass, or rather it mutated into something else, equally uncharacteristic.

"I just think," Virginia continued, "that you ought to remember where . . . your loyalties really ought to lie."

"Well, of course I—"

"Because I'm alone too. Not in the same way. But I'm alone here all day, with this awful thing going on." Edward moved to hold her, to take her in his arms. But Virginia continued to look away, and then suddenly her eyes met his and he stopped right where he was. "And besides, you really should be careful. To be seen to be . . . overattentive to her. Her being a divorcée and so forth."

Edward wanted to say again that this was not like her and was indeed not worthy of her, that it was mean-spirited and snobbish, the very kind of thing the upper-crust Protestant women she had no time or patience for might say. But he did not say these things, even though he was right. Because this was not like Virginia, and it was not worthy of her, if only because she was not saying what she truly meant to say, or at least was not saying it well: that she had never been so frightened in her life, and that Edward's parceling out of even an hour of his attention, no matter how well meant or even arguably necessary, towards someone else's fear was an hour too much.

So this was not like Virginia, but neither was Edward exactly like Edward. Nor was Jane the Jane she once had been. They were each altogether altered by what had befallen them. Crises are said to be occasions when one's true character is displayed or when virtues heretofore only rehearsed in the abstract may be pressed into real service. But whoever could have envisioned what had happened to them? Whoever could have planned for it and responded in a fitting manner?

What might be (what the *hell* would be, Edward was inclined to say at this point) the appropriate way to proceed?

The children might indeed have gone to California, but their parents were definitely in the woods. They were lost and walking in circles. The ice-breath of the windigo—the frozen-hearted cannibal of the boreal forest—was on their necks.

4

Thank heaven for practicalities, for work and for errands, for the lawn that must be mowed and the laundry that must be ironed, for the meals that must be put on the table three times a day, no matter what. Thank heaven, too, that there are things to be done about William and Emily's flight, or at least tasks that it entails, some of which may even be successfully completed.

For example, on the lieutenant's advice, Edward takes photos of the kids down to the bus depot to show to the ticket agents and drivers. No one has seen them, of course; there are kids traveling everywhere at the end of summer. This leads to feelings of defeat, but they are defeats resulting from having done something rather than nothing.

There is also the question of who ought to be told what the children have done and what explanation ought to be offered to the world at large. Among Jane's acquaintances, Frances already knows and offers the kind of hearty support that only one who is truly unsurprised by everything can muster. Otherwise there is no one who needs to know except William's father, and Jane will get around to calling him soon, one of these evenings, after the second or third round of drinks. There is, of course, the school to be notified, and Jane calls the registrar and says simply that William has been accorded a last-minute opportunity to spend the semester in California with his father, will attend school there, and will return in the New Year. The registrar wonders how the matter of taking the SAT and of getting William's college applications underway will be dealt with. Jane says that they have all that in hand; that a semester's worth of "masculine influence" is worth a great deal;

and that, in any case, perhaps William (whose grades are not stunning) will take an "enrichment year" before college. This is the best Jane can do, and, she thinks, as she puts down the phone and reaches across the kitchen table for her cigarettes and coffee mug, it isn't too bad at all, under the circumstances.

Virginia takes a different approach. She calls the Convent of the Annunciation and makes an appointment with Emily's adviser and favorite teacher, Sister Mary Immaculata. They sit in her classroom after the school day has ended with the door shut, and with Virginia's fretful hands clasped and perched uneasily atop her purse, it is a little like confession. She explains that Emily (How can this be true? she thinks even as she begins to phrase it) has disappeared, has in fact run away, and there is a boy involved, who has presumably gone with her. They have gone to California, or at least gone somewhere camping. She and Edward and, yes, the boy's mother too, have been to the police. A missing-person report has been filed, they have been investigating the matter themselves in accordance with police instructions, and the police lieutenant has told them that, really, this happens all the time nowadays and usually the kids come home; that they get bored or scared or lonely and they just come home. She feels very bad for the school, for Emily of course, and even for the boy and his mother. She tries to say these things with the air that they are temporary—that Emily will be back at school soon, that everything will be as it was—and not convey the fact that she has been more or less flayed, that her very skin feels sundered from her body, the very rawest and tenderest places open to the weather, to intrusion, to whatever the world pleases to torture her with.

After she is done, Virginia expects that the nun will say something sententious and comforting, and indeed she does. She says, "This must be a great affliction for you," and Virginia bursts into tears. After a time, she tries to speak. "I try to bear it—to let it be as God's will—to just offer it up. But I can't." She halts and dabs herself with the Kleenex Sister Immaculata has produced from her desk drawer. "Because I don't even know what it is. Where it came from—the whole thing— and where it's going to finish. Or even if it ever has a beginning and an ending. Does that make sense?"

"I think so. It's the feeling of great privation, of loss and emptiness. And so it feels very, very far away from God. Doesn't it?"

"Yes. It does. I guess." Virginia begins to sob again. The nun hands her another tissue, and takes Virginia's free hand in her own. It is an old hand, the skin glassy and drawn, weathered not by labor but by prayer, by taking on the world's misery, Virginia's misery and more, as its daily bread. "I'll tell the other sisters," the nun says. " No one else, of course. And we'll make it, Emily, part of our daily intentions."

"What about the other girls?"

"We'll just say she's away. Which is the truth."

"They'll think she's pregnant. That she's in a home."

"They'll think what they'll think. There are worse things."

Virginia gives the nun's hand a squeeze and releases herself from its grip. "I suppose you're right. And of course it'll probably be over soon, just like the policeman said, won't it?"

"I'm sure all will be well."

Virginia mops her nose and eyes again and stands. "Well, I suppose I should go," she says, and the nun stands too. She begins to move and turns back on one foot and says to the nun, "You know, I used to think that maybe Emily had a vocation. Isn't that silly?"

"No. Not really."

"For a while, when she was little, she was very keen."

"They often are. Most little girls. I wanted to be a nun and then I didn't for a while. But here I am."

"Well, with Emily, I guess that wasn't . . . in the cards. I suppose this just goes to show."

"Oh, I don't know what this would have to do with it," the nun says. "But, no, I never saw her as a religious. Her gifts are elsewhere. I saw her—I still see her—making beautiful things: writing or painting or music. And those are great gifts, gifts that serve God a great deal. More than most. But I think she might . . . chafe a little, being obedient to a rule, to a mother superior."

Virginia laughs. Perhaps it is the first time she has laughed in the last three days. She says, "Well, I must go. Thank you." She thinks of asking the nun for her blessing, but she cannot at that moment think whether it is appropriate to ask a nun for a blessing or whether she is entitled to it, despite having told the nun everything in her heart, the things she could not tell Edward and was sure he could not in any case hear.

$\mathcal{T}$hrough a kind of curious symmetry of gender, just as it had been up to Virginia to interview Monica Reardon and talk to the nun, so it had been Edward's duty to deliver photos and visit the bus depot. Now it fell to him to question Jim Donnelly, Edward being not only the liaison to male persons, but Jane's proxy in their investigation. Edward drove over to the Donnelly residence in the late afternoon, the hour for him already now redolent with quinine and lemon and gin. He walked past the infamous Pontiac (hunkered beneath a huge and diseased old elm from whose height various robins and starlings had applied a not inconsiderable impasto of guano to the vehicle's roof), went to the door, and rang the bell. It was answered by the young man himself, and he agreed without any demurral to tell Edward whatever he wanted to know.

Jim and Edward sat on the porch step together, and the boy was every bit as large as—perhaps even a little taller than—the man. Edward thought this was the damnedest thing, having no experience of sons or of young men since he himself had been one; and he could not say whether he was a little intimidated or perhaps simply nonplussed at that freak of nature which is the human male in its late adolescence. He explained who he was and his connection to William, and the boy seemed already to know all that. Then, without quite coming out and saying that the children had run away, he asked if William had ever said anything to Jim about the possibility of doing such a thing.

"Well, no," said the boy. "Not really."

"What do you mean, not really?"

"Well, he might have talked about doing something like that, but it would have just been . . . talking."

"You mean just shooting the breeze, b.s.-ing."

"Yeah. I mean we talked about driving the Beast"—Jim indicated the car under the tree—"to California, but, I mean, come on . . ." He looked up and shook his head. "Or Bill was going to get a new GTO. Right. Sure."

"Was he kind of, well, obsessed with going to California?"

"I don't think so. I mean, everyone talks about California." The boy turned towards Edward and opened his hands as though to elucidate a particularly difficult concept. "But maybe not the real California. More in the way of California just being wherever isn't *here*."

"So he wanted to get away from here?"

"I suppose. But then, it's like California. Everybody talks about getting away. About being free. It doesn't mean they're really going to. Or maybe even want to. You know?" Edward nodded. "Besides," the boy continued, "I think he was more interested in the north woods."

"More interested in going there than going to California?"

"Maybe not going. Just talking about them."

"But he'd never really gone?"

"He went to camp. Two summers ago, I think."

"Yes," said Edward. "I think that's right. And he was interested in woodcraft."

"In what?"

"Camping out. Living off the land."

"Oh. Yeah. He was."

"But he'd never really done that either."

"No. But he had all the gear."

Edward decided he ought to make his questions a little more pointed. The boy was willing, but willing in an insouciant manner that was a little hard to read. "So he never said anything like 'I'm thinking of taking off'?"

"No, not like 'I'm leaving tomorrow.' Not like that." Now Jim was genuinely trying to explain something which he understood completely but could not precisely articulate: that he and William or any other young person in that time and place might talk about freedom as their fathers might talk about money. They might have endless discussions about how to acquire it and what they would do with it if they had it, but it did not follow from this that any particular plans were afoot or were even being considered. (Jim's father talked about what he would do as the owner of a quartet of McDonald's franchises, but went right on working as a sales manager for the Toro Lawn Mower Company until his retirement.) At the same time, these meditations were in no way mere pipe dreams: They were in deadly earnest.

"So when was the last time you talked to him?"

"Maybe three weeks ago. We weren't really hanging out together so much." The boy paused. "He was, you know, pretty much always with . . . Emily."

"And how was he then?"

"Fine, I guess. He was mad about losing his job."

"So he was unhappy?"

"I don't know if he was . . . unhappy. I don't know if that's really it. He was just bummed out. About everything."

"About everything?"

"Yeah. Like the whole society. The draft. The war. The cops."

"The cops? So he had run-ins with the police?"

"Bill?" The boy laughed. "No way. I mean, just the cops hassling people. Or beating up protesters and students. Like in Chicago."

"That bothered him?"

"Sure. The whole system bothered him. I mean, it bothers everybody. Not letting people be free. Not letting anybody change anything."

"I guess I didn't think things were so . . . dire." Edward shrugged. "Like the end of the world. So rotten."

"Maybe not so much rotten as not really . . . real," the boy said. "Does that make sense?"

"I don't know. This . . . here isn't real?"

"No. Not the way you'd want it to be."

"I guess I'll have to think about that." Edward stopped and then he said, "Listen, Jim. Don't take this the wrong way. But that really was the last time you saw him? Or Emily?"

"Yeah."

"Because you have a car, so maybe they would have asked you to take them somewhere. Maybe you just took them to the fair or something."

"I went to the fair. Four times. But never with them," and the boy looked deeply at Edward as he said this. "Machinery Hill. It's really cool."

"Tractors and combines? That interests you?"

"Sure. They're really cool."

Edward stood. "Well, it's very good of you to talk to me." He moved off the steps, and then he said, "Let me ask you one more thing. Where do you think they might have gone?"

The boy put his fingers on his lips. "Well, they could have *really* gone to California. Or to the woods."

"Maybe the woods in California?"

"I think those are more like mountains. And they have snakes. Bill doesn't like snakes."

"But those are the likely places. California or maybe the north woods. Maybe up near where he went to camp."

"I don't know about that. I mean, that was only up as far as Brainerd or something. I think he'd want to go further. Somewhere *really* up north."

"Like the Lake of the Woods?"

"I don't know. I mean really, Mr. Byrne, they could have gone anywhere. Or California."

"Same thing, right?"

"I guess."

Edward shook the boy's hand and went to his car, and the boy went back inside his house. His parents were not home, and he had wondered what he would have told them if they had been at home, or had come home while Emily's father was there. He might have told them Mr. Byrne was Mr. Byrne, or that he was a private eye, looking for these kids who had run away, about whose flight everybody already knew; or at least Monica had known and she had told her brother Mike, who had told Jim, oh, maybe two or three days ago.

*I*t was on the third night, the Thursday after the children had gone to the fair, that Jane called the man that used to be her husband. She was not much accustomed to making long-distance telephone calls, and when the phone was answered and the familiar voice answering sounded not much farther away than Minneapolis, she was caught a little off guard.

"Frank?" she said. "Is that you? It's Jane."

"Well. Well. Well," the voice said, deep and round and insinuating (Jane had always felt her husband was insinuating something, but had never quite determined what it was). "Are you out here, or back there?"

"Back here. But Billy's—this is why I'm calling—not. He's run away. We thought—I and the police and the parents of the girl he's with—he might go out there. To you."

"Jesus Christ. He's run away? Why?"

"I don't know. It's something they all just *do*. That's what the police told us."

"Well, Jane, they obviously all don't just do it. That's an exaggeration."

"The point is, he has, and he might come there. To you or somewhere out there. San Francisco or something."

"Jesus, Jane. I'm worried sick." Jane did not believe he was worried sick. She did not believe anyone in California was capable of worrying overmuch about anything. She pictured his house, his yard. The steaks on the grill. The salad on the redwood table under the cabana. The palm leaves crisping in the sunset, in the smog. The water lapping in the pool. The woman, fifteen years younger than Jane, lying beside the pool.

Frank's voice shifted from concern to annoyance (not, however, because he did not, in fact, have a pool or, at present, a girlfriend). "How did this happen, Jane? I mean, *where* were you?"

"I was in Chicago. No. I wasn't in Chicago. I had been in Chicago, at the convention. I came back. Everything was fine. And then a week later, he and his girlfriend said they were going to the State Fair and they just disappeared. Two days ago."

"How, Jane, could everything have been fine? Obviously things weren't fine, or they would not run away. It kind of defies logic, doesn't it?"

You, Jane thinks, defy my sanity.

"That's neither here nor there," Jane said. "The point is, they may come in that direction. They may even come to you. I want you to be aware of it. I would like you to be *helpful.*"

"You are the custodial parent, Jane. I'm just trying to point that out. That as such, you have some responsibility. *The* responsibility."

"Don't you dare tell me about responsibility."

The phone was silent. "Look. I'll keep an eye out. Of course. Maybe I should go to the police here. Alert them."

"The police here are supposed to have sent them the missing-person report."

"That's good. I'm glad somebody's on top of this stuff. And I'll do anything I can." His voice became soft, urgent. "I mean, I would die for that kid."

Jane said nothing in response, nothing at all. The triumph, the irrefutable retort of her silence, came down the line and crushed him more or less flat. Or Jane surmised. "Look," he said at last, "just keep me posted, okay? And vice versa."

"Sure," said Jane.

"And hey, Jane. I'm really sorry. Okay? You must be going nuts."

"Yes. I am. I mean, sure."

"Goodbye, Jane."

"Goodbye, Frank." Go to hell, Frank.

5

ON FRIDAY MORNING, AS IS HER CUSTOM, VIRGINIA goes to visit Emily's grandmother. She is Edward's mother but she could easily be Virginia's. Not when she was young, perhaps; certainly not when she was raising her children (which she did with a certain casualness Virginia's own mother would have found rather lax); but now, in her capacity as the repository of the past, as the white- and frizzy-haired sun around whom her grandchildren revolve like merry planets, as the venerable saint whose daily attendance at mass (until last year, when her hip went) and ever-ready rosary are quietly saving the world. This is who Virginia is going to lie to.

Virginia has not decided to lie when she enters her mother-in-law's house, but it is, anyone would have to admit, a good bet that she will. For Granny Byrne, within a minute of hobbling back to what she calls the "parlor," after settling herself in her chair and raising her feet onto the ottoman (which also serves as her desk and telephone table), will ask, "And how are the children?"

That—quotidian as the cup of Sanka Virginia will volunteer to brew for Granny Byrne five minutes into her visit—is the occasion of sin. The rationale for it is twofold, one very good reason and one very bad reason, whose intentions can only nullify each other, leaving the sin— which is itself no more than a nullity in motion, numskull privation staggering about its business like the walking dead—still a sin.

The good reason is that any other answer to her habitual query than "Fine—couldn't be better" would worry her; and the actual truth would probably kill her, Emily being her "special pet," her "Emmybug" and other such endearments which bespeak Emily's role as the Biblical sister Mary who sits at Granny's feet while Susan's Martha polishes the silver and slides a baking sheet of meringues into the oven for what Granny is still pleased to call "tea."

The bad reason consists of Virginia's conviction that she will be blamed: not simply for Emily's disappearance, but for an entire chain of faults and defects leading up to and away from it, starting with the fact of her being Emily's mother and ending with the fact of her not being Granny's daughter; of on the one hand being what will in ten or so years be called Emily's chief "role model," and on the other being the alien element in Emily's bloodline and thus the likely source of all things inexplicable or disagreeable in Emily's demeanor and behavior.

A decade later she may learn to believe that she finds herself in this position because she is a woman: mother, wife, and daughter-in-law. But it is too soon for that, at least for her. The closest she can come to it is the inkling that her position has something—perhaps everything—to do with her not being Edward, and of Edward's position in the world of being, vis-à-vis his family, responsible but not accountable; of being charged with providing for and protecting them without being held much liable for the net results, for how the children "turn out," for the burden of what will be their history.

That, she senses, is deeply unfair. Then, after Granny does indeed ask the question and Virginia does indeed tell the lie, while she is in the kitchen waiting for the kettle to boil for the Sanka, she reflects that the lie might need to be confessed. She imagines herself saying, "Father, I confess that my daughter ran away from home," and knows that the priest would offer her consolation for her predicament, not impose a penance. And it would go without saying that he would not ask her to avoid the occasion of sin. For the occasion of sin in this case is that of being Edward's wife; of being Emily's mother; of being, unlike Emily, the daughter who is Martha rather than Mary.

She knows Edward has his burden, but it is a burden that entails doing rather than, in her case, merely being—merely standing by as the agony of the cross is imposed—and everyone at the moment agrees that there is nothing to be done. So Edward gets off scot-free, while she—and Virginia notes this with an emotion heretofore almost unknown to her, bitterness—is pierced through the heart by a sword.

On Friday afternoon, at the end of the day, Edward found reason to drop by William's mother's apartment. For one thing, he had a little news—or rather a little more evidence for the conclusions they had already reached. For another, a woman who was facing such an ordeal alone, without (unlike him and Virginia) benefit of spouse, of family, of church, deserved a little support. For a third, he felt he could use a drink. On account of the heat, the length of the day and the toll of its labors, and the perpetual overcast of worry, fear, and longing; but also because of a novel sensation, a weight at the back of his throat, a shortness of breath, a hunger that was—what? He could not name it even as he felt it like a boulder in his gut—being able, really able, to use a drink.

This was something that Jane understood in a way that Virginia, he imagined, did not. It seemed to Edward that Jane's house was more or less consecrated to being able to use a drink; that where St. Luke's Church had a tabernacle for the Eucharist and 919 Furness had, say, a breadbox, 475 Laurel had an ice bucket. It was likewise furnished in the service of being able to use a drink, right down to the music Jane played, which evoked nothing so much as longing and need; right down to Jane herself, who in some way Edward could not yet put his finger on might very well cause one to be able to use a drink.

Jane answered the door and greeted him without apparent surprise. "Ted," she said. "Come in. Come into the kitchen. Let me fix you something."

"Gladly," Edward said. "With pleasure."

After they had gone down the hall and Edward had sat down and watched Jane busy herself with the lemon and the paring knife, with the ice and the gin, they began to talk. "I don't really have any news," Edward said. "I talked to Billy's friend, the Donnelly boy. Nice enough kid—a little vague, I suppose, but who isn't?"

Jane made no response, and Edward continued, "He just kind of confirmed what we'd been thinking: that nobody said anything about going off, that there was no particular reason they might have gone off, but that that was no reason for them not to. So they probably did." Edward sighed. "All very helpful."

Jane sat down opposite him and put his drink down in front of him. He took it, drank, and said, "Virginia talked to Emily's best friend. She didn't know anything either. But then they hadn't been talking much lately. Apparently she felt she had been thrown over when Emily got involved with Billy."

"Girls feel that way," Jane said. "With reason. A girl meets a boy and forgets all about her friends. Then, afterward, you realize one decent girlfriend is worth any six men you could find."

"That's rather sad."

"Well, I suppose it doesn't work out that way for everyone. But for me it did. Speaking of which, I spoke to Billy's father. No sign of them. But he said he'd keep an eye out, that he'd alert the police there."

"How did he react?"

Jane drank, and put down her glass. "I don't think he was really upset. He was more affronted. Put out. Which is exactly like him."

"I'm sorry," Edward said. "It must be awfully hard to go through this . . ."

"Alone?" Jane said. She smiled. "Still beats going through it with him. With Mr. Franklin Lowry."

"I take it you didn't part amicably."

"I wouldn't have wanted to. Then it wouldn't have been worth going through all the trouble to get divorced in the first place."

"Oh, I see," Edward said.

"Sorry. I'm sounding like Frances. She's *my* girlfriend," Jane said. "She—and you—have been getting me through this."

"Glad to help. I can't say that you haven't been getting me through it. You and your excellent G-and-T's."

"What about . . . Ginny?" Jane paused. "I mean, how is she holding up?" This secondary question seemed to both of them a hastily added and unconvincing addendum to the first, which was not really about Virginia's present state of mind but about Edward's current estimate of his wife. It was in this instant that they realized they had stumbled out onto the thin ice of intimate disclosure; and that, in retrospect, they had been there for some time. And if they were going to make a retreat, they had better do so now. For unlike flirtatious talk, which either party can declare to be nothing more than jest at any time without causing undue offense, the manner in which Edward and Jane had been speaking was premised on a certain interest, concern, and commitment to each other: to knowing each other and doing well by each other.

"On the whole, she's fine. And so am I," Edward said, and this was a shrewd response, one that both answered and diffused each of Jane's questions while honoring their underlying intentions.

"I'm glad," Jane said, and added, "Why don't we move out to the living room?"—this change of scene being her own contribution to easing the strain. It was, however, more of a regrouping than a retreat, a lateral move, although they did not know this at the time, any more than they originally understood the area upon which they had earlier trespassed when they first entered into it.

On the way to the living room, carrying their drinks, Jane picked up Emily's two letters to William from the hall table where she had left them after reading them over several times. She wanted to talk to Edward about them. They concerned the children—perhaps, properly interpreted, could even help find the children—and this was surely the real and legitimate ground of Jane and Edward's relation. It was imperative and wholly blameless to explore it.

Upon entering the living room, Jane thought she ought to turn over the record that had been playing just prior to Edward's arrival, and she went to the record player to do this. Having started the machine and adjusted the volume, she moved without thought towards the couch, her habitual music listening post, and only after rounding the coffee table and being within two feet or so of her perch did she realize that Edward was already seated there. She saw the problem in going forward with her original unwitting intention, but understood that the alternative—turning around more or less on a dime and moving back to the easy chair opposite him—was more awkward still. So she sat down next to Edward on the tiny couch.

"I've been reading Emily's letters to Billy," she said. "I hope it's okay."

"Of course. I don't suppose they're very revealing."

"Well, not about what they've done. But about each other, maybe." Jane extracted one of the letters from its envelope. "For example, she mentions Bobby Kennedy in both of them. That he could be for kids their age what JFK was to their older brothers and sisters."

"That's funny. I mean, that's just what Billy wrote to her."

"I guess they're just echoing each other. Thinking the same thoughts." Jane paused. "Of course, I was a little surprised to think that Billy was a crypto-Kennedyite. Right under my roof." She laughed and then she drank. "But you can see how it might make an impact on them. Even though he never got near to being president. I mean, everyone—everyone our age knows what they were doing, where they were, when they found out Roosevelt had died. And I suppose it binds us together."

"So where were you? When Roosevelt died?" Edward asked.

"I was at college. Back East. In a class. Comparative religion. Someone came in and gave a note to the professor. He said, 'The president is dead,' and said he was going to stop for the day." Jane stopped and drank. "We all went outside, mostly just standing on the grass, and we were all crying. Female hysteria, I suppose." Jane looked directly at Edward, and Edward saw there was a tear running down her cheek.

Jane suppressed a sob and cleared her throat. "I guess I haven't changed one bit. Not in twenty years. Still hysterical." Jane laughed, but it came out in a strangled tone, as though the laugh were being forcibly held down, underwater.

Edward said, "I don't think that's it at all. I mean, under the circumstances. With everything you're going through—"

"We're going through," Jane said.

"Yes. That we're going through," Edward said. "All of us."

Jane cleared her throat again. "So where were you?"

"When he died?" Edward asked. Jane nodded. "I was in Germany. Well, barely. They'd bridged the Rhine, but I was way to the rear of that. I was just waiting."

"And what happened? How did all these men react?"

"I don't remember any weeping. Just a lot of silence. Men just not talking."

"Maybe silence is the male version of hysteria."

"Maybe," Edward said. "I suppose maybe there should have been. Some of them were scarcely eighteen years old. He'd been president for pretty much their whole lives. It might as well have been their father or grandfather."

"And what did you do? Did you cry?"

"No. I'm sure I didn't. It's hard to explain. There was a war. And I suppose you just can't let yourself get carried away."

"Do you ever let yourself get carried away?"

"Me personally?" Edward asked. "Or men in general? I can't say. Not really. I can't say I ever really feel the need."

"Not even now?"

Edward had been lulled by the drink, by the tailing off of the afternoon, by their easy and somnolent wading through the past, through memory and crystallized sentiment. But he saw now that he and Jane were back in the territory they had broached in the kitchen, and deeply so.

It had heretofore always seemed to Edward that talking about the past was the safest of conversational refuges, that you could not get into much trouble reminiscing or being nostalgic, whereas the present— with its conflicts and tensions and differences of opinion all in progress, all real—was a minefield. Yet now the past, too, was treacherous; what history disclosed was as naked and galvanic as a kiss. It said not simply "This is how I was" but "This is how I am. Taste it."

Edward could therefore only try to change the subject, and he grasped the nearest matter to hand, the music that, by turns sweet and strident, was playing on the record player. It was to no avail, for art is just as raw and intimate as history, and perhaps is nothing more than history a little ahead of itself, the germ of it, its translucent, pulsing embryo.

"So what's this you're playing?" Edward said, and it was only after the fact that he realized that this could be misheard too; that it might be understood to refer to some putative motive or strategy Jane was pressing forward with, some kind of game that was afoot.

"It's Bernstein," Jane said. "Not just conducting, though. It's his composition, too."

"Called . . . ?"

"*Age of Anxiety.*"

Edward laughed, almost barked. "You . . . you really have a knack. I mean, considering everything . . ."

Jane now also laughed, at first politely and then freely, as though she had now peeked over the same fence as Edward and seen that everything beyond it was utterly absurd. "I suppose I do. I didn't even think of it. It's just the kind of thing I . . . like," she said with almost a snort. She rocked forward and back, laughing.

"Something light. To while away the hours."

"Exactly." Jane began to try to settle herself, to steer the talk away from levity. "But, I mean, really. It's . . . profound."

"Oh, you bet your life it is," Edward said, and roared with laughter, as did Jane. And as they rocked and hooted and gradually calmed down together, they might have fallen into each other's arms, in relief.

They did not, of course. They collapsed into their respective corners of the little sofa, and caught their breath. There was still something Jane wanted to say, and she persisted in feeling it was important. So she raised it, even though she knew that in doing so she risked their succumbing to a further bout of, yes, hysteria.

"I really am a great admirer of Bernstein." She also had the good sense not to refer to him as "Lenny," although this was her custom.

"He's very talented," Edward agreed, and without any visible sign of mirth.

"I think he's almost . . . the preeminent man of—no, not of. The preeminent man *for* our time. Do you understand? He's a symbol, he exemplifies, I don't know, all these qualities. He's a musical genius and he's popular and classical and he's active in politics and social change. He's suave and brilliant. He's a star. For thinking people."

"He's a Jew, isn't he?" Edward offered this not with any malign intent, but as a further remarkable fact.

"He's a *sexy* Jew." Jane had warmed to her subject, and having also been warmed by her gin, lowered her guard sufficiently to make it clear that this was the nub, the ground zero of Lenny's appeal.

Edward's guard was also down. He thought he had already steered clear of the shoals when he had gotten them away from the past, from Jane's tears. "It sounds like you'd make an exception to what you said about six men not being worth one girlfriend."

"For Lenny I would."

"Lenny? It sounds like you're already . . . on intimate terms with him."

"Oh, if only I were," Jane said, and they both laughed, not uncontrollably, but heartily. It seemed, just then, that if they could mock each other a little and discuss sexual attraction solely in relation to others, as cousins or brothers and sisters might, they would be safe, they would pass through and beyond this awkward moment like a bout of fever and come to rest on the far shore as simply friends.

But then Jane said, "I'll tell you something that's a secret. A little-known fact. Frank—Billy's father—is a Jew. Well, partly. Maybe a quarter or something."

"Really?" said Edward. "Lowry sounds like one of those ordinary names. English or Irish."

"That wasn't their real name. It was Lowen. They changed it."

"I see."

"And that explains everything about Frank. Pretending to be something he's really not, right at the core."

"But you didn't care?"

"Oh, he always insisted I did. That underneath everything else, it bothered me."

"But you knew? Before you were married?"

"Of course. So did my parents. It did bother them a little. Especially my mother. But beggars can't be choosers."

"Beggars?"

"Oh, my, yes. I was the beggar maid. We Burdens had fallen on hard times. And it was a good marriage, an advantageous marriage. Frank got what he imagined was blue blood and I got security." Jane paused. "I wasn't really raised to work. My mother, her sisters, me. We didn't have the slightest idea."

"But you do work. Now."

"Oh, after a fashion. But mostly I live on alimony, on Frank's largesse. Of course, he calls it blood money."

"That's a charming way to put it."

"He's a charming man. Why do you think I married him?"

They realized, in the way that people do, that the lull in the conversation which just then presented itself marked a natural and easy point of departure in which they might move to another room or mix another round of drinks or say their goodbyes. It was the latter course they took, and as Edward drove away he reflected that any unease he had felt within Jane's home was unwarranted; that he had escaped without harm or incident, and, in fact, had had a marvelous time.

$\mathcal{E}$dward chose not to mention his visit to Virginia when he got home. If you are a scrupulous sort, you might say this omission—the kind of convenient, self-deluding sleight-of-hand casuistry at which adolescents are so adept—amounted to a lie; that it was a lie with a twofold rationalization undergirding it, just like the lie Virginia had that very morning told her mother-in-law.

Certainly Edward believed that he was in some way sparing Virginia from pain or at least unnecessary distraction; and he also had the rather less altruistic reason of sparing himself from suspicion and a possible interrogation of his motives for once again choosing to take refreshment on Laurel Avenue. At any rate, he was doubtless right in assuming that announcing it to Virginia would not do much to improve the mood in his own home.

That mood struck him as soon as he opened his front door—struck him as tangibly as the cooler air of the interior of the house struck him—as almost a change in the barometric pressure. He found himself wanting to flee, and the sensation was not unlike the one that accompanied being able to use a drink. Here, in his house (all but paid for come next year), the fact of Emily's absence was glaringly, implacably present; that and his failure or incapacity to bring her back. The rooms stank of dread and impotence.

Yet there is nothing much to being an adult if not the ability to whistle past (or even through) the graveyard. So Edward passed through the hall and down into the kitchen, where Virginia was waiting for him like, he felt, the sphinx with the impossible riddle, the one that must be answered and in which the penalty for an incorrect answer is death.

Virginia stretched out her arm to him, to summon his kiss on her cheek, and then said, "Would you like a drink?"

"Not just now. I had one after work. With old Dr. Fields."

"Okay. I thought I'd just do some hot dish for supper. That all right?"

"Lovely. Wonderful."

Virginia moved to the refrigerator, to the cupboard, to the sink, and then to the counter by the stove. "I talked to Susan today. She was very upset. She volunteered to come home. To help out while this is going on."

"And you said?"

"I told her there was no point. That there were enough of us . . . standing vigil. That she ought to try to put it out of her mind. That we'd keep her posted."

"That's good. Good counsel."

"Then I went and saw Granny Byrne," Virginia said (and one may infer her relative equanimity from the fact she did not say to Edward "your mother"). "She's fine."

"Did you tell her?"

"No."

"Don't you suppose we'll have to? I mean, she'll expect Emily to come over sooner or later."

"Maybe. But maybe she'll come back sooner rather than later and there won't be any need to mention it at all."

"I'm afraid that might be wishful thinking."

"Well, if you want to tell her, I'll leave it in your hands." Virginia took a can of mushroom soup, propped it on the automatic opener on the counter, and slapped down the lever. The can spun, the opener whirred.

"Let me just think it through."

"That's fine. But we don't want her having a stroke or something. I don't want the responsibility for that, too, on top of everything."

"She's my mother. She's my responsibility," Edward said. "I'll take care of her. Like I do everything. Don't worry about it."

Virginia turned around, the can in one hand, the ragged-edged disk of the lid in the other, looking at him. " 'Like you do everything'?" Then she said nothing.

"I don't mean everything. I mean . . . the kind of things that I'm . . . responsible for."

"Oh, just those things." Virginia opened the door beneath the sink and flung the lid of the soup can into the trash. Then she said, "I'm not sure I wouldn't be perfectly content to do them. Instead of this." She gestured around the perimeter of the kitchen, as though to point out what a mess, what a state, it was in, although it was immaculate. "I don't know that I wouldn't prefer to chat with doctors all day and have nice *cocktails* with them. As opposed to being here. Waiting and waiting and waiting."

"This isn't by anyone's choice, Ginny."

"Or for relief, I can go over to Emmy's school and, say, break down in front of her teachers. Just fall apart. Or go over and play-act for your mother. Tell her lies."

"Look. I have a job. Nothing would please me more than to stay here with you," Edward said. "Not that it would do any good. But we still need money and groceries. That's a fact. So I have a job."

Virginia was scooping the soup out into a casserole with a big stainless-steel spoon. "You have a life. Outside this house. You can do something besides wait. You can accomplish things. Or at least distract yourself."

Edward moved a foot closer to Virginia. He lowered his voice and let his hands hang at his sides. "I can't do anything about what matters. It kills me. But I can't."

"I can't either. I can't even pretend it's not my fault."

"It's not anyone's fault."

"Maybe it should be. Maybe then somebody could do something."

"And who should that be? Me?"

"I don't know. I just think maybe something could have been done. To prevent the whole business." Virginia lifted the cover of a saucepan on the stove, saw that the water in it was boiling, and poured in a half-packet of egg noodles. Edward watched her do this, and saw that she did it with a kind of offhand grace or perhaps fastidiousness.

"I was the one who didn't like the look of him at the start," Edward said. "I told you that."

"But you changed your mind, didn't you?"

"I changed it partly because you seemed to think he was just fine."

"What was I supposed to think? Good family. The Academy. What was there to be wrong with him?"

"What would that have to do with anything? I would have thought his being Protestant would concern you a little."

Virginia leaned down to pull a colander from a cabinet, and still bent, looked up at Edward. "You're the one who puts such store in being ecumenical."

"Better that than some kind of . . . social register nonsense. Which we don't know anything about."

Virginia stood, holding the battered aluminum colander in her hands like a begging bowl. "You have to go on something," she said.

"They're not even really a prominent family. Not to speak of. The father's name isn't even real. He's a Jew."

Virginia regarded him with what seemed to him a faintly amused expression. "Does that concern you?"

"Not at all."

"So why bring it up?"

"I'm just saying, they—he—isn't what they seem. You could say we were taken in. Maybe you ought to feel better about that. That we gave them the benefit—"

"Why do you keep saying 'they'?"

"I just mean the family."

"Not much of a family. The boy and that . . . suffragette." Virginia set the colander in the sink. She went to the stove and gave the noodles a poke with her spoon.

"I thought you didn't mind her," Edward said.

"I didn't mind *him*, not her." She took the saucepan from the stove and poured the boiling water and the noodles into the colander. She was briefly shrouded in steam, and as it began to clear she said, "And I'd just as soon stop hearing how lonely and all-suffering she is."

Edward said, "I don't know that it's even something I've brought up.

And maybe her situation *is* a difficult one. Maybe it's not unreasonable to acknowledge that."

Virginia had a can of tuna in her hand, which she inserted into the opener, once again slapping the lever, sending the can carouselling around the machine. "It's not. But our concern—your concern—ought to be Emily."

"I think you really mean my concern ought to be you, just you."

Her back was still to him. She took the can and emptied it into the casserole and then she dumped in the noodles. She turned around and said to him, "I'm *not* feeling sorry for myself. I'm just quietly, slowly dying of worry. I thought you might care to notice."

"Oh, God, Ginny. Why do we have to do this? To make more problems where there aren't any?" He put his hands up, imploring her. "I know all of this. You know I do. You know how I feel. I know how you feel. But it doesn't change anything."

"Maybe it should."

"Should what?"

"Change things. Make a difference. Instead of doing nothing."

"I'm not doing nothing."

"I didn't say you were."

"That's the implication."

"Then it's in your mind." Virginia turned back to the counter. She stirred the contents of the casserole, opened the oven door, and pushed the casserole inside.

"I've done everything I can," Edward was saying. "I call the police every day. I prowl around the bus depot. I talk to these idiot teenagers. I come home and try to have a smile on my face and you just . . . ambush me. With this stuff."

Virginia turned back around, giving the dial of the kitchen timer in her hand a twist. "I'm sorry. I really am." Edward nodded to her. Then she said, "This is all going to drive us mad, isn't it? And there's nothing for it—to drive it off. Nothing. I can't even get myself to pray. To go through the motions of it."

"Maybe you could go talk to Father about it."

"That's not doing anything. That's just more biding time."

"It's only been—it hasn't even been a week. It could be over tomorrow. Just like that."

"Or never."

"You're despairing," Edward said. "This isn't you, Ginny."

"This isn't us. This whole business. But it's happening to us. Whether we like it or not."

"I know. I know. But you have to . . ."

"Have to do what? What? You tell me."

"I know. I know how you feel. Just bear with me. We'll do something. We'll manage. You'll see. Okay?"

"Okay," Virginia said. "I'll try. I'm sorry."

Edward nodded and with no small relief went to the living room and sat in his chair, the one adjacent to the big sofa where Virginia and the girls customarily sat. He took up the evening paper, scanning the pages blankly, not reading but looking out upon them, as though they were a view he was watching from the window of a bus. He lost himself a little in this way for about twenty minutes, and then he heard the kitchen timer ring, calling him to dinner, to his wife and their life together once more.

6

IT WENT ON FOR DAYS AND EVEN WEEKS, BUT DURING these times Edward and Virginia did indeed find moments of peace, of consolation, and some of them were with each other. They made love ten days after the children had gone, and afterwards, as they lay in the dark and the silence, they both felt a curious languor, as though they had never been lovers before; or perhaps had been once long ago. Maybe Edward had been away at war; maybe Virginia had been confined in a sanitarium with a debilitating ailment, a rare disease of the nerves.

But in the morning, and the mornings to come, it was the same: The very house ached from Emily's absence, seemed to be wasting away, did not so much breathe as shudder and wheeze. When Edward came home each afternoon he expected to see signs of dereliction: vines insinuating themselves through the doors and windows, blistering paint, shutters flapping on rusted hinges, a glaze of dust on the furnishings, strands of cobweb hanging from the fixtures and doorframes like phlegm.

Of course, it was not like that at all. The house was, if anything, more immaculate than usual, since Virginia had learned that even a moment of idleness invited despair, and so cleaned like a woman pursued by furies, which indeed she was. She took up attending daily mass, not because she had changed her mind about its accomplishing anything, but because it was one more thing to fill the day. She had learned, contrary to her expectation in the first week, that things did not get worse but stayed the same; and it was precisely in this way that they did get worse, without alteration or surprise or hope, resisting all surmise or speculation, pressing the inexorable conclusion that—since nothing, after all, did, could, or would change—Virginia's child must be not merely missing but, in fact, dead.

Edward's mind had not taken this turn, at least not yet, at least not in its waking state. Rather, he found the means to persuade himself that it was too early to conclude or assume anything at all, although this was in itself a sort of conclusion that kept more definitive conclusions at bay. He figured they were probably still in transit to California, or, if they had gone camping, were going camping for two weeks—for why bother to go on such a trip for only one? Later, he upped this to three weeks, and put this supposition to Virginia, to Jane, and, when they at last saw each other and Edward confessed what had happened, to old Dr. Fields.

It was the third Friday in September, and it was late in the afternoon. The doctor was refilling their Dixie cups, for the second time, and Edward told him the whole business, which he could now recount in less than thirty seconds.

"God, Ed, I'm sorry."

"It's been very hard on Ginny. On the boy's mother, too. It's bad enough not knowing where they are. Then you think, why?"

"I'd imagine."

Edward downed perhaps a third of the whisky in the cup in one pull. "So what do you think?"

"I don't have the slightest. It makes me feel very old and dull. I never heard of kids doing such a thing. Except for Huck Finn, I suppose." Fields took up his cigarette pack and took out one for each of them, handing Edward his without comment. Then he lit them. "During the Depression, I guess kids ran away. Poor ones. On the trains. Other than that, this is beyond my ken. What do the police say?"

"Nothing at all. I call there every week, and every week they have absolutely nothing to offer. No facts, of course. No theories either. Just that it's a sort of trend among juveniles. Jane—the boy's mother—thinks it has to do with politics, with thinking the whole society's crumbling with riots and assassinations and wanting to get back to nature, to innocence."

"For a cause? I don't see it. But what do I know? I can only think of . . . Hansel and Gretel, or some Grimms thing. Where the kids wander off into the woods and get baked into cookies or some such."

"Ouch."

"I'm sorry." Fields paused. "I do suppose it somehow belongs to the realm of the irrational. Just blind love, perhaps. Maybe this is just how kids elope now."

"I can't imagine they just wanted to get married. She's only sixteen."

"That's exactly my point. And surely there's some benighted place—Idaho or whatever—where they could legally get married."

"I suppose. But I don't think so."

"I'd still say it's all to do with love. Love and sex."

"Sex anyhow. We found out they'd been at it before they left."

"And you were surprised?"

"No, I guess not. Teenagers are just awash . . . in hormones. We should put saltpeter in their food. Lock them up when they're in heat. Except that's all the time."

"You don't think it's all just sex, surely?" said Fields. "Not in your own daughter's case."

"You mean that would dignify it? If she'd been feeling some noble sentiments towards this boy? I suppose. But then it just complicates things that much more." Edward inhaled and drank. "The idea that it's just stupid instinct is cleaner. It's like an infection she could get over, get back to normal afterward. But love—love you have to reckon with."

"I'm not terribly clear on the difference between sex and love. As distinct entities, I should say. Never could get that straight. Because I really can't help but believe it's always love—this complex, profound thing rather than this simple brute base thing—and even when people say it's just lust, just this itch that wants scratching, they're not being truthful: that it's something deep and frightening, and they don't want to look at it too closely. So when somebody says 'It's just sex,' it's really a species of love they're not prepared to admit to. Shamefaced love."

"This is all very . . . idealistic. For you." Edward laughed.

"But it's true." Fields smiled and quickly sipped from his cup. "I know about these things. Take a man with a prostitute, an ugly prostitute, if you want. It happens all the time. He reaches his climax and he calls out, 'I love you.' To this stranger, this wretch."

"It's just the heat of the moment."

"But then why say that? Just then? It's hardly a moment when one's likely to be calculating. Why not just grunt? Or tell her how dirty and low she is?"

"It's wishful thinking. It's pretending that it's love. To dress it up, ease the guilt."

"Why pretend? How could one cook this whole charade up when your whole central nervous system is going into a state of total . . . release? It makes more sense that, just then, we'd be inclined to call things by their real names."

"I don't see it."

"The guilt, if there's guilt, comes afterward. I'd agree it happens. Although maybe it's shame. Or embarrassment. That you did in fact love this person, just for an instant. That's what's a little unbearable about it: not that you just ejaculated into this person at a convenient moment, that maybe you used her, but that you did love her for an instant, and then you reneged. So you're ashamed. It strikes me that you should be. It's blasphemy, isn't it? To renounce love, to renounce God? Isn't that what your people say? Bishop Sheen or whoever?"

"I don't know. I'm not a theologian," Edward said. "I'm pretty sure the church frowns on sex with prostitutes."

"That's exactly what I'm addressing. Hypocrisy. Of the gravest sort. Hypocrisy against love."

"I'm not following this." Edward paused. "And that's kind of the point. Because my own experience doesn't jibe with any of this. Ginny and I met. We loved each other. And we had sex. All at the same time, the sex and the love, I mean."

"You said you'd been with prostitutes."

"Did I?"

"Yes, during the war."

"So I did."

"And you felt nothing for these fräuleins or Polynesians or whatever?"

"I wouldn't go that far. I don't know what I felt."

"I don't believe you. I think you're cheating me a little."

"I was very young."

"So much the better. For intensity. For sensation that leaves a mark."

"All right. I was . . . floored. Swept away."

"That's better," Fields said. "So you see. You communed with the beautiful. Nothing paltry about that. You wished for nothing more than that girl's total existence—for her to simply *be*. The fact of her and you. That's love. You were swept away. You felt the swoon, the swoon of liberty."

Edward sipped the last of his drink. "You certainly ran away with that ball."

"You don't believe me?"

Edward smiled. "How could I want to? It's too much."

"It doesn't matter what you want. Joe Louis, blessed be his name, said a very wise thing once: 'You can run, but you can't hide.'"

"So be it," said Edward. "It beats me."

7

DURING ALL THIS TIME, THROUGH THE END OF September and into the first week of October, Edward continued to see Jane. They had a certain routine. He came by perhaps three times a week, Monday, Wednesday, and Friday, and they had two drinks and sat in the living room and talked and listened to music. Normally he arrived around four-thirty and in no case left earlier than five-thirty; and this schedule put him at his own front door at about the same time he would have arrived there if he had not stopped at Jane's at all.

They had, some weeks before, exhausted the topic of the children, their whereabouts, and their intentions, and in fact, the main point of their meetings became the very avoidance of this topic. Although Edward continued to check in weekly with the insouciant and contemptible Lieutenant O'Connor—if only to radiate contempt and disgust back at him as best he could over the telephone—there was no news from this quarter and so nothing that bore mentioning. Thus freed (however temporarily, however uneasily) from the perpetual cares of the last month, Jane and Edward found they genuinely enjoyed each other's company. It seemed to Edward that they had finally become friends and that they could discuss even fairly personal matters without awkwardness, without untoward or bothersome sensations arising.

This may have come about, at least as far as Edward was concerned, because Jane was meeting him on a more equal footing, not as grieving mother or damsel in distress or flirty ingenue of a certain age, but as a chum, even as a teacher. For example, she taught him a great deal about music, and they often listened together. More and more they did this without speaking, for the music seemed to require it of them, and they had become easy enough in each other's presence to manage it.

Of late, Jane had put Edward onto the works of Gustav Mahler, and she did this as though initiating him into a Gnostic cult. She said of Mahler, "He is Beethoven for our time," and said this in deadly earnest. With equal intensity and rather more glee, after her second gin-and-tonic, she liked to say, "There is but one Mahler, and Lenny is his prophet."

Jane quoted Bernstein on Mahler, how his music "foretold all," the bomb, the holocaust, and all the rest, and this could not but raise the question of whether, say, the Fourth Symphony somehow foretold the disappearance of the children, or at least the world—California or the forest or the underworld—into which they had disappeared. Jane felt it did—that they had run away from exactly the horrors and repression of the present age. Against that, Edward had only Dr. Fields's stupendous notions about love—the erotic holocaust, the existential bomb—and his own about an extended camping trip, about the children getting waylaid at the Greyhound station in Elko, Nevada.

Yet Jane and Edward took comfort in the music too. In what it said in its brutal marches and tender adagios; and, with Jane quoting Mahler again, in the dilemmas the composer had said he was trying to address: "What did you live for? Why did you suffer? Is it only just a vast, terrifying joke? We have to answer those questions somehow if we are to go on living—indeed, even if we are only to go on dying."

Perhaps it was Virginia who most epitomized this last state; Virginia, from whom life was ebbing out each day, for she had lost her child and now it seemed she was losing her husband too. She and Edward might have been two castaways—heretofore strangers to each other—who found themselves washed up on the same island, sharing a common plight, behaving with courtesy towards each other, but helpless to effect any change in each other's condition. But because, of course, they did have a history together, had pursued a common purpose in tandem for twenty years, they could not simply amicably bide their time. Edward, deep in his heart, believed that Virginia must now hold him in contempt; and so she did a little—not, as he thought, because he was somehow failing to rescue Emily, but because he was failing to save the two of them; to believe in her and their life together. He had thought their marriage and family had survived by luck and by labor, whereas Virginia knew it perdured chiefly on faith; and Edward, because he could *do* nothing, had lost his.

Thus it was that Edward came to prefer Jane's company over Virginia's. He had no obligation to Jane—there was nothing in her home it was his job to fix—and so whatever he brought to her was purely a gift, freely given. Even his sorrow and despair were a gift, for they made no demands on Jane, save that she acknowledge their existence. By the same token, they spent many hours talking about Jane's life; about how, by virtue of her family's fallen position, her divorce, her failure to make either much of a career or a home—an entire life of doing the wrong thing for the right reasons—and now her son's abandonment of her, she was more or less spoiled, even rather ruined as a woman of any serious consequence or worth. And Edward heard these stories—for to him they were stories rather than problems in search of solutions—with sympathy and a certain pleasure that they should be confided to him. The pity of these stories, the very thing that was unbearable in Virginia, was endearing in Jane.

None of this need have precipitated a crisis. Certainly there are many storms in life that couples weather best by sheltering in the company of others (be they friends, spiritual or psychological counselors, or even unattached members of the opposite sex); and Edward was not such a fool as not to know that under the circumstances it would be easier to like almost anyone better than his wife. But he had not counted on liking Jane so well, or, in what initially seemed to be only an afterthought, on finding her beautiful.

By conventional estimates, Jane is not beautiful: She is what is called handsome, just as Emily is thought "cute" rather than pretty. In fact, in the opinion of most persons, she is not as beautiful as Virginia. It must be said that this thought has occurred to Edward more than once, and he has taken comfort in it, believing that this among other factors will prevent their relation from moving where it should not go. But beauty, as Dr. Fields has tried to tell him, is but one aspect of being, and love is another; and the apprehension of being is much the same thing as the apprehension of beauty, and in either case love almost inevitably must follow from it.

Certainly not all of this has been lost on Edward. As he sits with her, as the music plays, he is aware of what he might call her darkness. Where Virginia is chestnut or auburn, Jane is umber; where Virginia is blue (as in her eyes), Jane is brown; where Virginia is evenly sunlit, Jane is chiaroscuro. Like the music she favors, she is a little stormy and mer-curial, whereas Virginia is placid: Even her anger trickles in and out like a shallow tide. At the time he married Virginia, Edward would have described Jane as "trouble." But how much we change, or are changed, by the beautiful. Jane's problems are not Edward's problems—or rather they are the same problems, but independently borne—so why should she be "trouble" for him? He is not going to marry her. He is not, up until the moment he does so, even going to kiss her.

When he does, on the Wednesday of the first week of October, as they sit on the little couch, listening to music, perhaps midway through their second drink, he cannot even say how it has happened. It is like a manhole in the sidewalk upon which he is walking, whistling, hands in pockets, which opens where no manhole should be. He simply falls in feet first. It was not headlong. They were perhaps two feet apart, and what must have happened was that both of them happened to be lean-ing back, resting their heads on the back of the couch, and one or the other of them turned his or her head to the side and found the face of the other, waiting.

If a decision was made, it must have been along the lines of "Oh, well, what could be the harm?" But once the kiss was accomplished, it seemed more the result of a decision taken long ago; or of some inevitability they had quietly accepted months before. There was, as it were, a crack, a chasm in the ground they had been sharing all this while, and at some point they were going to tumble into it.

They pulled apart slowly after the kiss. Jane smiled at Edward and arched her eyebrows, which might be read as saying "Well?" or "What did you think of that?" or "Shall we continue?" Edward understood all of these possibilities and his answer to each of them was "Yes indeed."

He had not a moment of compunction about kissing her again, about beginning to touch her with his hands, and when that kiss was done, he wanted her as he had wanted no one since his wedding night. Curiously, it was Jane who hesitated, and did so on his behalf, if only in her mind. She wondered if he understood what he was getting into, but decided she could not be the one to weigh his obligations against her needs. She is, after all, the beggar maid. She is already ruined. Edward's ruination must remain Edward's business.

It is hard to believe that Edward at no point halted, at least for a moment, and considered what he was doing. This is not like him, almost anyone would agree, but his hands are already upon Jane's breasts, his mouth set upon hers as if he were going to swallow her whole. Jane's own hands have plowed down his back and now her thumbs are in his waistband, and it is easy enough, given the fashions of the day, for the thumbs and then the fingers too to find their way around to the front of Edward's trousers to where his erection already stands high and taut. One hand is grasping the shaft of his penis, and then the other is pulling at his waistband, tugging at him to rise from the couch and toward Jane's bedroom.

The transit from the couch to the bedroom might have afforded another interval to reconsider. But Jane is long past that. It has been four years since she has been with a man, and much, much longer since she has wanted a man as she wants this man, since she has felt the two tremendous weights bearing upon her as they do now, the one pressing the breath from her chest, the other pressing up and into her below, florid, heated, and thrumming.

As Edward follows Jane down the hall, one of her hands still in his waistband, he knows where he is going, but insofar as he thinks anything at all, believes he is already pretty much there. The lovemaking of the married (or once married) does not proceed like that of the adolescent, through gates and doors that may or may not progressively open to higher intimacies. Edward figures rightly that once their kissing became deep kissing and certainly once they were touching each other, their mutual intention was to take matters to their conclusion. That is not to say that Edward has no capacity for self-restraint at this point—that he is, by his own definition of the species, himself no more than an adolescent—but now he is in the hands of destiny, of a chain reaction launched on the little couch scarcely four minutes ago. If you could get him to listen, if you could get him to stop for an instant, and asked him, "Would you give up everything to penetrate this woman and ejaculate inside her?" he would say, "Yes." He truly would, just then.

Once in Jane's bedroom, they do not undress each other. There is no time for that. Jane is naked in fifteen seconds, her shift and bra and underpants fallen to the floor. Edward takes longer. He has shoes and socks to negotiate. They regard each other for a moment. Jane's breasts are freckled and dark-nippled, as Edward thought—hoped—they would be; Edward's shoulders are broad, his penis heavy and arced as she wanted them to be. She lies down on the bed and Edward maneuvers himself inside her and begins to thrust. They call out to each other. At the final moment, which comes in hardly more than a minute and a half, Edward hears himself say, "I love you."

*A*fter they were done, after Jane had pulled herself a little toward the head of the bed with her fingers still in Edward's hair, with him collapsed on his side, his body curled up and facing away from her, she thought, What was that? That we did? And she felt blissfully, girlishly happy, and she thought, I never want this to end. She wanted to put Edward in her bed and sleep with him there and then, in a little while, rouse him and have him fuck her again.

Edward was trying to collect, if not his thoughts, then himself. He saw he was indeed naked, lying on a made bed in a strange and shadowy bedroom. He saw his bare leg—cratered and flecked with pores, freckles, moles, and spots, pierced by coils and threads of hair—and that it ended with his foot, whose sock he had indeed removed, even in his haste. Beyond that, looking into the gulf past the end of the bed, there was a closet, half open, and on the door was a mirror. In it, at last he saw himself entire, and a little way behind him, the woman. She was looking down, perhaps at her hand, her face somewhat abstracted, sitting, one knee bent upward, and upon this she set her chin, and her dark hair swaddled her cheeks. He—the man—looked like he had crumbled here, as though he had been struck by a vehicle or simply shot. Together in the mirror, foreground and background, he in the shadow, she in the light, objects fallen together on this spot, in this composition, Edward saw they looked like a painting. He saw then that, from that angle, it might have been a scene of great devastation.

Edward regarded his watch. It was ten after five. He had ten minutes to dress, to say goodbye, and ten more to drive home, during which he might consider or construe what it was that had taken place and what he needed to do about it. He was not after the meaning of it. He had the feeling that this was a great event, a miracle or a catastrophe, whose occurrence subsumed all other meaning, that made everything else around it mean differently.

He turned on his side and looked up at Jane.

"Hi," she said, smiling. "How's tricks?" She didn't wait for an answer. She slid down to him, made her body parallel to his, and pressed against him. He could feel her breasts and the mat of her pubic hair, the first soft and yielding, the second coarse.

"I'm fine," Edward said. "Just fine."

"You ought to be. You're not just fine. You're magnificent." She slid her hand over his buttock. "I'd like to keep you here all to myself. Fatten you up and just . . . eat you."

"That'd be nice. But I'm fat enough and . . ."

"You have to go."

"I do." He put his own arm over her and held her a moment, smelled her, smelled them, and wondered whether this scent (for between Jane's wetness and his own flood of semen, they were nothing if not lubricious) would persist, all the way home. Then he realized that, against all reason, he was becoming aroused again.

Jane pressed her hips a little tighter against him, against his hips. "Seems like somebody else has a different opinion." She pressed again. "A strongly held opinion, I'd say."

"And well-informed, too," Edward said at last. "But I still have to go." He sat up. "I wish I didn't have to. But I do."

"Of course you do," Jane nodded.

Edward stood. He put his hands out in a gesture of inquiry. "I wonder if I could use . . . "

"Of course. On the hall, just to the right." Jane watched him walk away, naked, his fine body treading barefoot, delicately, across the wooden floor and into the hall. She heard him urinate and then water ran for a time. She thought she should not be naked when he returned; that although she would happily be naked with him all day and night, she did not want to be exposed, to be—she supposed—vulnerable, when he dressed, when he bent to tie his wing tips, in order to leave.

She had just pulled the shift over her head when he returned, gathering his clothes from the floor as he went to the foot of the bed. As he pulled on his socks, as he wriggled into his underwear and threaded his arms into his shirt and began to button it, she sat behind him, and as he did up his cuffs, she kissed him softly on the neck. He stood and pulled on his trousers, fastened his belt, and sat again to put on his shoes. She kissed him again, and asked, "You'll come again soon, won't you?"

"As soon as I can," Edward said.

They walked together to the door, and before she opened it, she hugged him and he kissed her in return, not on the mouth but on the cheek. He rested his cheek pressed to hers for a while, and, Jane thought, very sweetly for all that.

After he was gone, she went into the living room to collect their glasses. The record player had shut itself off, and she slid the record into its paper envelope and then into its sleeve. She carried the glasses and her ashtray toward the kitchen, and thought of what he had said as she was having her orgasm, as he was having his, no doubt, and wondered whether she had imagined it.

*E*dward might have skulked into his house, having carefully checked himself in the rearview mirror of the car for telltale signs, lipstick on his neck perhaps from Jane's nuzzling; then swaggered unnaturally, with forced and strained normalcy, into the kitchen, where with his dry lips he might have given Virginia the faintest of swipes across the cheek and then backed away, his hands in his pockets, his eyes missing no chance to avert themselves from hers. And because Virginia's whole consciousness was perpetually tuned to the frequency of their relation, to the weather inside the Byrne household (and also because she was nobody's fool), she might have sensed something amiss.

But that was not how it went, for Edward had a good talk with himself in the car, in the ten minutes it took him to drive home, and came to one conclusion: that he had claimed something, found something for himself, with Jane, and he might give it up or he might not. But as against Emily, as against Virginia, as against the career which he had never even bothered to assay for any point beyond a paycheck, this was his, and he was not about to set it aside without careful consideration. Even if, on closer inspection, it, too, turned out be nothing rather than something.

So Edward entered the kitchen with nearly a bounce in his step, as though he were the preordained victor in an unanswerable argument, full of righteous, almost jovial anger. He did indeed kiss Virginia lightly, but not for fear of giving something away, but because that was the sort of kiss he felt like offering. He dealt with her usual queries in offhand style, as though they were of no consequence, but he was perfectly happy to oblige her nonetheless. As she worked at the kitchen counter, turning this way and that in a light cotton dress, he regarded the contour of her breast, the concavity just above her hipbone. He thought of coming up behind her and resting his hand there; and then of lowering his zipper, extracting his stiff cock, lifting her dress, sliding down her panties, and taking her right there, from behind, as she slowly begins to bend, as she calls out to him, her palms and fingers splaying out on the edge of the counter.

Virginia turned again, and he saw her face and realized it was not Jane and that it was Jane that he wanted. He saw Virginia's face had fine and delicate features, that after all these years his wife was still pretty, but her prettiness bored him, as white linen and porcelain and Parker House rolls bored him. He wanted Jane's beauty, her dark and arcane beauty.

Sometime between then and dinner—pork chops with spinach and applesauce—it begins to dawn on him that the conclusion he arrived at in the car is mistaken; mistaken because it rests on an inoperable premise. He has pictured his life as a void he is going to fill with his own desires and devices—Jane chiefly among them—when it is in fact already full; he has a history, a hand dealt to him long before Jane, and it is both substantial and substantive. It will not exist easily alongside this new thing, nor will it permit him—assuming he could bear to do so—to simply choose between them.

This comes to him when, midway through dinner, he realizes that the meal Virginia has prepared occupies a special position in their history: It is his "favorite," and she serves it at least every ten days. It calls for some acknowledgment: It calls for him to like it, and to say so. But now it does nothing for him. Yet there it is. It is not nothing after all. It is not so easily displaced, even by beauty.

What an aching and weary thing is beauty, really, save in the instant of its perfect apprehension (at the moment, say, when Edward called out, "I love you"). The rest of the time it is tired to the bone, just like memory, dutifully enacting its rituals and quotidian chores, which are never quite caught up on. For there is altogether too much of it—too much past and not enough present to give it its due, too much loveliness and not enough love to lavish on it—and so we are always a little short; and that is the pity of so much of our lives.

Edward pushes away his plate an inch or two, and that is also part of what he does after a meal. Then he says, "Thanks for making that, honey. I always like that. It always hits the spot."

8

IF VIRGINIA SUSPECTED NOTHING, WE MIGHT SAY that Jane suspected everything: every ring from the telephone, every suggestion of a foot tread at her doorstep, every thing present or absent under the sun that might be a sign—and what, in love, is not?

Surely that is going too far: to say, scarcely sixteen hours after they first parted as lovers, that Jane and Edward love one another, are in love. If Jane were to seek the guidance of a professional (such as herself, in fact) the therapist/counselor would likely attempt to help her see that what she feels today is at best infatuation (albeit without exactly using that word), perhaps even pure sexual desire—lust (without, needless to say, using that word either)—which, mind you, under the circumstances is a perfectly normal, natural, and healthy response to her recent experience.

But Jane would not be having any of that. Assuming she had told anyone. Which she has not and will not (not even Frances) for the foreseeable future. Because this is hers, and she is damned if she is going to share it, parcel it out, pass it around like a bowl of Triscuits. And that is why she is going to call it love if she calls it anything at all; which she is not going to do at this point, for just now she is keeping it even from herself. She is not saying anything about it to herself, not in words. She is keeping it entirely in her heart, and there it sits, spinning.

Edward, too, is thinking along these lines, when he is not thinking the other thing: the one that struck him over his pork chop; that he is trying to make two different objects occupy the same space, and will come to grief for it.

Edward has stopped work early—he could not sell an ice cube to an

Arab in his present state of mind—and is driving up the hill at three-thirty to tell Jane this very thing. Or some other thing he has yet to determine. It will amount to "This is wrong and we have to stop," but first he is going to make love to her, one last time. He is hard already, in the car.

"You came," Jane says as she opens the door.

"I said I would. As soon as I could." Edward elbows the door shut and seizes Jane by the hips, pulling them together at the waist. He lowers his face into her hair, just above her neck by her ear, as though he is taking shelter there; as though bullies or demons have been chasing him, and he has evaded them only by slipping quickly through her door and bolting it fast.

Their lovemaking is not as hasty as the day before, but still pointed, purposeful. There is something akin to a backlog in their relation—the love they had not made on the day they met in the Medical Arts Building, and all the days thereafter until yesterday. Then, the following week, the lovemaking (and surely that was the right word, for if they did not love one another at the start, they did by the end) becomes aimless, which is to say truly loving; propelled not by desire but by its own internal gravity, its being, its own forward unmoved motion. They do things neither had ever done before or scarcely even thought of, things undreamt in the mind of Harold Robbins himself, as Frances would have said, had she known, which she does not.

Edward does not speak to Jane of the matters that are weighing on him that day or on succeeding days. That is not to say they did not make themselves felt. Every time Edward leaves—more or less five days a week, around five-fifteen—she knows she is only borrowing him from Virginia, from the woman he belongs to. Yet what they have, what they make, is to Jane's mind so much better than nothing or even the best of what she has had before that she does not begrudge this. The woman she was born to be—a woman like her mother at the start of her life—would not countenance this so easily; would probably find Jane a pathetic figure, sad and disreputable, living on the table scraps of another woman's life.

Jane knows who she is (she is the beggar maid) but she is not disgraced, but graced; gifted, because with nothing left, not even her only son, she has Edward Byrne for ninety minutes at a time, as long as he will come, as long as heaven allows; and it seems to her that they are their very own heaven, that this is what they make when they make love, so it might well last forever.

So it is, when Edward does leave, she is content. She straightens the living room and the bed. She takes their glasses and their ashtrays to the kitchen and washes them, and as she does so, she sings a song of Bernstein's: *We're neither pure nor wise nor good/We'll do the best we know/We'll build our house, and chop our wood/And make our garden grow.*

9

ONE EVENING, PERHAPS A WEEK AFTER THAT FIRST Wednesday when Edward and Jane had been together, Virginia said to Edward, "You know, darling, I can't help but notice you've been smoking more. I can smell it."

Edward said, perhaps a little too suddenly, "Well, what can you expect? Under the circumstances? I'm a little nervous, to say the least."

"Oh, I understand. And if you feel the need to smoke here, in the house, that's perfectly fine with me."

"That's okay. I don't really feel it outside of work. It's awfully hard to concentrate then. With these other things on my mind."

"Of course," said Virginia. Maybe she should have detected something more than this, if not by way of physical evidence (for Jane and Edward have taken to having baths together. He loves to soap her white breasts, their tawny nipples and aureoles) then by his demeanor. But this has, if anything, returned to a more characteristic mode, more like that of Edward before Emily's disappearance; more grave and taciturn, more preoccupied, but also more steady and unremarkable. He can even be cheerful, and he is affectionate toward Virginia. They make love with some frequency. Perhaps this defies expectations—that Edward ought to be consumed by guilt or find Virginia unappealing— but for the moment, libido has begotten more libido and love yet more love, or have at least made Edward adept at feigning them.

He is throughout all this time in a dream that feels as if he is awakening from a dream or breaking the surface of a pool in which he has been for a long time submerged; coming into consciousness, jarred awake and into action. And it was then, in mid-October, that Edward told Jane and then Virginia, "I think I'm going up north this weekend and see if I can find anything out about the kids. Put up some flyers. Ask some questions. I know O'Connor would say it's pointless. But it's better than waiting for the police. It's better than doing nothing at all."

Edward feels—as he has always felt—that he and Emily have a special connection, and that he ought to know her mind and its reasoning; know it better than her mother or her sister or her friends; certainly better than the police. He ought to be able to find her.

He also feels in a curious way that he understands the boy's mind too: by spending time among his things; by recollecting the kind of boy he himself was; by, perhaps, making love to the boy's mother.

All this solidified into a hunch, if not quite a conviction, that the kids had gone north, into the lakes and woods, where both of them had once gone to camp. He had another hundred copies of the missing-person flyer duplicated and he planned to distribute them around the border country of the north-central and northeastern part of the state. The police and sheriff's offices, of course, already had them; have done, of course, nothing about them. Edward would go to the grassroots, to the bulletin boards of post offices, cafés, and grocery stores.

He left that Saturday morning before dawn and by nine o'clock he was in the country beyond the head of Lake Superior. By ten-thirty he had made three stops—a post office and two coffee shops—and he was feeling pleased with himself. When he asked if he might post a copy of the flyer, people of course said yes; were indeed deeply solicitous, helped him out with thumbtacks and offered him coffee. Edward was pursuing a good cause, and it made people feel good to help him further it. By lunchtime he had had a day's worth of coffee, and distributed fourteen posters.

Edward had not bargained for the fact that a good portion of the businesses—bait shops, boat rentals, motels and rental cabins, three-point-two beer and burger bars—in this part of the world had already closed for the winter, their owners departed for warmer, more lucrative climes. The farther he drove north and west, the emptier the country became until there were fifteen or twenty miles between one disconsolate post office/filling station and the next. These were perfectly agreeable about posting his flyer and volunteering that, no, no one had seen anyone or anything related to the kids, but they sure wished him all the luck in the world.

But as he went on into the afternoon, as he penetrated deeper into a land the rest of the world seemed intent on fleeing, he wondered if he was merely an object of pity. Both Virginia and Jane had visibly warmed to him (were in fact more ardent) when he told them his plan, and he had passed not a few minutes of the day's driving lost in erotic fantasies of him and Jane. But now, as the population thinned and the woods grew thicker, there was less and less to do; it was harder to escape the aimlessness and even futility of the course he was embarked upon.

He wondered what the waitresses and filling station attendants and postmasters who took his flyer, who looked at him with a deep gaze of compassion and then seemed suddenly to avert their eyes from him, truly thought of him: if they wondered what sort of man it was who could not keep a sixteen-year-old at home, by force if not by pure affection; whose hearth was so cold, whose fatherly gravitas was such thin gruel, that she would prefer to shelter here, where pretty much no one wanted to be.

By the time he was just fifty miles southeast of International Falls, he had had enough. It was six o'clock and the sun was going down. He had stopped at a filling station/café/post office/trading post (this last indicated by the availability of beer, fish lures, automobile deodorizers, and jerked meat products) at the junction of the highway with a dirt road leading to a place called Lac La Cache, twenty miles distant. There were two men inside, one evidently the attendant/postmaster/cook, and he began to say what he had by now said three dozen times that day.

"I'm wondering if you could put this up on your board," and here Edward held out the flyer. "We're looking for two kids. One of them is my daughter, actually. We think they might have come camping up here. Late in August or early September."

The man behind the counter looked at him in the way people had been looking at him that day. "Gee. You mean they're missing? Maybe got lost?"

"Yes. Maybe someone saw them."

"Well, I don't know of anyone. Of course, it's late in the season. Not much of anybody around. And they've been gone all this while?"

"Well, this is just one place they might have been."

"So they might have gone some other place? You don't know?"

"Not exactly. But this seems likely."

The other man finally spoke. "Oh, so it's like they ran away. Or they didn't say where they were going."

"Yes. It's like that."

The man behind the counter looked at the flyer. "Girl looks awful young to be on her own." Edward nodded, and the man addressed the other. "You seen anyone up at La Cache, Arnie?"

The other man took the flyer in his hand. "Now let me have a look-see here," he said and studied the photograph. He said nothing for a time and then shook his head. "Seems to me there were a couple of kids end of the summer"—and here he paused again, and Edward moved a step closer to him—"that hitched a ride in with Fred Peterson, came into my place. That's Nelson's. I got a little store up the road here at the lake. Said they were going canoeing or something."

Edward could not but interrupt. "Who's this Peterson? Is he around? Do these look like the kids?"

The man behind the counter spoke first. "Fred's away. Until next month. Down in the cities. Don't know exactly where."

The other man, whose feral aroma Edward had begun to take note of, continued to look at the flyer and then shook his head again. "I don't know," he said, saying this in a tone less of wonder or ignorance than of indecision about whether he ought to bestow a favor or make a discretionary purchase. Finally he said, "No, I don't think so."

"You're sure?" asked Edward, his heart collapsed into his stomach. "You're sure?"

"Yeah," the big man said. "Those kids were meeting up with their folks. They said so. Bought some supplies. Some candy. And that was that." He looked at Edward and shrugged. "Never saw 'em again. Sorry." He stepped away from Edward. "Wish I could help. I truly do."

"Well," Edward said, "thanks all the same." And then he turned to the man behind the counter. "Maybe you could get this Mr. Peterson to have a look at the poster when he gets back."

"Oh sure. Anything we can do, we'll do 'er."

"Thanks very much," Edward said. "We appreciate it."

"Oh, no problem. Least we could do."

The big man nodded, and said, rather loudly, "You take care now."

Outside, as Edward went back toward his car, it was full dark. The moon was up and the stars had yet to begin filling in the sky. In the distance between the door and the car—ten yards—you might almost have gotten lost in the shadows and the rising chill. Edward walked a little farther, towards the place where the dirt road to the lake met the highway.

He stood and looked down the road into the darkness; across the open field—cleared decades ago by someone foolish enough to believe he could farm here—to the great wall of the forest rising in the north, a blackness always three shades deeper than the gathering night. Somewhere, beyond it, was Emily.

He now believed this with almost perfect conviction, and at the same time saw the impossibility of finding her in that immensity, in a country without light or limit. He thought there ought to be the sound of crickets, the pulse of the summer night, but it was too late for that. There was nothing but a little wind, and that was distant, far off in the trees. He bowed his head and cocked his ear and thought he heard voices in it, the singing of loons or perhaps the howling of wolves. He listened and for a moment he might have started to call back, to howl Emily's name, but he merely began to weep.

Edward shuffled back across the gravel in the direction of the car and the amber flare of the windows of the store. He had thought his pain could set these woods ablaze, because there is so much of them and he wants so very little and would give up everything he has for it. But he is even paltrier than he imagined; and he is asking something from what, for all its infinite starlit desolation, is nothing at all.

He has planned on driving on to International Falls and spending the night there, and then heading back in the morning. But he steers the car southward, homeward, for the next five and a half hours. When he stops weeping, he thinks about the three women in his life, and how he misses them; how he feels tenderness and different species of desire for each of them; all of which might be called love, but most of all loss—of what he has already lost, is losing even now, and will yet lose.

Edward comes home a little past midnight, and when he gets upstairs to the bedroom, he sees that Virginia is sitting up in bed; that the sounds he has made in the house, so late and unexpected, have frightened her.

"I couldn't stay up there. Out there. All night, I mean."

"So there wasn't anything?"

"Not a sign."

Virginia patted the spot on the bed beside her. "Come sleep. You were very good—very brave—to go up there and look."

10

IT WAS NOW THE THIRD WEEK OF OCTOBER, AND there was no pretending that summer was not over. The gutters of the streets were filling with leaves, and as Edward walked from his car to Jane's door, the long and stark shadows of autumn fell upon him. His and Jane's lovemaking seemed also to have changed rhythms, to be less characterized by sheer ardor and, it must be said, playfulness than by the need to keep warm, to sustain one another against the coming days, the lengthening nights. Sometimes they would lie in bed a long time simply curled together, and although sooner or later Edward would enter her, perhaps as they lay on their sides, face to face or with Jane's back to Edward, and they would rock one another to climax, it was as a tiny shudder in their napping, in the long winter's rest they were sleeping.

One afternoon, on yet another Wednesday, they were sitting in the living room, drinking (now scotch-and-water rather than gin-and-tonic) and smoking cigarettes. They were listening to a Mahler song cycle, which Jane called merely "The Mahler Songs," thinking it was perhaps better to leave its true name unsaid. She had played it for him more than once, and Edward thought it was pretty and sad, dark in the way that Jane herself was dark. They were not listening with any great attentiveness. For Edward to make out the words—assuming he even could do so with his rusty German—would have been laborious, and the point of Edward and Jane's time together was not labor but solace and rest.

Jane asked him, prompted by nothing in particular, "Do you still think about why they did it? I mean, their reasons."

"Not really. It doesn't really seem . . . either here nor there anymore. Not germane."

"But it was all you thought about at first, wasn't it?"

"I guess so. Why they did it. How they *could* do it."

"To us. Funny. It sounds kind of selfish. On our part," Jane said. "I mean to be more concerned with how they could *dare* to do this to us than with their welfare."

"I wouldn't say it was quite like that. It was more shock. Befuddlement."

"And now?"

"I don't know. But I care less. Not about . . . them. About knowing. About understanding. I mean, didn't they know how we'd worry? How we'd suffer?"

"I don't think," Jane said, "it's a matter of their knowing. I think maybe they can't even imagine it—that we're even . . . vulnerable that way. That's not how we seem to them. If you think back, imagine yourself thinking that your parents or your teachers or all these other grown-up authorities were privately going around weeping or being confused or insecure. Instead of being totally composed and assured. It would just have been beyond your ken."

"I guess."

"I had the strangest thought a while ago. I was thinking about demonstrations like the ones I've gone to. And they have them outside the White House all the time, and people are chanting, 'Hey. Hey. LBJ. How many kids did you kill today?' "

"Very articulate, that one."

"It's simple. Maybe even a little crude. In order to make a simple point," Jane said. "Anyway, I thought, how does Johnson feel when he hears them saying that? About him? Does he hear it and wince? Does he lie awake at night crying? I can't imagine that he does. I'd love to think he does, but I just can't see it. But who knows? Maybe he does. But you just can't picture a man in that position feeling anything."

"So that's how you think the kids see us?"

"Similarly, yes."

"That's very sad. For all of us."

"But at least you can make yourself believe they really don't intend any harm."

"I suppose." Edward put his arm around Jane and squeezed her shoulders. "They've done what they did. What they had to do. And I guess nobody ever intends any harm. I don't."

"You couldn't hurt a fly."

"That's debatable."

"You're sweet as can be."

Edward cocked his head towards the record player. "*This* is sweet. In a sad way."

"The song? I suppose. It's as sweet as things get these days. When they're sweet at all."

"So what's it saying?"

"You tell me. You're the German scholar."

"Scarcely. And I bet there's a translation. On the jacket notes."

"Try it anyway." Jane went to the record player and moved the needle back to the beginning of the song.

"Okay." Edward screwed up his face as though this would in some way increase his comprehension, as though he might suck in the words like a strand of spaghetti. What he heard, at least in part, was this:

Oft denk' ich, sie sind nur ausgegangen!
Bald werden sie wieder nach Hause gelangen!
Der Tag ist schön! O, sei nicht bang!
Sie machen nur einen weiten Gang!
Jawohl, sie sind nur ausgegangen
Und werden jetz nach Hause gelangen!
O, sei nicht bang, der Tag ist schön!
Sie machen nur den Gang zu jenen Höh'n!
Sie sind uns nur vorausgegangen
Und werden nicht wieder nach Hause verlangen!
Wir holen sie ein auf jenen Höh'n!

Im Sonnenschein!
Der Tag ist schön auf jenen Höh'n!

"It's something about how 'They've only gone out for a little while, for a walk, in the beautiful hills, and they'll be home soon.' That's about it."

"Not bad," said Jane.

"So now tell me. What the translation says. To see how I really did."

"Okay." Jane took the notes out of the record sleeve and laid the sleeve back on the floor. Then she read, " 'I often think they have only gone outside and soon they will come home again. It is a beautiful day, do not be anxious. They have only gone out for a long walk. Really— they have only gone out and they will be coming home now. Do not be anxious, it is a beautiful day. They have only gone for a walk in the mountains. They have only gone out ahead of us, and they do not want to come home again. We will find them, up there in the sunshine. It is a beautiful day up there.' "

Edward said nothing and then he asked, "So it's about . . . ?"

"Children. Mahler's children, I suppose."

"And do they come home?"

"I don't exactly know. It's a poem, not a . . . newspaper story. But it's hopeful, isn't it?"

"I suppose it is. Very apt. For us."

"And like Bernstein said, 'Mahler foretold all.' So maybe it's a sign— don't be anxious. They're coming home."

"It would be nice to think so," said Edward. "So let me see." He took the sheet from Jane's hand. He glanced at the top of it and saw the title. He looked at Jane and said, "This is about dead children, Jane." He felt that a very cruel trick had been played on him. "I mean, you have a knack for these things. But this is a little close to the bone." He handed her the sheet. "It really is."

Jane looked distressed, in the way she might have looked distressed many, many years before, before they were all ruined, as a child. She said, "They're only songs, Ted. I thought you might think they were beautiful."

"I guess they are. But what did you think I'd think? How was I supposed to react?"

"I wasn't thinking of the title. I was thinking of the words. The part that says they're coming home. I thought it would be a sort of . . . consolation. Art can be a consolation, can't it?" Jane had begun to cry, silently, two paltry tears running down her face. "It wasn't meant to be, I don't know, a prediction."

"You just said, 'Mahler foretold all,' " Edward said. "Or did I hear that wrong?"

"I wasn't thinking of it that way. I just thought we could share it together. Like all the other music."

"So did you want me to cry? Or what?"

"I never thought about any of that."

"So maybe you wanted to me to cry? Like LBJ or somebody?"

"God no, Ted."

"So what did you want?" Edward stopped. "What is it you *do* want? You and your art and your sexy conductors? From me?"

"Just to go on. Like we have been. Together." Jane had now begun to sob, but she was able to add, "Is that so much?"

"Go on together. Contemplate the beautiful and the true. You think this stuff is so important and profound, but really it's just a lot of show, a lot of sentiment. Like the idiotic stuff the kids wrote in their letters. Like their silly poems." Edward looked at Jane. "You want me to be serious. This music says the kids are never coming back. I suppose that's what it boils down to, isn't it?" said Edward, looking away from her, up and behind him; glaring at the framed print on the wall, the winter cityscape, the dirty snow. "That's not pretty. That's just cruel. To me, at least."

After a long silence, Edward heard Jane say, "As though you had the right to say that. As though you knew. You make one pathetic day trip up there to look for them and you think you can moralize at me. As though you were the martyr in this."

Edward turned back and faced her, although she was crying silently now and looking down at her hands. Finally she said, "Let's just pretend I didn't say that. I didn't mean it. I got upset." Now she was looking at him straight on. "Because really, this is all we have now." She halted. "Or at least all I have."

Edward felt himself possessed by a great sense of purpose, although he could not say whether it was impelled by courage or fear. He said, "I can't do that, Jane. I can't pretend that, even for you." He found himself rising, getting to his feet. "I have to go now. I really do."

11

EDWARD KNEW, AS SOON AS HE BEGAN TO DRIVE, that he was giving up Jane, even if he did not know quite how this was going to happen. Nor could he say he was going to do it for Virginia, or even for Emily: It seemed to him that he had been in flight when he and Jane had come together and he had taken shelter there, and now he was in flight from that refuge; and what drove him on, now as then, was self-preservation, perhaps sheer terror.

He wondered what the mechanics of extricating himself consisted of. Could he simply stop going to Jane's, or did he have to make a speech? And if the latter was necessary, was it necessary for his sake or for Jane's? Was it necessary simply because it was the right thing—the fair or perhaps noble thing—or because he owed it to Jane; because, in fact, he loved her—and if that was the case, why was he doing it at all? But that was the labyrinth which he was attempting to flee, and to examine it further—to try to parse the grammar of his and Jane's love— only made him more lost.

He called her the next afternoon from a pay phone at the state hospital in northeast Minneapolis. When she answered, he thought of mentioning this fact by way of lightening the mood, but that was scarcely his purpose. He quickly told her what he had decided, and she said, "Well, I'm not surprised. I suppose I've been expecting this."

"I hadn't. Not really," Edward said. "But it seems the only way."

"That's how it seems." Jane paused, and said something, and she herself could not say whether she said it out of spite or rancor, or simply as a statement. "You know, I never once asked you to leave her. Or even if you'd thought of it. Not once."

"I know."

"I suppose that was rather kind of me, wasn't it?"

"Don't get into this now, Jane. For your own sake."

"And I won't ask you if you love me," Jane said. Edward thought he heard her sigh, but that might have been the noise from the wards, from the patients flailing in their agonies of loss—of seeing into too much too clearly—floating on their chains of Pneumanol. "I know anyway. You said so once."

"I guess I did," said Edward. Then he said goodbye. He had a long drive home. He had done the first thing. Now he wondered about the second thing: about what if anything he needed to do in relation to Virginia, and in particular whether he ought to or needed to tell her. He wished he could talk this over with someone, and he knew that there was no one suitable except Dr. Fields. But that would mean admitting that Fields had been right: that Edward could indeed love so suddenly and so deeply, and then just as suddenly, just as deeply, forsake it entirely. He had supposed he would be and ought to be ashamed of himself for what he had done with Jane, and for many reasons, but not, until just now, for this one in particular.

*A*fter she had talked to Edward, Jane went and sat on her bed, sitting upright with her feet on the floor, looking down, supporting herself with the palm of her right hand. Then she patted the bed once or twice, as if she had just finished making it up and was smoothing the coverlet. Although there was a telephone right there in the bedroom, she went to the kitchen, to the table, and sat down and called Frances.

"I was wondering what became of you," Frances said.

"Come over. I'll tell you everything. About my adventures."

"In Wonderland?"

"Through the Looking-Glass."

When Frances arrived, they circled the matter at hand for a little while. Frances said, "Well, I was rather beginning to think that you'd really done it: that you'd really gone to Canada. Or gone off to join Billy in San Francisco. If that's where he is. I don't suppose you've heard anything?"

"No. But I'm beginning to think they had the right idea all along. But I suppose I'd better stay here in case he changes his mind and comes back."

Frances let a suitable pause elapse. "At least until the election."

"You come over. We'll watch the returns. We'll fortify each other."

"You root for Humphrey. I'll root for Nixon. It's not like we'd be on opposing sides."

They went back to the kitchen, and Jane made drinks. After they were reasonably tight, after they'd agreed that a girlfriend was worth any six men, Jane told Frances everything. They finished the evening in the living room. Jane went to the record player and put on *Candide*, the very last song. She sang along: "We're neither pure nor wise nor good/We'll do the best we know/We'll build our house, and chop our wood/And make our garden grow."

Jane put her hands on her hips and turned towards Frances, a little unsteadily. "It was our song. He didn't even know it. But it was."

*I*t took Edward four days to decide to talk to Virginia. He was not sure he was going to tell her about him and Jane, not exactly. But he needed to talk to her, to speak about things that were out of the ordinary: to tell her that he loved her. He had no doubt that he did, although it was undoubtedly not the same love as had been there before. It was not seamless, no longer twenty uninterrupted years of mutual regard not unlike, say, twenty profitable years in business together, serving the public while growing ever more content and comfortable. Nor, as he looked at her intently for the first time in nearly a month, could he say she was beautiful in the way he once would have said she was: prettier than Jane. For the whole of the autumn had taken its toll, from the last day of the State Fair onward, and there was gray in her pretty auburn hair, which itself seemed thin and drawn, like her face, like her arms and ever fretful hands.

But he had determined to speak to her that evening, the last Sunday in October. He had rehearsed it. He had even spoken the words out loud while he drove the car that morning to the hardware store to fetch a new catch for one of the storm windows he was just finishing hanging.

He went into the kitchen and faced her across the counter. He smiled and prepared himself to begin. And, as it will do whenever a man is trying to effect something crucial—as it did for William and then for Emily five months ago, just before the crest of summer—the telephone did something untoward. In this case, it rang.

Virginia went to answer it. She listened for a while, and then she smiled and held out the phone to Edward. "It's a sheriff's department from up north." She beamed. She offered him the receiver like a trophy. "They have news about the kids."

With that, his chance was lost, and he never did try to raise the matter again. It returned to where it had begun, to the chasm in his life into which he had that one time fallen, although it was scarcely forgotten.

It is said—perhaps in one of William's books, perhaps in one of Jane's Mahler compositions—that the nothingness that reveals itself in agony is not a nothingness that is part of being, but a break in being, a crack in the existent. So that is Edward's agony and that is where it rests, in the crack where this love came from, where its memory still lives. He will always remember it, if not at all times. It will be among the things he thinks of while he waits at stoplights, the things that in their enduring absence give him pangs.

But now, as Edward takes the telephone, it seems they are all going to get their lives back; not their old ones, unaltered, of course, but lives that can be reasonably and even sometimes happily lived. They are going to know what happened to the children: what they did, if not why they did it. And they will have all the years that have been allotted to them in the future to decide what to make of it. All but Emily, and who can say what she might have thought?

Three

The

Briar

Wood

1

EMILY HAD GOTTEN ON THE NUMBER THREE BUS at a little before six, just after she mailed her postcard. William boarded four minutes later, opposite the Lawton Steps. He hoisted a green duffel bag up the steps, paid his fare, dragged the bag behind him through the aisle, and sat down next to Emily.

"Hi," William said.

"Hi," Emily replied.

He leaned close to her and whispered in her ear, "I love you."

"I love you too," Emily whispered back to him. Then they held hands, saying nothing as the bus rolled down the hill, into the rising blue of the morning.

They had agreed they would board the Greyhound (final destination: International Falls and Fort Frances) separately, although this was a precaution that was scarcely necessary, for on this day there was a larger than usual complement of young people passing through the depot and traveling by bus to and from home, camp, vacation, school, or visits with friends and relations. Two more—neither remarkable, save that William might pass for college-age while Emily looked sixteen at a stretch—traveling separately or together would not make the slightest impression on anyone.

Nonetheless, should anyone ask, they were brother and sister and were meeting their parents and younger siblings at Crane Lake for an end-of-season family camp-out. The rest of the family was already there. They had been finishing up their summer jobs in town and were thus joining Mom and Dad, and little brother and sister, a few days late. They would be bringing more supplies, and Dad—having decided this was a piece of equipment they really needed in their vacation arsenal—had given them money to buy a canoe in the nearest town, and they were to paddle it out to the campsite. Such enterprising, trustworthy, reliable children, anyone hearing this story would doubtless remark. Such a credit to their parents.

Emily and William sat five rows apart and tried not to look at each other. They tried to read. William had brought a novel by Herman Hesse and its narrative had sufficient appeal to absorb him for some minutes at a time. But Emily had brought poetry—Gerard Manley Hopkins and Hart Crane, whom Sister Mary Immaculata was going to be teaching that fall, whom she would therefore be missing out on—and she was not making much sense of it, neither on its terms nor hers. Her present terms were, of course, scarcely terms at all, so unformed and unfamiliar were they: They might as well be traveling to California, to the south pole, to the dark side of the moon. They were on a wilderness expedition. They were homesteading on the frontier. They were fleeing for their lives.

Emily wished she could sit with William. He, after all, knew why they were doing this and where they were going. But as the miles passed, as the fields and farmhouses gave way to mining country and the desolation, after many hours, became studded here and there with pines and birch and finally patches of deep forest, that mattered less. She was afraid, and yet her mood was not unlike what it would be if she had simply been returning to this country again for another session of summer camp: This, she thought, is going to be fun. Why should it not be? The forest was a curtain behind which they might disappear and do exactly what they wanted. And then she felt herself positively excited.

The bus stopped for lunch some sixty miles south of International Falls, at a roadside café, and it was here that William and Emily got off for good. They ate their lunches at the counter, their bags at their feet, still sitting apart, finishing before most of the others. They left the café, turned into the county road that ran behind it, perpendicular to the highway, walked one hundred yards, and stopped, standing together at last.

This was the part of their journey that William was most concerned about: the twenty miles to the water, to the end of the road, to Lac La

Cache. They were either going to have to walk it (with William dragging the heavy duffel bag behind him) or hitchhike, and perhaps risk questions, suspicion, and discovery. But walking seemed impossible—could they manage even half a mile?—and at the sound of approaching wheels on the gravel, William thrust out his thumb, and the pickup truck stopped.

The driver, a middle-aged man in a white T-shirt, flung the door open and said, "Where to?"

"We're going to Lac La Cache."

"Oh, Lac La Cache," the man said after a momentary pause, having flattened the word William had pronounced along the lines of "lock" into a firm "lack." "Not much of anyplace else to go on this road. Well, put your stuff in the back and climb in."

With some effort, William shouldered the duffel bag into the cargo box of the pickup, and pitched in Emily's somewhat lighter bag after it. Emily climbed into the cab and then William, although William wished it were he and not she who was sitting next to the driver. He felt, correctly, that Emily's youth and sex were more likely to attract notice. So when the driver, having released the clutch and set off, spoke, William was sure to preempt any reply from Emily.

"So, going camping?"

"Yeah," said William. "With our folks. They're already up there." William completed the rest of their story, including the purchase they were to make, figuring that would forestall other questions.

"A canoe," the man remarked. "Betcha Nelson's ought to make you a good deal this time of year."

"Nelson's," William said.

"The store. Only one in La Cache."

"The only one? But they have canoes?"

"Sure. Don't want to get stuck with 'em all winter. That's why you ought to be able to get your dad a good deal. Nobody likes to sit on inventory. That's where I'm fortunate. Being an independent professional. No inventory. Just my tools. My hands. My brain. Such as it is."

"You're a . . . ?"

"Handyman. Contractor. Wood cutter. Logger. Guide. All that." The man took a cigarette from the pack sitting on the dashboard, put it in his mouth, and punched in the lighter. "You and your dad like to fish? I could show you some good spots. Muskies big as your arm."

William felt himself in a dilemma. There was nothing so odd in this corner of the world as a man indifferent to fishing (or at least to discoursing about fish—their psychology, habits, and lore—and fishing), yet he in no way wanted to encourage this man to entangle himself in their affairs. Then he stumbled across a brilliant parry.

"Oh, we're nuts about fishing. But Mom hates it, doesn't she, Em?" William turned to Emily.

"Detests it," Emily said.

"Doesn't like me and Dad going off. It makes her feel like a widow, she says. So she said, this trip, you want me to come, no fishing. So that's the law."

"Tough business, that," the man said. "But you got to keep the womenfolk happy, don't you?"

"Sure do," said William.

"Well, you'll have yourself some fun with that canoe. Best time up here's right now. No bugs. Practically no people."

"That's the way we like it," William said.

"Yeah," Emily said. "The serenity. The peace."

"God's country. Truly," the man added.

They drove the rest of the way in silence. Emily looked out the back window of the pickup, at the plume of dust fanning out over the road behind them. They were putting the whole world behind them. They were going deep into creation, as the man had said.

$\mathcal{L}$ac La Cache consisted of a boat ramp, a couple of summer cabins (the septic tank of one of which the man in the pickup was here to investigate), and Nelson's store, a building not much more prepossessing than the warming hut at St. Clair Park. There were, as promised, canoes lying inverted on the grass outside and, sheltering under the eaves of the roof, an old soda pop cooler that was full of live minnows. Next to this sat a fuel tank in a cradle and sundry cans, some full, some empty, of oil for blending into outboard motor mix.

The proprietor, the eponymous Arnie Nelson (and it would be difficult to say, in their mutual dishevelment, their air of a temporary project having gone on longer than anyone might have expected, where Nelson's the store left off and Arnie the man began), had come to his front door on hearing the noise of the pickup's arrival. When he saw that the passengers pulling their bags from the rear were kids, he cursed ("Dag-nabbit") under his breath, for being kids, they either had no money or would be unlikely to spend it on anything. Maybe a candy bar, and Arnie had several of these—no matter that their carapaces had reached melting point several times during the summer—he'd just as soon dispose of before he closed up for the season at the end of the month. No one came to Lac La Cache without trading at Nelson's. There had been a Hudson's Bay post as long as 150 years back, though there was not much about Nelson's to suggest anything of the voyageurs and beaver pelts: Rather, it had the look of a henhouse superintended by a fox.

Emily and William approached the door and Arnie swung the screen open to admit them. "Hi, kids," he said. "What can we do for you?"

"We need some supplies," William said.

"We got 'em."

"And I heard you might be able to sell us a canoe."

"Well, yes indeed." Arnie was happily thunderstruck. The sale of a canoe, properly regulated, would cover the better part of his passage to Tampa, Vero Beach, and points south, upon which he planned to embark no later than noon on October 15. "I think we might arrange that. Come around the side here, and I'll show you what we've got."

What Arnie had were five aluminum canoes of various antiquity, none so blatantly dented as to suggest porosity and any one of which might be deemed to be serviceable. "Take your pick," Arnie said. "I maintain 'em all myself."

"I was kind of thinking of fiberglass. Because of the weight," said William.

"Well, weight's one thing, I suppose. But toughness is another. You hit a rock, it'll stove fiberglass clean in. And there's lots of rocks around here. That's why I don't have 'em—fiberglass. Not durable."

"I guess you have a point."

"You going to be making a lot of portages?"

"I don't know exactly. I don't think so."

"Well, there you are. You're better off with something that can stand up to the country."

"So how much are they?" William asked.

"Depends on which one you want."

Emily pointed to what was doubtless the least distressed-looking of the five. "This one looks okay," she said.

"So how about that one?" William said.

"You know how to pick 'em. That's the newest of the bunch—the one I like to use myself." He hesitated, as though weighing whether he could bear to part with the object of such sentiment. "I don't know. It's a lot of trouble just to get 'em trucked in here. I paid three hundred for her."

"Boy, that seems a little high," William said. "I mean, I worked at a sporting goods store and I don't think any of ours were that much."

"Well, you see, it's the freight. It'll pretty near double your cost. That and the maintenance. You got to recognize, you're a long way from anywhere up here."

"I suppose. But still, I don't know."

"Tell you what. I'll let it go for half of what I paid. One-fifty. You can't get fairer than that."

"I think that's about what they go for new."

"Well, I explained how it is," Arnie said. "Heck, I don't know why I should even bother. I just got to get another one in here next season. It's a losing deal for me, when I think about it." Arnie put his index finger on his lip to indicate that he was, indeed, thinking, and moreover, rethinking.

Emily looked at William and shrugged. William shrugged in return and said, "Okay, I suppose. Since it's such a good canoe."

"I think you just made yourself a good deal," Arnie said. "I must be a little loco today." He knocked on the gunwale of the canoe. "Now, I suppose you'll want paddles. Life jackets."

"They're not included?" Emily asked.

"They weren't included for me. When I bought her. It's just another thing to get hauled in here next season."

"How about we throw in ten bucks, then?"

"Ten bucks'll get you the paddles. The life jackets I can't do for that. I'd have to get ten more. These are Coast Guard–approved, you know. I can't just give 'em away."

William was already feeling a little humiliated by the course this transaction had taken. "We'll manage without them, I guess." He gestured toward Emily. "My sister's a Red Cross lifesaver."

"Suit yourself," said Arnie. "Want to come inside? Get your supplies?"

"Sure."

"Hang on. Let me get your paddles." Arnie selected two, seemingly at random, from an oil drum next to the minnow tank. "These okay?"

William looked at Emily, and Emily nodded. "I suppose," he said.

Arnie leaned the paddles against the canoe, and William and Emily followed him into the store, a store perhaps only in the sense that there were shelves fastened to the walls and items resting on these that were apparently for sale. There was no cash register, no scale. There was a Hamm's beer lighted clock on the wall, and a large refrigerator which contained, along with Arnie's personal groceries, a large stock of this product.

"So what do you need?" Arnie asked.

"Well, we're going camping. With our folks."

"Didn't see them."

"Oh, they're already here."

"Haven't seen anyone in a few days, actually."

"Oh, they put in last week. With the boat. Over at Crane Lake."

"They going to pick you up here?"

"No. We're going to paddle over to them."

Arnie Nelson was not himself a gifted liar, but he was a connoisseur of the liar's art, and he was interested to see where this tale the boy was telling him would go if he bore down on it a little. "They came over from Crane?" he asked. "Through the pass, I guess." There was no pass. "Since you said you weren't doing much portaging."

"Yeah," said William. "That must be how they came."

Arnie was disappointed in so lame a response. Amusements were hard to find at Lac La Cache. "Beautiful stretch of water, the pass," he could not resist adding. "So how about your supplies?"

"Well, do you have hardtack? Bannock? Pemmican? That kind of thing?"

"Afraid not. We got what you see. Canned hash. Chili. Stew. Vienna sausage."

"I suppose we'll have some of that then."

"Help yourself then."

Emily and William plucked cans from the shelves until both their arms were full, and turned back to Arnie. "Set it all down here"—he indicated a table already occupied by an unwashed plate and a beer can—"and we'll ring you up."

"Do you have any bacon?" William asked. He looked at Emily. "We kind of have to have bacon."

Arnie shook his head. "All I have is what I keep for myself. Of course, I guess if you really needed it, I could get more. It's a long drive to town, but you guys are good customers now."

"Well, if you could . . ." William said.

"I suppose. But I got to charge for my trouble. For the freight, and so forth."

"Sure."

"Say five bucks."

"That's an awful lot."

"Whole pound. Costs me five bucks in gas just to drive to town."

William said, "Okay, I suppose."

"Well, there you are then. Let me just ring you up." Arnie went to work on a pastel-colored notepad. "That's one hundred and ninety-two dollars, with the canoe, of course. There's tax, of course. But we can let that go, by the by. Nobody much watching up here."

William nodded. He went outside, followed by Emily, and Arnie watched him dig inside the duffel bag sitting on the ground. He returned with two hundred dollars in twenties.

"I don't know if I can change that," Arnie said.

"You'd only need eight bucks."

"So I would," Arnie said with a note of surprise. "Well, let me see." He felt his pockets, and then dug inside one of them with an expression that intuited he was working a dry hole. "Well, what do you know," he said, extracting a tangled five-dollar bill. "Here you go." He unfolded it and passed it to William. "I'll have the other three dollars for you when you come back through."

"I don't know that we will be," William said. "We'll probably go out with my folks."

"Oh, through that Crane Lake pass."

"Yeah."

"Well, you just swing by. It'll be here."

"Okay." William and Emily began to move to the door, laden with cans. Arnie went to the refrigerator and extracted a packet of bacon from what seemed to be a half-dozen such packets. "Don't forget this," he said, and set it atop William's armload of groceries. "And don't forget to come back."

*W*illiam and Emily were afloat at last, at four o'clock in the afternoon, a beautiful clear afternoon, untroubled by wind or heat or insects. The canoe sat a little low in the water, being filled amidships with the duffel, Emily's bag, and the two dozen or so cans they'd bought at Nelson's. When the canoe was launched, that was to be the true beginning of their voyage, of their new life, but for William it was a little sullied by their transactions with Arnie. He allowed how Arnie would fit right in with Mr. Murkowski in the back room at Brower's.

"We still have a lot of money," Emily said. "Which we don't really need."

"I guess." And then they began to paddle, north and east, parallel to the shore of the lake. In twenty minutes they could scarcely see Nelson's store; in thirty, it was gone. There was nothing at all, save the seethe of the canoe sliding through the water, the drops that fell from their paddles, that rang on to the lake surface. They thought they might have heard an outboard, but it might have been a gust of wind.

"This is far enough. For today," William said, and they turned towards the shore. They found a spot where a long shelf of rock cut into the lake; that made, after a fashion, a little dock next to which they could berth the canoe before pulling it up onto the shore. Next to this there was a low area that might almost have passed as a beach and behind it, where the forest began, a clearing where they could camp; where there was indeed the remains of a fire ring, laid, for all William and Emily knew, a century before.

After they had disembarked, they stood together ankle-deep in the water and pulled the canoe up as far as its not inconsiderable weight would allow, and then they began to unload a few things from William's duffel. It was a sunny and cloudless afternoon, so they would not pitch the tent. William would merely lay his tarp on the ground — on a high spot, under the trees, close to the fire ring, but not too close — and spread out his big sleeping bag on top of it. When he had done this, he and Emily stood at the edge of the tarp, their bare feet still a little wet from the lake, and began to undress each other without so much as a word passing between them. They were half in dark, half in light — great swaths of shadow and sun scudding over their bodies — and Emily might run her hand round the edge of William's hip and back onto his buttock and seem to lose sight of it entirely; even as her own breast glowed, gold and rose, perched in William's palm.

They lay down on the flannel of the open sleeping bag. They kissed each other's chest, and still lying on their sides, William pushed himself into her. They had not been together for over a week and William thrust hard and deep, but they were not done for some time; long enough that Emily clenched her jaw and quivered and grasped William's shoulder not once but twice; long enough that when William could contain himself no longer and withdrew to release himself all at once, all over Emily's belly and breasts, her body and most of his were completely in shadow, the sun having moved some distance down the lake.

Emily raises herself onto an elbow and ponders what to do about the fluid, congealing but still thin enough to find channels through which it might run down her waist or into her navel. But William takes her hand and they walk down to the water. The water is warm, as warm as it ever gets (it being late afternoon, at the very end of the season, when every drop of winter has been wrung out of the lake, just before the next winter begins), and they walk in, up to just below Emily's waist, which is just above the top of William's thighs. They wash each other. The soap is still in Emily's bulging flight bag, but they are not very dirty: some dust, sweat, William's semen and Emily's lubrications, and the fusty, near-forgotten residues of the bus, the pickup, and Nelson's store. When they are done, even the sour and greasy odor of Arnie's greed is washed away, together with not only the memory but the very fact of his paltry machinations, the sham of his lies, of his pathetic efforts to make nothing into something.

William goes back to the shore, to the big slab of rock, and leans against it. He watches Emily continue to brush and splash herself with water, to lower herself to shoulder depth and then dip her head under completely. She emerges, working her fingers through her hair, unknotting its tangles, combing the water out of it. It is a great labor to be a woman, to do all this tending and polishing of one's beauty, and it has, William sees, nothing to do with conceit or fastidiousness or vanity. He has never seen Emily naked from such a distance or so unframed by other things, by rooms and doors or even the tall grass of the park. Now there is just the sky above her and the water below and the rising of her arm as she scoops water or rakes her hair with her hands.

Heretofore, he has seen her mostly piecemeal, in parts, and those parts—her face at rest, her breasts and their nipples, pink as candy Valentine hearts—have moved him and aroused him; and he has thought, as perhaps every man has thought at some point, that were he to apprehend them all at once he would be overwhelmed, overcome by a sort of paralysis of wonder and eros and—why this last should be, no one can say—pity.

But now William sees Emily whole, or at least as one thing, one part in something greater: the sky and the water, saturated with the accumulation of all the day's light, which just now and just here is the world entire. She is in it and also of it, but her beauty remains. She is still, for William, the most beautiful thing in it; perhaps she is the door, the crack in the ordinary, through which he can enter into it fully.

Emily is still merely standing in the water, the water lapping against and eddying through her crotch, bearing the last trace of her and William's lovemaking away. She knows William is watching her, and she does not care. She does not worry that her breasts are too small or her stomach and her fanny are too big. She feels herself in the center of his gaze, and she pictures what he sees—the water and the girl in the water—and she, too, sees that they are beautiful. She cups another handful of water and pours it over her shoulder, lets it run down her arm, mixing them altogether: the girl, the water, the light, his looking.

*T*his was all surely freedom, but being utterly at liberty has its entailments, its queries and demands. If nothing else, William had to gather wood. They would need a fire, if not for warmth then for cooking. No one had camped on this spot for a very long time, so he could gather everything they would need right off the ground, within a twenty-yard radius of their campsite, in scarcely fifteen minutes. He was in the midst of setting down a load by the fire ring when Emily came up out of the lake naked and beaded with water. He thought how much he loved her and how fine and good everything was and then that he might cry. He brushed his fingers under his nose, and he could not say whether the scent was Emily's or the wood he had been carrying or the water of the lake.

Emily dressed and William built a fire, a little box fire, branch stacked on branch to make a square crib upon which one might set a pot without using a trivet. He got his cast-iron Dutch oven from the duffel—this being one of the chief sources of its weight—opened a can of hash, scooped it out into the pot, and let it heat on the fire. One can was enough for the two of them, or would have to do, because, although William would begin fishing and trapping tomorrow, the stocks of food they had brought in—the cans and an enormous supply of rice—would have to last a long time; long enough at least for them to set up their permanent camp and make a return run to Nelson's, should that unsavory prospect become necessary.

When the hash was heated up, when it had taken on—as things

cooked outside inevitably do—the savor of the fire and the air and the trees, Emily and William ate their dinner, each using one half of William's mess kit as a plate. Then, because they were unimaginably tired and because the sun had indeed gone down, they went to bed. They slept naked in the sleeping bag, so tired when they slid inside it that it did not even occur to them to make love. At first, it seemed so dark and so quiet that they might have drifted off to sleep immediately, but then the night began to open itself, to begin its rustling and twinkling. Their heads were pressed together, supported by William's rolled-up red-and-black Hudson's Bay blanket, and they looked up, and where it had seemed a moment before totally dark and blank, there were tens of thousands of stars; and beneath them, coiling up towards them like smoke from the forest, the sawing of insects, the heart-struck plainsong of loons, somewhere out on the water.

They held each other closer, not because they were cold, but to make themselves a little more of everything else; a pair of stars, a brace of waterfowl, two alternating notes. They were totally free, at liberty, and not yet afraid. William tried to give voice to what he knew Emily was also seeing, to the harmony subsisting with the chaos, the order in the infinite, to the transcendent; that word featured so prominently in the books on William's shelves on Laurel Avenue, the word William had never quite understood even as it had impelled him to come here. Perhaps he was rather wise not to pretend to know what it meant, for surely among the meanings it overleapt was its own.

He put his fingers in Emily's still damp hair. Then, before he could say anything, Emily said, "Do you want to count them? The stars?"

"I thought you meant the hairs on your head."

"You can do that too, if you want."

"There's too many. Of both," William said. "So many. More than anyone could count. But even then, they're all perfectly . . . arranged. Not like controlled. Just being exactly what they're meant to be. Each one. There's no system, no rules. It's perfectly free, and perfectly fine, just the way it is. No police, no army, no government." William paused, to look again, to collect his thoughts about what he saw. "Maybe there's no God here."

"Or maybe," said Emily, "maybe there's no one here but God. No one at all. Except us."

Afterwards, when they had begun to drift off, William thought he heard Emily talking in her sleep, chanting in a breathy, singsong manner. They had never slept together, all night long, in the same bed. When the speaking continued, he became a little worried, and whispered in her ear, "What is it? What are you saying?"

"I'm saying my prayers," Emily said.

"You don't need to do that," William said. "We don't need any help. Everything's fine."

"I know. It's just what I do. Every night. Just kind of singing myself to sleep. Just kind of thinking."

"Don't worry. Everything's great. Everything's good."

"I know. I'm just thinking about it, thanking . . . God for it," Emily said, and then neither of them said anything more.

2

SOME FAVORABLE HAND WAS UPON EMILY AND William the next day and the next, and for some weeks to come. There was scarcely a cloud in the sky or so much as a gust of wind until October. Their greatest piece of foolishness, that they might live off the land, proved not to be so foolish, for William caught fish and Emily picked blueberries and with the addition of a little rice, their appetites wanted for almost nothing.

They had found their permanent camp the very next day after their arrival on Lac La Cache, a little after noon. It was perhaps one mile north-northeast of their first camp, well inside Canadian waters by William's reckoning, and well out of sight of any other habitation, excepting an empty summer house on the shore just beyond the spot they had camped their first night. It was an island, big enough to appear on William's map, but without a name.

The island was perhaps fifty yards long and fifteen across, less land than an outthrusting of stone, albeit with enough soil in places to sustain some large spruce and pine and a bit of groundcover. On the southwest end, there was a little cove, just big enough to stow their canoe out of sight. Most of the surface of the island was a good ten or fifteen feet above the surface of the lake, and from most points other than the cove, you would have to scale some fairly sheer rock faces. They would be safe here.

They would also be comfortable, or at least enjoy the impression of comfort. There were big trees to shelter them. Better still, there was a hollow snag of a pine and a cave as well. It was not a cave in the techni-

cal sense (these being rare in northern Minnesota or, as William supposed, southwestern Ontario), but a crotch formed by the abutting of
two huge rocks. But it was deep enough and wide enough to allow both
Emily and William to sit in it, upright, pretty well sheltered from either
wind or rain.

The hollow tree was less capacious—big enough really only for
one—but merely the fact of being in possession of such an amenity
seemed to place a seal of benediction on their entire enterprise. The
island afforded little in the way of soft spots to bed down, so William
made them a bower of spruce boughs just to one side of the cave (six
feet before whose entrance was a recess almost preternaturally ordained
to serve as a fire pit), and this, once William had picked through it and
removed the harder and sharper branches, was their bedchamber. For
their larder, William's duffel, now pretty much emptied of everything
save perishables, was suspended from a high branch of a jack pine by a
rope; for their stove, he removed the middle seat from the canoe, and
this, inverted, made a support for the Dutch oven, the aluminum frying
pan, and the little teakettle atop the fire.

Emily watched William set up these improvements to their camp,
and was more than a little impressed. She had been inclined to believe
that William's aptitude for woodcraft was of a limited kind (he had
been to camp but once, whereas she had been twice, and to canoe
camp, not far from these waters, at that). She had not been much
encouraged by his inability to master the J-stroke of the paddle that was
essential to keeping their craft on a straight course.

So she was pleased when he proved so adept at making them a
home in the woods. Now William had of course read and reread the
sections relating to this in the *Book of Woodcraft and Indian Lore* and
the *Boy Scout Handbook*, and he had rehearsed them countless times
in his mind's eye. He had dreamt them for nights on end over the previous months, and so, when it was time to enact them in actuality, they
unfolded without a hitch. For the next three and a half weeks, their
days passed as they might have done in paradise, leisure and labor,
diversion and routine; even—on September 23, the autumnal equinox—day and night were in perfect equilibrium.

Every day they ate a breakfast of rice cooked the night before, reheated in the frying pan over the banked coals. Then they paddled the quarter mile to the mainland shore and gathered wood and dug worms (although William discovered that the fish were just as happy to be baited with the innards of their previously taken cousins), and on the way back, William fished and Emily read and corrected their course as necessary. In the space of two hours, William would easily catch as many fish—middling perch and trout—and that was sufficient for their lunch, their main meal of the day. In the afternoon they napped and made love (sometimes with William withdrawing himself, sometimes availing themselves of one of the three dozen prophylactics purloined from William's drugstore), and afterwards they bathed in the lake together. They dried themselves on the southwest-facing rock at the entrance to the cove. Sometimes they returned to their bower and made love again, love without aim or climax, William lapping and kissing Emily's sex, Emily tonguing and sucking William's. They learned to do this together at the same time, heads entwined in legs, and sometimes they fell asleep, exactly in this fashion.

That is not to say they gave no thought whatever to the morrow, that they had no concerns or desire to improve their lot. At first, their wishes were frivolous. Emily pined for cocoa and licorice, William for chocolate and more bacon (although they now had a stock of bacon grease sufficient to meet their needs almost indefinitely), and they both agreed that if they obtained flour and sugar, they might make some flatbreads in the Dutch oven.

These matters arose at the end of the first week, and with them the question of when or if to make a return journey to Nelson's store. There were several problems involved in this, not the least of which was Emily and William's ardent wish to never set eyes on Arnie Nelson again for the rest of their lives. Then there was the issue of a visit raising awkward questions, of its attracting unwanted attention: How would they explain their again being unaccompanied by their parents or siblings or, if they waited much longer, their lingering presence in the district of Lac La Cache long after virtually all other visitors were gone for the season?

It seemed to William that if they explained they had been sent by their parents for a final batch of supplies for use on the way back out the Crane Lake pass, this would raise no suspicions in Arnie Nelson. And it would not, because Arnie had no interest in any aspect of Emily and William but their money. He was indifferent to the mysteries of their minds and hearts as well as to the attractions of their bodies.

On a Thursday afternoon, the children paddled into Arnie's view, Arnie having decided he ought to take a little more sun before heading south lest he startle the tanned natives with his white-as-a-fish's-belly north woods pallor. He rose from his chair, and as was the custom of the country from voyageur days, helped pull the bow of their canoe ashore. "So," he said, a little out of breath after this exertion, "you're still here. Where are those folks of yours? Get here faster in a boat, I imagine."

"Oh, they sent us up to get a few things before we all leave," William said.

"We thought it would be fun to have one last outing in the canoe," Emily added.

"How's she holding up?"

"Oh, fine," said William.

"Actually," Emily interposed, "it kind of leaks. In the middle, in the bottom."

"Oh, it's supposed to. Keeps the joints and seams . . . cured. In trim," Arnie said. "And a little bailing kind of comes with the country."

William hoped Emily would not choose this moment to expose, via the expertise she had gained at canoe camp, this baloney for what it was; and she did indeed hold her tongue, much to his relief.

Arnie went on, "So what did you need? Or have in mind? Stocks is kind of low, it being the end of the season." The three of them walked towards the store. "And of course when supply falls, prices rise. That's the law of the market," he added. "But you kids are good customers. Regulars."

They went inside. It seemed to William and Emily that nothing had been taken or removed from the shelves since their previous visit. They took two or three cans each of the items they had previously purchased and to these they added a few cans of soup, together with a bag of sugar and two of flour.

"You planning to enter the bake-off or something?" Arnie queried.

"No. We just eat a lot of pancakes," William said.

"And Mom bakes bread," Emily added.

"Probably want some baking powder and some syrup then." Arnie reached for these without waiting for a reply.

"Yeah," William said. "We do. I forgot."

"We need cocoa too," said Emily.

"I got this here that you just mix with water," Arnie said. "Don't suppose you got any milk."

"No."

"Anything else?"

"Maybe a little candy," William said. "That, and some bacon."

"Oh, I'm down on bacon," said Arnie. "On account of which I ought to charge you more. But I won't. I'll give you a break. Charge you the same as last time." It went without saying that Arnie recollected this figure to the last decimal. "So with the bacon, that makes fifteen dollars. How many candy bars did you want?"

"I guess we'll take them all," William said, turning to Emily, who nodded her concurrence.

"Suit yourself. I'm all but closed up now. Come the middle of next month, I'm heading south."

"So who's here then? In the fall and the winter?"

"Nobody. Nobody at all," said Arnie. "Maybe Fred Peterson, the guy who drove you in, comes up once a month or so. Checks on the summer people's cabins. Makes sure the pipes ain't burst." Arnie had counted out nine assorted candy bars. "So that makes eighteen dollars."

William reached into his pocket, removed a ten and a five, and handed them to Arnie. "There you are," William said.

"You're three bucks short."

"No. Not really," said Emily. "You owed us three from before."

Arnie shook his head. "So I did. Imagine me forgetting."

After they had loaded the canoe and pushed it out as Arnie looked on—"I'd help, but I think I put my back out hoisting her earlier"—they paddled back the way they had come. They spent the night at their very first camp, doing without a fire, supping on a tin of Vienna sausages and then splitting a Nut Goodie. They settled into the sleeping bag on the selfsame spot they had slept before and watched the last of the sun set into the lake, into the selfsame spot where Emily had stood naked, washing herself. Already, it seemed long ago, in a time when they were very young.

3

THEY HAD, BY NO FORMAL CONSENSUS OR EVEN
discussion, agreed not to mention the winter: what they would do
or where they would go, if they went anywhere at all. It seemed to
them both that the goodness of each day was contingent on assenting
to it from the start without reservation, to presuming that all would be
well; and thus far—after more than three weeks—all indeed had been
well. If they looked neither forward nor back, it seemed a good bet that
time would stop altogether, that the ease and bliss of these days would
continue without end.

It was not that nothing changed, or changed only for the better.
Emily could not but notice on the long paddle back from Nelson's
store that the canoe was leaking more; and in the ensuing days that,
while William fished, she bailed nearly as much as she read. That was
not so bad: There was the rhythm of the poems (and these were as
prayers, lapping, rocking on waves) and that of the bailing and the paddling. Their whole life consisted of beats and strokes and ticks, the
notes struck by a clock that need never be wound.

But sometime after the equinox, there were unmistakable signs: The
maples began to pale and yellow, and a wind began to sing in them,
coloring them amber and red and shaking the leaves free a handful at a
time, and these skittered across the rock face of the island, collecting
here and there in little piles they might come upon unexpectedly, like
a lost mitten in the street.

It was then that William began to think about building them a
house. He had already strung a tarp over their bower to keep the morn-

ing damp off them, to baffle the wind that was beginning to gust during the lengthening nights; and he supposed they might soon have to pitch the tent. But he had also begun to collect what might be called building materials, the odd plank or two-by-four he had found along the shore during the various expeditions to the mainland.

It had been William's intention, when the intention was still a little unformed, more liquid than solid, to build a house of logs. But he had not an ax, but a hatchet, and no stone to hone the blade. The edge was already getting dull and ought to be preserved for cutting and splitting firewood, which even before shelter, he knew, must be a woodsman's highest priority. So William began to conceive what he might fashion out of the materials at hand, all varying in length and thickness and finish, using no nails, but only a little wire and a little rope. He had no saw, and he took everything that fell into his hand as given, as unalterable in form; and so he tried to build a house, foursquare and in three dimensions, with the jumble of obdurate jigsaw pieces nature had provided. Eventually (owing to the special boon of a largely intact sheet of plywood found on a beach half a mile to the north of them) he assembled a lean-to shack between the cave and the hollow tree. The plywood roof was supported on a grid of two-by-fours and slender logs strung between rocks and weighted down on top with yet more rocks. It was walled at the back and the sides with the planks he had found, and the gaps in these were filled with yet more log lengths and, as both insulation and exterior siding, covered over with spruce boughs. The roof was covered over in the same fashion.

All this was finished by the first days of October. There was no obvious moment of completion, no occasion at which William might carry Emily over the threshold and begin settling into their new home. Emily had been watching the whole structure going up—accumulating, really, like the fuel for a bonfire—and had provided assistance where she could, although this was difficult since both the blueprint and the tools to execute it were present only in William's imagination. While she was pleased, as always, by the ingenuity her lover had once again displayed, the lean-to was not quite what she had in mind.

Emily had also pictured a cabin of logs, one with generous eaves, two square mullioned windows, and a real front door, a Dutch door, in fact. Now she saw that this was an unreasonable expectation, and with the residual happiness of their Indian summer still warming her, she tried to make the best of William's lean-to, which had no front door — no front wall, for that matter — at all. And when it was fully covered over with boughs and they had laid their bed inside and the golden light of the fire lapped upon it in the early evening, she saw it looked just like a Christmas manger.

That night, a Wednesday in October, the first night they slept in the lean-to, they made love at great length, watching the firelight lap their bodies, casting their shadows on the back wall: William atop Emily, Emily astride William, William's head rising to kiss Emily's breasts and then turning over again, Emily's hands on William's buttocks, driving him, driving him deeper.

When he knows he is going to come and begins to withdraw himself, Emily holds him fast, pulls him back in, says, "It's okay. It's all right"; and then he goes on a little longer and floods into her, and as he does she imagines the force of him, having watched him ejaculate so many times, the long strand of semen flinging itself out of him like a whip, like a line cast out and over the lake.

They have always been very careful — excepting two or three times (the first time in the park, another in William's mother's apartment, the last by the balcony in Emily's attic). But Emily knows the night is long, and for the first time, on the following morning, she will wake up a little cold, not merely brushed by a cool wind, but chilled, as though an icy fog has crept down her throat while she slept. Winter is coming, and she needs a reason to stay.

The next day William is especially happy, happy with the house he has built, with the day that is brilliant and cool, with the night before, when Emily drew him in. Regarding this last matter, he imagines that Emily's period is due, that she knows what she is doing. The fishing takes a little longer — perhaps the fish have gone to ground, so to speak, swimming deeper, down at the bottom of the lake, where maybe it is still summer—and even with Emily's assiduous bailing, there is enough water in the bottom of the canoe, chilling their feet, for both of them to understand that the lake is cooling.

When that was done and they had cooked and eaten their lunch, they made love, and again Emily held William inside her when his time came. As William pushed on and loosed himself, Emily saw that this furious labor, the pleas and cries that accompanied it, the exhaustion into which it crumbled when it was done, was all truly for her, on her account. William remained inside her afterward, and when the imperceptible contracting of what had been his erection threatened to separate them, they jostled and pushed together so that they remained joined.

They lay quietly for a time and then they began to talk and at one point William said, "You know the book I brought? That I've been reading? It's about enlightenment, about being connected with everything."

"Yes."

"And how hard people struggle for that. But the whole point is, it's not really about struggling. It's about just being with what already is."

"Yes."

"So maybe that's what this is. Right now."

"You mean it's enlightenment?" Emily did not have the same notion of enlightenment that William did, of infinite calm. Insofar as she had pictured such a state, it was more along the lines of Teresa of Avila struck by the arrow of divine love.

"Yeah," William said. "I mean, everything is perfect. It's itself. And you and me—we're . . . one. One with everything."

They had in the course of this turned a little on their sides, and now Emily rested her head in the little hollow just below William's shoulder. She said, "Tell me more."

"So," he started, and with their limbs tangled up and his hands caught in the wedge where his sex and hers met and perhaps his legs starting to fall asleep, he really could not tell where one of them left off and the other began. "So, it's like we're in union with everything. And the union of everything is God, right?"

"I guess."

"So, in a way, we're God—doing this, being this way." William clasped Emily very, very close. "This is it. This is God."

Emily felt the joy and the triumph in William, and she loved it as she loved him. She did not disagree with it: She just couldn't see it. She said, "I think God is supposed to be love. And this is love. So . . ."

"This is God, right?"

"Or maybe is *like* this."

Just by speaking of it, it was getting away from them. And Emily felt William's semen on her leg and as they rolled away from each other, she might have seen, through one of the innumerable chinks in the back wall of the lean-to, the plane of cloud and wind from the north, infinite and gray as ashes, sliding down over the lake.

4

IT MIGHT HAVE BEEN THE CHILL THAT PENETRATED their hearts in the night, the miasmas that formed from their own breath, condensing on the ceiling of the lean-to, dripping down upon them in the early morning hours, but by then, in any case, all winter's creatures had begun their work.

Emily and William talked of weighty matters a great deal—rather abstract things by grown-up lights, but almost fleshily concrete in the mind of a young person, for whom conviction is the very bread of life—and how was Emily to know which topics were best left alone? So it was that they were talking one day of how things might be going "down south," with the election campaign fully underway, with the inner cities perhaps in flames in the wake of the latest horror, another assassination, a fresh campaign of police repression, the all-but-formal imposition of martial law by National Guard troops.

"Do you ever think," Emily asked, "that maybe this is running away, hiding from everything that's terrible?"

"You mean that I ought to be there? Like fighting against it?"

"Maybe. Or trying to do something to change it."

"I thought you knew," William said, "that it was too late for that."

"Maybe," Emily said. "I just don't think people ought to give up so easily."

"This isn't giving up," said William, and thought how he might retrieve the amity between them. "And I thought you thought it was good here?"

"I do. I do," Emily said, and felt how unconvinced this sounded even as she said it. And then, because they did care about what it was they were trying to persuade one another of but had no means to advance it any further, they fell silent. They were silent as William fished, and even though silence was supposed to be conducive to successful fishing, fewer fish than usual came. Emily bailed and the cold water in the bottom of the canoe felt weightier, seemed thicker than it had a week before. She tried to read her poems, but the lines would not hold together: The words bounced around like Ping-Pong balls, spastically, like popcorn popping.

The night was worse. They did not make love, although they held each other. It seemed there was not a sound in the lean-to, not even that of breathing; only a faint ticking that Emily was sure she could hear, the sound of William aching or seething.

Finally she pressed up against him and said, "I love you. I love you more than anything." This was yielding everything she had to yield, if not, she felt, conceding everything she believed that William did not believe. For were she to do that, who would have been left to love him?

William turned over and said, "I love you too. I just want us to be together. Forever." He put his arms around her and pulled her close, as though he was cradling her, reassuring her.

But it was Emily who replied, "Of course you do. And so do I." Then they began to make love, very slowly, cautiously, their flesh seeming to each other a little tender and sore. Even as William thrust toward his climax and, signaled by the way she gripped his neck with one hand and his buttock with the other, Emily rose to hers, they did not move very fast; no faster really than their usual canoe stroke or Emily's bailing, scooping and pouring, the last of the bilgewater dripping heavily onto the blue-black oil of the gelling lake.

In the morning, all was well again; as it was before, save that it was colder today than the previous day, even as yesterday had been colder than the day before it. Because the fish had been a little recalcitrant in their usual places, William thought that they should try paddling southwest, down the shore in the direction of Nelson's store. They certainly would not travel that far, but at the point (perhaps a mile out from the island) where they were about to turn around, they noticed the house on the shore, the same summer cottage they first noticed five and a half weeks before when they first paddled in, the only habitation between them and Nelson's store.

It was clearly closed for the season, just as it had been before. There was no smoke from the chimney and, looking closer, it was apparent that the shutters had been fastened. William looked back to Emily in the stern of the canoe and said, "Let's go look." And Emily nodded her assent.

They landed the canoe on the stony beach. There was a wooden stairway ascending the bluff on which the cottage was situated, and at the base of it, several sections of dock, removed from the lake and stacked for the winter. William and Emily pulled the bow up onto the shore—even with nothing in it except the three small fish William had caught it seemed heavy—and then they climbed the stairs.

At the top, the house sat in a grove of big jack pines and the ground was covered in their rusty needles. There was a front door giving onto a little porch, but Emily followed William, who was tracking slowly around the side of the house. At the back was another door, a propane tank, and a road leading into the woods bordered by electrical and telephone poles. There was a little shed that housed the well pump, and another in which firewood had been stacked.

William was surprised to find a real house—not a shack or a trapper's cabin—so deep in the woods, and more surprised when he tried the door to discover it was unlocked.

"I wonder if it's a good idea to go in," Emily said.

"If they were so concerned to keep people out, they'd keep it locked," William said. "Besides, I read how it's the custom in the far north to leave these places open. In case somebody needs to hole up during a blizzard. A trapper or somebody."

"I don't know."

"We're not going to hurt anything. Or even touch anything, okay?" And William pushed the door open and Emily followed.

There was nothing remarkable about the interior of the cottage, although it was a little difficult to see by the single long rhombus of light the open back door let in. William tried a switch and to his surprise found that the lights went on; that they were standing in a kitchen, paneled in pine, giving onto a larger room, similarly paneled with a big hooked rug on the floor, a fireplace, and three doors that probably led to bedrooms. There was a stack of lawn furniture by the front door, and, next to those, a croquet set, paddles and oars, fishing gear, and inflatable rafts and water toys.

Emily sees all this, but she sees more, or perhaps at a slightly different level of magnification than William. She sees—or, really, senses—that this is not the house of an Arnie Nelson or Fred Peterson or some other local person, but belongs to a family, and it is a family more or less like hers. She can tell this from the same gear that William has seen, but also from the potholders (made from stretchy loops on a frame at summer camp) in the kitchen, the olive-green napkins and place mats piled on the counter, the unused components from Chinese dinner meal-kits in the cupboards, and the epigram burned onto a tranche of diagonally cut birch log, coated in shellac, and hung on the wall.

Entering one of the bedrooms, Emily can also tell that this is the room of a girl just like her. She can tell by the smell of Noxzema mixed with some other scent—of damp or unwashed hair?—the smell of a girl her age. She sits on the bed for a moment, fingers one of the knobs of chenille on the bedspread, knows that if she opens the nightstand drawer inside there will be one pinecone, a couple of Betty and Veronica comics, and paperbacks of *The Great Gatsby* and *The Spoon River Anthology* from last summer's school reading list. She gets up and looks in the other bedrooms: One tiny one is clearly that of the boys (she thinks there are two) and the other belongs to the parents, which bears the scents of grown-up sophistication; of hairspray, medicine, and mothballs.

All this is making Emily unaccountably sad. She misses these people, these people whom she does not even know, but who are just like her; who, for all she knows, sit two pews back from her every Sunday at mass; who travel in the same model of station wagon as her family does; who play Scrabble and Clue and do crossword puzzles (but only here, only together, during the summer); whose mother is pious and good; whose father is a hero, who regards his daughter with naked adoration.

The house affected William too. It disturbed him. In fact, it diminished him when he thought of everything he had done to bring himself and Emily into the wilderness and to make a home in it—to make it a real and authentic experience—and here sat, not a mile away, this exhibition of bourgeois living with its septic tank, its charcoal grill and Scotch cooler, and its three-horsepower Johnson outboard.

"We'd better go," he said, and Emily nodded. They switched out the light, slipped out the back door again, and returned to their canoe, to their three fish, and paddled wearily back to their island.

5

THEY ATE THE FISH IN THE LATE AFTERNOON, AND that passed for both lunch and dinner. Later, in the early evening, they each read a little and then Emily read aloud.

William liked it when Emily read to him, and he did not much care what she read. They were, of course, pretty limited with scarcely six books between them. William's Alan Watts did not lend itself very well to this, so mostly Emily read her poetry, Hart Crane and Gerard Manley Hopkins.

William liked the Crane better. It was sonorous and striving, moving through and beyond great things and spaces, while the other seemed to stand in one place, throbbing and flashing, singing like a bird. Not that he necessarily understood one better than the other: Understanding was not the point. It was more like listening to music.

That night Emily was reading Hopkins. "He didn't really write this one," she said. "It's a translation. From an old Latin thing, a hymn or a prayer really." And the part that stuck in William's mind was when she read, " 'But just the way that thou didst me/I do love and I will love thee.' " That was the part she wanted him to hear, the part that might have been about them.

When she finished, she said, "I suppose at school they'd make us translate it back into Latin."

"So that's another good reason to be here instead of there."

"I suppose," she said. She did not know what to say next, because she sensed it could cause trouble, that it could take them back where they had been yesterday. Because the truth was, she found herself missing school a little. She found herself missing a lot of things. But missing them seemed to go against her loving William; against the very thing she had meant for him to understand from the lines she had just read. It had never occurred to her that there might be something she dare not say to him; still less that there might be something she might want that he would not want.

"Should I read some more?" she asked.

"Oh, it's awfully dark," William said. "I suppose it's awfully late." The one watch they possessed, Emily's, had been allowed to wind down, and of course now there was nothing to reset it against, except approximately: the rough time they supposed the sun rose this time of year.

"It's getting cold." After she said it, Emily realized that this, too, was another thing it might not be wise to say.

William understood what she had intended not to mean. "It is. But we have good blankets. And the tent. And we could always go to that cabin, if we needed to."

"Oh, I wasn't even really thinking that," Emily said, and understood that her love might ask her not merely to not say certain things but to tell lies.

William loved Emily as much as Emily loved him. He sensed her worry. "We'll see. Maybe we'll go someplace else for the winter. Maybe to California. Wouldn't that be cool? Wouldn't you like that?"

"Oh, yeah. I would," Emily said. She felt terribly sad. She would have liked to crawl over to William and have him hold her while she cried a little. But how could she have explained? There was no place for her to go, not California, not even right here, to William's body.

6

T HE SILENCE DESCENDED AROUND THEM AND EACH day it grew deeper. By the second week of October, everything was perfectly still. It seemed that the loons had ceased their yelping, that the last string of geese, moaning and nattering as they flew overhead, had passed many days ago. Then, in the night, the howling began, icy, stony silence racked by cries.

William and Emily both knew it must be wolves. Neither had heard a wolf before, but there was no mistaking the sound. It was a howl blending hunger, sorrow, desolation, and ardor, not plaintively, but ravenously. It was terrifying. William told Emily, "We're on the island. They're on the other side of the water," but wondered, in his own heart, what would happen when the lake iced over, as it must in a month or so.

William and Emily were hemmed in by their own sentimentality about wolves, which was a little different from the sentimentality about wolves that prevails today. For Emily and for William the crucial thing about wolves is that they are carnivores of a special kind: that they do not merely eat humans—and human children in particular—but eat them *up*, this last intensifying adverb serving to underline the wolf's relish in this act, his lusty capering as he tears his dinner limb from limb, greedily masticates it, and, yes, wolfs it down.

Both William and Emily took in this notion of the wolf almost with their mother's milk, in fairy tales and songs; and in recordings of *Peter and the Wolf*, chiefly that narrated by Arthur Godfrey, whose own rather folksy but unmistakably lupine voice—normally employed in pitching Chesterfields and Oxydol—carried a special frisson. So the howling, which was both attenuated and reechoed as it passed over the water to their ears, was not merely disconcerting, but, as it went on for hours each night, buttressed before and after by devastated silence, unbearable. It ripped through the black night sky and sawed through their teeth and bones, cleaved them skull to toenail, flayed them alive; left them wishing to be dead rather than have it go on.

On the morning after the third night, William conceded that they had to go. They would not leave Lac La Cache, not yet, as Emily hoped, but William agreed that they could take refuge in the summer cottage they had explored the previous week. Maybe then, after a while, they could go to California, although William would rather winter here.

Emily did not like this compromise: She would have liked to get clean away, and did not like the idea of trespassing, even if there was no one to catch them, even if, as William insisted, they would treat the cottage as their own and leave it clean and tidy. This was the best William could do. He was afraid of losing Emily, but he was also afraid of losing what they had made here together; losing what they had become; losing what the north and the woods and the lake had made of them.

They broke camp. The lean-to had to be partially demolished to remove the tarps on its floor and roof. The dozens of empty tin cans went in the fire pit together with fish bones and the other trash. It made a smoky, mean-spirited, halfhearted fire. They spent the morning at those tasks and at loading the canoe. When it was filled and they climbed in, it was very low in the water, and piloting it to the cottage was like rolling a boulder across uneven ground. They worked at their paddles without comment, having become inured to the canoe's sluggishness, which seemed just another part of the world's cooling, of the onset of deep winter. In fact, on account of the canoe's loose riveting, the front and rear flotation compartments contained as much water as they did air. In complaining of the trouble it took him to hoist the canoe's bow when they landed a few weeks earlier, Arnie Nelson had for once not been prevaricating.

7

THEY DID NOT SETTLE EASILY INTO THE COTTAGE. Despite William's assurances, Emily could not help continuing to feel that occupying it was wrong and that they might get caught. "Suppose that guy that looks after these places in the winter comes around?" she said as they began to haul their things up the bank.

"Then we'd tell him it was an emergency. That we were lost or we got soaked in the lake or we ran out of matches or something." Emily accepted this without being convinced by it. She followed him up the bank and into the house.

Once inside, William dragged the duffel and their sleeping bag towards the parents' room and its double bed.

"I'm not sure we should sleep there. I mean, since we're not supposed to be here at all, the least we could do is not use their bed. It'd be warmer out here. By the fireplace."

William turned around and looked at her. "You're afraid this is like Goldilocks or something? Like 'Who's been sleeping in my bed?' "

"I'm not afraid of anything. I just think it would be more considerate."

"Suit yourself," William said, and set down the duffel and the sleeping bag next to the fireplace, with stiff, exaggerated movements.

Then they went in the kitchen to eat. William looked through a stack of papers on the kitchen counter. "Their name is Jorgensen," he said, "these people you're so worried about."

Emily made herself a cup of boiled rice from the last of her supply. William munched from a can of chow mein noodles taken from the Jorgensen's larder. They said nothing to each other for most of the

afternoon, and that evening William laid himself down with an osten-
tatious sigh onto the sleeping bag on the floor. It was the first night they
had ever spent together that they did not make love. They said good
night woodenly, and rolled away from each other and feigned sleep.

They could still hear the wolves, more dimly, insulated by the great
forest between them and wherever the wolves were. In the morning the
inside of the house was sepulchral because of the shutters. William, trying to be agreeable, volunteered to open some of them, then insisted
upon it and just went ahead and did it. Now Emily had to wonder if anyone would notice the shutters (not to mention the smoke issuing from
the chimney); if anyone would come and peer in at them while they
slept, perhaps even the wolves, with their hungry, liverish yellow eyes.

William tried to do and say the right thing, and so too did Emily. They
uttered pleasantries to one another, but silence was easier, less treacherous. The fish weren't biting, so they spent most of the day in the canoe,
where they were accustomed to not speaking. In the house, it was not so
easy. It seemed to William in their mutual speechlessness and paralysis
that Emily's every action, and still more, her inaction, was an irritation or
an insult. When without much thought she switched on the table radio in
the living room and a basso voice tumbled out of it from Duluth or some
such place, William barked at her, "Turn that fucking thing off."

The following day, William tried to calculate the day and date using
the calendar hanging on the kitchen wall, having lost track. His best
guess was around the last week of October. Emily volunteered that she
had been, in fact, making a mark for each day since they had arrived
on the flyleaf of her Hopkins.

"Counting the days until you could get out of here." William glared
at her.

"No. Not at all," Emily said firmly. "Maybe just counting the days
we've been *together*."

"You should be honest enough to admit how badly you want to go.
To get rid of me," William replied, and Emily looked to see if his teeth
were bared, if his eyes were hot yet empty of feeling. "That's what this
was supposed to be all about," he added. "Being honest. Being real."

"You're the one that's not real. Not now. Not acting like this." Emily saw the telephone on the wall—neither of them had tried it but presumably it worked—and thought of what would happen if she picked up the receiver, of the howl of pain and outrage William would make. But she stood still, saying nothing.

"So you see. You want to leave."

"Maybe I do. When you're doing *this*."

That was, Emily realized the instant she had said it, the wrong thing to say. Yet it had a pacifying effect on William, for it gave him a choice between calling Emily's bluff—inviting her to leave—or backpedaling in the service of what he truly wanted, which was for her to stay. "I'm sorry," he said after a long silence during which they stared at each other. "I just got really upset. Because I know you're unhappy."

Emily went to him, put her arms around him. "And I know you're unhappy." And, going a little further than she was sure she had the heart for, she said, "And I want us both to be happy. Together."

They held each other in the half-lit kitchen, and they repeated these things, chiefly "I know" and "I know you know," and took great comfort in these affirmations, these acknowledgments. It was as if they had illuminated each other, made one another visible again, put flesh on what had been mere bones.

As they began to make love, it seemed to them almost as though they were new together; that they had never done this before. William cried out, "I love you," and Emily echoed him. William thrust and loosed himself inside her, without a thought. Then they lay at last in the Jorgensens' big bed, at peace, and they began to talk. Emily had a gift for asking William questions that he liked to answer, that made him feel special, and now she asked him, "When was the very first time you ever saw me?"

"You told me I must have seen you when we were little. At a birthday party or something. But I don't remember that." William paused. He settled into the thing he was going to say. "I remember seeing you in St. Clair Park. The summer before this one."

"And what did you see? What did I look like?"

"You were sitting with Monica. And some other kids. They were smoking, but you weren't. I think you were wearing cutoffs. And your hair was longer or something."

"It was. Back then. And I liked to tie it back with this sort of fat, fluffy yarn."

"I remember that," William said.

"So what else?"

"That you were pretty."

"Prettier than the others?"

"You were the prettiest. To me." William said this, and thought that it sounded a little stupid. He tried for something more, something truer, although the truth was he could not really recollect what he had been thinking all that time ago. "There was something about you that I wanted . . . that I wanted to see. And touch."

Emily thought of William looking at her all that time ago and of her not even knowing that he was looking.

"Touch," she said. "Now."

*T*he following day, Emily and William were pretty much back where they had been on previous mornings, the good mornings. The fishing was good, and Emily was less punctilious about their occupation of the house. When William took logs from the woodpile rather than gather deadfall in the woods she said nothing. She felt freer and more confident, more like herself, the girl in the park, the girl William had been looking at. At lunchtime, as they stood in the kitchen, she picked up the telephone receiver for no particular reason, save that it was there. "Hey, it works," she said. "We should call somebody."

William looked at her rather gravely. "You'd better hang it up," he said. "And who would we call, anyway?"

"Maybe Jim. Or Monica. We could say, 'Hey, we're up here with White Fang. With Babe the Blue Ox.'"

"Nobody knows. Where we are. Or even what we're doing."

Emily felt the way she felt when adults said she was "impetuous"; as if there were carbonation flowing through her. "They know we went away together. I sent my mom and dad a postcard."

William took a step toward her and then stopped. "You sent them a postcard?" He paused again. "I mean, what did you say?"

"Just that we were going away together and not to worry."

"That we were coming here?" William's voice rose.

"No. Of course not."

"How could you do that?"

"Do what? I didn't say anything."

"They might have figured out something," William said. "That was a really stupid thing to do. A really reckless thing."

"I don't see how." Emily bit her lip and rested her hands on her hips, and then she put them out, towards William. "I mean, I had to say something. So at least they'd know I wasn't dead or something. That's not very much."

"It wasn't being very careful."

"Was I supposed to act like I hated them? Like I didn't care what they felt at all?"

"You were supposed to care about us more," William said, and then he looked away from her.

"It's not . . . all or nothing. I still love them. I mean, don't you ever miss your mom? Or your friends?" Emily paused. "Don't you ever just want to go home?" And then her eyes began to flood.

"This is home. Our home, that we made for ourselves. Or we could go to California."

"We just . . . stole this place," Emily said. "And I don't want to go to California. I'd rather just go home. To my real home."

William was gazing at the floor, shaking his head, his arms dangling. "We're supposed to be our own home, for each other. Or don't you believe in that anymore?"

Emily said, "I believe in everything. There isn't anything I haven't done for you. For us. I give everything to you. I want everything. When we make love, I want . . ."

After a moment, William understood. He looked at her and said, "Well, that's reckless too. You—we shouldn't. . . . It's careless."

"It's the most I can do. It's everything. Isn't that enough?"

"But you want to go back. You don't want to be free anymore."

"I don't know," Emily said. "Maybe what's free for you isn't the same as free for me. I really don't know."

---

*A*fterwards, they didn't fight. They were merely confused and sad. In the span of a few weeks, they had traveled a course it often takes grown-up lovers years to transit. Maybe it had been the cold, or something akin to it. Like discussions about God, talk about love is conducted by analogy. We can never quite put our finger upon it, our knowledge of its location, appearance, and history being at best approximate. Clever persons—and persons have grown very much cleverer since that winter—are perhaps rightfully impatient with terms like "approximate" and "mystery" that look like camouflage for thinking that is vague and sentimental. But "God" and "Love," we cannot but feel, have some great affinity—the truism that "God is Love" must also mean that "Love is God"—but the fact that we make fools of ourselves (rather as love is said to make fools of us) in struggling to ascertain their relation does not mean that they are themselves nonsense. Sometimes we are too clever by half.

Say it was the cold—something *like* the cold—that caused this change, this cooling, in their relation. They had found enchantment in and with each other in a thoroughly disenchanted world; and they had come to the north woods to discover a place commensurate with what they had discovered in each other.

William had told Emily about the windigo, the native daemon that freezes the heart and graces its victims with a fate that ends in cannibalism and self-annihilation. And perhaps, far from having gone the way of the story's creators, the windigo was still at large in this country; for when William's ancestors depopulated it of Indian persons, they could not help but populate it with ghosts, and the windigo is first of all a spirit creature.

So perhaps their hearts were frozen, and they scarcely even knew it. Or it was what Emily understood as the hardened heart, the heart that is embittered, unfeeling, and uncharitable: that lacks mercy, which is no small component of love—which is, on many a day, all the love we shall ever want or need. It is also an unseeing heart. It turns away, averts its eyes, is blind to pity, always looking away, shamefaced. It wills itself not to love, knowing all the while it is precisely for love that it is made. Thus does it grow cold. It is perhaps only a great failure of imagination, a loss of faith.

It was surely something like this that happened in the cottage or on the island. William and Emily had not reached the point of not being able to stand the sight of each other. But neither could much bear to look upon the other, for they knew they were each killing the other, that they were each dying before the other's eyes, if they would dare to look.

8

EMILY NEVER DID REACH THE CONSCIOUS CONCLUSION that she must leave. But the morning before—the last Thursday in October—it began to snow. William brought her outside to see it fall. He raised his face to the snowflakes and began to twirl, to do a kind of dance, to let the flakes catch in his eyelashes, to catch them upon his face and tongue. He reached for her hand to bring her into his dance, to make merry with him, to celebrate the first snowflakes of the season. And she could scarcely do it. It seemed false. She felt pity for William because he wanted to do it at all, and wanted her to join him. She felt that in another day, perhaps in another hour, the pity would turn to scorn. She could feel her heart going cold, growing hard.

But when she did go, early the next morning in the indigo light that comes just before dawn, it was the wolves that drove her on, drove her out. It had seemed to her for three nights running that they were coming closer, and perhaps they had, or perhaps her hearing had simply become more acute. She had dressed very quietly in the kitchen, where she had left all her clothes under the pretense of washing them in the sink. It was very cold outside and she put on every item she could, finishing with alternating layers of sweatshirts and sweaters, surely warm enough for both the lake and the long hike from Nelson's to the highway. When she was done, she stood for a moment, amazed that William had not heard her, was even now sleeping contentedly in the far bedroom; was not going to stop her or even know she was gone for another couple of hours. He was, she could not prevent herself from thinking, *that* stupid, that great a fool.

Emily opened the door and the air was as cold as she imagined;

colder still, for it seemed that when she breathed she inhaled not air but drafts of ice crystals, of freezing fog. Then, as she rounded the side of the cottage, the howling began, unmistakably near. Her boots scraped and brushed against the cold-brittled pine needles, and she could not tell where the sound of her own footfalls left off and that of the stealthful, onrushing paws and pads of the wolves began. And with that she began to run, to run hard for the beach, for the refuge of the canoe.

There was a glaze of ice on the shore, on the pebbles and rocks that constituted the beach, and once she overcame the canoe's inertia, its keel slid almost effortlessly into the water. Once it was gliding forward, she leapt into the bow, scarcely moistening her feet, only to be surprised at feeling her boots penetrate a crust of ice and perhaps four inches of water in the bilge.

Emily waded through the ice and water to the stern of the canoe, took her paddle, and brought it around on a course headed out into the lake, roughly northwest. She paddled hard, straight out towards deep water. She did not bail. She wanted to put some distance between herself and William, between herself and the wolves, and—in the unfathomable silences between the howlings—she imagined the bailing might be noisy, that William might hear the tin can scraping on the bilge, the water pouring out into the lake.

Once she was a hundred yards out, the dawn began to gather, or perhaps her eyes had adjusted themselves to the light. In either case, she saw how high the water was in the bottom of the canoe and how low the canoe sat in the lake. She began to bail, rapidly, expertly, efficiently, for she had spent hours, perhaps days, bailing during the last two months. She bailed rather as Ulysses' wife wove, for the bailing was always being undone, not by her hand, but by entropy, by the unwinding of time and motion and the canoe's aching joints and seams.

Emily saw after a few minutes of bailing—halted every twenty seconds or so to lay down a few hard paddle strokes to keep the canoe moving and on course—that the water level in the bilge did not seem to be receding and that the canoe was riding no higher. Her hands were white with cold and so were her knees, and as she kept bailing, she began to lose the feeling in her fingers, which was already gone in her feet. And this was when she began to feel alarmed, because she understood that her ability to bail was becoming impaired by the cold, that the chill in her numbed hands was spreading up her arms and into her shoulders.

She took up the paddle again and began to try to turn the canoe a little towards shore, or at least parallel to it, but just then there was another burst of howling, magnified by the water, seeming to come from everywhere on the shore, from anyplace she might land, if she could reach it, the shore now two hundred yards distant. When she put down the paddle to resume bailing, she saw that the water was now shin-deep in the bilge, that the canoe was half swamped. She did not so much panic at this as she puzzled over it, for there was no logical explanation for the rising water, and the fact that it continued to rise confounded her, teased her to figure out, to fathom, how this could be happening. But her brain was nearly as cold as her hands and her arms, and when she decided to give up wrestling for an explanation and to begin bailing again, she saw that the can she had been using to bail had floated away into the other end of the canoe.

Emily believed that even a swamped canoe of this construction would still float: There were flotation compartments both fore and aft and these were supposed to be watertight and sometimes also filled with buoyant material, to prevent the canoe from ever sinking entirely. But the seams of Emily's canoe's flotation compartments were as porous as those of the rest of the craft, and contained mostly water and, now, ice; and the combined weight of this, the nearly knee-high water in the bilge, and Emily herself was more than the canoe could support.

When Emily saw that the bailing can had floated away, she reflected that she was happy she had not let go of the paddle, for it was now clearly time to leave off bailing and paddle hard, straight for shore or the shallows, wolves or no wolves. And with all her might, now restored a little by the adrenaline that was finally being released into her arteries, that was what she did. But by this time Emily was not so much on the lake as in it, no longer afloat upon it, and so she might as well have been paddling against air. Her paddle had nothing to push against, or rather, everything to push against, and so she could scarcely make the canoe move at all.

This dawned on her more quickly than the earlier phases of her predicament, came to her as quickly as the water reached her waist. But the cold was moving through her faster than any thought or even feeling, wicking up from the now immersed lower half of her body through her torso, past her heart and into her shoulders and the very last means of locomotion she possessed. So it came to her very slowly, as though she had been in a fever which had broken and from whose troubled sleep she was now just awakening, that she must swim for it.

Emily found some relief in this realization, for she knew that she was a good swimmer; that she was expert enough not only to look after herself in the water but (on account of her lifeguard training) to look after others. And in this case she had only herself to worry about. That was in her mind as she pushed off into the lake, the water now nearly up to the gunwales of the canoe, and began to swim.

She was surprised to find that the water did not seem much colder than the canoe had. Of course, she was wearing a great deal of clothing, but once this was soaked through, she was less conscious of the chill than the weight of the sodden clothes; and it was then that she recollected the Red Cross instruction that one should not enter the water so heavily attired.

When it first came to her that she might die, the thought arrived in the form of a negative proposition: that because she was such a strong swimmer, she would *not*, even so greatly laden, die on account of drowning. In this supposition, she was correct, and it followed from it that the true cause of her death would be the cold.

Already her body was in shock, and even then she could make a little forward progress in the water, the shock helping insulate her from the cold, or at least the sensation of the cold. But she was still well over 150 yards out from the shore, in the lake, on whose surface the sun was just now flaring up.

It seemed to Emily even then that she was still paddling or rather still swimming, still propelling herself onward, but in fact she was scarcely moving at all. She was going to die in a manner pretty much like falling asleep, by cold, gradually, almost painlessly, dark covering everything else over. She was going to die as lovers are meant to die, not from passion but from languor.

Emily must have comprehended at some point, however dimly, what was happening to her: that she had indeed died for love. What exactly she made of this cannot be said; whether it was worth dying for. There had been two loves in Emily's understanding, earthly and spiritual, and she had always thought you ought to be able to tell them apart. But she had not begun to reckon with there being two deaths to go with them. She would have supposed that if divine love—the love of God and, for example, Saint Teresa—required death, it would be a sin to refuse it. Of this love, that of her and William, she had no time to be able to say yes or no, but she had surely not refused it in any way. She had given everything for it, and taken everything from it that it could offer her in return, down to the fetus inside her, which went on living for some minutes after Emily had begun to breathe water and then ceased to breathe at all.

9

WILLIAM AWOKE A LITTLE BEFORE SEVEN O'CLOCK, and he woke slowly, as he usually did; as did Emily most days. He did not notice her absence for some while, and when he got out of bed he imagined he would find her in front of the fireplace, stoking the banked coals of the previous night with fresh wood, or in the kitchen.

When he saw that she was in neither place, he was alarmed, for in the last two months they had scarcely been apart. Emily had taken the canoe out by herself a few times in fine weather and had of course walked the perimeter of the island many times and found, in the lap of one tree or another, places where she might happily read a book.

But none of that history accounted for her not being present now, on a bright but deeply cold morning just after dawn. William tugged on his clothes and his boots and went quickly out the back door. There was still some residue of yesterday's snowfall, and he saw Emily's tracks rounding the side of the house, and then, the strides much longer, bounding down the hill to the water. He saw the canoe was gone, and he began to scan the water for a sign of her. He saw nothing, and he ran back up the hill and into the house to fetch the binoculars that sat upon the mantelpiece. He took them outside, stood at the crest of the hill, and again searched the surface of the lake, all the way to the horizon. At one point, he glimpsed what appeared to be a long length of driftwood huddling low in the water, except that unlike most such logs this one gave off an almost metallic glint. But that was not what he was looking for, and he gave it no thought.

He spent more than fifteen minutes surveying the lake, and then he went inside. He had to rebuild the fire from scratch, having failed to feed it when he awoke. Once it was aflame, he sat before it and contemplated what must have taken place and what he ought to do about it. Twice, he heard what seemed to be footsteps outside, and raced out to investigate them. Only the second time did he realize that these sounds were nothing more than the dripping of melting snow from the eaves, and that it would persist and increase as the day went on.

William did not worry that danger or evil might have befallen Emily. He knew she was on the water and that she was a better swimmer and canoeist than he was. Whatever she had done, she had deliberated, and it took him no time at all to comprehend what action it must be. He had prophesied it all, seen it all, well before she had herself done so. She had, from the very beginning, unlike him, held back a little from their relation, withheld some part of herself, and now she had left. He had, it seemed to him, always known this: right from the moment of their second date, when she had withheld her kiss. He had known this. He thought he had forgiven her that, had forgotten it, but here it was, palpable as the oily scent of the pine and spruce and the drip of the melting snow.

It was a clear, cold day, and he put on more clothes. He saw that hers, save for some underwear, was gone. He went back down to the beach to wait and to look and to plan. It occurred to him to call out for her. The sound would carry across the water. He shouted and then bellowed her name. "Em-me-lee!" it came out, and he felt foolish. Then, as he saw how pathetic he was, how forlorn in his abandonment by a smart and pretty girl, he felt humiliated. And with that he stopped calling out for her.

The plan he devised was this: that he would walk to Nelson's on the road going out behind the cottage (for surely that was where it had to lead). There was no place else she would have gone, and perhaps he would find her there, or some sign of her. He left her a note on the kitchen counter, on the back of a used cribbage score sheet: "Dear Emily, I went to Nelson's store to look for you. If you come back, just stay here. I hope you are OK. Love, Bill."

It took William not much more than an hour to walk the road to

Nelson's. He scoured the whole vicinity of the store, from the beach to the edge of the woods into which the county road disappeared. He looked into the windows of a half-dozen summer cabins, but there was nothing and no one inside them, and not so much as a footprint anywhere. He saw that there was no sign of the canoe on the beach or out on the water in any direction.

William decided that before taking any further action he ought to go back to the cottage to see if Emily had returned. He wondered if there was a telephone at Nelson's, or anything else that might help in his present situation, and with no small pleasure he knocked out the window in the door using one of the paddles in the barrel under the eave. The interior of the store seemed identical to the last time he and Emily had been there six weeks earlier, if damper and more foul-smelling. There was indeed a telephone, but when William picked up the receiver, it was dead. Arnie Nelson had also turned off his refrigerator, but the little chest freezer next to it hummed quietly in the half-light of the store. William opened it. There were a couple of canisters of frozen orange juice and four packets of bacon. William took one of the latter, only one, shut the freezer, and went back outside, leaving Arnie Nelson's door—which after all now had a broken window—hanging open.

He began to walk back to the cottage, and it was dusk by the time he came near to it. It seemed darker, because the road was deep in the woods. Just before he reached the cottage, a shape ambled across the road, stopped, and turned towards him. William stopped and moved to the shoulder, and as he did he could finally make out what it was: shaggy as he imagined, a little smaller perhaps, long in the legs, with a lascivious mouth, and deep and muddy amber eyes.

He thought—or perhaps he said out loud—"Come on. It's all right. Just take me," and he took a step forward to indicate the nature of the offer he was making. They stood regarding each other a long time, and William thought surely the wolf would at last surge toward him, for he showed not the slightest fear. But after a time, measured out in the forest's dripping and the wind rising off the lake, the wolf, being merely a wolf, skittered away.

Four

Love
Among
the Ruins

1

IT WAS THREE DAYS LATER THAT EDWARD WENT TO
see his daughter's body. The day after she disappeared, the boy had
had the good sense to use the telephone in the cottage. The operator
contacted the sheriff's office and the sheriff came out to Lac La Cache.
By that evening they'd found Emily on the shore, not very far south of
the cottage. And that was when they called Edward and Virginia. They
said they would be calling the boy's mother too.

Virginia did not want to go, to see, and so he went alone to the
undertaker's, which was housed in a mock-Tudor building not far from
the river. He did not hear, or could not later on remember hearing,
anything that was said to him by the morticians, although he at some
point assented to a modest coffin and minimal preservation of what
they called the "remains."

They had, he had been assured, done nothing to her—had scarcely
touched her—as yet, and he assured them that he had seen corpses
before and that they could leave him alone with her.

She was cold, naked, and refrigerated, and covered with a light green
sheet. He pulled the cloth down to just below her shoulders, and he
thought, as though he were saying it aloud, and smiling kindly while he
said it, "Don't worry. I wouldn't do anything that would embarrass you. I
won't look . . . there. I just want to see you. Just this one last time."

She was white as a pearl; as the inside of a fish's mouth. Her hair
looked redder than it had since she was five or six. On the undersides
of her arms and on the lower parts of her sides, spreading upward from
her back, there were dapplings and whorls of violet and green, as

though her flesh were turning to marble. It was, he knew, only bruising and the pooling and settling of the fluids that her heart had once pumped through her, thoughtlessly and effortlessly, or so it had seemed at the time.

He had not known he was weeping until a tear fell and beaded on her skin, near her collarbone and just to the side of her armpit. "I'm sorry," he said, and he realized that he had said this out loud.

Edward dragged his hand across his eyes and then, for only a moment, he rested his hand, very lightly, on the round of her shoulder. "There," he said. "There." It all came down to this, to the body; this slight and created thing that was supposed to be a splinter of being joined to love. It all came down to a great deal, or not much at all; in either case, merely this.

That was what he had come to see: the body and its inexorable gravities, that drew down hunger and desire and pity and joy upon itself as it drew his eyes; as it had drawn the boy's. It was every bit as good as the soul, and the soul, created with and for it, was nothing without it. The soul would languish, however comfortably, without the body; and the body would waste away for want of the soul. They would pine for each other until the end of history when mercy would bring them together again, these sundered lovers.

Edward took his hand off Emily's shoulder and brought it to his face. It was cold, but it smelled of Emily, he could swear it did, as Emily always smelled. He pulled the sheet over her head and to himself he said what he always said to her at bedtime, and they had a little laugh about that. But out loud he said the thing Virginia said, for his sake and all their sakes: "Pray for me."

2

THERE WAS A REQUIEM MASS FOR EMILY BYRNE, aged sixteen, of this city, three days later. Virginia wore a black, Spanish-style veil, and sometime afterward she realized that this was the first time she had worn a veil since she and Edward were married, in this very church; where she had not too long ago begun to picture Susan and then Emily being married to young men as fine and handsome as Edward had been twenty years ago.

There was not much to Edward today. He looked pallid and slight. His hand was in hers, but it was brittle and weightless and inanimate, like a dried leaf. She stole a look at him, although she could rest her eyes on whatever she chose without discovery from behind the veil. He was not the man he used to be, or at least the man she had pictured him being when she was, twenty years ago, still almost a girl.

He had gone to see Emily at the funeral home, and that was, she knew, no small thing. She had looked at peace, he said. He had given her both their blessings. Virginia had not wanted to go. She had known how it would be; that she would merely be seeing what she already felt inside. She had lived in Emily and Emily had quite truly lived in her, and then, at birth, had been parted from her. Now she had been torn from her body again. Virginia could feel it. Really, palpably. There was a sensation in her gut, in her womb, of something moved, displaced, and pressing against the rest of her, an absence that was a presence. There was no need to go down to the mortician's to see what it was.

Virginia had always believed God had given her two daughters,

Martha and Mary, Susan and Emily, one steady and practical, the other
headstrong and rather too curious. And one tended the kitchen and the
hearth, and the other sat at Love's feet, listening. And who knew, thus
enchanted and charmed, what she might pick up and do, where she
might go?

Now she had one daughter and a husband, and it was her lot from
this day forward, for better or worse, to tend them and care for them no
matter how diminished she felt. She could see, still gazing at him,
Edward's diminishment, and she supposed her own was visible to anyone who cared to look.

The mass went on without incident. Virginia could scarcely say she
was even there, although she went through all the motions and heard
the beads of a rosary clattering in the pew behind, Granny Byrne's,
with Susan alongside her. She heard the Dies Irae, clearly in Latin;
and she remembered this the following year because by a coincidence
or vast pretense the protests that occurred in Chicago just then took the
same name, the days of rage. These were in reaction to the prosecu-
tions brought in the aftermath of the events at the convention the previous summer.

Virginia, too, knew something of rage. It had been the most natural
intuition for her last October to drive by the boy's mother's apartment
on several different afternoons and see that Edward's car was parked
nearby. She had spent forty years being nobody's fool and she comprehended precisely what was taking place. She had planned on saying
something, and was in fact going to do so the very night the police
called about Emily. But then what Edward had done was no longer the
very worst thing that had ever befallen her.

Virginia's grief was very deep, but it was also broad, and lent her life
a capaciousness, a sympathy for the larger world and its troubles, that it
had perhaps before lacked. She took it in and made herself at home
with it, and while it claimed her life entirely for a while, it gave it back
more or less whole, if not intact; altered not entirely for the worse. She
could imagine how losing Emily, and the other matter too, might also
be the worst things ever to happen to Edward.

But Virginia and Edward both kept their silence, not about Emily, but about the other thing for as long as they had left together. It is so hard to be alone and yet so hard to be with others, to speak the truth without doing injury, without unraveling the net of memory—of the sweet and delectable past, but also of slights and secrets set aside, of bonds we wish had never been made—upon which all our affections rest.

3

THE CORONER SPARED EDWARD AND VIRGINIA the news that Emily had been pregnant; Edward and Virginia spared Granny Byrne the news that the circumstances of Emily's drowning had been other than a late-season school camping trip; and Jane and William spared everyone concerned by not attending the mass or otherwise making their presence felt. (It would be "in poor taste," Jane explained to William, invoking a moral logic she had last heard from her own mother perhaps thirty years before.) Thus are we spared not so much pain as agonies of the imagination; so we are spared, if not the death of our loved ones, the death of our love for them as they were, as we need them to remain.

Two months later, after the hearing, William and his mother were driving home. It was a cold January day, the twentieth of the month, almost as cold as it gets at Lac La Cache. They rode in silence, not an angry silence, but one born of relief. William was, for the moment, in the clear. The court officials up north had agreed to have the matter— consisting of various counts of breaking and entering—transferred to the city, and there (with a little help from the fact that Jane's father's name still carried some weight, if only in the form of nostalgia, among the city's legal community) it had been dispensed with. William was to finish school on good terms and thereafter either attend college or enlist in the service, the choice being up to him. Provided these conditions were met, his record would be cleared and he need never revisit the court again.

So that was, if not a triumph, at least a conclusion; an end to the matter. But it was hardly worth exulting about, and so they rode in silence. William turned the radio on, and upon hearing the voices—and one voice in particular—issuing from it, Jane groaned. William tried to find another station, but virtually all of them were carrying the same broadcast. So they listened, even as Jane punctuated the air with sighs, sputters, and mild expletives. But William truly listens, and he hears.

Each moment in history is a fleeting time, precious and unique. But some stand out as moments of beginning, in which courses are set that shape decades or centuries.

This can be such a moment.

We see the hope of tomorrow in the youth of today. I know America's youth. I believe in them. We can be proud that they are better educated, more committed, more passionately driven by conscience than any generation in our history.

We are caught in war, wanting peace. We are torn by division, wanting unity. We see around us empty lives, wanting fulfillment. We see tasks that need doing, waiting for hands to do them.

To a crisis of the spirit, we need an answer of the spirit.

To find that answer, we need only look within ourselves.

Until he has been part of a cause larger than himself, no man is truly whole.

As we measure what can be done, we shall promise only what we know we can produce, but as we chart our goals we shall be lifted by our dreams.

No man can be fully free while his neighbor is not. To go forward at all is to go forward together.

We have endured a long night of the American spirit. But as our eyes catch the dimness of the first rays of dawn, let us not curse the remaining dark. Let us gather the light.

When the speech was done, when these and the other things in it had been said, William turned off the radio.

"So?" his mother said.

"It doesn't sound so bad. It sounds like what anyone would say. Anyone good, at least. Maybe even Bobby. Or Gene," William added quickly.

"From him it's all lies."

"You mean he doesn't mean it?"

"He doesn't know what he means."

"I thought he was supposed to be smart. Or kind of . . . wily."

"It doesn't mean he's sincere."

"So he's . . . a sort of hypocrite."

"It's way beyond hypocrisy. Beyond meaning one thing and saying another. He doesn't know *how* to mean anything."

"So he doesn't mean anything. Anything at all."

"I think that's it," said Jane. "I think you put your finger on it."

Now many people believe that in the intervening thirty years, pretty much everyone has taken on the character of the new president inaugurated that day, Richard M. Nixon; that pretty much everything means nothing, or means no more than the particular construction put upon it by its speakers; that every life is a shabby, embarrassed thing, unwitting pretense outwitted by unwitted outcomes, by events.

But we are a little inclined to forget, despite what the world, thirty years on, seems to have become, that we live still a village life: that the most raw and pertinent facts of our lives are recorded in the vital statistics of the town hall and the local press; that the most emphatic marks we leave on earth may well be initials inscribed in wet cement or the shade of a tree that we, now parents of children ourselves, took the time to plant. Our losses are constant but ephemeral, signified at most in moving vans and vacancies, one-way tickets and funerals. The world is yet something rather than nothing, and ourselves more the sum of our graces than the subtractions of our faults, by however scant a margin.

4

VIRGINIA DIED OF CANCER SEVEN YEARS LATER, in 1975. What she had felt beneath her heart the day of Emily's requiem never went away, but persisted, as did Virginia herself for much longer than anyone thought possible once the nature of her pain had been discovered.

It took a long time for Edward to find a way of living, and it was by a roundabout path. Not surprisingly, he begin to drink rather more, and also to sample some of his own wares, and in particular various sedatives. His life had made him miserable, so he turned to these palliatives, and then the palliatives made him miserable but since life had nothing to offer him, he turned again to the palliatives, and with a vengeance. After four years, he realized he had to stop—that he had managed to construct a new life far worse than the one that had been afflicting him—and with the help of a treatment program (these being something of a specialty in his part of the world), he did. He also found in it a way of explaining his life to himself. He became convinced that he had fallen into his affair with Jane (he had also convinced himself it was not really love that he had felt) as a result of his drinking.

It was a little different for the children, for the next generation. Their time made great claims for the idea that this must be so; that these children were different from their parents as no children had ever been. Perhaps there was some explanation for this view in their respective histories. Consider, for example, the leadership of the nation and the society; how Roosevelt, the president that accompanied Edward,

Virginia, and Jane into adulthood, was the embodiment of ennobling tragedy, whereas he who ascended to the office just after Emily's death embodied nothing so much as tragic ignobility.

Emily's sister, Susan, and William and their cohorts did not have much use for tragedy, it having been so spoiled for them (even as, perhaps, they spoiled idealism for their own children). Nor did they have any truck with the concepts of "human nature" or the accidental. Everything could and must be explained, at least as some variety of curse—either deserved or unfairly inflicted. Thus did Susan take up Emily's cause. The specific narrative changed over the years, but its denouement was always William's fault: because he had controlled and oppressed her in the manner of the male sex; then because he must have introduced her to drugs; then because, in a variation of the first, he had abused her—mentally, of course, but also possibly physically— and she had stayed only because she was in terror or because, in the manner of victims, she had formed a perverse bond with her oppressor; finally because Emily was only sixteen (and a very young sixteen at that) and William was older—nearly a legal adult—and what he had done amounted to abduction and child abuse.

Susan believed, as many people nowadays do, that every misfortune has an author, and that once you have dug down past mental illness, addiction, familial trauma, and incompetence, you will find evil—evil personified; an evil person who either is the perpetrator or who has in some manner impelled the perpetrator to do evil as his proxy. William fills this role convincingly enough for Susan, but perhaps only because they have never met. Indeed, were Susan to meet someone authentically evil, say, Arnie Nelson, she might be a bit disappointed; might find the devil cuts a rather unprepossessing, even pathetic figure.

Susan meant well, but in all this—in her great efforts at displacement, at substituting explanations for happenstance, for replacing mere life with the machinery of history—her thinking would have been alien to Emily herself, who would no more have comprehended the new sciences and philosophies Susan was employing than her Irish greatgrandmother. Surely it had been easier for her parents, who grew up with so much innocence and therefore a surfeit of meaning in their lives, and who on that account perhaps did not feel the need to always grasp at meaning so hard. Perhaps a generation, like that of William and Susan, that feels a bit dispossessed of history will find that a history—shorn somewhat of the requirement to keep faith with it—is exactly what it craves.

5

FOR THE REMAINDER OF HIS LIFE, WILLIAM has been forever distracted. He is simply not very good at living. His heart is somehow not in it. He has been married and divorced and has two children and, although he believes they do not love him, in fact they do. It is merely that they detect the strong scent of failure upon him, of something a little like death on his hands. They would like not to be so wary of him, but they cannot but feel that to come too close would be to invite more sorrow than they are ready to bear.

William has had troubles similar to Edward's, but he has never been able to focus tightly on one particular avenue of self-destruction. He spent a long time talking to a considerable number of professionals about the course of his life, and of late had found some ease in a medication. He felt a little weighted, a little heavy, but the medicine kept him going.

William's current therapist had pressed him for a long time to try to establish a modus vivendi with what had happened at Lac La Cache and thereby to put it behind him. She proposed he might consider visiting the place again, the lake and the island, and she pressed this idea over the course of a year until, in the autumn of 1999, he finally agreed to do it.

At their next session, after he had returned, she asked him how it had felt.

"It didn't really feel like anything. I mean, I could see it was the same place. I even found a couple of things we must have built or left behind on the island. The cabin was still there too. Pretty much the same. Same people own it. But it all seemed smaller, less real."

"But of course it was real."

"But not the way I imagined."

"Maybe because what you imagined really *is* imaginary. It's not real anymore. It's gone. It's past."

"That's very . . . apt," William said and looked at her. He did not look at her most of the time. "But I feel like it ought to have felt real. That it kind of . . . dishonors what happened. Dishonors Emily. Or her memory. Not to be able to see it as it was."

"Which is not how it is now. Not really. Not it. Not you either."

William realized he was still looking at her and turned his head away. "I know," he said. "I know. But I feel like I need to sort of embrace it before I can get beyond it."

"Which is good. Which is exactly right."

"So what do I do?"

"Well, if you're willing, you could do something. A kind of exercise."

"For example?"

"You could write something. To Emily. Like a letter. Tell her what you saw."

"Like she was still alive?" William was looking at her, and he did not avert his eyes when she answered.

"If you want. Whatever way would make it real for you. That would allow you to say what you need to say."

"Okay."

*W*illiam returned the following week with a letter he had written to Emily. He read it, and when he was done, he looked up at his therapist, a little slyly, he could not help but feel.

The therapist was looking at him and their eyes did not part until she said, "You've made her very real. Like she's still alive. Like she has a life."

"That seemed to be the way to do it. To make it real for me."

"So it was?"

"I cried when I was done. I haven't done that for a long time." William turned his face away, as though in modesty.

"Maybe you're finally grieving. And then, after you've finished, you can move on. Be done with all of it."

They talked about this possibility for the remainder of the hour. William said he would try writing more letters. And at the end, his therapist made a suggestion.

"Maybe after you've done that—after we've worked on it a little— you'd consider something else. To get some real closure."

"I suppose."

His therapist spoke slowly. Her voice seemed softer, more musical than usual. "I wonder if you'd ever consider contacting her family? Just to talk about this."

"To apologize?"

"Not even that. Not with any expectation at all."

"There's just her sister and her father. And what would be the . . . pretext? Why shouldn't they just hang up?"

"There doesn't need to be a pretext. And maybe they need to talk about this too. Maybe they think about it, just like you do. It would be strange if they didn't." When William looked back at her, he saw she had cocked her head, her brown hair, to one side, as if she were thinking very hard, trying to help him. "You could just tell them you'd gone up to visit the lake. That maybe they'd like to know."

"I suppose," William said, and he saw that she smiled at him just then.

*W*illiam did indeed write some more things, and then, one evening in early November, he decided to call Emily's father. He had never met her sister, and had heard that she had a low opinion of him. But he remembered—from where, he could not quite say; perhaps the picnic they had all had together once—that the father had seemed affable, or at least relatively approachable.

He dialed the number—he was pretty sure it was not the same number—and waited. It rang many times, and he was sure an answering machine would engage and he began to think what if anything he would say to it. But then a voice, male and a little tired, answered.

William spoke. "Mr. Byrne?"

"Yes."

"This . . . this is . . . William Lowry," he said, very quietly, and then he waited to see what happened.

After a time, the voice said, "Oh," and then, rising and a little less hushed, "I see."

William did not know quite what to say, but knew he must say something before Mr. Byrne hung up or, worse, said something like "What can I do for you?" So he began, not knowing quite where he would end up, "I went up to Lac La Cache a couple of weeks ago. Just to . . . kind of remember. To remember what happened. To reflect on it."

"I see."

"Anyhow, I just thought maybe . . ." And here William found he had exhausted everything he could think of to say. He would have hung up himself, just like that, if the voice had not said something; and this thing in particular.

"So you've been thinking about Emily, I gather."

"A lot. All the time."

"Me too, Mr. Lowry."

William did not know how to take this. He quickly said, "Please. Call me Bill."

"Of course. As you wish. Bill." And then Edward said, "She must still mean a great deal to you. For you to have gone. For you to have called."

"Yes," and then William added, "I just thought . . ." although he did not quite know what he thought.

"It's good that you did. That you called. That you went." Edward paused, and then he said, "Did you know I went up there that fall? That I got within twenty miles of you two?"

"No. I never knew."

"Oh, yes. But that's where I stopped. Where I gave up. Right there." Edward then added, "I always wondered what became of you."

"I always figured you must hate me." William felt a kind of relief at saying this, or in being able to say it first.

"I suppose I did at one time. We all did. Susan, of course. Even Emily's mom."

"I heard that she passed away. I'm sorry."

Edward said, "It wasn't that long after . . . the other. Not that there was a connection. They said the cancer would have started way before that."

"I'm still sorry," William said, and then he seized the chance. "I'm sorry about all of it. I really am. I just wanted to say that."

There was another silence, nearly as long as the very first one. "I know you are." Edward paused again. "I'm not going to say anything beyond that. Not 'apology accepted.' Or anything about forgiveness. I'm not holding back. It's just taken so long to get here. And it's good enough."

"I understand. That's fine. Really it is."

"It's enough that we can just talk together like gentlemen, isn't it? That's no small thing."

"Maybe sometime we could have a drink or something—"

"Oh, I don't drink anymore. Can't."

"I suppose I really shouldn't either."

"But it's a nice thought. It truly is," Edward said. "When I was your age I used to have a lot of nice visits with a doctor friend of mine. I suppose he was the age I am now. It was during that autumn. It helped me get through it. It was a consolation." Edward paused, and then he said, "He was a fine man."

William knew it was his turn to speak, but he felt no pressure upon him. Finally, he said, "I see."

"You end up keeping your own counsel," Edward said, and then he added, "How's your mother?"

"Oh, she's fine. Pretty happy actually."

"That's good. You know, I thought of her the other day. I heard Leonard Bernstein had died. Not that recently, but news gets to me slowly. Anyway, she was very big on him. So I thought of her."

"She was. Still is, I guess."

"You tell her I said hello. You tell her I said—let's see—" Edward stopped. "Tell her I said, 'Mahler foretold all.' That'll give her a tickle. She'll know what I mean."

"Okay, 'Mahler foretold all,'" William repeated, and paused. "And did he? Foretell all?"

Edward thought and then said, "Mostly. But I don't know. We're not quite done yet, are we?"

*F*or Jane, not a great deal changed in all those years. She was not entirely surprised that she never heard from Edward, even after his wife was gone. She pretty much gave up politics, commiserated with her friend Frances, and went on living at 475 Laurel Avenue, where she still lives today. And if you pass by her apartment (as people are wont to do so as to have a peek at F. Scott Fitzgerald's birthplace, which is right next door) on a summer day when the windows are open and the air is thick and resonant, you may well hear a snatch of Mahler or *Candide*.

William had been told, and knew full well, that he remained a prisoner of certain beliefs which would remain the primary obstacles to his recovery. He believes a little too strongly in romantic love or at least holds an unsophisticated view of its powers and importance in human affairs. But the fact remains for him that he only saw how very much God loved Emily, and could not but love her too.

His mother lives as if it were always 1966 or thereabouts; and for William (for whom at the best of times Emily lives, in California, with her children, near the tennis courts) it is always just now. In this way, they keep the intervening years—the history, the ruins among which their loves transpired—at bay.

Acknowledgments

My infinite gratitude to Peter, Jeff, and Trish;
to Alane Mason and Colleen Mohyde;
and, as ever, to Carrie most of all.